★ ★ ★ ★ ★

MADAM
VICE PRESIDENT

★ ★ ★ ★ ★

JULIAN MANN

ISBN 978-1-954345-42-3 (paperback)
ISBN 978-1-954345-43-0 (hardcover)
ISBN 978-1-954345-44-7 (digital)

Cover Art: Jan Michael Labra
Design and Photography: Copyright © Daniel Grill, Getty Images

Rushmore Press LLC
1 800 460 9188
www.rushmorepress.com

Printed in the United States of America

CHAPTER ONE

July 1980

From across the dining room table, Ben Ochman dropped the top edge of his newspaper and peered at his daughter.

"Vera, my sweet child, is it possible for a man to die of a broken heart?" Before the dawn of another sweltering day in New York City, fate would answer Ben's question. But Vera surely would not.

In their cramped two-story Brooklyn home, two identical archways connected the tiny eating space between living room and kitchen, but neither exit offered Vera an avenue of escape. She watched her plate fill with tiny streams of melting vanilla ice cream that trickled down the sides of the white frosted cake, yesterday's bargain from the A&P bakery.

Uncomfortable and nervous, Vera squirmed. An arid breeze whisked through the dining room from the back screen porch, momentarily cooling the tiny beads of perspiration that glistened on her forehead. Vera had suspected her eighteenth birthday would soon lead to unanswerable questions about her mother, but she was unprepared for this one. Any response whatsoever to her father's question would elicit an endless, totally uninterruptible discourse on love and death. Her time did not allow for such a conversation.

Vera grieved for her mother, but not like her father. Ben's grief bordered on madness. His melancholy questions lured her into his tormented mind, but Vera knew not to go there. She, instead, preferred to escape into a forbidden world outside.

Silence became Vera's answer. She quickly stuffed her mouth with a gigantic spoonful of the saccharine dessert that quickly dissolved into near-intolerable sweetness. The diversion worked as her father's eyes disappeared behind the headlines of the *New York Times*. He often argued with the newspaper. His next question likely would come from what was written in the headlines. Vera strained to read. "Mayor Questions Carter's Ability to Win. President Refuses Comment"; "August Heat Wave Blankets the City"; "Summer of '80 . . ."

Vera's chin and head tilted almost at ninety degrees as she strained further. Her jet-black hair fell over her shoulder as her contortion continued and then abruptly returned to symmetry. Ben coughed to clear the congestion caused by fifty years of smoking, but no question followed. Vera's hair framed a darkly tanned and perfectly proportioned face, dominated by piercing blue eyes that returned to focus on the soupy mound of birthday cake, drenched completely by the heat into liquefied ice cream, which was melting away the same as her time.

Ben muttered unintelligibly from behind the paper, an unconscious reaction to something he had just read. Vera took her spoon and mashed the liquid ice cream and frosted cake into a single consistent mixture. A frustrated sigh of impatience and desperation escaped upward from somewhere deep inside. Vera squinted through the haze of her father's cigarette smoke and searched for the hands of the grandfather clock in the living room.

By nine o'clock, she would be late! Vera thought.

Opposite the grandfather clock, above the fireplace mantle, hung a stunning portrait of a Latin goddess, encased in dark mahogany. Brightly burning candles stood watch over her mother's shrine, causing shadows to dance in the rich oils of the canvas. The canvas goddess held a single long-stemmed red rose across the front of her black sequined gown. Vera's blue eyes stared back through her mother's face, a haunting similarity that served only to heighten Ben's grief.

The grandfather clock droned in D-flat the first in a series of electronic chimes.

Displayed on a side table below the mantle were Ben's neatly arranged, professional-quality photographs. A younger version of Ben Ochman beamed down at his veiled bride as she arrived at the altar in St. Patrick's Cathedral. She was a mere teenager in contrast to her balding fifty-year-old groom. The clock chimed four. From her hospital bed, her mother adoringly cradled her infant child, just a few hours after birth. Vera was at the center of her father's attention in a series of five-by-seven-inch photographs, the first taken atop a playground sliding board, sitting on her mother's lap, and followed by a collage from childhood to adolescence, all of Vera and only of Vera. Her mother smiled faintly from another hospital bed. A desperate regimen of radiation explained the erasure of her color and hair. Six chimes. Two priests sprinkled holy water over a veil-draped casket again in St. Patrick's Cathedral. Ben retired from his career as a municipal architect in the New York City's Building Permit Office. The grandfather clock finished its toll.

In the dining room, Vera marked nine chimes in a cupped hand beneath the table. She was late.

"I am heartbroken that your mother did not live to see her beautiful daughter turn into a woman today." Ben folded his paper, gulped his wine, and searched earnestly for his daughter's reaction.

Vera spoke back sharply to her father. "It's Saturday, Pops. My birthday is Saturday. In two days I'll be eighteen. If mi mamá were here today, she might have recalled a little anticipation eighteen years ago, but that's about all. Ask me Saturday. Today's Thursday, a school night, senior year, Pops, and I have homework assigned. Here, finish your wine while I go upstairs to study."

Vera bolted around the table and kissed her father on his forehead. Rubbing her eyes from the smoke, she crushed her father's cigarette in the ashtray and said, "Haven't we had enough cancer?"

"Don't you want to see your gift?" Ben said.

"No, Pops. Wait until Saturday." Vera escaped through the living room archway and bounded up the steps by twos to her bedroom.

Ben's head fell into his hands. Tears dropped like tiny bombs into the liquid ice cream below.

Vera slammed the door to her bedroom and barely avoided a headlong fall as she hopped on one foot to her closet, yanking off shorts and T-shirt simultaneously. First with one arm and next with two arms extended, she fumbled for garments in the hidden reaches of her closet. Both arms returned empty-handed. Vera plunged her entire body into the four-by-five-foot closet and disappeared inside. Suddenly she reemerged and dropped to the floor, twisting painfully back and forth into a pair of skin-tight leather pants. Up from the floor, she pulled the sleeveless top effortlessly over her head. Her face descended within inches of the lighted clock radio as she pulled and twisted her hair into a ponytail.

"¡Ay, Dios!" (Oh, God!) "9:12," Vera whispered aloud.

Nervous fingers fumbled with the bands. She pulled her jet black hair upright into a ponytail. The azure-blue bolt of lightning tattooed on the back side of Vera's neck was in plain view.

Black boots were on. 9:14. "Pops, please be dead asleep!" Ben Ochman's evening ritual was to weep uncontrollably. Absent Vera's solace, he rapidly fell into a deep sleep, a clocklike routine spawned most every evening by two bottles of wine with dinner.

Vera, transformed, switched the bedroom lights off, rushed to the back window, threw up the sliding lower frame, exited onto the back porch roof, and left the window fully open for her return. Arms extended for balance, Vera descended to the roof's edge, slid over the side, and disappeared. The sturdy rose trellis, adorned with her mother's favorite Mr. Lincoln Rose, so sweet in the night air, made a perfect ladder. She climbed down, protected from the thorns by her leather armor. 9:16. At the bottom, Vera cupped both hands around her eyes and pressed them against the porch screen. Across the porch and through the window-paneled kitchen door, she had a direct view of her father's chair in the dining room. Slouched and listing, Ben was fast asleep in his grief.

Vera dashed in a full leather sprint to the front sidewalk, down the street, and around the corner intersection into a vacant lot. Her leather slacks turned a darker shade of black, saturated in sweat, but she had not been left. Steel black bikes, arranged neatly in a semicircle, rumbled at idle with ominous red and yellow lights that glowed in the darkness. Breathless and voiceless, she climbed on behind a male rider, as slurs in Spanish greeted her tardiness.

"¿Porgué Sanchez, esperamos por esta gringa? Nunca esperamos por nadie. Posiblemente ella ya es muerta. Vamos a beber rum y esperamos para ver!" (Why, Sanchez, are we waiting for this American girl? We never wait for anyone. It is possible she's going to be dead. Let's go drink rum and we'll wait and see.)

"¡Silencio, vamonos!" (Quiet, let's go!)

With the deafening thunder of the combined high-performance engines at full throttle, all straining to make up eighteen minutes of lost time, the gang roared out of the lot and down the street. Each member wore a lightning-bolt insignia on his back that matched Vera's tattoo.

CHAPTER TWO

August 1980

The steel bikes stood at rest in a semicircle at the foot of an isolated and abandoned one-story house near the waterfront. The serpentine entourage had rushed to make a timely arrival for a business purpose that was not evident to Vera. Nevertheless, she was relieved. The aluminum engines intermittently popped and clanked as they cooled in the night air.

From the darkened and dilapidated living room inside the house, Felipe Sanchez complimented a bearded brute with the gang name of Black Beard, shortened to BB, on the near-perfect trajectory of the bottle he had just flung end over end across the length of the room through the right upper panel of the picture window. "You know, BB, you should pitch for the Mets."

The drunken voices in the living room filtered down through the muggy night air to a solitary lookout who smoked in the darkness below. This sentinel provided the only security from a surprise attack by a rival gang. He would have preferred to have been inside drinking and carousing with his companions rather than searching the night's shadows from his lonely outpost, but failing his watch would have been worse than death. Moments earlier, he had ducked his head to the side just after the empty rum bottle rocketed through the shattered glass and crashed onto the driveway beside him. A chorus of raucous laughter trailed the spinning projectile through the opening left by the shattered glass.

Sanchez chugged the last shot from his empty fifth of rum, wound up like the pitcher that he used to be before he turned to a life of crime, and hurled a perfect strike across the room through the center pane of the same window. "But Sanchez should pitch for the Yankees." Shrill laughter erupted again as the second bottle sailed down the hill, past the head of the nervous sentinel before it shattered just inches from the first.

Felipe Sanchez, who was born in the inner city to impoverished Puerto Rican immigrants, stood about six-feet-two with biceps that bulged and protruded through his sleeveless T-shirt, just like the arms of a Yankee hurler. His wavy hair matched the black leather of his jacket, and his brown eyes reflected the color of rum.

Sanchez was a violent man when he had to be, but the violence was balanced with a sarcastic charm. He was older than the rest, due mainly to a five-year stretch in the state pen for a failed armed robbery. Sanchez enjoyed the power and respect he wielded as the leader of his inner-city gang, but these fringe benefits were secondary to the real object of his game: controlling territorial profits generated from drugs, prostitution, and extortion. He was not just a second-rate criminal disguised as a motorcycle thug, but he was a racketeer who knew how to compete in the professional ranks of gangsters and he was now getting noticed by both organized crime and bunco cops. He brutally crushed his minor-league competitors, took over their turf, and defended himself from their counterattacks. It was not just violence that got him noticed but a shrewdness that was born out of lessons learned in confinement and on the streets in New

York City that brought Sanchez success as he entered the lower echelons of the city's major racketeers.

He had learned from baseball, both as a childhood player and a fan. He loved the Yankees, and he recruited like the Yankees. Only the best could play for his team, and he filled each position with the best. Without hesitation, he raided the key talent of rival gangs, luring them away with promises of top dollar and huge signing bonuses, a baseball strategy that produced a team filled with professional players of the highest quality. Sanchez kept his financial promises, which engendered fierce team loyalty. Besides the specific talent required for each position on his team, he looked for two characteristics that all held in common.... shrewdness and violence.

Without a hint of indecisiveness, Sanchez cut players for poor performance and replaced them with better performers. Performance was measured in terms of brutality. Hesitancy to use violence in the heat of a turf war caused the swiftest exit of all, but a close second to poor performance was to break one of Sanchez's disciplinary rules. Earlier that night, the team witnessed an uncharacteristic departure from the strictest of all Sanchez's rules as he patiently waited eighteen minutes for the late-arriving Vera Ochman. All knew that lateness evoked brutality. Sanchez once stabbed an underperforming player for his tardiness, but Vera escaped without consequence for a reason. Quite simply, she intrigued Sanchez. True, she remained the unfulfilled object of his sexual interest, an interest intentionally subverted to his objective efforts to evaluate her potential for his team. Sanchez knew she was the best female talent he had ever seen—unsurpassed shrewdness wrapped in unsurpassed beauty—worth at least a one-time exception to the Sanchez tardy rule for an answer to the second prong of his minimum test: could she also be violent?

As a silhouette in the darkness of the abandoned living room, Vera inhaled deeply from a neatly wrapped joint and held the smoke down in her lungs for a full thirty seconds before she exhaled, then chased it away with a slug of cheap rum from a fifth that circulated from hand to mouth in the darkened living room, barely illuminated by dripping wax candles. She did not like the taste of the rum without the cola, but she could not contain the outburst of laughter that emerged from the narcotic within the marijuana. She joined the gang's spontaneous laughter—a laughter she dreadfully missed at home since her mother's death.

Vera was the only child of a Polish-Catholic immigrant father, who was almost three times the age of her mother. Vera's mother would have been only thirty-seven had she lived to survive cancer. Vera knew it was a marriage of necessity for her mother, who arrived in the city from Puerto Rico at age sixteen, not knowing a word of English. Her mother's beauty captivated her father, who fell spellbound in love with his Latin bride and worshiped her more than the Holy Mother. Vera's split heritage bequeathed genetically her father's intelligence and her mother's beauty. She admired her mother's skill in the inner-city marketplaces of Brooklyn, turning the heads of all the vendors, who were blinded by her beauty and prey to her shrewdness. Vera was her mother's only child. They were close. They went everywhere together in the city, and shared everything, including her mother's native language. Now Vera shared a home with a father who lived in the paralysis of grief for a woman he depended on for the fulfillment of his every emotional need. Vera, in contrast, was consumed with all the energy and expectations of a rising high school senior. Her father incarcerated himself inside his home in a despairing retirement after advanced lung cancer took his wife to a Long Island grave a mere five weeks after diagnosis. In response to her father's anguish, Vera diverted the grief that she felt for her mother by enrolling in summer school where Felipe Sanchez helped her escape the confinement of her father's prison and the pathos of her mother's death.

From the very first, Vera fell captive to the Sanchez mystique, a fascination shaped in rebellion. One scorching afternoon in early July, Vera crept silently into the shade of a weeping willow tree tucked away at the far end of her school's parking lot. There, motionless, lay a man stretched out asleep across the leather of his behemoth motorcycle.

"Can't you read, hombre peligroso?" said Vera. "This lot is reserved for students."

Vera had accepted the dare of a classmate whom she did not know. "Go ahead, I dare you. Wake up the sleeping demon, and tell him he's trespassing on school property." Sanchez had planted the dare. Vera had been scouted as a potential replacement for Amber Morelli, an underperforming current team player.

Standing next to his parked chopper, Vera nudged Sanchez with the point of her finger on his shoulder.

No response . . . nothing . . . is he passed out . . . dead maybe? she thought. As Vera turned to retreat, Sanchez mocked her with his sarcasm, without looking up. "Who are you, the parking lot cop? Let me warn you, señorita cop, be very careful if you try to arrest me." Sanchez looked up and grabbed Vera's wrist. "Maybe I'll just arrest you."

"I wouldn't do that if I were you. You might have more on your hands than you can handle. You are very lucky that I'm not a cop."

The two were a pair, connected from the start by a smoldering sexual attraction. There was no shortage of guys who attracted Vera's sexual interest, but they were all adolescent boys compared to this man. The allure for Sanchez was grounded in the forbidden—the powerful attraction of a real man so unlike the childish schoolboys who surrounded her. Only Felipe Sanchez, straddling his black steel stallion, could sweep her away from her own grief and a father consumed by death.

Besides, what did Sanchez imply that afternoon when he said, "Summer is made for more than summer school. Climb on my bike to see how it feels"? Vera climbed on and liked the way it felt. Over the next several days, a series of provocative invitations followed in rapid and escalating succession, all accepted. "Let's take a slow ride around the parking lot. Now ride with me around the block. I promise not to go fast."

Initially, Sanchez kept his promise not to go fast, but that promise was soon forgotten. The ride was totally exhilarating, like the rides she took with her father on the old wooden Cyclone roller coaster at Coney Island. Vera, in no time, became molded to the back side of the bike and the biker. She was hooked on a drug called "excitement." Each afternoon after summer school, Vera met Sanchez in the parking lot for her afternoon dalliance. Soon the gang arrived as well—rugged, wild, misunderstood—all similarly and strangely alluring. Sanchez controlled everyone with his charm and intimidation. She admired his power and the gang's unquestioning response to his authority. Sanchez transitioned with ease between charm and intimidation. She never knew which he would employ, but Vera was attracted to both.

Vera's first night venture out with the gang was to a garbage dump outside the city on another hot July evening. This excursion required a clandestine escape from her grieving father, accomplished with the same ease as tonight's escape but a more timely rendezvous in the vacant lot down the street. For the first time, Vera met other gang women, including Amber Morelli, a well-endowed blonde bimbo who rode in the saddle behind Sanchez. Amber and Vera hardly spoke to each other except through a sneer and a glare. On the ride out behind BB, Vera enjoyed the cool night breeze against her face and the vibration between her legs of the motorcycle at high speed.

Sanchez handed Vera a .38 revolver and challenged her to shoot aimlessly into the air. Vera took the dare and soon was blasting empty beer bottles at close range. Her accuracy at longer range was errant and, according to Sanchez, attributable to poor form. Vera welcomed his instruction but not just for the reason of mastering the technique of small arms fire. Standing behind Vera with his left leg planted squarely between her legs, shoulder-width apart—ostensibly to illustrate the proper spread of her feet—Sanchez held Vera's outstretched right wrist with his left hand and their index fingers entwined over the trigger, pointing the .38 downrange. Their sexually suggestive entanglement unexpectedly accelerated Vera's breathing, causing the barrel to wobble perceptively.

"Sorry, Felipe. Guns make me nervous." This was partially a lie.

"Try a rum and cola." Sanchez handed her the rum bottle, and Vera slugged down the rum. "Now, chase it down with this." She took the cola and repeated the sequence. "Now, let's try again," Sanchez said.

Sanchez blanketed Vera's firm breasts with his left forearm as he pulled her backward against the length and feel of his body so the two were merged as one. Sanchez held Vera in this position for an exaggerated length of time before he pulled her hair away from her right ear and whispered firing instructions in a soft voice. "Exhale, aim, now fire." Their combined breathing distracted Vera and caused her to miss her initial glass target, but the correct firing technique was burned forever into her mind. Together they fired with greater accuracy at the garbage-eating wharf rats in the distant dump beyond the glass bottles. The rats' eyes turned an eerie red when curiously attracted to the high beams of the motorcycle headlights, most often their last view of the world.

No matter whether the targets were bottles or rats, Vera, independently of her coach, became a sharpshooter. In fact, the absence of his hands-on instruction improved her breathing and accuracy. As with most tasks taken seriously, she quickly excelled. Her marksmanship promoted her immediate acceptance among BB and the gang. Vera was surprised at her need for the gang's acceptance. She had retreated to herself in the aftermath of her mother's death, and without the gang's acceptance, Vera knew she would lose Sanchez. She yearned for more of his private sessions, but wondered why it took him so long to become sexually aggressive. Vera's face and contours attracted an endless procession of aggressive boys at summer school. "Why not Sanchez?" Vera exhaled and whispered audibly. She steadied her breathing and rapidly blasted three consecutive rats at fifty yards.

Vera signed on with the gang after that night in July, and as an initiate she was required to emblazon her body with the azure lightning-bolt tattoo. Vera lay motionless in the squalor of the backroom tattoo parlor in Queens. The emblem was to adorn her statuesque neck. The design extended down about two inches behind her right ear and reached almost to the top of her shoulder, concealed from the world and her father when her hair fell to her shoulders, but there for the gang and the entire world to see when her hair was pulled up. The vibrating needle bloodied her neck with piercing discomfort for the two-hour procedure, but the results were stunning and permanent. Sanchez, BB, and the gang applauded their approval, all except one. Vera was getting too close for Amber's comfort.

Armed now with more empty rum bottles, the pitching duel continued with no one matching Sanchez's skill and accuracy. The revelry in the darkened living room increased proportionately with the consumption of rum and now hashish. Vera knew she had to surpass Amber tonight, her principal competitor. The role Amber played on the Sanchez team was obvious. Apparent, too, was her lack of shrewdness that Sanchez demanded of each player. Her team play was sloppy, diminished by her constant state of drug and alcohol inebriation. Even Amber, through a veil of chronic intoxication, knew the risk Vera presented, and so Amber watched Vera's every move.

Aware that Amber neither spoke nor understood a word of Spanish, Vera tiptoed past Amber to a position immediately behind Sanchez, pushed her torso upward to its fullest extent, and planted a kiss on the back of his neck, followed by a feigned congratulatory message for his bottle-pitching duel. "Muy bien, Felipe. ¿Cuál es major para usted, béisbol o qué?" (Very good, Felipe. What is better for you, baseball or what?)

Through Vera's body language, Amber interpreted the move for what it was and exploded with a fist directed at Vera's nose, but just as Vera descended from her tiptoes, Amber's drunken punch erred a fraction of an inch over Vera's head and landed squarely on an unintended target: Sanchez's nose, just as he turned to face his Spanish-speaking inquisitor.

"Oh, God . . . I'm sorry," Amber said.

Vera instinctively retaliated with a right cross to Amber's chin. The first punch of her life was fast and light. The excitement of watching brawls in the school cafeteria often broke her daily boredom. What Vera learned as a spectator was the importance of landing the first punch. The result buckled Amber at her knees and dropped her to the floor. Laughter and cheers erupted from the encircling gang, who exhorted Vera to continue her feline attack. A strange feeling of power and dominance, never before experienced, surged over Vera as she taunted Amber, "the sorry bitch," to get up from the floor. In a moment of uncontrollable rage, Vera sensed she was capable of killing Amber, but fortunately she would not find out tonight if that was true. Sanchez grabbed Vera by her ponytail and planted his foot onto Amber's chest, pinning her shoulder blades squarely to the floor to foreclose any possible risk of retaliation. Twisting Vera's head by turning her ponytail in the opposite direction so that her lips were within inches of his, Sanchez complimented Vera. "Buen golpe muchacha, por otro tiempo, no por esta noche." (Nice punch girl, for another time, not tonight.) The answer arrived to the second prong of the Sanchez test. Vera was violent.

Sanchez released Vera and Amber simultaneously. "We are about business tonight, amigos. Midnight is payday. It was to be a surprise, but you need to know why the cheap rum and catfighting must end. We have delivered some of New Jersey's finest ladies to the back bedrooms of the Wicked Whiskey Bar. The patrons have been generous, but it's time for our ladies to return home across the state line and for us to collect our management fees for such lovely vice and protection. ¿Comprende ustedes? We have work to do. ¡Vamanos!"

The gang understood the urgency of *vamanos*, particularly those who had witnessed the Sanchez propensity to stab the tardy, and transformed itself into a team of professional racketeers.

All heeded the directive, except BB, who headed down the hall to the back bathroom ostensibly to relieve himself before the long ride. Secure in the filthy premises bathroom, with the door locked, BB, carefully coiffed in biker disguise for his undercover assignment, pulled back the lapel of his black leather jacket and spoke into a hidden wire. "Did you copy that? Repeat. Did you copy that? Wicked Whiskey Bar . . . midnight. No time for further direction or communication. All backup must be in place by 2400 hours to take down Bike Leader on numerous felonies. Final transmission . . . copy . . . Wicked Whiskey Bar . . . backup in place by 2400 hours."

Abruptly, from the other side of the door there was a loud, forceful banging and twisting of the doorknob. The knob fell harmlessly to the floor. BB folded back his lapel just as Sanchez busted through the door, shrieking, "Nothing but trouble since the day you arrived, Señor Black Beard Hombre. You've moved up too damned quickly. Guess I'll have to kill you. The rest of us wait while you take a leak. What the hell's wrong with you?"

Sanchez smacked the undercover agent sharply on his face with the back of his hand while yanking BB by his beard out of the bathroom. Sanchez regretted that he had left his knife in his saddle bag. "Piss on yourself next time. When I say move, you damned well move in the direction of the choppers, not the bathroom."

BB's enmity smoldered but abated. This was the night for a bust, not to settle a score.

"So what about your pretty woman? The rules don't apply to her?"

Sanchez raised his fist to strike again, but stopped and smiled.

"I don't have time to kill your tardy ass now, but you just guaranteed that I'll kill your tardy ass tomorrow, so live to enjoy a few more hours of life before I kill you. But right now, you must earn what I've already paid for. Shoot straight tonight, compadre. Who knows? I might only stab you a little bit. You can take a good stabbing, BB, can't you?"

Before releasing his beard, Sanchez sarcastically patted BB on the cheek. "¡Vamanos!"

Outside, Sanchez and BB mounted their bikes, propelled their right legs almost simultaneously on the kick start, and brought their machines to life. All engines rumbled in thunderous unison as drivers and riders roared to their business appointment . . . and because of Amber's second-place finish, Vera rode astride the lead bike right behind Sanchez, her night's championship prize.

CHAPTER THREE

August 1980

Expressionless riders straddled steel choppers that stood in a semicircle, barricading the entrance to the Wicked Whiskey Bar. Hot engines rumbled at idle, all facing away from the entrance, except for one. Sanchez and Vera had dismounted, making their way inside to collect the weekly fees hidden inside the wall safe of the manager's interior office. The marauding gang outside was engulfed in humidity and concealed in darkness. Their black bikes and leather jackets blended into the night. Absent, though, in the darkness were the ominous parking lights that earlier silhouetted the bikes in the abandoned lot near Vera's Brooklyn home.

The riders watched the procession of cars, loaded with drunken patrons spent from a night of whoring, exit at the rear of the unlighted parking lot. The very last one, a cherry-red '57 Chevy convertible, top down, sped away, leaving a trail of thick white smoke belching from its dual exhausts and the stench of burning black rubber pealing away from its oversized tires. The convertible slid nearly sideways onto the highway while the passengers tossed empty liquor bottles high into the air, each landing in a sequential explosion on the concrete pavement.

Only minutes before, the gang had rounded up the last of the night's revelers, five drunken sailors, and ordered them off the premises. The sailors wanted more of the whiskey and women before their shore leave ended, but for BB, it was too close to midnight, so he bloodied the nose of the drunkest objector to illustrate what it would be like for the rest to delay. All left.

The manager's office was a windowless room that served as a connecter for two hallways. One hallway led to a back entrance past several storage rooms crammed full of lounging prostitutes and illicit vice. The other led past the premise toilets to an elongated pine bar that stretched the length of a sprawling room.

The Wicked Whiskey Bar was a converted diner that once served the guests of the Moonlight Tourist Court. The bar fronted twenty-five detached motor court units with quaint stepped-front porches. The units no longer provided rest for weary travelers on the two-lane Empire State Highway out front. Isolation from motoring families and competition from the chain hotels on the new interstate caused its demise. Every night of the last week, the musty bedrooms, leased by the hour, served the bar patrons and their hired women. Sanchez skimmed 50 percent of the gross as fees for providing sexual entertainment for the patrons and kickbacks for the cops to look the other way while the crimes were going down inside the tourist court bedrooms.

The old diner booths were now completely empty and the bar darkened, except for the reflection of a single red neon light configured in the shape of a tilted whiskey bottle that illuminated the window above the double push-through aluminum doors.

Whores, now off the clock, lounged around in plain view and jabbered among themselves in Jersey accents laced with vulgarities. Although finished for the night, the women were still dressed in provocative attire designed to allure the bar patrons into propositions for an assortment of sexual favors. Their intimate apparel and perfumed bodies added to the sexual tension that filled the hot August air.

Vera stared at one woman passed out on a brown leather couch, her veins tracked on both arms by countless needle injections, and she knew what made this woman sell her body for money. Another prostitute spun Sanchez around with her left arm just as he passed by and unzipped his fly simultaneously with her right hand. "For twenty-five dollars I'll suck your cock dry in less than a minute. It won't take long, honey, but fifty, if you make me wait. The best part of the deal is it won't cost you a dime extra to let your pretty bitch watch." She glared directly at Vera. "Maybe she'll learn something from a real pro, or maybe you would like to watch us! That might cost you, depending on how good she is!"

She laughed uncontrollably through tobacco-stained teeth until she began to cough up phlegm. Sanchez rejected the overt invitation to make himself the last trick of the evening as he pushed past the hacking whore, pulling Vera through the back hallway with him.

Outside the entrance to the manager's office, Sanchez turned suddenly and pinned Vera forcefully to the wall with both his muscular arms flanking her shoulders. He leaned forward and pushed his lips onto hers. Vera, momentarily caught-off guard, resisted, but then yielded. She thought, *Hadn't this been what I've been waiting for since the night at the dump? If not now, then it will be Amber later.*

Vera had fantasized in great detail what it would be like with Sanchez. This was her chance. She opened her mouth and kissed back with a passion that signaled she was ready for more.

Just as quickly as Sanchez became aggressive, he stopped. The business at hand was the collection of the weekly split soon to be lifted from the manager's safe just on the other side of the door. So Sanchez pulled back a matter of inches from Vera's lips, dropped his arms to her sides, and then moved his hands around and underneath her jacket to the flesh just above the small of her back and whispered, "Mi pequena campeóna de boxeo, nosotros debemos ser pacientes hasta que nuestros negocios terminen, pero yo siento que usted está lista a mover a Amber de mi campo de juego cierto. ¿Verdad?" (My pretty boxing champion, we must be patient until our business is finished, but I feel you are ready to remove Amber from my playing field. Right?)

"I'm ready when you are." Vera smiled. "A woman like me prefers pleasure before business, but if your business is that important, señor, let's not leave this open for business all night. Too much for the ladies in the back room!" Vera reached down and tugged his fly upward, using both hands.

Outside, the night riders throttled their hot engines, blasting the silence with unmuffled thunder and raising the temperature of the humid hot air. BB, atop the bike nearest the entrance, searched for any sign of backup in the darkness beyond the parking lot. Sweat poured down from his armpits, soaking the inside of his jacket. BB wondered whether the wire transmission had been received. He revved his engine. Instantly, the tachometer needle bounced to the right and then, after a second time, shot well over the red line. Any agent concealed beyond the tree line could not possibly mistake his position in the darkness.

OK, just where the hell are they? he thought to himself.

BB questioned whether there had been enough time to organize an assault team in such a remote location, miles outside the Manhattan headquarters, which was tucked just blocks from the Twin Towers of the World Trade Center.

"Nothing!" BB blurted in frustration.

"Did you say something, BB?"

"Not me, man."

BB could smell the scent of his wife's perfume and the talcum of his infant twins from just a few hours before when he left home for his undercover assignment. If backup was not in place, he alone would be left to make what could be a life-or-death decision. Time was running out. The transaction was going down now!

Desperate to receive some kind of a sign, BB flipped the switch to his headlights to signal his position in the night. No observable sign returned from the outer darkness.

"BB, tell me, man, just what in the hell do you think you're doing?"

BB flipped the switch off. "Sorry, man, just a nervous habit . . . won't happen again."

A faceless voice responded, "Amigo, if you should experience the misfortune of this nervous habit again, I will have to break out your headlight . . . with your head!"

Laughter erupted from the bikers.

"I've got to take a leak." Not waiting for permission, BB dismounted and made his way inside the bar.

Vera, oblivious to any possible danger, thumbed mindlessly through a fashion magazine as if she might have been waiting in a beauty salon for a hairstyle instead of the interior of the manager's office to witness a felony that could land her in the slammer for years. Sanchez watched the night manager, a man with ruddy fingers, count out a large stack of bills removed from the safe hidden in the interior wall of the windowless back room.

"Fifty thousand," the manager said, extending the stack of bills to Sanchez. "Not a bad take for a week's work. Who says drugs, whiskey, and prostitution don't pay well, man? But too damned bad our ladies must return to New Jersey. Some of those whores are pretty damned good at what they do for a living. You ought to try one, but there's no use pressing our luck, right, Sanchez?"

Sanchez ignored the manager's question as he was counting the stack of bills. Vera looked up from her magazine. "It's always business before pleasure with him."

With his FBI service revolver drawn, BB slipped silently past the johns to the end of the hallway, stopping outside the manager's door. As he listened to the voices through the solid oak panels, BB knew immediately that he would have to act or lose his opportunity to witness the incriminating transaction going down on the other side of the door. BB hesitated a few seconds longer to calculate the consequences of his decision. As he held his service revolver at the end of a V with both of his arms extended straight up, BB whispered, "Where in the hell is backup? Odds are good that the assault team is in place right now, listening to my wire, and knowing exactly when to move. They don't want to blow my cover before I have the goods on Sanchez. But maybe not, maybe they're not out there at all."

BB listened through the door, but there was no conversation on the other side.

"Can't be the right time," he whispered again.

He could have returned from the john with no one the wiser, still undercover as Black Beard, gang mercenary, and waited for another time and better odds. But act now and Sanchez was snared, caught red-handed counting out the cash, the guaranteed removal of a serious racketeer from the streets of New York. Even better, if he acted now, Sanchez would have known the sting of an undercover FBI agent who was not the cowering minion whom Sanchez intimidated less than an hour earlier. BB pictured Sanchez's face and his look of shock.

BB whispered, "But do nothing and both opportunities could be lost forever."

BB impulsively kicked through the locked door with badge and gun. A quick check of the room revealed three individuals, but no visible weapons. Sanchez was still counting the stack of bills. Vera was reading her magazine, and the night manager was standing next to the wall safe.

"FBI . . . Drop to the floor, face down, discard all weapons you have on your person, and do it now," BB announced in a calm voice unbefitting his tenuous circumstances. "Felipe Sanchez, you are under arrest for extortion, racketeering, felonious sale of narcotics, and violation of the Mann Act, just to name a few."

BB concluded, no matter what, the present situation was manageable, one armed against three unarmed. His life depended on the correctness of his assumption that a flanking backup would charge through the rear door in a matter of seconds. His lapel wire clearly signaled that he was making a solo arrest. Premature gunfire would be fatal. A discharged weapon changed the equation with a minimum of ten gang members pouring into the office ahead of backup, way beyond what he could control.

"Are you tardy again, man?" Sanchez said, ignoring BB's command. "Maybe you gotta take a leak and mumble something into a wire. The bathroom is down the hall on the left. So, Señor FBI agent, where are your buddies now? Oh, I'm sorry—that's 'backup'? Seems to me you're here all alone, amigo. You know what that means, don't you? You're a dead man, BB. So *you* better drop your gun and surrender to me, and I'll just take you hostage. Exchange you maybe for my freedom."

Doubt crept into BB's mind as he thought again. *Time for backup. Where the hell is my backup? What if Sanchez is right? But, no, there's a reason. They're waiting to record the evidence of the crime on tape. The FBI would never leave an undercover agent in such a predicament.*

BB knew he was in a standoff with his life in the balance. He would have to stall and squeeze out another minute.

"Please give me even the slightest opportunity to . . . let's see, how did you say it, Sanchez? 'You can be sure I will kill your tardy ass.' Well, Sanchez, why don't you try to kill my tardy ass right now? Maybe I'll just stab you through that hand while you're counting out the cash . . . make sure you and the evidence don't walk away, or maybe just watch you bleed to death."

BB walked over to Sanchez and smacked him with the back of his hand, knocking him backward into the wall.

"I will be pleased to accommodate you, Señor FBI agent," Sanchez wiped blood from his lower lip and replied, "but first you must drop that muy grande FBI pistole so we can fight like men with knives, the winner takes all, including the pretty woman."

BB continued. "You tick me off, Sanchez. You know that? I love undercover work, extra pay, everything about it, especially when I can rid the streets of a creep like you. It makes it all worthwhile, but now you've made me blow my cover. I could have nailed a bunch of your sorry-assed goons tonight from inside the holding cell 'cause they all think I'm a slimer like you. But what the hell, I'm going to take you down tonight, Sanchez. Oh, sorry, for the sake of those listening to my wire. That's 'Bike Leader.' That's your official FBI name, you know. That's how I'll refer to you at trial, right before the judge salts your ass away for twenty years to life. Wonder what you'll look like after all that time, Sanchez, busting rocks in maximum security?"

Vera, frightened now, her back pressed firmly against the opposite wall, sensed the room in front of her was about to explode. She knew how Sanchez talked about prison. He would never go back there. BB turned to face Vera to buy more time.

"Now, Vera, do as I say. Drop to the floor, remove and throw down your weapon. I just can't figure exactly what the hell an uptown girl like you is doing in the middle of all of this, but I like your chances if you cooperate. I bet the DA will respond to your innocent good looks."

Vera did not know what to do with the dangerous standoff unfolding in front of her. Her idea of gang fun was strictly as a daredevil diversion, certainly not witnessing the murder of an undercover cop or spending the rest of her life in prison. Surrender and cooperation seemed to be the better way out. Vera withdrew her .38 from her jacket pocket and threw it down behind her as she dropped to the floor. She stretched out face down.

"Smart move, Vera," BB said, relieved to see there was one less gun to defend.

"Señorita, how easy you give up," Sanchez said. "Nervous chicks like you often turn into stool pigeons at the police station. Tell me, how easy do you turn into a pigeon, Vera?"

In the instant BB reached to secure Vera's gun from the floor, the manager moved his hand farther into the safe to the trigger of a concealed .45-caliber pistol, withdrew it slowly, and pointed it directly at the agent's head.

"Don't mean to interrupt, but I've got you cold. You can die or drop your gun. That's my best offer."

At the same time, Sanchez pulled his gun from his jacket and aimed it at BB's chest. Both had dead aim. BB looked down at Vera, then Sanchez, and back to the manager. He knew he could not drop both of them before one of them shot him. BB also worried that a stray bullet might hit Vera, so he was left no choice.

"Offer accepted." BB dropped his gun. He thought for the last time to himself, *Where the hell is backup?* He knew all too well that the time for help was over. He regretted his decision, but BB made one last attempt at a stall.

"All I have to do is give the signal and fifty armed and very pissed-off agents will come rushing into here! So while we wait, let's fight with our knives to see who takes the woman."

With a big smile breaking across his face, Sanchez ignored BB's offer to fight. "Guey, esto es obvio, yo deber haber sabido." (Man, you were so obvious, I should have known.)

Sanchez's eyes narrowed as he retrieved Vera's pistol from the floor and walked calmly behind his victim. "Now, Vera, get up. Here's your gun. Show me just how much you hate the cops."

In the next instant, Sanchez coldly shot BB in the back of his head, his knees buckling as he dropped face down on the floor, blood spewing from the back of his skull.

"Good work, Vera. You shot a rat, just like at the dump," Sanchez said clearly. Vera stared in a stunned silence. Sanchez dropped down and lifted BB up by the head and looked into his open eyes. "Now, see, amigo, I told you. You *are* a dead man."

Vera recoiled, not fully believing what she just witnessed. In that instant she knew Sanchez was an animal without human emotion. Sanchez dropped Vera's pistol and sarcastically said, "Vera, bet you didn't know that your gun was loaded. You only wanted to scare señor. Now look what you've done."

Vera's fear turned to anger. "You are a sorry murdering bastard!"

Sanchez lifted up BB's jacket lapel and ripped out the wire.

Once the unmistakable sound of the solitary gunshot escaped the interior of the Wicked Whiskey Bar, the FBI's automatic weapons, inexplicably delayed, blazed red in the night from every direction at the scattering and diving perimeter guard. The gang's training was of no use, to the badly outnumbered bikers who returned scattered fire instead of just riding off while Sanchez remained inside. They were paid to perform. The extra bonus for holding the perimeter did not compare to the physical cost of hightailing it if Sanchez were to make it out alive. No matter, the gang was surrounded on all sides, outnumbered five to one, with every avenue of escape blocked. Their choice was simple: keep firing and die, or give up and live. All were quickly arrested, cuffed, and forced to the ground.

In seconds, the agents swarmed like ground hornets over the inside of the bar shouting, "Agent down, agent down!"

Sanchez placed the cash inside his jacket and fortified the entrance to the office by dragging an armchair in front of the door. The manager, fearing the advancing army of agents, blindly opened fire in the general direction of the attack coming from the hallway on the other side of the barricaded door—a poorly reasoned decision. A hail of bullets from a chorus of automatic weapons splintered all of the furniture and glass in the small room. In an instant, the night manager was shot dead with a bullet into his temple, dropped to the floor with his eyes open, as if he were staring right into the back of BB's shattered head.

Vera grabbed her discarded .38 from the floor and fired through the partially obliterated door at the animated targets on the other side, curiously contrasting the slower-moving agents with the faster-moving wharf rats at the dump. The gunfire from Sanchez and Vera unexpectedly pinned the advancing agents in the narrow corridor. Sanchez shouted to Vera over the deafening barrage, much louder than the fire at the dump, "Cover me, Vera, while I make a break for the back, and then I'll cover you."

Vera heard nothing but exploding weapons and continued firing her .38. Sanchez miraculously made it through the opposite door, down the hall to the rear flop room, flushing the screaming brothel on his way to the back window and wishing he had brought Vera with him, but only as a hostage to broker his own freedom. Every whore in the brothel was useless to him as a hostage. Sanchez had no intention of returning for Vera. All that mattered was his own escape. As he pushed his head halfway through the back window, a team of flanking agents greeted him.

"Throw down your weapon. Place your hands behind your head and drop to the ground. Now, Felipe Sanchez, your options and ours in the next few seconds are very limited." Sanchez, vulnerable and defeated, was still able to formulate an avenue for his ultimate escape in the seeds of doubt that he had planted through the FBI wire, so he complied fully. "The bitch shot BB. Never for a second did I believe she would do it. Must have been some mistake. I swear if I hadn't ditched when I did, she would have shot my ass, too."

Inside, Vera's revolver clicked mechanically, empty of bullets. She, without a clue as to how to reload, tossed her pistol out the door to the charging agents and surrendered. Vera tried to hold her hands up but had to rub the tears from her eyes from a room suffocating with the residue of spent gunpowder. She announced to the agents, "Thank God you are here. That son of a bitch is a cold-blooded killer!"

CHAPTER FOUR

August 1980

"Mr. Benjamin Ochman."

These were the words that Ben Ochman awakened to as he silenced the ringing telephone beside his chair in the living room as the grandfather clock behind him completed the fourth chime.

"Yes, this is Ben Ochman. Who is this?

"This is Special Agent Ramirez with the Federal Bureau of Investigation. Do you have a daughter by the name of Vera Ochman, whose eighteenth birthday is tomorrow?"

"Why, yes, I do," Ben responded, still half asleep. "Is there something wrong? Why on earth are you calling me at this hour?" Ben turned around and looked at the grandfather clock. "For Christ sakes, it's four a.m."

Clumps of white wax, still melting from the flickering candles, accumulated on both sides of their holders, dripping all the while on the mantle above. The dining room chair proved too awkward for a bed and the table too cluttered for a pillow so Ben, sometime during the night, had moved a few feet to the living room to be with his wife, momentarily alive, in the canvas above the mantle.

Agent Ramirez continued the conversation in his monotone. "She's being held in the jail at the Manhattan

Federal Courthouse on multiple felony charges, including the murder of a federal agent. Because she's a minor, the law requires immediate parental notification."

"Murder? Did you say 'murder'? That's totally crazy. There's been some mistake. This is some kind of bad joke. My telephone number is unlisted. My daughter is asleep upstairs in her bedroom," Ben said curtly and prepared to hang up.

"No mistake, Mr. Ochman. You better go check your daughter's bedroom."

Ben rubbed his head that ached from too much wine and reached for a cigarette from a crumpled pack beside his chair, knocking it off the table with the back of his hand when he discovered it was empty. He placed the telephone down, labored to get up from his chair, sat back down, finally managed to stand up, lumbered to the stairs, grasped the rail, and ascended to his daughter's bedroom. He knocked gently on the door, a standing courtesy that Vera demanded of all who wished to enter.

Ben knocked a second time, his ear inclined against the door to hear his daughter's sleepy voice whisper permission to enter. Ben spoke in his normal tone. "Vera, I need to speak with you. There's a crazy man on the phone." Ben waited, but no response came from the interior. His voice and knock elevated, "Vera, my sweet child, open the door, please," but the silence continued from the other side. "Vera, I said, open the damned door." The quiet knocking turned to pounding. His daughter apparently must be awakened from some deep sleep, or so he thought.

Ben turned the doorknob, pushed into her room, and flipped on the light. He first noticed Vera's shorts and T-shirt crumpled in a pile beside her closet, then the fully opened window at the far end of the room. Next his eyes fell onto her neatly made bed. Vera was not there. Vera was not anywhere! Ben's breathing quickened. He walked over to Vera's telephone and picked up the receiver.

"I don't know where she is."

"Mr. Ochman, you better get dressed and come down to the courthouse immediately."

"I'll be right there." He hung up.

Stunned, Ben crossed the upstairs hallway to his bedroom, his mind transitioning from sleep into reality. "Surely, I'm still asleep in the chair downstairs. This is some sort of a damned nightmare. Yes, that's it, I'm having a nightmare. Wake up, Ben, but damn it all to hell, I *am* awake!"

Ben, now at his bedroom closet, could barely concentrate on finding his clothes. He seldom dressed to go anywhere. He never knew what to wear.

"This can't be true. My daughter jailed in the Manhattan Courthouse. What did he say? *Murder?*" Ben talked to himself as if someone were listening. "Holy Mother of God, you know I can't take this."

His hands trembled as he pulled from his closet a collared white shirt and long brown slacks. "I'll ask her mother." As often happened, Ben acted as if she were alive and often directed audible questions to her about Vera, but the terrible apprehension nagged at him again—a second incomprehensible tragedy to face alone.

Sitting on his bed, Ben's heart raced as he slipped on a pair of brown shoes, laced them up, and almost passed out from the sudden rush of blood to his head when he leaned over. He regained his composure, stood up, spread his arm in a circular motion over his marital bed filled with passionate memories, and walked out of the bedroom.

At the top of the stairs, Ben turned halfway around hesitantly and questioned whether to return for a necktie. He heard, as he often had before, the voice of his wife beckoning him to join her in the living room below, or was that just the operator's recorded voice intoning mechanically through a receiver left off the hook too long?

Ben dropped his right foot down the first step, grasping the rail, and began to descend. Suddenly, he swayed as a penetrating pain knifed its way through his heart. His hand, grasping the rail, flew up to his chest as Ben's consciousness turned to black. His knees buckled, and he was instantly dead even before gravity could smash his head into the railing and drag him tumbling to the bottom of the stairs.

The candles burned much smaller but still flickered above the fireplace, illuminating the dark canvas. The Latin goddess smiled. Through the window over the stair landing, the faint glow of an early dawn preceded another sweltering day in the city and cast a dim light over the worry frozen on Ben's face.

CHAPTER FIVE

November 2007

Friday, November 23, 2007, was the date displayed in black Roman letters on Victoria's military desk calendar. For the third time in less than an hour, she rechecked the calendar to make sure the day and date matched correctly, and then her eyes returned to the work on her desk. Her fingers fidgeted nervously with the pages in a large black policy manual. Unable to concentrate on the fine print, she pushed back and swiveled her high-backed black leather chair 180 degrees, staring impassively through the windows behind her at the falling snow blanketing the parade field outside Marine headquarters in Stuttgart, Germany. Last night's snowfall added at least eight inches to an existing base of almost two feet, and it was still snowing. She swiveled back and glanced across the room to the ashen logs flickering in the stone fireplace beneath the wide hickory mantle that stretched along the entire north wall opposite her desk. Eight double-hung paned windows, concealed behind closed burgundy draperies that served also to insulate the interior from a freezing subzero east wind, ran the length of the adjacent wall and stood in contrast to the windowless west wall, divided evenly in half by a pair of glass French doors with glass handles that opened into the outside corridor.

Victoria's military dress jacket with an assortment of colorful ribbons pinned above the left pocket hung neatly on a wooden coat hanger on a stand behind her desk. The name tag read, "Brig. Gen. Victoria Pierce." Her eyes returned to the thick manual on the top of her highly polished dark mahogany desk. The bottom edges of two brightly colored military flags, standing at attention on each side of the mahogany desk, dropped within an inch of the wall-to-wall carpeted floor that matched perfectly the burgundy draperies.

With an audible sigh, Victoria slammed one side of the manual over the other, shoved it back into a bottom drawer, and turned to stare blankly at the photographs on the credenza behind her desk, wondering if Sam's military flight would be delayed by the snow.

The collage of neatly arranged photographs visually narrated the last twenty-five years of Victoria's life in the military. In the very back, a slightly discolored snapshot, encased in green plastic veneer, framed three figures standing on the south lawn of the White House. Sam and the president, both smiling, were pictured pointing to the medal just awarded to Lance Corporal Pierce immediately after the Rose Garden ceremony over twenty-five years ago. Vera remembered in perfect detail that hot August day in 1981, the day she first met Sam Eagan, his shocker of a dinner invitation that followed the ceremony under the pretense of discussing ROTC scholarships, when his real objective was a steamy night of romance with a very attractive and somewhat naive lance corporal.

> In the Rose Garden, assembled dignitaries milled around, some smoking a last-minute cigarette while they waited for the president. Standing out among the older men in dark suits about twenty-five yards away was one quite handsome younger

man dressed in a light gray suit wearing a bold red- and-white-striped tie. I wondered who the handsome gentleman might be and could do little other than ogle the man, when, suddenly without warning, he stared directly back at me. To my astonishment, this man was crossing the garden and in a moment was right beside me.

"Good morning, Corporal. I'm Sam Eagan. I've been reading about your heroics and actually asked the president if I might attend your ceremony. Do you mind?"

Mind? Before I answered this inquiry, I thought to myself, *How could I possibly mind the attention of this man? Six-feet-two, black wavy hair, penetrating blue eyes, and positively up close the best-looking man I've ever seen.*

"Well, Mr. Eagan, sir, I don't know you well enough to object, now, do I? Is there some reason why I should mind?"

Before Sam could respond, we were interrupted by the aide in charge, who was pointing to the group that Sam just left behind. "Senator Eagan, please rejoin the other lawmakers behind the ribbons over there. The president has just lifted off from Camp David." Sam retraced his steps back across the lawn.

I remembered saying in a whisper to myself on the way to taking my place in the center of the color guard, *So the quite handsome Mr. Eagan is Senator Eagan. Well, well.*

After the President of the United States pinned the Medal of Honor above my name tag, the ceremony abruptly closed. I watched intently. No one came. A minute passed and still no one.

The press corps left. Everyone left except Senator Sam. He made his way back across the lawn to my side. Senator Eagan stopped to exchange handshakes and a few polite words with the president. His aide tried to pull the president by his arm toward the White House to meet his next engagement. Sam pulled a small camera from his jacket pocket and asked the aide to snap a photo of the two men flanking me on each side and pointing to my medal. The aide complied, and Sam acknowledged, "That will be a great photograph." The president whispered words of congratulations in my ear and quickly disappeared into the West Wing of the White House. I stood alone and wondered if or when the FBI would close in for an arrest. Sam turned directly toward me and looked me straight in the eye. "Congratulations, Corporal. Well done."

"Thank you, Senator Eagan."

"Please, call me Sam."

"OK, then, Sam."

"Where to from here, Corporal Pierce?" Sam must have thought that I might reply, "Please call me 'Victoria.'"

"Oh, back to Bogotá and a light-duty station."

"Seems a waste to me, Corporal. Ever give any thought to finishing college? Some of the best universities in the country have officer candidate programs that lead to commissions in all branches of the military while earning bachelors' degrees. We have plenty of scholarships to offer the right candidates. Seems to me you would be a shoe-in for such a program after today's award."

"You seem to know a lot about this."

"I'm on the Senate Armed Services Committee, which has a great deal of oversight of these programs. Look, if you are interested, why not have dinner with me tonight, and I'll explain more?"

I certainly did not expect a dinner invitation from a United States senator. I hesitated and looked into Sam's eyes for a clue as to his motivation. His blue eyes were soft . . . kind . . . so what was the harm in having dinner? I did not realize at the time that anyone who wanted to advance a career in the military would have leaped at the chance of dining with a member of the Senate Armed Services Committee. But I hesitated a bit longer.

"As I said before the ceremony, Sam, I don't know enough about you to object. Shouldn't I mind having dinner with a man I just met today?"

"Strictly educational business, Corporal. Besides, I greatly admire your valor and want to express our government's appreciation by taking you out as the guest of the United States Senate."

I looked again at Sam's eyes and saw no guile. *What would be so wrong dining out with such a handsome man before boarding a plane back to Bogotá?* I thought to myself. The decision was made. "I'm staying at the Mayflower Hotel. I can be ready at seven. And please call me 'Victoria.'"

Sam smiled. I smiled back. "Well, then, it's settled, Victoria. Look for my limousine in front of the Mayflower at seven sharp."

Victoria's eyes refocused on a dark framed photograph that sat to the side and slightly in front of the ceremonial photo and showed a young officer candidate, soon to be Lieutenant Victoria Pierce, in a black gown receiving her bachelor's degree in military science, summa cum laude. Victoria, though now much older, nevertheless appeared no less striking than the day she graduated from college. Sam snapped this photo of his proud graduate almost four years to the day after Victoria's initial conference with Dean Saunders, where she tried to explain her relationship with a young U.S. Senator fifteen years her senior. Victoria clearly recalled that tense conversation with the dean of admissions.

At exactly 3:00 p.m. that August day, I remembered sitting calmly on the settee across from Dean Saunders, a thin man of limited humor who was dressed in a gray suit with matching thin tie.

"Miss Pierce, how do you know Senator Eagan? You must be a constituent?"

I was uncertain as to the exact meaning of "constituent," but quite certain of the implication, so I slowly uncrossed my legs and replied, "Let's just say that Sam and I are good friends."

The implication of the gesture and response confirmed the dean's suspicions and ended the conference. Dean Saunders stood and extended his hand, "Well, now, Miss Pierce, any friend of Senator Eagan is a friend of this university. With the senator's recommendation, your admission here is assured."

So I stood up and asked, "And what about a scholarship?"

"A federally subsidized military scholarship will cover your entire tuition and all living expenses. You will be admitted into the best naval ROTC program in the country. After completing the general curriculum at the end of your sophomore year, you will elect your bachelor's program that will lead to a degree from one of the best universities in the country. You will graduate as a lieutenant in the United States Marine Corps, but then you will be required to fulfill the terms of your military scholarship by completing at least two years of active military service. Do you have any questions?"

"Only one, Dean Saunders. When do classes begin?"

Sam's explanation of the relationship to Dean Saunders and all other inquisitors in the intervening years was quite simple: "Victoria is the daughter I never had." But for Victoria it was not so simple. She could not even feign to believe that Sam was even remotely a father figure. She had a father, albeit deceased years before. Asked again today, she still could not and would not rationally express her long-standing relationship with the handsome Senator Eagan. Why should she be made to disclose her second-most-private secret? Why should she have to explain the fact that she was not married after twenty-five years? Their long-term affair was a closely guarded secret buried deeply within her heart. But the explanation of the affair was in reality quite simple. She fell madly in love with the handsome United States Senator who bedded her that searing August night in his Connecticut Avenue apartment.

By 7:15 of the evening that followed the afternoon medal ceremony in the Rose Garden, I was riding in the backseat of the senator's limousine on its way down Connecticut Avenue to one of Washington's most exclusive restaurants. The chauffeur offered to open a bottle of champagne, chilling in the backseat refrigerator, an accoutrement of the service. I was perched upon the leather cushion right beneath the rear window in my neatly pressed dress uniform, positioned almost twenty feet away from the driver, so it was difficult for the driver to hear me politely decline. I made matters worse by managing to turn the interior television set on at maximum volume as I fidgeted nervously with the remote control. Unfamiliar and fumbling with this electronic gizmo, I instead quickly turned the TV off manually. "No, thank you, sir," I shouted, far louder than necessary, to the driver.

At the restaurant's private entrance, Sam waited just outside the door and greeted me surprisingly with an embrace and kiss to my right cheek.

"Thank you for accepting my invitation."

"I thought this was the invitation of the United States Senate?"

"Well, of course, it is, my dear."

We followed the restaurant's head waiter into a private room at the top of the stairs. The senator wore no special-occasion cologne at the afternoon ceremony, but that evening Sam's captivating fragrance suggested romance could be in the air, a suspicion confirmed by the brush of his right hand to the small of my back and then gently lowered across my hips, all under the guise of assisting me into the intimate private dining room. The head waiter seated me first as Sam took his seat on the opposite side. The table was elegantly adorned with gold-rimmed china, eight pieces of the house's finest silverware, and an assortment of crystal goblets. Two white candles stood erect, flickering upward bright yellow flames and yielding a hint of cinnamon. Freshly cut flowers filled the room with an incredibly perfumed fragrance.

"May I present a rose to your guest, Senator?" the waiter inquired, knowing the answer before he asked the question as he laid a perfect long-stemmed red rose across my dinner plate. He also lifted a chilled black champagne bottle from its stand, wiped the ice residue with his towel, and presented it to Sam, who nodded his approval. With the bottle partially hidden beneath the towel, the waiter popped the cork and said, "Will the lady start the evening with a glass of our finest label?" This waiter, never bothering with a response, filled my champagne flute and stepped around to fill Sam's glass before returning the elegant bottle with French cursive lettering back into its chilled container, splashing water and ice against the sides.

Sam lifted his glass, "To the Marine Corps' most decorated woman, and to my humble attempt to honor her presence at this table." Sam downed his glass. I sipped the bubbling wine slowly, knowing I had never tasted anything as extraordinary in my life. I could not resist the nectar of the remaining ounces and was not sure if I would be able to resist my dinner companion across the table so handsomely and impeccably dressed in a white dinner jacket. The waiter lifted the bottle now neatly wrapped in a white linen napkin and refilled each glass.

The waiter next recited the choice of appetizers. Sam sensed my confusion and signaled the waiter to make the appropriate selections.

"Victoria, making the right career decisions could lead you into an extraordinary military career. But you must become an officer and you must earn the right degree from the right university. I can help. Please allow me to make an appointment with my undergraduate admission's dean at my university. He's a personal friend, and he would be doing our university a great favor by recruiting you into a program leading to an officer's commission."

This sounded like my father's advice, and I could not help but recall my own father's continuous and constant urgings for me to earn a college degree. How circuitous my path to college had become, beginning with college preparatory classes in high school, which quickly terminated at the hands of Felipe Sanchez and the lure of forbidden adventure. But I knew my father would approve of Senator Sam's proposal, and perhaps following his advice would atone for the decision that so obviously led to my father's death. I had matured remarkably over the most notorious year of my life from August 1980 to August 1981—beginning with Sanchez and ending with a special Marine Corps assignment in Bogotá that led to my decoration.

"No more poor decisions! I will be happy to meet with your dean. I have been struggling for some time with a career path, and this just might be the right direction. I have succeeded in the

Marine Corps, and I can be a good student when I want to be."

"Well, good. It's settled. You can meet with Dean Saunders Monday afternoon at 3:00 p.m. I've already made the appointment. I knew a smart Marine like you would make the correct choice. Will you be free by 3:00 p.m.?"

"Of course."

"Here's his card and campus address. The dean will be expecting you." Sam reached the short distance across the table, taking my palm in both hands, placing the card in the center, and momentarily caressing the underside of my hand with his and sending a tremor from nowhere down to my toes. Sam raised his glass again. "To your future academic and military success." He downed his glass and I, without hesitation, followed.

"Tell me, Victoria, what else are you good at when you want to be?"

I smiled but did not answer. I had a sudden ravenous appetite. The excitement and stress of the last forty-eight hours left me no time or desire for food of any kind. My appetite returned and nervousness abated with each glass of champagne until the waiter turned the finished bottle upside down in its container with a splash. I was completely relaxed and comfortable in the hands of such a distinguished dinner companion. The champagne followed by a sweet rosé fueled a stream of nonsensical gibberish that not even I could follow. In silence, Sam just stared, bemused.

The meal, four courses with carefully selected wines, culminated with Bananas Foster, followed by a light after-dinner port. Standing up was an uncertainty. The fragrant mixture of petaled flowers, scented candles, and expensive cologne, blended with the exhilarating chemistry of French champagne, sweet wines, and rum marinades left me weak-kneed and enamored with my dinner companion. Sam rounded the table to assist me from my chair. From behind me he leaned over and whispered in my ear. "Thank you for a lovely evening," brushing his lips against my ear in what I thought was a kiss instead of a whisper.

"Return with me to my apartment for a cordial. The night is young, and you can rest there before returning to the Mayflower." I leaned my neck to the side and Sam kissed its length. My silence signaled consent. The rest was a blur.

At near four the next morning my eyes shot wide open and my mind questioned, *Where was I?* The man next to me brusquely snored. I had to think. *How did I get here? Where am I?* I retraced my last memory: the journey from the restaurant to Sam's fifth-floor apartment on Connecticut Avenue. Like a hypnotic dream it rushed back at me. Embracing in the elevator, fumbling with keys, tumbling onto the living room sofa, kissing that without warning turned wildly passionate, and caressing impeded only by the stricture of a Marine Corps dress uniform, somehow effortlessly unbuttoned, removed, and discarded to the living room floor. Bra and undergarments yanked free and laid in a trail from sofa to bedroom, followed by a passionate union, coupled with loudly embarrassing feline shrieking. "Please, don't stop!" And all this before we could even reach the top of his bed, which was the size of a football field. A relentless surrender turned into the irresistible pleasure of the moment—more details flooded backward— the night's unending searing waves of passion combined with the August humidity, which seemingly enveloped my guttural eruptions of joy, loudly reoccurring at each of his thrusts, reaching a series of screams at the crescendo that could have been easily confused for a woman caught by surprise during a criminal assault. The uninhibited sexual ecstasy was made more uninhibited by the sedation of intoxication. It was a night shrouded in seduction, surrender, and obsession, but in the morning no regrets— not one. Now it was over. It was time to find my crumpled garments, escape the dawn, and swoon in dreams between the sheets of my canopied bed. Why make parting awkward by fumbling through inartful conversation, totally opposite to the pinnacle of sexual intimacy, certainly never before and, perhaps, never again to be experienced?

Where are my panties . . . my bra . . . my stockings . . . my blouse . . . my skirt? I planned for my lover to mourn my absence if only he would, left alone in a bed filled with my scent to stir his morning's sexual imagination.

If he failed to give chase, my heart would forever cherish the night's memory, a memory incapable of enhancement, a memory undiminished through time to a winter's day in Stuttgart, Germany. I remembered the inexpressible feeling that came over me as my breathing quickened again just by looking down over my lover's body. A thrill shot upward, like that I had experienced falling down the tracks on the Coney Island roller coaster. I thought, *I must leave before my passion erupts to break the morning calm.*

Twenty-five years later, Victoria remained in love with that same man, perhaps even more so, and it mattered not that her lover was married to Mrs. Elizabeth Belvedere Eagan, the senator's wife of forty years, quite healthy and undivorced, with whom she must coexist.

A larger framed photograph, taken by Senator Sam while on a congressional junket to the Middle East—in actuality a seven-day tryst with his military liaison, Captain Pierce, but officially designated by the Senate Armed Services Committee as the chairman's secret tour of battlefield conditions—clearly dominated the rest of the photographs displayed on the table. It featured Victoria saluting the camera while standing in the foreground of an armored personnel carrier. Her fingertips touched the edge of her steel combat helmet, which matched perfectly her camo-desert fatigues. The muzzle of her strapped M16 rifle protruded from behind her left shoulder at a forty-five-degree angle; its barrel, descending downward, appeared to point directly to her twin captain's bars pinned neatly on one of her shirt collars. This photograph unmistakably demonstrated that Victoria was a combat-tested Marine officer fighting an enemy in an actual war zone, accounting for its prominence among the other photographs.

To the right of the combat photograph was a framed picture of Senator Eagan clad in a dark blue business suit and Colonel Pierce in full dress uniform standing together outside of Victoria's Pentagon office. A desk job at the Pentagon for Colonel Pierce was the setting for the final photograph, which leaned ever so slightly backward in front of the others, showing Victoria, again in full dress uniform, seated alone at a long conference table in front of a microphone before the Senate Armed Services Committee, whose members had just unanimously approved her flag rank promotion to brigadier general in the United States Marine Corps. Senator Sam was not featured in this photograph, but certainly without Sam, there would have been no promotion for Victoria, at least not to the coveted rank of brigadier general.

Sam's nocturnal visits diminished considerably since Victoria's overseas command, and this long-awaited visit would be delayed further if his military transport could not be cleared to land in such inclement weather. This night's encounter, like all the others, would be emotionally charged, but perhaps this one would be lightened to a degree by an intriguing and teasing one-sentence cable sent to Victoria a few days earlier. "I have a proposition to make, General!" Victoria knew instantly the distinction between a "proposition" and a "proposal." Sam carefully avoided the word "proposal."

Victoria flipped open a rounded pocket mirror retrieved from the center desk drawer, checked her lipstick and makeup, and sighed, "Fine," in a whisper. Every red-blooded Marine under her command lusted after his commanding General. Beneath her muted green dress uniform protruded legs that would make a fashion model proud, and not even Marine fatigues could conceal her centerfold figure, superior to most pinned to the inside of a soldier's foot locker.

Victoria was constantly pursued by a parade of high-ranking generals, consuls, and diplomats, both foreign and domestic, all of whom she spurned and discouraged with ease. Victoria would kindly accept social invitations for dinner and even the opera, but afterward her suitors were rewarded with a polite handshake and a closed door. Victoria faithfully remained monogamous to Sam, but certainly it was not for lack of a stream of these unrequited suitors, some of whom, in a final act of desperation, would sprinkle exiting conversations with proposals for matrimony linked with the security of a lavish dowry. In hopes of leveraging even a hint of jealousy from Sam, Victoria would inform him of her suitors' foolish schoolboy proposals but never a hint of such a proposal emerged from the betrothed Senator Sam Eagan. Politically, he could not and would not leave Betty, although he had no hesitation straying outside his wedding vows, particularly with Victoria. The Eagans bore no children, but Sam's infertility spawned in Betty a disinterest for his insatiable sexual appetites. They married, more from an arrangement between aristocratic families than spontaneous love, five years after Sam earned his juris doctor degree from the University of Virginia, preceded by Betty's conversion to Catholicism from agnostic-Protestant, a mere formality for Betty, who aspired to share in Sam's textile wealth and considerable prestige as partner in Smith, Lee, and Eagan, one of Roanoke's finest insurance defense law firms. Within a few years, Sam ran successfully for Congress and later was appointed by the governor to fulfill the unexpired term of the junior U.S. senator from Virginia, whose private plane missed Charlottesville's fog-enshrouded runway by almost a mile. Sam was immensely popular among Virginians and now was in his fifth elective term as a U.S. senator.

When not with her real lover, Victoria was full-time mistress to her second lover, the United States Marine Corps. As post commandant and later commander, she ruled like a wartime monarch. She had served under some of the military's worst post commanders, even worse than the dictators they were sworn to kill, but no dictator on either side of a war could compare to her murdered mentor, Felipe Sanchez. It was his style she emulated: combining charm with intimidation. If she failed in her command, she knew she would have no one to blame but herself. Besides Sam, who knew virtually nothing of military command, Victoria had no other confidant, so she played her cards close to the vest. Her orders were her own, totally dictatorial, and never fashioned by committee or delegation. She was the boss, and her subordinates had better faithfully execute her orders to the letter. God help the officer who failed to follow every detail of her directive. The consequences were ruthless and immediate. Just like Sanchez, her inferior ranks were littered with busted officers who ignored her orders. The men beneath her in rank expected and anticipated her failure. How could any woman succeed in the Marine Corps, particularly one rising through the ranks from political largesse? These chauvinists repeatedly underestimated Victoria's intelligence and determination. The best way for her to succeed was to threaten her with failure, and failure was never an option. Constant preparation was her routine. She arose long before the winter's dawn, pored over every minute detail of the coming day, inspected personally her admiring troops at every formation, and was the last to turn in after taps. This was her routine, every day, seven days a week—except, that is, when Sam arrived. That's when life in the military came to a halt.

The buzz of the desk telephone shattered the silence. "Yes, Sergeant, what is it? Good, the flight was not delayed. . . . Well, tell the senator my car will meet his plane at 1330 hours. . . . What? . . . Yes, of course, Sergeant, tell him I'll be in the backseat." She hung up. "God, the senator can be such a baby!"

As the enormous green C-17 cargo jet glided to a stop at the end of the runway, a civilian dressed in a gray herringbone overcoat disembarked and crunched briskly through two feet of the snow-white blanket toward a parked and idling, matching green, Mercedes limousine. The right back door swung open as Senator Eagan slid into the embrace of General Pierce and then into a long, passionate kiss that suggested the absence between lovers was too long. "Why do you have to always keep me waiting, Sam?" She stroked his cheek with the back of her hand and fidgeted with his tie, followed by another long embrace and another kiss. The Mercedes rolled away, circling back to the general's private quarters along tracks in deep snow that paralleled their arrival.

* * *

"OK, Sam," Victoria asked, smiling as if she were about to tell a joke, "so what is your 'proposal'? "Oh, I'm sorry," she chided. "I think you actually said 'proposition.' You did say 'proposition,' didn't you, Sam? Not 'proposal,' right?"

Ignoring completely the implication of Victoria's question, Sam spooned out the last cluster of fresh red berries embedded at the bottom of his sorbet glass. This signaled the end of an exquisite dinner, meticulously planned in every detail, in Victoria's private dining room tucked secretly away in her living quarters.

"That will be all for the evening," Victoria said as she waved her hand, dismissing her dinner staff just after the waiter cleared the final pieces of dinnerware from the table and poured the remaining ounces of an exquisite French Burgundy. The staff knew the general required complete privacy while entertaining the senator. The remainder of the evening was completely off-limits to all personnel, except under the most dire circumstances. God help any would-be intruder who entered her private quarters armed with no less than an announcement of impending nuclear war.

Sam and Victoria were finally alone.

"So what is your proposition, Sam?"

"I have decided to declare my candidacy for the presidency of the United States, and I need your help."

Victoria's first thought was that this decision would further complicate their already complicated relationship. But the announcement, otherwise, came as no real surprise. Widespread coverage, even in the foreign press, speculated that Senator Eagan would be a logical candidate to make a run at the presidency based upon his lengthy tenure in the United States Senate and his vocal opposition to the incumbent president. His strident criticism of the increasingly unpopular lame duck, occupying the White House in the waning years of his second term, seemed to have struck a popular chord with the American public, and no other candidate had emerged as a clear front-runner in either party.

"Congratulations, Sam, to you, and, of course, also to Betty, your future First Lady. But I cannot see what this has to do with me."

"First and foremost, my dear, I trust you with my life. You are and have been my chief advisor on military affairs. As you know, I have no military credentials, and several of my opponents will use that to their advantage. The military represents a huge block of voters. I must develop relationships with base commanders who can be persuaded to support a president who will have a pro-military agenda. Military men trust veterans, and they certainly know I am not one, so they must be reminded of my long-standing record of support for military spending and weapons development. You have successfully fashioned much of that policy already and would be the logical campaign liaison between me and your comrades in arms. You're captivating, persuasive, and believable. These guys will listen to you."

"Look, Sam. It's true that I owe my entire military career to you. But I know war, not politics. Frankly, the military is run like a dictatorship, not a democracy. To a military commander, democratic decision making is irrational and inefficient. I know nothing about the niceties of political campaigning." Victoria's tone sharpened, "Besides, don't you have a wife for this sort of thing?"

Sam, now sensing a shift to an all-too-familiar issue, stood up, circled the table until standing behind his dinner companion, and placed both hands on the back of her chair. He leaned down and whispered in her ear. "You are absolutely correct, General, you do owe me your entire military career, and I'm calling in my chips." Sam caressed her shoulders and kissed the back of her neck beneath her hair. "This will be the most exciting ride of your life."

"What happens when the senatorial candidate turns president," Victoria chided, turning around to search his face for an answer, "and my military debt to you is paid in full?" She leaned her head forward again, exposing her neck, "and the ride of my life is over? What then, Senator Eagan?"

Sam cradled Victoria's neck under one arm, turned to silence her lips with his, placed his other arm between her seat and bended knees—lifting her upwardly with a single effortless motion that carried her from her chair across the adjoining threshold—and gently laid her on top of her brightly colored quilted bed. Passion soon overtook lovers too long separated and ended the frustration of questions that could not be answered.

CHAPTER SIX

March 2008

"No, that's not what he meant!" A deep drag off a long, thin, white-filtered cigarette, exhaled quickly through his nostrils, interrupted momentarily the voice pleading into the telephone receiver. "I know what he said, but that's not what he meant. Look, you must have read Senator Eagan's policy position on military affairs. It's on our website. Anyone can plainly see that . . . well, of course . . . of course, I can see how his words might be misinterpreted. . . . Yes . . . but just opposite from his stated position . . . but that's why we write the positions down. . . ." The cigarette, half finished, was crushed into a cocktail glass, full of white butts and gray ashes, sitting isolated on a wet bar right beneath a sign that reads, "This is a smoke-free facility. New York City Ordinance #46763 strictly prohibits smoking of tobacco products in this suite. Violators will be punished to the maximum extent permitted by law."

"Well, you're talking to Tom Pearsall, Senator Eagan's national campaign manager. I should know his first-strike position on nuclear weapons. It has nothing whatsoever to do with provocation."

Victoria uncrossed her legs, stood, stretched, yawned, and walked across the conference room window to view Lower

Manhattan, fifty stories below. She glanced over to Ellis Island, the Statute of Liberty, across the Brooklyn Bridge to Brooklyn, and then down to the right to view the Manhattan Courthouse. To this day over twenty-five years later, no one knew her connection with that courthouse. Victoria filtered out everything around her as she remembered her sterling performance before the grand jury in August of 1980.

I promenaded down the interior corridors of that courthouse on my way to the grand jury room. My finely coiffed hair bounced off the top of my shoulders. Kenneth Berger, my lawyer, and I walked along. I had been rehearsed, dressed to kill in a perfectly coordinated unsubdued crimson dress with matching heels that Berger had selected. A few blocks north, I could have just as easily been mistaken for a model who sashayed down the runway of a chic fashion review, instead of one who testified as a stool pigeon before a eighteen- member grand jury, who plotted to snag Felipe Sanchez in a coerced plea to save my own skin by convincing two-thirds of the grand jury to indict Sanchez on first-degree murder.

What good fortune, I thought, that the grand jury panel had been all male. Berger knew this beforehand, which explained my afternoon attire. My job was to charm and persuade two-thirds of these gentlemen—all thoroughly fed up from nearly a year's worth of performing a thankless civic task locked behind the closed doors of the grand jury room and all looking for any opportunity to break the monotonous routine of another boring day of testimony—to convince these gentlemen to return a true bill of indictment against Sanchez for the murder of an undercover FBI agent, the man I had known briefly as BB, and every other member of the gang on a number of felonious racketeering crimes.

Sanchez, under subpoena, sat beside his creepy mob lawyer, Angelo Siffo, in the hallway in front of the grand jury room, waiting for his turn to refuse to testify before the grand jury. Siffo inhaled an unfiltered cigarette and exhaled the smoke through his nose. He stood up, stretched, and yawned, his bony wrists extending through the sleeves of his long black sharkskin suit. His skinny black tie matched his cheap black Italian loafers. His greasy hair dripped down over a forehead that topped a greasy face indented with pockmarks dating back to his adolescence. Angelo Siffo mostly represented second-rate gangsters, retained by the Mob, mostly to protect organizational interests and not that of clients, but he was adequate as a criminal defense lawyer. Siffo's theory of defense was to cast the blame on me for the accidental shooting death of the agent, with Sanchez being minimally connected to the crime scene. The fictional defense was flimsy and unbelievable at best, but Siffo was left no choice after his client's uncoerced statements made the night of the shooting, an unfortunate admission made to FBI Agent Ramirez that admitted Sanchez's role as an accomplice which, under the best circumstances, would have guaranteed him hard time for a second felony conviction. Sanchez was going to maintain the lie that I had pulled the trigger, although, according to Sanchez, it was accidental. Sanchez's testimony before the grand jury was to have been brief, consisting of a number of calculated Fifth Amendment refusals to answer the U.S. attorney's incriminating questions, but what Sanchez did not know was that his denials were going to be contrasted with my open, honest, and detailed testimony of what really happened that night, which, when completed, would leave the gentlemen of the grand jury little alternative but to indict Sanchez under a true bill for first- degree murder.

As I rounded the corner in the hallway, I had been told by Berger that Sanchez and Siffo would be seated in tandem across from the grand jury room, as part of a staged arrangement to pressure Sanchez into a plea. Siffo was the first to glance up at me. His jet-black eyes narrowed and focused over his bifocals at me, approaching in my crimson red dress, with high heels, aflame in an even deeper shade of red that clicked and resonated off the marble floor as I promenaded down the hallway. Berger insisted that I wear the outfit. It had worked for another of his clients who had used the same costume to walk free after a unanimous all- male grand jury had refused to indict under equally questionable circumstances. The outfit had been tried and true. Siffo stared at me like I was a barroom stripper. He had not recognized me until Sanchez rose from his chair and bowed sarcastically with one arm extending across his waist as he pretended to hold an invisible sombrero, "Buenos dias, Vera mi muchacha vestida de rojo." (Good morning, my little Vera dressed in red.) Siffo's black eyes narrowed into an expression of worry as he looked at Sanchez. I was told to completely ignore both men, as if they were not there, before staging my life-saving performance in front of the grand jury.

Siffo's face revealed the shock of betrayal. He knew that his client had been set up, strategically placed in the steel chairs across from the grand jury room to observe me about to testify against Sanchez. Unknown to Sanchez, I had flipped from loyal biker girl to the prosecution's star witness. Siffo turned deathly serious as he further understood the ploy. I was to precede Sanchez in the grand jury, where I was about to disclose in vivid detail the whole sordid truth about the execution-style murder of an FBI agent. Siffo would have to explain to Sanchez the sober reality of my testimony and that any attempted plea to a lesser-included offense in exchange for his testimony against me was off the table. This explained why U.S. Attorney Michael Brandon had turned a cold shoulder to Siffo for any discussion of a plea bargain and why, without fail, Brandon had never returned a single one of his telephone calls. My treachery, a betrayal made worse as his former girlfriend, was fully explained to Sanchez while the two sat waiting for their turn before the grand jury. They were there to hear my muffled testimony escaping through the quarter-inch space between the marble floor and closed door of the grand jury room.

"No, no, no, I'm telling you that's *not* his position! You can't print that. Just wait for the senator's press release. . . . It clarifies everything. What's your fax number? . . . It's on the way now. Please wait. I know it's about press time, but don't ruin our campaign a week before the New York primary by printing something so totally inaccurate and inflammatory. The *Times* is better than that. . . . Yes, I do know what he said, but that's not what he meant. . . . Yes, I promise he will call you directly in less than fifteen minutes to clarify this entire misunderstanding. Yes, good-bye."

Pearsall exploded, "Just who the fuck is responsible for putting such an incredibly stupid gaffe in the mouth of *my* candidate? Sam, surely you must know better than that! Get him on his cell phone *now!*" A staffer punched in his number and handed Pearsall the telephone.

"Sam, you gotta call Pete Riley at the *Times* . . . and I mean right now. . . . Pull up our military policy statement from the website and click on 'Nuclear Weapons.' Read it, Sam, quickly and spit it back to him, almost verbatim. . . . You've got to make the call now. Don't wait. . . . Tell him the campaign's latest press release that I just faxed him correctly states your position. . . . *Do it now, Sam!* His deadline is less than half an hour away. Have you got his number? Call now. OK . . . Let me know how it went, and I'll do the follow-up myself." Pearsall sailed the cell phone against the back cushions of the couch behind him.

"Maybe, just maybe, we can modify this story just enough before press time to save our ass at the last minute or at least control the damage. Now, which one of you pricks is responsible for such a preposterous position statement? I know one of you fucking amateurs did it, so who did it?" Pearsall stared around the room at each face, searching for a confession.

Victoria turned from the window, facing Tom Pearsall, and said, "Look no further than right here . . . and it's not a preposterous position. It happens to be the correct position and could save this country from nuclear disaster. The United States must be able to deter a first strike by a rogue hostile country without consulting the UN, NATO, or any other alliance for that matter, if reliable reconnaissance information confirms that an attack on the U.S. is imminent. We need to deter a first strike by making a first strike ourselves."

Silence filled the room. Everyone stared at Victoria.

"Excuse me, can someone please tell me who the fuck she is?" Pearsall searched the room again for an answer. No one responded. "Oh, wait a minute. Yeah, yeah . . . you're that military dame that Sam insisted on bringing in as his military consultant at the last minute."

"Yes, I am, and believe me, I don't want to be here anymore than you want me here."

"Well, Sweetie, you don't have to worry about any of us being here much longer with such disastrous tripe that came spewing out of *my* candidate's mouth just a few hours ago that you call a position . . . because *my* campaign will be over by next week. . . . Hell, we're all but finished right now. In case you don't get it, we cannot win without carrying New York City. Do you have any clue as to what New Yorkers will think about your preemptive first strike? Are we talking, here, conventional bombs? Why, hell no. We're talking about the queen mother of all the bombs, the big nukes. And what city exactly do you think will be the recipient of an immediate nuclear counterattack? Well, it won't be Podunk, USA. Right fucking here . . . so if you're intent on losing this trench warfare for New York voters all by yourself, may I suggest that you at least take a look at *my* candidate's stated position on nuclear war and nuclear first strikes before spewing out some foolhardy policy position totally inconsistent with the carefully crafted language of his express campaign policy—a policy, no doubt, you have no idea that exists and certainly have never read."

Victoria was stunned. She was only doing what Sam had asked of her, advising him on what she believed was sound military policy.

"Look, your gaffe will be the fodder for each of our combined opponents' thirty-second attack ads, being put in the can right now, probably already leaked by the *Times*, all to be aired Sunday night right before the election, all designed to bring down the front-runner, an opportunity that everyone in this room, with one notable exception, has scrupulously avoided handing them, but not anymore. Just imagine the fear that will be spun out of your gaffe. You think maybe New Yorkers aren't aware that they are the biggest fuckin' nuclear target in the world?"

"Wait a minute, Mr. Spinmeister. Sam's position makes New Yorkers a whole lot safer because it could very well protect their city from a first strike and nuclear disaster."

"Do you really think I give a rat's ass about the correctness of your policy, coming from a political novice like you?"

"Look, it's Pearsall? Right? Well, Mr. Pearsall, I'm United States Marine Corps General Victoria Pierce. My subordinates address me as 'General Pierce.' Now, Mr. Pearsall, Sam took my advice on this military issue because nuclear war is just too damned important to be left to civilians like you."

Pearsall clapped his hands in mocking applause. "Well, well, well, what a fine piece of political commentary. In case you don't know it, General Sweetie, my first job is to win political campaigns . . . and we had a shot at winning this one, too. Of course, that was before this horrendous statement came spewing out of *my* candidate's mouth, completely unrehearsed and without my knowledge, in his position conference with the editors of the *New York Times*, no fuckin' less, and exactly one week before the election. I can see tomorrow's headline now: 'Senator Eagan Proposes First Strike,' or how about this," spreading one arm above his head, 'Eagan OKs Nuclear Surprise Attack,' or how about 'Nuclear Bombs Away, Says Eagan'?"

The cell phone on the couch chimed Sam's special ring. Tom walked over, stared at it for a second, and then flipped it open.

"Yeah . . . did you make the call? How did it go?" There is a long silence. "Good . . . Great . . . Go on. . . . So what you're saying, Sam, is that Riley is not going with the story the way he said. . . . No, I've never known him to go back on his word. . . . Much softer story . . . They will go back to your express statement on the nuclear issue, because that was your official position. Did your conversation with him make it in before press time? Good . . . Great, Sam! You are a master. . . . Yeah, it does. Five terms in the Senate does teach one a little about dealing with a negative press. We can all start breathing here again. . . ." A cheer went up in the room as Tom turned his back, "Tell me, Sam, what exactly does this military broad mean to you?"

Victoria walked across the conference room to the door that opened out into the hallway. "Do you mind waiting a second, General?" Pearsall dragged off the desk a voluminous document, bound in a green binder, about the size of the New York City telephone book, and handed it to Victoria. With his other hand he opened the door. "Now, please, listen very carefully because I'm only going to say this once. I am in charge of this campaign. Understand? I outrank you and everyone else in this room. The reason is that I know how to win political campaigns. You do not! In the future, you clear every single word of advice that you give *my* candidate before you even suggest something as simple as a dinner entrée or the color of the shirt he wears. Get it? Every position statement he has, and yes, right down to what he wears and what he eats, is determined by me and this polling data."

Victoria took the polling data as Tom patronizingly continued, "It's top secret . . . so don't let it out of your sight. I suggest you read it. . . . Read every word that's in here. So maybe, just maybe, you won't create another firestorm like you did today . . . some bullshit policy that's directly in conflict with what I know appeals to the voters of this city. This copy must be returned to me personally by 8:00 tomorrow morning." He opened the door. "Good-bye, goodnight," he said, and under his breath after she exited the room, "Good fuckin' riddance."

Down the hall, Victoria disappeared into her bedroom, slamming the door behind her. "Just what in the hell is a Marine doing here in the middle of political warfare? How could any Marine tolerate such political hypocrisy? How could anyone say that they don't care about the correct first-strike nuclear policy? That's just insane! Why can't we just tell the damned truth around here?"

Victoria threw the polling manual on her bed, took off her jacket, sat on the bed, and calmed down long enough to realize that she was not serving on the campaign as a general in the Marine Corps. "I told Sam I don't know the first damned thing about politics, and probably came pretty damned close this afternoon to losing Sam's campaign in New York. The prick could be right. I've got to know and understand what's in this manual." She picked it off the bed with both arms and flopped it down on the hotel room desk. The first half of the book quoted the numerous polling questions with the answers broken down by age, gender, ethnic origin, and numerous other categories. The second half contained statements of political strategy based upon the polling results. Victoria could follow the second part better than the first, so she concentrated on the second half.

She read meticulously, turning each page slowly, and then went back to the front. Hours passed. "So all polling really is . . . is mathematically predicting the universe from a subset within a margin of error." Victoria recalled similar concepts from her college courses in math and statistics to underscore the validity of what she was reading. "Amazing! You really can alarm voters with complex information about a topic that can be easily manipulated by your opponent. Wait, what is this? Sam is not polling well with New York women, who are likely to vote, between the ages of thirty-five and fifty . . . across party lines, religions, and ethnicity. Why not? Surely this must be wrong." Victoria quickly turned to the second half to look at the political strategy to combat this weakness. She read, underscoring key words with her pencil and silently moving her lips. "This will never work! How patronizing! If he says these things, it will only make matters worse. Don't they know that?"

Although it was past midnight, Victoria folded the manual in her arms, bolted out of her room, and marched down the hall to the conference room. She banged on the door, and when Pearsall opened the door, she's shoved past him into a smoke-filled room. Sam put his glass of scotch filled with ice cubes down on the coffee table and stood up to greet his secret mistress of over twenty-five years. "I hear you've had quite a first day on the campaign trail."

"It won't work, Sam."

"What won't work?" Sam turned up his glass, sucking down its contents.

"This strategy to attract women voters . . . right here." She unfolded and tumbled the telephone-book-sized manual onto the coffee table in front of Sam, rattling the ice cubes in his empty glass. "Just read this. It will never appeal to New Yorkers. In fact, it's a sure-fire recipe to lose their vote. I'll say again, this will not work! These women are the most independent women in the world. The slightest hint of a suggestion as to what and how they should think on any issue, much less reproductive rights, will backfire. They have to arrive at their positions independently. Your positions are not far off. It's the way you are trying to persuade them that will be offensive. The more you follow this strategy, the more your support among women in this range will erode."

Pearsall, ameliorated by several vodka nightcaps, did not explode as he normally would in the face of such amateur analysis. "Look, General Pierce, we all appreciate your efforts to help Sam, but this manual was prepared by the best pollsters in the country at a cost of . . . well, you don't want to know about the cost. The strategy has been reviewed and is sound. We are still a few points down in this segment, but it's because we have just started airing our final ads and it will take a few days to saturate. . . ."

"Look," Victoria said, showing equal restraint, "Mr. Pearsall . . . Let's drop the formality. . . . Tom?" Not waiting for his response or permission, "Tom, do you mind telling me how many New York women have looked at this strategy?"

Pearsall did not offer a direct answer. "First, do you mind telling me exactly what a farm girl from the plains of Oklahoma knows about the women voters of New York? You see, after today's near and total disaster at your hands, I reviewed your bio, and you do not appear to be an expert on urban voters."

Victoria, knowing on paper she was not from Brooklyn, reeled backward from the shock of the Oklahoma revelation. Nevertheless, she saw a grave political danger, perhaps even greater than an incorrect first-strike position on nuclear arms, in terms of an impact on Sam's potential victory. Victoria would not retreat again. Instead, she bristled.

"This strategy is so misguided that even a farm girl from Oklahoma can see right through it."

"OK, just what in the hell do you know about the women voters of New York?"

"Obviously, a whole lot more than you and your pollsters! Sam, you need me right now more as a woman than a military advisor. I'll lead the counterattack directly onto the streets of New York. You need the correct advice on how to appeal to these women voters and a correct strategy *now*! Put me on the sidewalks of Manhattan, and you'll get those votes." She turned to face Pearsall. "You doubt me on this one, ol' boy, and you'll lose this city . . . and you will be lucky next year to manage the campaign of the Podunk dog catcher."

"OK, OK, Victoria," Sam said. "I've got to fly back to Washington for a roll call vote Saturday. I cannot miss another vote. I'm scheduled for an address in Central Park, kind of a family day out in the park. Why don't you take the walk up Seventh Avenue to the park, campaign along the way, and make my speech? Let's see what you can do. Besides, I will be back Saturday night, but if I miss another roll call vote, I'll be reading about it. Tom, you know we are not closing these numbers. She's right. We've talked about this. We have to have this vote. What's the harm? She might be right and the right person to pull this off. What do you say, Tom?"

Tom's answer came in the slam of the door as he stormed out of the conference room, and from down the hallway he could be heard screaming at the top of his lungs, "Absolutely un-fucking believable!"

CHAPTER SEVEN

March 2008

Grace Brandon was a cub reporter for the *New York Times*. Uncomfortably restricted and quite overdressed in comparison with her peers, Grace chatted on nervously with her photographer while waiting beside the curb in Times Square to cover her first- ever real political assignment. In perfect hindsight, Grace would have chosen the beige slacks and white blouse among the array of discarded garments that lay scattered on the floor of her tiny apartment instead of the red matching wool suit and blue winter coat. Under the exigencies of expiring time, Grace finally deemed the outfit appropriate enough to question Sam Eagan, the senior U.S. senator from Virginia and presidential candidate, as she mimed the interview in the reflection of her full-length bedroom mirror. Her shortly cropped blonde hair fell to the top of her cheeks, this morning pancaked in makeup that would make a flight attendant proud, but even through the stiffness of an uncomfortable-looking face, Grace remained diminutive and cute.

She had talked her way into her first-ever real assignment to cover Senator Eagan's speech in Central Park, or so she thought. No one at the *Times* cared much for Saturday's slow local news, particularly since the real fireworks would come later Sunday evening at the candidates' forum debate. The senator's canned Saturday speech in the park was bound to be fluff, so none of the senior reporters wanted to expend their energy working furiously on an early Saturday deadline for a story likely to be cut completely on the editor's floor or vanquished to the wasteland between the weather and obituaries. But for Grace, this was an opportunity to cover a serious contender for the presidency and definitely not her ordinary courthouse beat, where cub reporters like her labored in journalism purgatory. The last-minute swap was a snap. It would be her day to cut her teeth on a real story.

Grace was the only child of prominent United States Attorney Michael Brandon, now retired. She grew up in the federal courthouse. She knew by first name all of the important news sources there or they knew her. Her mother died of a stroke the week before Grace graduated with honors from the University of Missouri's School of Journalism. She declined a job at the *Los Angeles Times* to return to New York to help her father through a difficult time.

But as the senator's cab jerked to a halt and the back door swung open, legs ordinarily sheathed in the pants of a man's blue suit turned out instead to be legs sheathed in the stockings of a woman's sheer pantyhose. "What is this all about?" Grace whispered aloud. "Where's Sam Eagan?" Simultaneously, cameras clicked furiously as this unidentified woman proclaimed that she was the senator's last-minute surrogate. *What was she saying? Senator Eagan had to be on Capitol Hill for an important roll call vote?*

Not even Grace's layered makeup was able to conceal burgundy cheeks flushed with anger and betrayal as she watched this stand-in candidate, not even of the correct gender, feigning equality with a U.S. senator. Grace snatched her cell phone from her outer coat pocket and speed-dialed back to the *Times* news desk for an explanation.

"Where's Senator Eagan?" she demanded, turning her back to the cab and plugging her left ear with her finger. "Yesterday? You mean the campaign sent out a press release late yesterday announcing that the senator had to be back in Washington? . . . Well, hell no, no one bothered to tell me. . . . No damned wonder the swap was so easy." Grace flipped her phone off and back into her pocket. Others in the media obviously did not get the word either as the sidewalk thinned in front of the talking head stiffly addressing the press as if they were troops in formation.

"Listen up, press. Today you will be following Brigadier General Victoria Pierce of the United States Marine Corps. Last month, I was a base commander in eastern Germany, but I am today, having elected active-duty status in the Marine Corps Reserves, Senator Eagan's full-time military policy advisor and spokesperson. He, as I just said, has to be on the Senate floor today for an important military spending roll-call vote."

Victoria watched as the press dissipated right in front of her, disregarding completely her prepared remarks and disassembling their equipment as if she were invisible. The veteran press was certainly not about to fight the crowded sidewalks following some complete unknown campaigning in the place of Senator Eagan on the long walk up to Central Park. A few might show up to cover the speech later, but that depended on other local breaking news, particularly for the broadcast media looking for more colorful footage that could easily supplant a political novice talking from a podium on a slow news Saturday.

Rudely abandoned by the others, Victoria and Grace were now face-to-face. Grace clutched her photographer's sleeve to prevent his flight and in her mind quickly reshaped a political story into a feature. Grace's assigned photographer, Lennie Callahan, age twenty-seven, tall and boyish, sported curly black hair that almost reached his shoulders, shoulders today that are crisscrossed with an assortment of camera straps suspending three expensive cameras. Grace thought Lennie was handsome but that he lacked initiative. He, too, was uncertain as to what to do, so he readied himself to abandon his assignment in favor of a Knicks basketball game later that afternoon. Grace imagined an attractive general debating military policy with disinterested New Yorkers crowding the sidewalks on a cold Saturday morning. Grace was intrigued by the vision of the pedestrian encounters and the potential for an interesting feature, but there was no time to win the approval of her editor. She would just have to go with it and argue her case later.

"General Pierce, tell me a little about your background and how you came to the campaign?" Grace asked as a first question.

"I've been in the Marine Corps for over twenty-five years, rising through the ranks to brigadier general. I have admired Senator Eagan's career in politics and his support for the Marine Corps, and all the other branches for that matter. He really cares about the well-being of our soldiers in uniform."

As Grace scribbled in shorthand on her reporter's pad, she asked a follow-up. "And what about your background? Where are you from?"

"Is that really important?" Victoria responded.

Grace nodded affirmatively, not looking up, and waited for the answer.

"Well, if you must know, I grew up on a farm out on the plains of Oklahoma in isolation, was homeschooled there, enlisted in the Marine Corps, and later went to college on a military scholarship, graduating as an officer, and the rest is history. Can't we talk about Senator Eagan?"

"Actually, right now, General, I am more interested in you," Grace responded, imagining what it would be like for a farm girl from Oklahoma turned Marine Corps general trying to delay hurried New Yorkers long enough to plug her candidate.

Victoria, looking at her watch as would a field general about to synchronize an assault on Central Park, responded, "Well, can we at least start off? Otherwise, we will never get there in time for my speech."

Surprised, Grace looked up. "You know how long it takes to get to Central Park from here?"

Victoria paused to find the answer to a question she had known since she was a child. "Well, based upon the city maps, it looks to me to be about a twenty-five-minute walk with stops along the way, but you can tell me exactly how long it actually takes and then tell me your name."

"Today in the light Saturday morning pedestrian traffic it should take about thirty minutes, depending on the number of stops you make . . . and my name is Grace Brandon, but everyone at the paper calls me 'Ace' but it's such a cliché." Grace thought how unprofessional it was of her to volunteer her personal dislike of her nickname, which she truly detested, but the more she protested, the more her peers enjoyed ribbing her as if she were some sort of sorority pledge.

Grace resolved to be more professional as she shaped her next question, but Victoria was now way ahead of her, walking in the direction of Seventh Avenue before she could even blurt it out.

Finally catching up and still pulling Lennie along by the sleeve, Grace asked, "What was it like growing up in isolation on the Oklahoma plains?"

"Not much fun for a girl growing up on a farm with just my folks and me to do all the chores. My parents were religious purists who believed that any contact with strangers would be destructive to our faith, so we rarely came in contact with anyone in the outside world."

"So, where on the plains of Oklahoma did you live?"

"Iowa County, some fifty-five miles north-northwest of Lawton."

Grace saw the contrast sharpen. She knew that New Yorkers could be brutally intolerant of rural insophisticates, particularly an evangelical growing up in isolation on the plains. New Yorkers would have a difficult time listening to and then voting for a Virginian, much less a farmer's daughter from Oklahoma turned military general, campaigning in his place.

So the zealots' military daughter from the hinterlands is about to be devoured by irascible New Yorkers as if she were a breakfast entrée, and I'll be right there to record every second of the debacle, complete with unflattering photographs to prove it, Grace said to herself.

Victoria stepped away again in what was known to her in the military as fast walk cadence. For a second time, Grace was caught pensively daydreaming as if she were incapable of walking and thinking at the same time. Grace, waking up, ran to close the distance between the two, literally dragging Lennie along by one of his camera straps and committing the cardinal pedestrian sin of bumping several New Yorkers along the crowded sidewalks, rousing their vocal hostility, before she caught up with her subject.

Victoria encountered a cab driver waiting his turn for a fare in a long line of cabs underneath a hotel portico. Through his open window Victoria tried to hand the driver a small card with a black-and-white photograph of Sam Eagan on the front and a short list of his accomplishments on the back. "Are you going to vote for Senator Eagan in next week's primary?

As Lennie, the photographer, snapped a shot from the opposite side of the cab, Grace braced for the cab driver's profane expletives. Startled, the driver, trying to locate the source of the unfamiliar voice and thinking it might be a fare, twisted his neck around to face his inquirer and cupped his left ear, "What did you say? Vote? Vote for who?"

As the driver took the card from Victoria's hand, she said, "United States Senator Sam Eagan. He's running for president."

"Who the fuck? Never heard of him! But let me tell you something, lady," the driver seized the opportunity to pontificate upon a discourse normally reserved for a captive passenger. "I immigrated to this city twenty years ago from Beirut," the driver said in English that gave away his Lebanese origins. "Nobody works anymore. I've been driving a cab from the day I got here. I worked every damned day of my life fightin' this fuckin' traffic, and I worked hard, not like these ones that come in today," gesturing critically with his left hand in an upward direction. "Get on welfare and do nothin'. I own my house and a little other property . . . and today, I'm almost a millionaire . . . but these new bums do nothing. Tell that to," he squinted at the card, "to Senator Eagan, and I'll vote for him."

"Thank you, I'll do that," Victoria acknowledged before walking away and turning into a specialty seafood deli filled with early shoppers buying a variety of salads and fresh seafood. A photograph of the owner with his son hung behind the cash register.

"Hi, Mr. Margolis. I'm Victoria Pierce, out campaigning this morning for Senator Eagan."

"Come back when I'm not so busy, honey." A rotund man, who looked like he just stepped down from his photograph—with a black and gray mustache, dressed in a full-length white apron—dished up two pounds of lobster and shrimp salad into a smooth white container and lifted it up on the scales: exactly two pounds and an ounce, which he rang up on the register and handed to the customer. "Who's next?" his voice boomed. No one was ready to place an order.

"Hey, I like Sam Eagan. Good Catholic boy. He's done good for our country, too. Yeah, sure I'll vote for him."

As the *Times* photographer snapped a series of pictures, Grace could not find the name "Margolis" anywhere inside the deli. Grace filed away a mental note to ask Victoria how she knew the proprietor's name. The campaigning general was already fast out the door moving up the street to her next stop.

Victoria, remarkably at ease on the New York City streets for an Oklahoma girl, stopped outside the door of a sandwich deli where a strong waft of grilled onions and green peppers escaped to the sidewalk each time the front door opened. She spoke to a patron on the way out the door. "Gonna vote for Eagan next week?"

The man walked on, without looking up or hesitating. "You gotta be kiddin' me."

Victoria interrupted two middle-aged women in animated conversation as they left a coffee shop next door to the deli. "What do you think about Sam Eagan?"

One woman hesitated long enough to answer. "I like everything about him except he's Catholic. Can't have the pope in my bedroom, and that's final."

Victoria followed the two up the street and stepped in front of them, walking backward and impeding their progress up the sidewalk. "But wait a minute, do you know his views on women's issues?" They both stop, prevented now from circumventing Victoria's blockade. Grace stepped back with pad in hand, knowing the Oklahoma general would get an earful from these gals, complete with finger-pointing-in-the-face photographs.

One woman responded exactly as Grace anticipated, pointing her finger directly at Victoria's nose, "Know what, Butch Boy? You look like some sort of transgender faggot in drag!"

Victoria, angered, bristled, "You don't want to see me get upset, Doll-Face, because I can be one tough Marine." Victoria stepped back, regaining her composure. "I happen to be one of the few women in the United States Marine Corps who has achieved the rank of brigadier general."

Silenced, the other woman intercedes, "Can't be any good if he's Catholic."

Victoria continued, "Look, if there is anyone who understands what issues appeal to women it's me—a combat soldier who had to throw men off the ladder on her way to the top in the Marine Corps, a ladder marked 'For Men Only.' I understand what a woman has to do to make it in this world. I'm Sam Eagan's chief military advisor *and* his chief advisor on women's issues," an aggrandizement that surely Tom Pearsall would have adamantly denounced, had he been there, and he certainly would denounce if the quote made it into print from Grace's copious scribblings.

"Sam Eagan strongly believes that women's issues belong to women and most especially not to the pope." Even Sam Eagan would have avoided the irreverent reference to the pope, but he, too, like Pearsall, was far away minding his congressional duties in Washington while General Pierce spoke for attribution before a reporter and a photographer just waiting to pounce on her slightest gaffe. To Grace's surprise, both women were actively listening, with their once-folded arms now at their side. The previously silenced woman responded, "I bet you do know about a man's world, honey, and I might not vote for Sam Eagan, but I would likely vote for you."

"Look," said Victoria as she handed both women his cards, "go to his website and read his positions on women's issues. I'll think you'll be pleased. I was surprised, and I'll bet you'll be, too. There's no difference in how we view these same issues. Then read his other positions that are important to New Yorkers, like the right of women to walk the streets of New York free from violent and assaultive behavior." Both women took the card and continued walking, now unobstructed.

Grace was astonished at Victoria's poise. *How does this woman from the plains fit in so well on the streets of New York?* Instead of resistance, she felt compatibility. And, for the first time, Grace found respect creeping into her story.

Arriving next at the podium in Central Park to a scattered few, mostly resting in seats reserved for an audience thinned by the absence of the United States senator, Victoria walked along the rows of chairs talking up Eagan to anyone who would listen. The observant few who knew they were next in line gladly vacated their resting perches, preferring not to be pinned down for an unsolicited political spiel. Victoria wandered off down the sidewalk, looking for any unsuspecting pedestrian along the way, while Grace prevented Lennie's escape by forcefully towing him along by the sleeve as if they were now handcuffed. The next encounter would prove to be newsworthy far beyond what Grace could have ever imagined.

A circle of Puerto Rican bikers in black leather jackets completely blocked the sidewalk ahead while pedestrians walked around on the grass. An elderly Jewish couple stopped and motioned for them to get out of their way.

The elderly man raised his hand and said, "You're blocking the public sidewalk here!"

"Lo siento, viejo pasear el resto." (I'm sorry old man, walk around like the rest) responded the lead biker, spitting within an inch of the man's shoes. The gang broke out in laughter.

Victoria approached from the back of the couple, stood for a minute observing, nudged in between, and demanded, "You're blocking the sidewalk. Move!"

The young leader diverted his attention from the elderly couple to Victoria, dismounted from his bike along with two others, shoved the elderly man aside, and whispered, "¿Qué dices, Puta?" (What do you say, whore?) We have business to conduct this morning in the park." He grabbed Victoria's arm and began to push her off the sidewalk onto the park grass.

Grace, exhausted, caught up with Victoria as Lennie, obviously uncuffed, lagged about twenty yards behind. Grace, in disbelief, observed as Victoria took the arm of what appeared to be a pedestrian and flipped him over her shoulder, landing him squarely on his head, out cold. The others moved to aid their fallen leader and made a similar run at Victoria, who, combat tested, repelled them with several well-placed punches to the nose and finger gouges to the eyes, all occurring just as Lennie arrived, snapping the encounter in rapid fire. Victoria reached inside the biker's jacket, pulled out a clear bag of cocaine, a handgun, and a knife about the size of a machete. She noticed a suspicious man on a bicycle who tried to flee when spotted. Victoria suspected that he was the connecting buyer and chased him down at a full sprint, pushing his two-wheeled conveyance over, spilling a large quantity of bills on the sidewalk, which blew all over in the chill of a stiff north wind. Finally, a cop on horseback arrived to conclude the arrest, calling backup with a hand-held walkie-talkie, and in a matter of seconds fifteen squad cars surrounded the scene with the buyer and most of the fleeing bikers cuffed in the backseat.

Grace flipped open her cell phone and speed-dialed back to the *Times* desk.

"You are not going to believe the story that just broke out here in Central Park."

The next day's Sunday *Times* front-page headline read, "Central Park Gang Subdued by Lone Military Woman." Beneath the headline, dual photographs captured Victoria assailing an unidentified biker and lifting the machete of the lead biker while he lay unconscious on the ground and simultaneously holding a clear bag of cocaine in her other hand. The caption read, "Brigadier General Victoria Pierce intercedes on behalf of elderly couple and quells violent gang while campaigning in Central Park for Senator Eagan." The two-page story below the reporter's byline, "Grace Brandon *Times* Staff," described the general from Oklahoma in glowing terms: rising through the ranks to general; campaigning along the sidewalks to Central Park; conversing with the cab driver and deli owner; encountering the two women, whom she converted with the facts about Senator Eagan's position on women's issues; ironically talking with the two about public safety just twenty minutes before her lightning-fast defense of the elderly couple and her counterattack upon a totally unsuspecting gang that led, single-handedly, to a major drug bust in Central Park.

Sunday afternoon, preceding the candidates' forum, Senator Sam Eagan—flanked by General Victoria Pierce and campaign manager Tom Pearsall—seized the momentum in the approaching New York primary by delivering a major crime address in the exact spot of Victoria's bust to an overflowing and applauding crowd, while decrying drug violence and reiterating his long-held position for federal funding to underwrite support for local police in the war against drug-driven street gangs so families could be safe to enjoy the public parks and to walk the streets of New York.

Grace Brandon, sans makeup and comfortably dressed in yesterday's discarded beige slacks and white blouse, scribbled Senator Eagan's words onto her reporters pad as the follow-up to one of the *Times'* biggest local stories of the year, but it was her exclusive with her byline that launched her career.

CHAPTER EIGHT

Spring/Summer 2008

Senator Sam Eagan swept the New York primary exactly six days after General Victoria Pierce busted up the ring of drug-dealing thugs in Central Park. The incident also catapulted reporter Grace Brandon into the elite ranks of the national print media, first with her front-page eyewitness story in the Sunday *Times*, followed closely by a series of exclusive Sunday features. In the aftermath of the hyped-up publicity, popular interest in the previously bland presidential primary skyrocketed with every interview of the vigilante-general-turned-heroine. Polling results of urban voters suggested a lack of understanding as to why she would risk stepping into the middle of a drug deal going down when it would have been easier and safer for her, like so many other politicians, to have done nothing or looked the other way. With endless repetition, the national cable news channels were having a field day with the story. Likewise, the *Times* circulation soared with every feature that Grace cranked out of her private interviews with the general. Newsworthiness mattered little. The general's military image coupled with a front-page reference to a sectional feature was all that was needed to spike readership and advertising revenue.

Victoria rewarded the one reporter who stuck with her through that now infamous Saturday morning when all the others rudely abandoned her in Times Square long before she set one foot in the direction of Central Park. It mattered little now that Grace's angle that early Saturday morning was to photograph and feature the encounters of an embarrassed Oklahoman general suffering abuse along the sidewalks of New York at the hands of irritable pedestrians who resented being interrupted with a political pitch at such an early hour. It had nothing to do with the general's devotion to her candidate or the senator's military policy. What really mattered to Victoria was Grace's stick-to-itiveness. No one could have predicted how the political walk in the park would ultimately have turned out that day, not even Victoria. So the one reporter, despite her motive, who had remained at the side of the bare-knuckled campaigning general fell blindly into a sensational story and scooped a seasoned press corps that should have seen the possibility of conflicting chemistry between the rural and the urban, a chemistry that was readily apparent to a less seasoned reporter such as Grace. Grace, who had the added burden of forcefully dragging Lennie Callahan every step of the way and ironically forcing him at the same time to snap the most sensational photojournalistic series of his professional career, was the only one with the tenacity to follow her subject to its conclusion. With her tenacity now rewarded, she emerged as the only reporter in the country who knew her formerly obscure but now famous subject well enough to dial her up on her private cell phone to schedule an interview for her next feature story.

The novice general and cub reporter forged a partnership that thrust both into political stardom. One fed the other, and overnight Grace's features were the envy of every political journalist in the country, all of whom wanted a shot at covering the drug-busting general. The secondary stories spun off from these features made Victoria a household name and her face instantly recognizable everywhere in America, particularly on the Eagan campaign trail, so much so that the candidate's military advisor became the focus of the media's attention, upstaging the presidential candidate himself, ordinarily a violation of the most basic campaign strategy: staffers shall not upstage their candidate. Sam, however, delighted in sharing the limelight with his protégé, not just because of their long-standing amorous relationship, but for the significant fact that the press's clamor to know more about Victoria bankrolled millions of dollars in free publicity for the Eagan campaign.

Tom Pearsall, on the other hand, did not share his candidate's enthusiasm for what he saw as an unknown and uncontrollable quantity spewing out unrehearsed campaign rhetoric. He could not control her message. Besides, Grace completely ignored Tom when he tried to take over for Victoria to give his stock answers. Grace, instead, favored Victoria who could sensibly articulate the senator's position on both military affairs and women's issues. Grace learned quickly that all the journalistic nourishment she would get from Tom Pearsall was poll-fed pabulum. On the other hand, Grace enjoyed Victoria's honest spontaneity and the competent expertise that she brought to her side of campaign policy. Grace, also, noted the escalating tension that Victoria created internally between the candidate and his manager.

Tom Pearsall was a political operative at the top of his game. He always played to the percentages, knowing exactly how to interpret his elaborate polling data to safely pitch the Eagan message to the sizeable core of his base voters. That was his job. He knew how to protect a political lead and how to come from behind. He knew when to stay positive and when to go negative. Although Victoria's confrontation in Central Park sparked an unexpected connection with an expanding base of law-and-order urban voters stretching across a wide spectrum, her constant unrehearsed, off-the-cuff remarks had the potential to threaten the senator's simple message as the only candidate in the field with the political experience to lead the nation. Eagan was the front-runner, and the surest way to lose the lead was to carelessly stumble and fall before the finish line. Pearsall, learning the hard way from past political mistakes, knew the press always rode the bigger story, so the darling one day could turn into a goat the next day faster than a guard dog accosting an unsuspecting intruder. The senator's campaign might be overtaken by a late-charging candidate, riding the tide of some hot-button issue, but Pearsall was damned sure his candidate was not going down right before reaching the finish line, politically tripped up by one of Victoria's unrehearsed gaffes that could be used by his opponents to splinter the senator's base. But to Pearsall's astonishment, every time Victoria spoke out unrehearsed, she spiked the senator's overnight polling numbers. She was a natural, knowing instinctively what to say. Pearsall developed a bittersweet relationship with Victoria. But all of Pearsall's apprehensions proved to be just that— apprehensions, nothing more. Of course, Victoria gaffed up more than a few regrettable quotes along the way, but mostly she became the campaign's popular symbol for law and order.

Quick Victory!

In the end, Eagan convincingly won the right to be his party's presidential standard-bearer. Riding a spontaneous swell of urban support propelled by Victoria's media-popping performance in Central Park, the Eagan campaign not only won the New York state primary, but won it decisively. The campaign's connection with urban voters followed quickly into Detroit, Pittsburgh, Minneapolis, Miami, Dallas, Denver, and Los Angeles. Eagan ran away with the primaries in states dominated by metropolitan voters and locked into a majority of the delegates needed to propel him to the nomination. Two months before the senator's return to the party convention in New York in August, his victory was mathematically sealed, having completely routed his opponents by seizing 60 percent of the delegates in a lopsided victory in both the Texas and Pennsylvania primaries. The only mystery that remained for the televised national audience, tuning into the convention, would be the identity of his running mate.

The vice presidential selection, according to the carefully crafted Pearsall formula, would come to the floor as a well-orchestrated announcement on the next to the last night of the convention, somewhere between 9:00 and 10:30 p.m. on the East Coast, three hours earlier on the West Coast, at a prime time calculated to reach the largest possible television audience. But the precise time for the announcement remained open—to be pinned down at the last minute, based upon the analysis of the previous day's overnight polling data—in order to target the geographic region that would reach the maximum number of loyalists who were likely to make sizeable donations to the Eagan campaign in the days immediately following the convention, while their identification with and emotional attachment to their candidate was at its zenith. The selection of the time slot for the vice presidential announcement also had to be balanced by considerations of how to appeal to the largest segment of undecided voters, who, if the campaign were not constructing a targeted message formulated by pinpoint polling, might channel surf away onto unrelated entertainment programming. Plus, nominee Eagan had to persuade a certain percentage of those superficially committed to his yet-to-be-officially nominated party opponent, with a warning to abandon their foolhardy choice or to at least plant the seeds for their defection by forcing them to watch the most blatantly partisan seconding speeches, all carefully crafted to dislodge their superficial allegiance. All of these highly partisan speeches, identical in form to paid political advertising without a glimmer of substantive policy, were to be amplified in the familiar voices of public figures, in prime time no less, without costing the campaign a dime, through a perfectly legitimate stratagem known as "network news." It was a campaign manager's dream of a lifetime, and Pearsall was not leaving anything to chance.

"So, Tom, who will be the Eagan running mate?" Victoria asked point-blank, thinking perhaps that a direct question would produce a direct answer that had eluded her through several indirect approaches. Tom, as usual, was poring over polling data, crushing out his cigarette into a water glass beneath the identical sign warning of prosecution for violating the ban on smoking in this hotel suite.

"Don't you know," Pearsall responded, "that we have not finally determined who that will be, Victoria, and even if we had, we would not tell you or anyone else in the campaign because that's the surest way to leak the identity to the press and spoil the only convention surprise left? Might as well toss millions of free campaign dollars right out the window." Tom pointed, without looking up, to the picture window at the far end of the hotel suite as if he might magically pour a trashcan full of millions of dollar bills right out of the window.

"OK, OK. But you can at least tell me why Sam and you get to pick the vice presidential nominee while the voters get to select the presidential nominee."

As Tom was waving his hand in a dismissive fashion while reading and turning pages back and forth in the polling data notebook, he muttered, "Didn't used to be that way," his voice fading as Sam entered through the suite's bedroom door.

Pushing up his tie, Sam said, "I'll answer that question. The constitutional founders never contemplated resting such power in the presidential nominee. The first vice president, John Adams, was the runner-up to President George Washington in the Electoral College balloting, and some years later, upon the advent of political parties and their conventions—a partisan concept equally mistrusted and disfavored by many of the constitutional originalists— the vice president came to his position as runner-up to the presidential nominee at a time when party conventions actually nominated the president, while the country looked on through the eyes of black-and-white television instead of a modern party caucus or presidential primary election that left nothing really to do at the party convention except identify the name of a vice presidential nominee."

"I honestly do not remember black-and-white television, Sam," Victoria responded absentmindedly, eyes glazed over, focusing on applying a bright red fingernail polish to her extended right index finger.

Sam, acting presidential, buoyed by his nomination and relaxed after several days of rest, blithely continued his history lesson. Tom, too, was paying absolutely no attention because the topic held no relevance for him, and he had seen the senator filibuster like this before, sometimes for hours at a time.

"But the presidential nominees throughout history spurned the office of vice president, so often filled with a political challenger thrust upon the president by the party convention, and, thus, the vice president was cast off into the realm of oblivion and relegated to its only constitutional function, other than succeeding to the office of president, as the presiding officer in the United States Senate, ironically named the president of the Senate. The real function the vice president served was to step in as president in the unlikely event of the president's death while in office."

"So, who will step in for you, 'President' Eagan, when someone like me drops the commander in chief with a hairbrush thrown across the room because she can't get a simple answer to a pretty damned simple question?"

Undaunted, Sam continued his lecture. "Presidential history proves that a vice president succeeding to the office of president during a president's elected term is an unlikely probability. It has happened but only rarely. After President Nixon resigned from office, Vice President Gerald Ford became the president, but the last time a president died in office occurred about forty-five years ago when Vice President Johnson succeeded President Kennedy after his assassination in Dallas. Kennedy had selected Johnson, his bitter adversary, as his vice presidential nominee."

"Why would he do that?" Victoria's voice was laced with surprise and whimsy at yet another political absurdity.

"Johnson could deliver the solid South for a northern Catholic, but after the election, LBJ was so mistrusted by Bobby Kennedy that he was all but cast out of the White House to become just another weak vice president—not at all like Harry Truman, who was selected by the convention as a strong vice president. Everyone in the country knew FDR's days were numbered, and the convention was really nominating Truman to be the next president. True, the convention saw Truman as a compromise candidate from Missouri who southerners could vote for, but now that I think about it, maybe the convention saw something the people could not see, the man's inner strength. But I diverge. What was my point?"

Tom's eyes were staring off in a daydream, and Victoria's were focused on her nails. Sam asked the question to remember his point. It came to him.

"Why, of course. Johnson finished second in the convention balloting behind Kennedy, but he, not unlike Truman, but for different reasons, became a real asset to the country after Kennedy's assassination because he was someone of presidential timber who happened to fall a few votes shy of the convention nomination. Not like today—a vice presidential nominee could be of relative obscurity whose only strength is a personal connection to the president or who might deliver votes in geographical areas of presidential weakness."

Tom now looked up and pointed his finger directly at Sam. "Don't ever repeat any of this historical bullshit outside of this room!" Tom returned his attention to his polling data and moved to the couch at the far end of the suite.

"Will it be Tom?"

"Oh, God, no! Not unless I wanted to intentionally shoot myself in the foot for the sole purpose of losing this election!"

Tom nodded affirmatively without looking up, chuckling, "What's more, I don't wear a bra." Victoria paid attention to Tom for the first time, realizing that a substantive truth had been just revealed.

Ignoring Tom's off-color remark, Sam continued his lecture. "Most recent vice presidential selections have been made so as not to upstage the presidential nominee. This nominee was more of an ally to the president than an adversary and more likely one to share presidential power after the election, without concern for bringing a former political opponent into the president's inner circle. After the presidential election, the handpicked vice president could remain a titular head or be given substantive responsibilities depending on the reason or the motive of the nominee's selection of his running mate in the first place."

Victoria's curiosity demanded an answer to her question, but, try as she might, Pearsall and Eagan would not disclose the identity of their front-running nominee. Concealed between the two men, a leak was not likely. What Victoria knew was that they had narrowed the list to one finalist from a broad field, although technically this candidate lacked their final confirmation. Pearsall's selection was, politically speaking, bulletproof, already confirmed by months of secret and targeted polling with only a focus group evaluation remaining to verify the polling results.

"So which is it?" Victoria inquired. "Are you looking for someone to shore up a weakness or someone to share presidential power?"

"What do you think, General?" Sam leaned over, looking Victoria straight in the eyes with a glint of passion.

"You are still weak in two areas, Mr. Want-to-Be-President. If you expect actually to be elected president, you need to attract a lot more women voters, right, Tom? And alleviate the fears of those voters who are concerned about your military experience as a draft dodger, right, Sam?"

"I was not a draft dodger. A torn ligament in my left knee, an old football injury, prevented my service, so please quit saying I was a draft dodger."

"That's right, General, for the love of God, never refer to Sam as a draft dodger again, but you are close on the vice presidential issue." Tom responded seriously now, exhaling cigarette smoke through his nostrils, without looking up, but still focusing on the polling material in his lap.

"You need a strong woman on the ticket with you, Sam. It's really that simple."

Tom looked up suddenly and winked at Sam. They both nodded approval without saying a word. Victoria had just spontaneously confirmed what months of analyzing and synthesizing scientific polling data had already established, once again validating Victoria's natural political instincts.

"So, who is this super woman?" Victoria flashed a smile, acknowledging hitting the bull's-eye.

"We'll get back to you, General, with *his* name," Tom responded to Victoria before Sam could blurt out the super woman's identity.

Surprised, Victoria responded, "'His name.' You mean 'her name.' A military man would only be half a loaf!"

Victoria had declined to be featured by Grace for a story on the subject of Sam's potential selection of a vice presidential candidate and the intimation that the selection might be her. This was a subject way beyond her expertise and came on the heels of Tom's repeated and not-so-subtle chastisement to stay away from all political topics, except for military and women's issues. But Brigadier General Victoria Pierce had been the product of a lifetime of powerful decision making. She could have easily made such a powerful decision to become the vice president of the United States, had she been interested. She was good at politics, but she wanted out. Her mission had been to help Sam win his party's nomination and then elect him president of the United States, thereafter forsaking politics and returning to the military and her role as Sam's lover, knowing that Sam the president would never divorce Betty, the First Lady. Nevertheless, Grace had planted the seed of her suitability to be the vice president, a subject originally fleeting but a subject that Victoria could no longer ignore because of so much media focus during the lull before the convention on the one remaining mystery. Who would Sam pick as his running mate? Without fail, the editorialist always listed General Pierce in the short list of predictions. The questions came to Victoria more often now. Her answer was the same. "I don't know, and I'm not interested."

It dawned on Victoria that Sam and Tom were missing the obvious. She thought, *I know more about the right choice than the supposed experts. A man, any man, was the wrong choice to attract the new core of professional women that Sam needed to win the election. Sam is weak in this category of potential voters. Everyone sitting in the room knows that. I know that. Tom knows that. Sam knows that. The pollsters know that. Wasn't this really the only reason that Tom even tolerated me in the campaign's inner circle in the first place, because I have made serious positive inroads into this very significant negative category of voters, particularly each time I'm featured in the* New York Times? *So what's all this bullshit about a man?*

"You're kidding about a military man, right?" Victoria continued.

Tom again responded before Sam could answer the question truthfully. "Let's leave it this way, Victoria. The campaign is not disclosing the identity of its vice presidential nominee. Not to you or anyone else."

Undeterred, Victoria continued her assault on the nominee's identity. "So what are this man's military credentials? At a minimum, he has to be a general or a former general."

"Historically, generals have made poor presidents," Sam responded as might a political science professor, refusing to depart from his appointed lecture, while driving his students into episodes of daydreaming.

"Here we go again." Tom looked up. "See what you've started now!"

"The founders feared generals."

Victoria momentarily looked up from her nails and interrupted. "OK, what about the father of our country, General George Washington?"

"Precisely, my point. The office of president had to be pushed upon General Washington because as the victorious

Revolutionary War general, he feared being perceived as a military despot, poised to overthrow the new government, much the way Julius Caesar, a conquering general, overthrew the Roman Republic in the first century. You see, General Pierce, at the time of our nation's creation, there was no pattern for a constitutional democracy. The founders' greatest challenge to an enduring constitution was to avoid the historical mistakes of the few republics that survived long enough to provide models for their demise."

"Well, General Washington was perhaps our greatest president, and what about General Eisenhower, a brilliant military strategist? I studied his tactics in college, and even cadets to this day study his tactics. Wasn't he a good president?" Victoria, knowing the answer, asked the question anyway to defeat Sam's point.

"The cigar-smoking General Grant better illustrates my point. Nevertheless, I will concede that Generals Washington and Eisenhower were both great presidents and great generals. But the founders still feared the commingling of presidential and military power. The president is the commander in chief of the military, but the Constitution reserves to Congress the power to declare war."

Tom, surrounded by volumes of polling notebooks, snored sitting upright on the couch with his cigarette still burning between his figures. Victoria walked over to the couch and removed the cigarette, without dropping an ash, and crushed it in the glass as Tom, without interruption, snored on.

Victoria stood next to Sam, breathed deeply, and whispered so as not to wake Tom. "Look, you need both a woman and a general. As much as I really can't stomach this political hypocrisy, that someone could be me. I am an outsider who appeals to strong women voters. These women, I am willing to bet, will cross over to vote for our ticket. I have strong appeal to male voters of all ages because I retain some beauty from bygone days. You know I will also appeal to male voters because I can lend a military balance to a presidential candidate who lacks military credentials. If not me, someone like me. Find that profile, and you'll find your way to the Oval Office. Forget this nonsense about putting some four-star blowhard on the ballot. Women will jump ship! Then you will have to deal with a carping and bitching mistress, full-time, instead of a dismissive vice president trotting around military bases."

Victoria pulled herself closer to Sam with her breasts neatly bisecting his upper arm and whispered in his ear, "Tell me, my lover, who is the bastard? I have ways of making you tell me your secrets just as Cleopatra had ways of making Julius Caesar tell his secrets."

"I can withstand sexual torture. Try as you may, I'll never tell you my secret."

"Oh yeah, we'll see about that," as Victoria dropped her hand from Sam's upper arm and grasped his hand, pulling him across the room into the suite's private bedroom, locking the door behind, and turning around as she unbuttoned her blouse. "In a few minutes, you'll be begging to tell me your secret. Maybe I'll listen to your answer right away, or maybe I'll make you beg. Then when you can't stand the torture any longer, I might listen or I might not . . . to what I know you're surely going to tell me."

Sam held out longer than expected, but wilted under Victoria's sexual torture. An hour later, the couple emerged from the bedroom into the conference room, where Tom was lying down on the couch, loudly snoring. Sam was smiling and Victoria bristled, "A half a loaf." Tom woke abruptly, automatically pulling a cigarette from his pocket. He lit it, trying to figure out what Victoria was saying.

"You got the woman part right, but she has no damned ability to solve your military problems."

"But that's your job, Victoria," Sam countered.

"I can't believe you fucking told her, Sam!" Tom—realizing now that Sam has just breached a confidence between candidate and manager—stood up, rubbed his eyes, and rushed to the center of the room in a panic. "Who else have you told, Sam? Look, damn it all to hell, you promised me." Tom turned, glared at Victoria, and said, "Look, Babe, you've just been let in on a $10 million secret. For God's sake, tell me you have not phoned that bitch at the *New York Times*."

Victoria flashed a smile at Tom. The smile revealed that Victoria had ways of gaining information that Tom could do nothing about.

"No one outside of this room knows," Sam responded sheepishly.

Victoria, dropping the smile, turned serious. "Well, how the hell is the Speaker of the House—right, it is the Speaker of the House?—going to appeal to anyone except a few Texans? Just because she helped us out in the Texas primary is no reason to put her on the ticket."

"She was more than just a little help. Sixty percent of the vote in a Southern state—unprecedented—sealed our victory. Cannot imagine how the most politically powerful woman in the country would gain my attention," Tom responded with dripping sarcasm.

"You guys got it only half right. You would be better off putting a hawkish, good-looking, young senator on the ballot than this woman. There are dozens of choices better than her. Heck, you would be better off putting me on the ballot than Margaret . . . Maggie . . . which is it? You were so hard . . . so hard to understand with all that groaning you were doing when you finally came out with it, Sam."

Sam's cheeks turned beet red. "Her name, officially, is Margaret O'Connor, but everyone calls her Maggie."

Tom's concern grew deeper than the revelation of the nominee. *What had Victoria just said? Something about she would make a better choice?*

"Look, everyone knows I don't have the same name recognition as Maggie, but I have the combination that you must have to win this race."

"Just what in the hell is she talking about now, Sam?" Tom fired the question to Sam in total astonishment. "I have been your political advisor for over fifteen years, waiting for the very day when you place your hand on the Bible and accept the oath as president of the United States. We're almost there, Sam. Don't do this to me!"

Victoria responded, "You're mistaking me for someone who gives a rat's ass about who is the vice president of the United States. I care enough about Sam Eagan to make him president of the United States, and I'm willing to sacrifice myself and my personal agenda, which, in case you haven't noticed, Tom, is a return to the sanity of military life. As a general, I know what it takes to win a war. To lose at war means death, for yourself and a lot of troops around you, so I am trained not to lose. It's the same in politics. Losing is not an option. You do what's necessary to win. You know what it will take, Tom, or do you need to see it again in black and white?" Victoria picked up one of Tom's notebooks off the couch and threw it in his direction. "Sam needs crossover professional women voters and the vote of men who fear his military record in order to win. I am the only person, not just the only woman, in the United States who can bring that combination to the ballot box."

"But you have zero political experience. You are a complete unknown, never held public office, no base, no constituency, and you're an Oklahoma farm girl with no urban background. At the very best, you are a high-stakes gamble." Tom stared again at Sam to ensure he's listening and comprehending.

"I will be the outside-the-Washington-beltway-candidate who will be viewed as a no-nonsense advocate not just for the military, but I will pitch law and order to every fire and police benevolence society in the country. I am a strong woman—actually a role model, in case you haven't noticed. I'll attract strong women voters."

Victoria now turned to face her lover with her final argument. "And I'll attract red-blooded American men who will have to lie to their wives about how much they admire you, Sam, when the only real reason they voted for our ticket was out of sheer lust for the vice president."

Victoria stood erect, facing the two men, legs planted shoulder-width apart and her arms attached to her hips like a schoolteacher scolding misbehaving children.

"Victoria, you know I love your spunk, always have, but that's why we have Tom. I've learned to never go with my gut when Tom's advice relies on his scientific polling data. There are just too many unknowns out there at this late date in the selection process. When the focus groups confirm the selection of the Speaker of the House, we will offer her the spot on the ticket. She knows she's the leading contender."

In the hours that followed, Tom Pearsall, with uncharacteristic speed, pushed his pollsters to conclude the focus group confirmation before Victoria had the opportunity to "torture" Sam into reversing his position on his vice presidential nominee. A day and a night later, the pollsters completed their final analysis, confirming that Margaret O'Connor would be the vice presidential candidate, as the senior member of Congress from Texas and the sitting Speaker of the United States House of Representatives.

* * *

The day before the convention, Tom, facing the hotel suite's glass view of the Manhattan skyline, spoke softly into his newly acquired cell phone, what Tom called "his secure telephone." "No, no, don't enter from the lobby. Take the back entrance through the kitchen to the service elevator up to the eighteenth floor, get off the service elevator, and walk down the hall and up three flights to the twenty-first floor. The executive suite is the first door to the right as you exit the stairwell. That should be sufficient to elude the press. Mobs of them are staked out at the front entrance. We will have several nominee-decoys drive up in limousines to the lobby entrance as a diversion while you slip in the back. . . . Yes, four o'clock. . . . A woman, you remember meeting Sam's military advisor, General Victoria Pierce. . . . Right, you met in Dallas. Outside of Sam and me, she's the only person who knows about this. She will be in the kitchen at the hotel's back entrance. . . . Right . . . the hotel kitchen at four o'clock. Again, this is only a formality. The senator wants to conduct your final interview and be sure we are all on the same page. . . . No, there is no other candidate under consideration. . . . The last interview is perfunctory. Your background check is complete. . . . No questions there. . . . Everything's ready to go for a Thursday nomination. See you at four o'clock." Tom hangs up his secure telephone.

"Confirmed at four, Mr. President. Now, Victoria, please be staked out behind the entrance to the hotel kitchen by 3:30 p.m. to provide escort for the Speaker."

"Why me? You know I won't be nice to the 'half a loaf.'"

"Ordinarily, a staffer would be assigned, but there's too much danger of a leak. No one will suspect you, and I don't have to worry about the Speaker's safety. You can crack heads with the best of 'em. Escort her up the service elevator to the eighteenth floor and then to this room. She's been told to come alone. No one, and I mean no one, is to accompany the two of you up to this room. The press can speculate all they want, but this is a $10 million announcement that cannot be upstaged by a last-minute leak! Got it? And you better be nice to her! No one should recognize you. Just try to look like a civilian. You do know how to look like a civilian?"

As much as Victoria resented Tom's condescending remark, she admired his attention to detail. She had her orders, and she would follow them. Besides, her role as escort would provide her with the opportunity to size up the Speaker.

At 3:30 that afternoon, Victoria, dressed in a white blouse and navy skirt, paced in high heels back and forth by a sink full of pots and pans as she recalled in a daydream a time in her young life when her job was to scrub such items spotless.

> Laboring at the back sink behind the commercial stoves, relentlessly scouring the black off of pots and pans, was an arduous job and clearly the worst duty station in the restaurant. Damned hard work! Fortunately for me, life on the Pierce Farm trained me for long hours and hard work. I still remember the smell of the cleanser and the chemicals. Nothing's changed. They still smell the same today.

Victoria reminisced and chatted in Spanish with the Latino dishwasher, becoming so absorbed with their connection that she completely missed Maggie's entrance.

"Excuse me, you are Victoria Pierce? I am supposed to meet you here," said a slightly rotund woman with dyed blonde hair in her fifties.

"Oh, God, yes. Why, yes I am. We met in Dallas. And, of course, you are Speaker O'Connor."

"Of course, I am, and this is my husband, Dr. Larry O'Connor."

Victoria extended her hand. "Larry, oh my, well, Larry, I am so sorry, but you must wait here. The Speaker should return with me in about a half hour. Our mission calls for us to go it alone from here. I am sure you must understand the need for the strictest confidentiality."

"Why, yes, of course. I'll just chat with the help in the kitchen until you get back. Hurry along, now, Maggie. I'll be fine. This should not take longer than about five minutes?"

"Well, I suspect I'll have to listen to their proposition for longer than five minutes, Larry."

"But we both know what your answer will be, so promise me you won't keep me waiting down here too long?" Larry kissed his wife.

The two women stepped onto the service elevator, the doors shut, and they disappeared. They exited, according to plan, onto the eighteenth floor, turned right down an isolated hallway to the stairwell, marked with a red lighted exit sign above the door, climbed three flights of steep steps to the twenty-first floor, and turned right into the campaign suite, with no one in the press the wiser.

"Mission accomplished," Victoria exclaimed as she breezed into the room. Maggie followed and extended her hand first to Tom and then to Sam. Under noticeably labored breathing from the steep climb, "How are you . . . good . . . whew, damn, Sam . . . good to see you, Mr. President." Maggie extends her hand.

Sam took her hand and led her to the couch. They sat down simultaneously.

"This will not take long," Sam began. "There're reporters crawling all over out front. Tom, here, has gone through all of the polling numbers, calculations, projections and whatever else he does. You know how detailed he is. To cut to the chase, Maggie, the bottom line is, Tom's data confirm that together we make an unbeatable combination. I want you to be the vice president of the United States."

"You do get to the point, Sam," Maggie responded. "Doesn't give a southern gal much time to be coy, does it now, Sam....remember you are talking to the Speaker of the House, who already sits third in line in presidential succession and who can only take a step up from third to second in the presidential rankings by accepting your kind invitation. But my acceptance may not be a sure thing, you know." Sam looked over at Tom. Neither expected Maggie O'Connor's equivocation. Her acceptance was a mere formality, they thought. If she said "no," there was no other screened successor to step up to Thursday's nomination. She had unexpected political leverage. The announcement must come in four days. What did she want?

"Well, Maggie, we are not asking you to give up the Speakership," Sam responded quickly. "You can run as both the vice presidential nominee and for reelection as the congresswoman from Texas, just like Senator Lieberman did as Al Gore's vice presidential running mate. Aren't you running unopposed in your Texas district? You'll finish no worse than third no matter what you do."

"Gentlemen, it's a good thing I don't have any major conditions to put on the table right now. Sam, as a senior United States senator, I'm surprised you would ever put yourself in such a compromised bargaining position," Maggie chastised. "But listen to me carefully, both of you."

Victoria, the fourth person who was alive and breathing in the room—reduced now to someone of insufficient stature to be included in this cautionary directive—sat down in an armchair, cleared her throat, thus alerting Maggie to her presence, and listened.

"I will not give up the Speakership, a position of genuine power, to become some figurehead. I want presidential responsibility. I know Congress. Together, we can enact your legislative agenda into law. But I will have to be both your vice president and your legislative representative on the Hill. What I will not be is a ribbon cutter!"

This was the first time Victoria had ever heard "ribbon cutter" in such a negative way. She may not have known how political insiders viewed ribbon cutters, but Maggie O'Connor made it abundantly clear she was not going to be one. What Victoria learned was a political lesson about vulnerability and leverage, not unlike what a military general might do to win a favored assignment—lessons she learned the hard way from Sergeant Goodheart and applied to NCO Rodriguez at an early military age. Victoria had just gained immeasurable insight into Maggie, a shrewd woman, sitting next to two outbargained men, who just prospectively conceded presidential power.

But Victoria—while observing Maggie, who scarcely paid her any attention at all—questioned to herself, *Can this woman do anything at all to shore up Sam's military image? Can she even be trusted? Her egotistical demands bordered on disloyalty. She has zero military credentials. Isn't she seeking to advance her own political agenda, not what's best for Sam or even the country for that matter?*

"We all know that you will make a strong vice president, Madam Speaker. It would be unthinkable to make you anything like a titular head." Sam immediately regretted using "titular," a term subject to a sexual nuance, so he immediately clarified, "Much more like a co-president, really . . . well, actually both my vice president and congressional liaison."

"Thank you, Sam, for accepting my terms as your chief legislative counsel while serving as president of the Senate. I did hear you correctly about that, Sam?"

"Right you are, Maggie! We have a deal!" The two shook hands.

Tom exhaled with a sigh. He never suspected that Maggie O'Connor might decline their offer. Of course, she had no intention of declining. She only leveraged the prospects of declining.

"Maggie, the announcement comes Thursday night. The precise time will be established based upon Wednesday's overnight polling numbers. Our campaign committee will coordinate with your people about the identity of your seconding speakers and content of your acceptance speech. Be thinking about who you want to make these seconding speeches. We have several people in mind, and I'm sure you do as well. But it's your choice, subject to our final approval. There's very little time left before Thursday, but we already have collected a great deal of your video footage from your campaign spots."

"I am going to fly back to Dallas tonight," Maggie responded, "and we can work from there. The more I hang around here, the more someone in the press will figure this out. I'll be ready by Thursday. By the way, guys, I intend for this ticket to win! We are unbeatable."

Victoria, snubbed again as the invisible nonperson in the room, realized the finality of Tom's mistake. No time for reconsideration or second-guessing or answering unanswered questions. Victoria checked the hallway. It was clear. The two women slipped out of the suite and down the hallway to the stairwell. Victoria eavesdropped as Maggie muttered to herself, "Really, it was too easy. I can see I'll have to assist Sam in delicate negotiations." Maggie laughed out loud.

She's already being disloyal to Sam, Victoria thought in a quiet rage. Victoria stopped abruptly, bristled in silence, and then raced to catch up with Maggie's fast-paced escape through the exit door. Victoria retook Maggie at the top of the stairwell, pulling her left sleeve to make a counterpoint about Sam's political toughness. At that instant Maggie reached to grab the handrail in her rushed descent down the steps, as if someone from the hallway above might yell down to her to withdraw the offer of her nomination.

Maggie fell, missing her grasp on the handrail by centimeters, tumbling, cascading headfirst down fifteen unforgiving concrete and steel stairs to the bottom landing.

Victoria's anger at Maggie had not subsided. Victoria knew what she must do, but she could not take the first step down. It was the same ambivalence she felt many years ago after she decked Amber Morelli. Anger trumped her compassion. Maggie lay unconscious and bleeding from her head, mouth, and leg. A jagged tibia extended through the skin above her left ankle. Victoria observed the lifeless form at the bottom of the stairs as someone certain to be dead. In a warped trance, Victoria saw herself as an alternative to Maggie as Sam's vice presidential nominee. She loved Sam and would protect him from a calculating vice president. Victoria would always act in his best interest—out of love, not ambition—not at all like the lifeless form below. *What if Maggie*, who lay in a requiem-like state at the bottom of the stairs, who looked to be already dead, *needed a minute longer to make this her final resting place?* The first minute passed.

Victoria knew the face of death. She had seen the faces of too many dead Marines. Could she wait a minute longer for fate to seal the right choice for vice president? *Wasn't this woman a potential enemy and a danger to Sam*, she agonized. The second minute passed.

Who, then, would be Sam's vice president? The third minute passed as Maggie's head moved. Her left eye was already badly swollen and closed. She groaned in semiconsciousness. She was not dead. Victoria, responding now as if Maggie were a wounded comrade gunned downed in combat, raced to the bottom of the stairs, took a handkerchief from her pocket and pressed it to Maggie's mouth, cradling Maggie's head on her lap. Victoria checked her vital signs. The pulse was weak; she was going into shock. From Maggie's purse she retrieved her cell phone and punched in 911. "We need emergency assistance right away." After giving her location as if coordinates on a battlefield map, she punched in Tom's secure telephone number.

Startled at the ring on his phone, Tom snatched up his cell phone. "Hello. Who is this? How did you get this number?"

Victoria blurted out, "Tom, you won't believe what just happened in the stairwell. Maggie tripped and fell down the stairs. She's badly beaten up, extent of her head injuries uncertain, at least one major break, contusions everywhere. Bleeding is now under control, but we could lose her to shock any time. Emergency help is on the way." The line went dead as Victoria hung up.

"What did you say?" But the message was clear to Tom.

Tom stared out the window, thinking, until Sam asked for a second time his absent-minded question, "Who's calling you on your secret-police phone, Tom?"

Tom slammed the phone shut. He could not help who he was. He thought only one way: politics. He walked over to the wet bar and poured a straight vodka, without ice, and drank it down like water. He quickly made another and then made a scotch on the rocks for Sam.

Leaning over the wet bar, Tom said in a whisper, "Maggie O'Connor could be dead by Thursday."

"What?"

Tom brushed his hair back with his hand, pulled out a cigarette, lit it, walked over to Sam, sat down again, and handed Sam his drink. Tom's face was like chalk.

Sam finished half of his glass. "It's a bit early for this, don't you think? You said something about Maggie. I thought I heard . . . dead?"

"No, she's not dead, at least not yet, but she's in real bad shape—may not even make it through the night or until Thursday."

"Where is she? Where is Victoria?"

"Look, Sam." Tom removed all personal thoughts from his calculus and gave Sam the straight political advice he must have. He secretly wished it had been Victoria instead of Maggie. "Look, Sam. You have no vice presidential nominee right now, one fuckin' day before our convention opens and three days before our vice presidential announcement. It gets worse than that—a potential press field day about our campaign's potential involvement in the demise of the Speaker, no less. And, yes, she is *the* fuckin' Speaker of the House of Representatives of the United States of America. Ooh, and it gets better, Sam—as if it couldn't get any fuckin' better for our enemies: Speaker O'Connor lies half-dead in the stairwell one floor below your campaign headquarters."

CHAPTER NINE

August 1980

"Vera Ochman, you have been charged by complaint with the murder of an agent of the Federal Bureau of Investigation."

From his perch high upon the ornate bench in the cavernous criminal courtroom of the Manhattan Courthouse, the young-looking magistrate judge barely even glanced down at defendant Vera Ochman. The hands of the giant pendulum clock hanging on the wall behind the judge indicated 10:30 a.m. It was the morning following the murders at the Wicked Whiskey Bar, and it was Vera's mandatory first appearance. The judge, cloaked in his black robe, was barely visible from the shoulders up. Vera stood between the counsel tables in the center of the room about fifteen feet from the judge's bench, her tight leather attire exchanged for an orange jumpsuit. Her hands and legs were shackled to ostensibly prevent her escape from a courtroom filled with twenty armed agents, all of whom had been called to silently protest the execution-style murder of their fallen comrade. But many were also there to assuage their own guilt for their failure to respond to an agent felled in the line of duty the night before. Print news reporters, who normally do not cover initial appearances on the federal courthouse beat, sat quietly on the front row taking copious descriptive notes as Vera stood before the magistrate judge to answer criminal charges for the first time in her life.

Vera broke the silence with a question for the magistrate judge. "Please, will someone let me see my father?"

Agent Ramirez, a kind-looking Latino man of diminutive stature, whose telephone voice was the last ever heard by Ben Ochman, sat at the counsel table beside the U.S. Attorney. He rose and asked to approach the bench. Normally, only attorneys were granted such permission, but Ramirez was a veteran and respected FBI agent who had won the trust of every judge in the courthouse. Waving Ramirez forward, the magistrate judge watched patiently as the agent crossed the room and approached the bench. Ramirez, because of his height, stood on his tiptoes and strained to reach the bench. With his arms folded, he leaned on the front of the bench, and the judge also leaned forward so that their faces were less than a foot apart. After about two minutes of whispered conversation, Ramirez stepped back. With no alternative, the judge exhaled and blurted out the bad news from the bench. "I am afraid that is impossible. Your father died early this morning of heart failure. Is there another relative that you wish the court to contact?"

The courtroom murmured as reporters scribbled. The uninflected words of the magistrate judge drifted down and past Vera as if she were not standing there. However, the content was crystal clear. She replied without looking up and tried desperately to retain her composure. "There is no one else."

"Do you wish to speak with a lawyer? If you qualify, I will appoint a lawyer to represent you."

Dazed, Vera recalled her insensitive response to her father's final act of love, her ice cream melting in the August heat, and her callous resentment of her father's grief. Had she remained at home last night, none of this would have happened. Like the ice cream melting atop her birthday cake, Vera's tears began to trickle down the sides of her cheeks and drop to the front of her jumpsuit unrestrained by her shackled hands. She nodded affirmatively to the judge.

"I'm sorry, Miss Ochman, do you wish for me to appoint a lawyer to represent you?" The judge spoke with a hint of compassion for the first time as he leaned forward, his eyes focused on Vera and his hand cupped beside his ear, as he was required to record her answer to this critical question.

"Yes," Vera responded barely audibly with her head down, attempting to conceal the tears now streaming down her face.

Ken Berger, a veteran criminal trial lawyer with wavy gray hair, streaked with black from an earlier age, and impeccably dressed in a dark three-piece suit with a bold striped tie, sat conversing in a whisper with another lawyer on the attorneys' bench behind the counsel tables. He had not expected to hear his name called out by the court as he was there to represent a client on another matter.

"Mr. Berger, will you accept appointment as indigent counsel for Vera Ochman?"

"As Your Honor knows, it has been years since I have accepted such an appointment. There are many other fine . . ." Berger stopped, looked at the young defendant and then around at the courtroom full of agents, and changed his mind. "Yes, of course, Your Honor."

"Please, then, arrange you calendar to meet with your client by this afternoon to complete the indigent counsel form. You can return it to the clerk for my consideration by tomorrow morning."

"Certainly, Your Honor. But if it pleases the court, would it be possible to immediately confer in private with my client before she returns to lockup?"

"Yes, Mr. Berger, you may use the side conference room and take a few minutes to discuss with Ms. Ochman the indigent request form so the court may determine her right to indigent counsel." The judge pointed to a federal marshal beside the entrance to the conference room. "Secure the conference room and permit Mr. Berger to confer in private with his client for five minutes."

Agent Ramirez whispered desperately in the ear of the U.S. Attorney for New York City, Michael Brandon, a ruggedly handsome and athletic man seated beside him at the prosecutor's table. Had it not been for the highly publicized murder of an undercover FBI agent, in the normal routine, Michael Brandon would not have been in the courtroom that morning at all. An assistant U.S. Attorney routinely ran the first appearance criminal calendar on Friday morning.

Brandon stood, facing the bench, and objected. "Your Honor, the government has neither completed its initial intake interview with the defendant nor determined the appropriate jurisdiction for the trial of this minor. It's all a little premature to appoint counsel at this juncture."

"Actually, the court will determine the appropriate jurisdiction upon appropriate notice to the defendant. And no determination has yet been made as to whether counsel will be appointed. Mr. Brandon, I am going to permit Mr. Berger to assist the defendant with the completion of this form. Objection overruled." The magistrate judge knew the precarious circumstances facing the frightened young girl standing before him, and just how fortunate she was to have Ken Berger consider accepting an indigent appointment to represent her.

Inside the small conference room, a drab space with an elongated table and four uncomfortable chairs, Vera Ochman and Ken Berger sat across the table from each other. Her tanned dark face, now pale and ashen, dropped to rest on the top of her cuffed wrists. Tears poured down the sides of her cheeks into a shallow puddle on the table below. She sobbed quietly and then wept uncontrollably. She was barely able to draw enough air into her lungs to sustain her crying. Berger waited. Vera finally spoke.

"My life's ruined. Oh God, what have I done? I want my father! I need him," she wailed.

"Vera, please sign these indigent appointment papers in blank. I'll fill them out, and you will have an opportunity to go over them later. But right now, we have only a precious few minutes, and I need to talk with you as your lawyer, so please listen carefully," Ken Berger said unemotionally. "You will be eighteen years old tomorrow, right?

"Who are you?" Vera tried to look up through a veil of tears at the dignified man sitting across the table who was pointing to a signature line on the form. Vera somehow managed to sign the form.

"I'm your appointed lawyer or soon will be. Now, Vera, please straighten up and listen to me with every ounce of maturity that you can muster under these dire circumstances because you are in the race of your life," Berger continued. "But there's good news. You have a jump on your co-defendant. The feds have not decided where or how to try you. You were a minor at the time of the murder last night, a fact that significantly complicates your prosecution. The first decision the government will have to make is to determine whether to try you as an adult on the murder charges in federal court or to turn you over to the state authorities who could try you as a minor. Improbable as it may be, the New York State Court might even allow you to walk free in a matter of days since, at the time of the murder, you were a minor, and normally the period of incarceration for a crime committed by a minor lasts only to the age of majority, which for you would be tomorrow."

"Can't you see my life is ruined? Just leave me alone."

"No, I will not leave you alone, Vera, so try to listen the best you know how. That's part of their dilemma. Had you not been involved in the highly publicized murder of an FBI agent, likely they would have done just that and bounced you over to state court and been rid of you. But they cannot risk a slap on the wrist in state court when there was a murder of an FBI agent merely because you happened to be a minor two days shy of your eighteenth birthday. Most certainly, Michael Brandon will argue to retain jurisdiction over you and try you as an adult, blocking your avenue of escape. The only choice you really have is to cooperate. Help them convict Sanchez because they need your eyewitness testimony, but you must make a deal quickly. You, my dear, are the only living eyewitness to this murder, besides Sanchez, of course."

Still crying, Vera looked up, confused by Berger's language, and said, "How do you even know who Sanchez is or what happened last night? Have you talked to him or something? You must know he's going to kill me."

Ken Berger pulled the late edition of the *New York Times* from his briefcase and flipped it open to the front page where Vera could see a grainy black-and-white photograph that showed BB and the night manager covered in sheets facing each other in the exact location where they were shot dead in the office of the Wicked Whiskey Bar.

"It's amazing how much detail is available in this story that took place just a few hours ago," Berger said, looking at the door. Ramirez was pacing outside trying to prevent exactly what was about to take place between attorney and client inside the conference room. Last night, Ramirez could not have interrogated Vera, a minor by definition, without a lawyer or parent present, thus the need to rush Ben Ochman to the courthouse, trusting Vera would incriminate herself and Sanchez after he arrived. Ramirez did not count on Ben

Ochman dropping dead before reaching the courthouse. Sanchez, by contrast, sang like a jailbird to Ramirez, but it was his version of the events, conveniently exonerating himself as an innocent bystander and asking Ramirez to imagine how shocking it was to witness Vera shooting BB in the back of the head. Sanchez was pretty sure it was an accident.

Vera stared at the photo depiction on the table before her. Her sobbing intensified. "Now, everyone in Brooklyn thinks I'm a murderer. I didn't . . . I didn't do it. He did!"

Berger saw that the newspaper article was only making matters worse, so he quickly returned the *Times* to his briefcase and pleaded with Vera to listen to him carefully.

"Your life, or what's left of it, Vera, may depend on what happens in the next few minutes. First, say nothing to anyone about the events of last night unless I am present. Promise me that, Vera." Vera nods. "Second, Sanchez has likely already pointed the finger at you for the murder of the agent, and if not, will soon do so because that's his ticket to freedom. Your gun fired the fatal shot. The *Times* story implicates you. However, the prosecution knows just how implausible it will be for a jury to believe that an innocent and attractive high school girl from Brooklyn, with no priors or motive, would shoot an undercover FBI agent in the back of the head. Besides, the ballistics evidence will assuredly point the finger at Sanchez. His attorney doubtless is having the same conversation with Sanchez, trying to elbow ahead of you to get his version of the facts before the prosecution. You probably are just a few minutes away from losing that race. Vera, you must act quickly before Sanchez can make that offer."

Ramirez banged at the conference room door. "Time's up."

Ignoring Ramirez, Berger continued. "Vera, authorize me to open negotiations with the U.S. attorney on a plea that could lead to your immediate release. There are so many factors that make it difficult for them to prosecute you. Believe me, they want Sanchez off the streets permanently."

"I can't testify against Sanchez. The gang will murder me the minute I get out and throw my body in the East River."

Berger paused to think and then snapped his fingers as his analytical mind soon found the solution. "You would be an excellent candidate for the Witness Protection Program." He stood up and began absentmindedly talking to the door, not Vera, almost in a whisper, rubbing his hands through his streaky gray hair. "There is no one now at home. The father died trying to respond to an incomprehensible chain of events set into motion last night. There is no relative anywhere to accept responsibility under any kind of protective release. OK, that's it." Berger snapped his fingers again and turned to face Vera directly. "The Witness Protection Program will give you a new identity, and you will safely live out the rest of your life in relative obscurity somewhere far away and unknown even to the feds—but free, not incarcerated, not even a criminal record. The gang will never find you, and you will be secure in complete anonymity."

"Not good enough," Vera responded shrewdly for the first time, clearing her mind, but sensing that Berger was headed in the right direction. "Look, Mr. Berger, you know they will hunt me down and find me no matter where I go, unless . . . unless . . . they think I'm dead. I have to somehow be made to appear dead. If not, it might be a whole lot smarter and much safer for me to take my chances here or, who knows, you might be able to talk them into getting me over to state court like you said, because to testify against Sanchez is a death sentence."

Ramirez banged on the door. "Time's up."

"Five minutes more. My client is having difficulty understanding the form, Agent Ramirez," Berger yelled back through the door.

"One minute. That's all. The defendant must return to lockup, or else I'm coming in," responded the authoritarian voice from the other side of the door.

Turning his focus back to Vera, Berger hurriedly thought out loud. "OK, OK. I'll try to arrange your death. . . ."

"What, have me killed?"

"No, no, no. Not your real death. It will be faked, only looking like you've been killed. That will be a part of the deal. That will certainly be a new twist under a witness protection deal, but, you know, it just might work with the threat of a Puerto Rican gang, tied to the Mob, threatening to kill the state's key witness. Now, Vera, if I can arrange both the Witness Protection Program and your feigned assassination, will you testify truthfully against Sanchez and the gang before the grand jury?"

Vera hesitated and started to cry again. "Let me think about it."

"God, Vera, have you not heard a word I've been saying? There *is* no time to think about it," Berger responded in whispered desperation. "The deal has to be made now because they will come after you if they have to. Someone is going to fall for the assassination of this agent, and it could be you, or worse, they won't even need your testimony to convict Sanchez on murder because of the strong forensic evidence, and they will prosecute both of you."

Ramirez inserted the key in the door and said, "I'm coming in."

Brandon pressed his shoe against the door.

"You've got five seconds, Vera, to save what's left of your life."

"OK," Vera relented, just as Ramirez forced his way into the room. He was instantly beside Vera, lifting her up by the arm.

In the courtroom, Ken Berger walked up to the prosecution's table and whispered in Michael Brandon's ear that he wanted to confer immediately about a deal. Brandon nodded but did not say a word. He concentrated instead on Sanchez, the real reason that he was in the courtroom that morning. Sanchez's first appearance was a mere formality to officially inform him of the reasons for his incarceration and to inquire into his legal representation. It would take less than five minutes. The federal agents were there to intimidate Sanchez with a show of force and resolve.

At that moment, Sanchez, similarly dressed and shackled, entered the courtroom through the side entrance. He did not know of Vera's planned betrayal as she passed by him on her return to lockup with Ramirez. Berger saw no sign of a lawyer for Sanchez and realized that Vera had a real shot at beating Sanchez to the U.S. attorney. Sanchez stopped, smiled, and winked at Vera before a federal marshal pushed him into position facing the judge. Such open disrespect for the proceedings caused every agent in the courtroom to murmur and sneer at Sanchez.

Directed by the banging of his gavel and the perceptible nod of the magistrate judge, the uniformed bailiff standing in the back of the courtroom announced in a thunderous voice, "Quiet in the courtroom. All quiet!"

CHAPTER TEN

August 1980

Later that same morning in the U.S. attorney's large, opulent office, Michael Brandon and Ken Berger, two capable trial lawyers advancing opposite interests, opened negotiations on a plea bargain. Brandon needed the testimony of an eyewitness for a conviction and swift retribution for a cop killer. Berger needed to win a second life for a teenage girl ensnared by her own naivete in racketeering and murder. They both postured.

"Look, Mike, you will have an attractive, believable, not to mention innocent, young woman as the government's key witness to ensure the conviction of the man who murdered in cold blood an FBI agent—a family man with a wife now widowed and three daughters, all fatherless." Berger lifted a framed photograph of Brandon's family off his desk. "Tell me, Mike, how old is Grace now?"

"She's three."

"Can you imagine what it would be like if this had happened to you, and your daughter had to grow up fatherless? This agent gave his life in the line of duty. You need my client's testimony for a successful prosecution. Vera Ochman will not only seal a first-degree murder conviction for this father killer, but she will send the remnants of this street gang, all serious criminals, to the pen for a long time. The minute that this thug, Sanchez, realizes that Vera has turned state's evidence, I'll wager you that he will offer a very quick plea to second-degree murder, before the ink even dries on our agreement. If Sanchez rolls the dice at trial and loses, he will spend the rest of his life behind bars, and he knows that."

Brandon picked up some papers on his desk and began to read absentmindedly. Berger stopped and waited.

"So, Ken, when are you going to tell me something that I don't know?"

"Look, Mike, without a quick resolution, your open case will just fester in the public's eye with the FBI hounding you every day to rush to trial, if for no other reason than to vindicate themselves for their hesitant performance last night—a trial, I might add, you could easily lose if the jury becomes confused as to which one pulled the trigger."

"Sorry, Ken, I've got them both cold," responded Brandon, bluffing, and knowing, because of the way Sanchez was recorded on BB's tape, that Vera's eyewitness testimony was indispensable to convict Sanchez, and knowing, too, that Vera, despite her youthful indiscretions, should have to do serious time for her active participation as an accessory to first-degree murder.

"As soon as the forensics come in, you can be sure that the gunpowder evidence will point unmistakably to Sanchez, and odds are your client is going away as an accessory for a very long time."

"Not a chance," Berger rejoined. "The jury will be confused."

"OK, why?"

"Sanchez used a gun with her prints all over it. Both have powder burns from the same weapon. Both will testify that the other did it. And what about the wire? What will it show?" Berger observed that Brandon avoided answering the question by looking down, pretending to fumble through the papers on his desk.

"Believe me, Mike, there will be such confusion as to which one of them pulled the trigger that a jury will either hang up or return a verdict of not guilty based upon a serious reasonable doubt."

"That's not the way I see it. I can prove that Sanchez did it, and she was an accessory. It's that simple, Ken."

"But what if you're wrong, Mike? You're not looking at your worst-case scenario. What if both walk out of the courtroom on the same day back to a life of crime? How bad will that look if I'm right? Now, my client will testify in detail before both the grand jury and at trial as to Sanchez's participation in the murder and salt this gang away on racketeering charges. What's more, if their lawyers have any sense, everyone should plead quickly and the press, public, and FBI will back off. In exchange, Vera walks."

"So the government caves in to a teenage girl, who, for all we know right now, might have intentionally murdered an FBI agent in cold blood, who by her mere presence on the scene—not to mention the *minor offense* of trying to kill several agents trying to arrest her—just damned lucky, I might add, that she did not shoot one of them—committed at least five other felonies, all of which we somehow just ignore? Really, Ken, that's a stretch even for you," responded Michael to the absurdity of the offer. "Face it, your client's going to do active time. You know that. Get real. You're wasting my time."

"All right, I'll get real," Berger continued, as he pulled off his silk-lined jacket and loosened his tie. "Sit back and listen carefully as this is the real deal." Michael leaned back in his chair, and propped his feet on his desk. "Vera does not walk. She dies."

Both of Mike Brandon's size-twelve black-laced wing tips landed with a thud on the floor as he leaned forward in his chair and said with dripping sarcasm, "I want to hear this one!"

Berger also leaned forward but from the other side of the desk and continued. "Vera's greatest fear is that the gang will execute her for her treachery. Not a bad assumption, you will have to agree. So she rats on everyone, coming as clean as a whistle. She will tell you things that no other human alive knows about this operation as long as she feels safe. She does not feel safe testifying and then returning to high school in Brooklyn. Besides, where will she live when she returns to school? There is no surviving parent, brother, sister, or even a distant cousin, for that matter, to offer even the minimum protection of a home. Ok, Mike, here's the real deal: after she testifies before the grand jury where her credible testimony will assuredly trigger a Sanchez plea to save the rest of his sorry-ass life—after this plea or later at trial if he does not plead—Vera is publicly executed in a faked drive-by shooting by gang members, or at least it will appear that way. She then goes into the Witness Protection Program and lives out the rest of her life in total obscurity and anonymity under an assumed name. That's her life sentence. Vera's death will send a message to every teenager in the city that if you screw around with these gangs, you'll wind up dead like her. Of course, you don't ever have to publicly explain the break you gave Vera in exchange for her testimony."

Michael Brandon did not say a word. He just sat there speechless and dumbfounded, captivated by the beauty and simplicity of the resolution. After minutes of staring into the back of his left hand covering both eyes, a smile broke out across his face, and his tough DA's mask dissolved into laughter. Berger could not discern whether Brandon's laughter signaled approval or ridicule.

Finally, Mike looked directly at Berger and conceded, "I like it. I really like it, nothing left to clean up or explain, a staged execution, been done before. There's precedent. Everything is nice and neat, and no one the wiser if planned and staged properly. Sanchez and his gang are finished; the press, public, and FBI placated. But we have to get past two conditions."

He pointed his finger at Berger from behind his desk. "First, the forensics must unmistakably confirm that Sanchez pulled the trigger, a fact we have both assumed. Vera has to be confirmed as the witness, not the killer, and second— listen very carefully, Ken—second, a jury trial is off the table. There's no guarantee that Sanchez will be convicted at trial, even with Vera's eyewitness testimony, so there's not going to be any trial. As you well know, her credibility will be seriously undercut by any plea bargain I give her in exchange for her testimony against Sanchez. Sanchez's defense will argue she actually committed the murder. She could make a lousy witness and Sanchez could walk. Then she's got to somehow be bumped off no matter what happens to Sanchez. No way, a trial is too risky, too messy, and too late. Her testimony before the grand jury must force Sanchez to plead or the deal is off. If she fails before the grand jury—let's say she makes her deal and decides not to be convincing, or for whatever reason the grand jury refuses to indict Sanchez on first degree—then she will have to plead as an accessory and do at least a year of hard time, but if we have to go to trial, her staged execution is completely off the table. That's the real deal, Ken."

"It's a hard deal, Mr. D.A., but my client will give convincing testimony before the grand jury. They will indict Sanchez on first degree, I'm certain of it. So I can accept and will recommend that my client accept," Berger said as he extended his hand across the table. The complex plea bargain was sealed with a handshake between two honorable lawyers.

* * *

One week later in the hallway across from the grand jury room in the Manhattan Courthouse, Vera Ochman ignored Felipe Sanchez as he bowed before her in mocking respect, in contrast to his lawyer, Angelo Siffo, who immediately understood that Sanchez had been strategically placed in the steel chairs across from the grand jury room to observe Vera and the other state's witnesses who were to follow as they came and went, all of whom would testify against Sanchez. Siffo excused himself and disappeared into the men's bathroom just as Vera disappeared behind the closed doors of the grand jury room. Lawyers were not permitted to be with their clients in the grand jury room. So Berger followed Siffo into the courthouse john, making sure there was no mistake in his mind about exactly what Vera was doing behind those closed doors. The two lawyers stood parallel in front of the antique floor urinals, staring straight ahead.

"Good morning, Andy, what brings you to the courthouse?"

"Oh, nothing much, Ken. Just investigating your client, that good-lookin' bitch, dressed in a red dress, who soon will be feloniously perjuring herself before the grand jury, lying because she's just copped a sweet deal with the D.A. to save her own ass. I wonder just what kind of deal she made, Ken. Maybe she walks out of the courtroom right into the middle of trouble on the street!"

Berger, looking down, replied, "Andy, it's easy to make a sweet deal when all your client has to do is testify truthfully to a premeditated murder. That makes murder in the first, Andy. The real problem comes at the trial before the jury of twelve when the forensic evidence rolls out so badly in such a serious case involving the cold-blooded murder of a federal agent that it's embarrassing for you as the lawyer even to look a juror square in the eyes, because every juror on the panel knows that the lawyer is lying his ass off, too. The jury will soon figure it all out, and when they do it just infuriates them. You, the lawyer, an officer of the court, trying to force them to believe a lie."

"Maybe, we roll the dice. Either way my man can't swing for this crime. It's just not on the books," Siffo responded.

Ken Berger finished his business, zipped up his pants, and stepped over to the sink to wash his hands. Soon Andy was again parallel at the sink beside him.

Berger reengaged, "A life sentence for first degree, without parole, is a long stretch behind bars, Andy. Sometimes a real stupid criminal defense lawyer loses a post-conviction proceeding for ineffective assistance of counsel by his client, following an unsuccessful appeal of a murder conviction, let's say for nothing more than just being stupid enough to roll the dice at a murder trial that he could never win, especially when a plea bargain to second degree was an easy deal to make, and particularly when everybody in the courthouse, right down to the janitor, knows his man pulled the trigger. A word of advice, Andy. After years of work at this, I recommend any defense lawyer rolling the dice like that to have a letter in his file to his client detailing the risks of a trial and being sure to make clear that he will spend the rest of his life behind bars if the jury figures out the truth. The convicted client always forgets that precaution when all you have in the record is a verbal explanation of such a logical outcome."

Andy stomped out of the bathroom through the swinging bathroom door, fuming, "That's assuming the lying bitch survives long enough on the street to testify at trial."

* * *

"Yes, Mr. Brandon, I was there on the night of the murder and saw everything." These were the first words that Sanchez and Siffo heard through the door, as Vera began to testify.

In response to Michael Brandon's series of questions, Vera—in the detail that she rehearsed with Ken Berger—nailed Sanchez and the gang with her answers to a nodding and note-taking group of male jurors, all admiring Vera's shapely sheer-stocking legs protruding crossed from underneath her red dress. Vera was calm, assured, and rehearsed. All she really had to do was to answer the questions and tell the truth. But she also had to be believable, and her sexual attraction was part of Berger's strategy. Vera repressed all thoughts of her father and a life ruined if she failed. During the rehearsals before her actual testimony, Berger became even more confident as he discovered just how intelligent Vera really was and how quickly she could answer a lawyer's questions without being tripped up.

"For what criminal purpose was Felipe Sanchez at the Wicked Whiskey Bar on the night in question?"

"Felipe Sanchez was there to collect his share of the profits from the sale of hashish, cocaine, and heroin sold to the men who had sex with the prostitutes brought in by Sanchez from New Jersey."

While Vera testified behind the closed doors, she could see that the men were both listening and responding to her. She made eye contact with each. Throughout her life, a life modeled after her mother, Vera saw how older men responded to her. Today was not different. Her expensive French perfume, supplied by Berger, must have intoxicated every man in the room. She was confident and convincing. The combination of her intelligence and sexuality was winning the day for the prosecution.

On the other side of the door, Andy Siffo would periodically cup his hand around his client's ear and whisper the legal consequences of Vera's testimony. But mostly the two sat silently locked together in the steel chairs across from the door as Vera's muffled voice, at times a tearful performance, escaped the quarter-inch space under the door, where they could easily hear her.

Near the end, Vera in a loud voice quoted Sanchez's prophetic words as she described how Sanchez picked up BB's blood-drenched head and stared him straight in the eyes. "'You know what you are, BB. You're a dead man.'"

Sanchez seethed at Vera's betrayal as she left the grand jury room with Berger in escort and erupted uncontrollably in a Latin fury as he pointed his finger as if it were a barrel to the gun he did not have, straight into Vera's face, and then pulled the imaginary trigger, "¿Usted ya sabe que es una mujer muerta?" (You know that you're a dead woman?)

Vera's scripted performance could have won her an Academy Award. The male jurors granted unanimously, well beyond the required two-thirds, returned a true bill of indictment against Sanchez for first-degree murder along with ten other felonious racketeering counts. No member of the gang was spared by the grand jury as numerous indictments were handed down, all flowing from Vera's truthful testimony, which detailed their conspiracy and racketeering activities. Truthful testimony for all, all except for one.

What shocked everyone in the gang, except Vera, was the serious indictments returned against the young and obscure Amber Morelli. Vera, vindictively, shaded her testimony in order to tag Amber with felonious interstate prostitution, describing her as the ring's madame who paid her hookers in daily doses of heroin, in addition to her role as Sanchez's chief conspirator in perpetrating the gang's other criminal activities. By the time Vera was finished with Amber, she was guaranteed more jail time than even Sanchez.

Siffo had no wiggle room between Brandon and Berger, and the pressure mounted both from the facts and the Mob's growing discomfort with reprisals that might flow against them for the death of an FBI agent. The Mob bosses instructed Siffo to accept a deal to get the press off their trail. Based on Vera's testimony before the grand jury, Sanchez could have easily never seen the light of day again except from the exercise yard of the worst federal penitentiary in the country. Sanchez suggested that Vera be silenced, but he just did not have enough standing or longevity with the right bosses for any professional hit man to sign on, and besides, the risk of a bungled amateur job would only have made matters worse. So Siffo, without an alternative theory of defense, retreated into checkmate. He agreed to plead Sanchez to second-degree murder with a guarantee of a hospitable federal pen in New England to serve out a twenty-year sentence. He would bide his time in lockdown so he could meticulously plan the demise of Vera the Rat either personally by strangulation upon release, or by some other equally nefarious pre-incarceration plot. With good behavior, Sanchez could theoretically be out in seven years, but then Sanchez did not meet the profile of a model inmate, except for the singular motivation of an early release to silence Vera forever.

* * *

Another week later, Sanchez was standing erect with Siffo slumped sitting beside him at counsel table in the same criminal courtroom of his initial appearance. Michael Brandon stood at the prosecution's table with Ramirez seated beside him. Ken Berger waited in the back of the courtroom for his client, just in case the judge wanted to take her testimony before sentencing, but he knew what was about to take place. Otherwise, the courtroom was empty.

Brandon convinced the visiting senior retired federal judge, seated high on the bench, to quickly accept the plea bargain, and neither of them needed a courtroom of vindictive FBI agents to spoil the deal. The white-haired federal judge, recalled from judicial retirement, had gone along with the Sanchez plea bargain and was concluding the standard review of the terms of the guilty plea. The rest of the gang pleaded earlier in the week and were well on their way to a long stretch in the federal pen for their part in the sordid mess of racketeering and conspiracy to commit murder. Amber was completely sold out and on her way to the women's maximum security penitentiary in upstate New York for a minimum of thirty years.

Sanchez paused when the judge required an affirmative answer to the last formal plea-bargain question prior to sentencing: "Do you, Felipe Sanchez, knowingly, willingly, and freely accept the terms of the aforesaid plea bargain, acknowledging fully your guilt because you are in fact guilty of second-degree murder without any coercion being exerted upon you from any source?" Siffo looked up and nodded at his client to affirmatively answer this last question. As Sanchez paused, a distant popping sound drifted through the courtroom.

Outside, Vera Ochman no longer existed. Halfway up the front steps to the Manhattan Courthouse on her way to testify against Sanchez at his sentencing hearing, Vera's contoured body was ostensibly riddled with bullets shot at her by a fully automatic machine gun protruding from the rear window of a speeding black sedan. She laid motionless, face down with her eyes closed, stretched across four of the white marble steps, as her left hand, unnoticed and hidden in her jacket pocket, pumped an oozing ketchup-like substance from the lapel of her jacket onto her white blouse just above her breasts. A peculiar and melancholy sensation invaded Vera's consciousness that day as she feigned the end of her life. She fought back tears, knowing the dead cannot cry, as she grieved her own demise. Images of her deceased parents flooded through her mind.

Flash cameras popped in the distance in the hands of photojournalists summoned there, unknowingly, to record the harsh world of gang violence and the ruthless consequences of such associations. Vera could just see her father now at the dining room table, pointing to such a photograph on the front page of the *New York Times* and lecturing her in sermonesque detail against the vagaries of such teenage transgressions.

Two federal marshals, with service revolvers drawn at the ready, swiftly drug Vera out of harm's way, like a rag doll bumping to the top of the courthouse steps, rolled her over face up, and shook their heads simultaneously at the absence of vital signs. The red ooze, which clearly and completely saturated the front of her blouse, dripped onto the top step and ran down the stairs. The synthetic blood and her motionless body would convince even the most serious skeptic that Vera Ochman had just been assassinated by the Mob.

Not knowing that the only eyewitness to the murder to which he now confessed lay silenced by assassination a few hundred yards away, Sanchez cleared his voice, answered the judge's final question, and confirmed his twenty-year sentence behind bars. "Yes, sí, señor."

CHAPTER ELEVEN

September 1980

"You will no longer be known as Vera Ochman. From now on and for the rest of your natural life, you will be known to all of the world as Victoria Pierce." These words were spoken through the tobacco-stained lips of Bill Slaughter, a federal marshal nearing the end of his professional career and were directed to an attractive blonde brushing her hair while incredulously gazing into a mirror that hung above a credenza in the interior conference room of the fourth floor of the Murrah Federal Court Building in Oklahoma City. The blonde woman was Vera Ochman, alive and very much transformed into her new identity as Victoria Pierce, a more mature-looking woman and oddly more striking than before.

Vera Ochman's metamorphosis to Victoria Pierce changed her appearance as much as a butterfly emerges transformed from the cocoon of a caterpillar. Mostly, the change was attributed to her shoulder-length dirty blonde hair that altered Vera's appearance the most. But there was more to it. True, her new contact lenses corrected minor myopia, but they more significantly altered her eye color from piercing blue to emerald green. Victoria's dazzling new look reduced Vera's disenchantment at losing her continuous eighteen-year Brooklyn identity. Besides, no one here was even looking for Vera Ochman, an obscure crime decedent who was murdered by assassination in a faraway city. Most Oklahoma Sooners could not have located Brooklyn on a map, much less ever met someone from there, so the odds of a casual identification of Vera, made over as a strikingly different Victoria, approached the impossible. Vera had to decide, for her own protection, whether she wanted more permanent cosmetic surgery to shorten her nose or enlarge her breasts. The feds were taking no chances.

Slaughter, the crusty, tobacco-chewing cowboy lawman, stood beside his new blonde creation, glancing sideways at her beauty in the mirror. Slaughter cleared his voice, realizing that his gaze was rising above a professional curiosity and about to cross a line that would have interfered with his briefing. He opened a manila file folder and tried to hand Vera the first in a stack of spurious documents, all created under the authority of the Federal Witness Protection Program that permanently created the fictitious Victoria Pierce and permanently eliminated the real Vera Ochman. Slaughter was unusually proud of his hard work bringing Victoria Pierce to life and was perturbed by her inattention to his carefully crafted legal documents. At that moment, all that interested Victoria was the woman staring back at her in the mirror. Slaughter finally gave up and tossed the manila file folder marked "Vera Ochman—Top Secret" on the conference table in front of him and sat down. Slaughter spat a dark brown tobacco juice into a tin can held for that purpose in his right hand and stained on both sides from errant spittle, cleared his voice again, and said to the new Victoria, "Let me know, Little Filly, when you're ready to get down to business." "Little Filly" was the name Slaughter used to refer to all young women. "Do you want," Slaughter looked in his handbook on the top of his file, "OK, it's called 'cosmetic surgery'?" Vera continued to look at herself in the mirror.

"Your brand-new parents should be in here 'bout right now, and you need to know about your new self and these two that will be raisin' you from here on out."

Vera continued to stare at herself and finally concluded, "I don't think I want the surgery. Tell me more about this made-up Victoria Pierce. Who is she anyway?" Vera turned to admire her right-side profile in the mirror but positioned herself slightly facing Slaughter so he could continue his briefing. Slaughter detailed the account of the fictitious Victoria Pierce who owed her existence to a life lived in complete isolation on the Oklahoma prairie, totally opposite from Vera Ochman's fast-paced life in the Big Apple. Victoria stood before the mirror for the first time as a completed identity, fully made up with a skillfully crafted past, meticulously documented to belie the truth of her nonexistence, continuously living a fictitious life from birth through the documented completion of her homeschooled junior year, exactly the same year as Vera would have been back in Brooklyn.

Slaughter first handed Victoria a birth certificate that attested to the existence of an infant baby by the name of Victoria Pierce, with no middle name or initial, weighing into this world at eight pounds, four ounces, the only daughter of Ezekiel and Lucinda Pierce, a miraculous conception and birth for such elderly parents. She was born on the same family farm where she lived in Iowa County some fifty-five miles north-northwest of Lawton, Oklahoma, on August 9th, 1962, a date that now appeared as the first date on Vera's gravestone in the cemetery on Long Island. Slaughter handed her more documents transitioning Victoria from birth through homeschooling, arriving fully grown and alive in the flesh, on Monday, September 22, 1980. Slaughter also handed Victoria a contract that required her to remain in the custody of Ezekiel and Lucinda Pierce, or their survivor, until she graduated from high school by taking the Oklahoma High School Graduate Equivalency Exam. Slaughter quickly admonished, "Now, Miss Victoria, you oughta stay on permanently with your new parents. That way you'll stay out of trouble and protect your new identity and your life." Slaughter waited for a response, any response from Victoria. He doubted that his subject had listened to a single syllable of what he had just said.

Victoria was quite the rising senior, looking more like a mature cheerleader from suburbia than her more homely neighbors living on the plains, none of whom lived anywhere close to the Pierce Farm and none of whom knew her parents, much less the daughter they raised in isolation, protecting her from them in a sinful and ungodly world.

Slaughter continued by presenting Victoria with complete and meticulously detailed records of her childhood vaccinations as required by the public health laws of the state of Oklahoma and next, the proudest of all, an Oklahoma drivers license already imprinted with a glossy color photograph of the woman standing before him now, admiring her pose from the left side in the same mirror. It came as a shock to Slaughter that Vera was actually listening. She interrupted, "Does this mean I can drive a car?"

"Why, hell, yes, you can," came the reply.

Slaughter had left nothing to chance. All documents, including her Social Security card issued the day before, were genuine and would surpass the strictest investigative scrutiny. Vera had died once and for all, reincarnated herself now as the attractive and very much alive Victoria, fresh from the rural plains of Oklahoma, some fifty miles outside Lawton.

Vera focused again into the mirror, this time not to admire Victoria but to disguise her daydream. She imagined the names of Benjamin and Vera Ochman etched beside her mother's on the Ochman gravestone sited just below the outstretched arms of the Virgin Mary, freshly chiseled from white marble. Vera remembered the time that she and her father climbed the elevated ridge of the Long Island cemetery where Ben Ochman, architect, scolded the backhoe contractors who disrespectfully sited the gargantuan monument of the Holy Mother with her arms compassionately extended to enfold the crypt of his divine goddess.

"No, no, you're doing it all wrong. It won't be in the right place. Stop, stop!" Ben cried.

"Pare, pare!" Vera translated her father's instructions for the Latino workers. Predictably, he was overcome by grief and tears at the mere mention of her mother's name, much less at such a reverent occasion as the siting of her monument. The grandeur and scale of the memorial that dominated the cemetery landscape paid final homage to a wife whom he loved in life more than a husband should. The occasional pedestrian mourner drawn to admire the imposing statue of the Holy Mother could not help but wonder about the unfortunate events that caused a father and teenage daughter to die three weeks apart. The real irony for the graveside visitor was that, unknown to anyone in New York except for Michael Brandon, Kenneth Berger, and her supposed executioners, no decomposing corpse lay in the vacant casket underneath Vera Ochman's name. Ending her daydream, Victoria focused again on her hair.

"What do you think, Marshal?" Victoria pulled her shoulder-length blonde hair up with both hands until it rested on the top of her head and turned her face from side to side, capturing in multiple poses the reflected images of a much shorter cut.

Slaughter stood up and stepped toward his subject for a closer inspection, not the least concerned about a shorter hair style but focusing instead on the back of Victoria's neck at the lightning-bolt tattoo now revealed to him for the first time. "Just what in the Sam Hill is this on your neck?" Slaughter exclaimed, scratching his head and squinting his eyes. "Since when did women start marking up their bodies with a man's tattoo? That one," pointing his right index finger at the offensive mark, "got to go . . . and for a lot of reasons—not just besides it ain't fittin'. There's a place downtown, 'bout a mile and a half from here, that can take that out. You'll, quite likely, be the first woman they've ever seen in the filthy place. Why, hell, you want to see my tattoo I got in the war?"

Victoria dropped her hair. "No," she quickly responded before Slaughter could roll up his sleeve. A subdued, tentative knock was heard on the conference room door. Entering the room were two of the strangest-looking and strangest-dressed individuals whom Vera had ever seen in her short life, rivaling even the strangest people she encountered on her fast-paced walks down Broadway on the way to New York's Theatre District. Marshal Slaughter jumped up and made the introduction. "Mr. and Mrs. Pierce, allow me to introduce your new daughter, Victoria Pierce."

They must be farmers, Victoria thought to herself. *Why else would anyone on earth dress this way?*

Lucinda was a slight woman with gray hair pulled back in a bun with tiny wire- rimmed spectacles, outfitted in an off-white gingham dress that fell to her ankles. Ezekiel, a tall, lanky man, wore a black vested dark suit either hand sewn or, at the very least, arriving from a mail order catalog sometime in the nineteenth century. And they were old. Vera thought that her father had been old, but these two looked like they might be a hundred years each, with matching leather complexions, no doubt parched by long days of work in the hot Oklahoma sun.

The Pierces stepped forward, not saying a word of welcome or introduction, and walked to either side of Victoria, examining her as if they were about to purchase a plow horse. They looked back at each other and then at Victoria. They seemed to reach a consensus that she would do.

Slaughter's assignment had not been an easy one. How did you create an eighteen-year-old girl with neither a friend nor a past? He concluded that Victoria would have to be the offspring of one of the many families living in total isolation on the plains of Oklahoma. The Pierces, whose name and history had been culled from agricultural statistical reports, met that description, and when presented with the arrangements seemed to welcome a generous offer from the government to pay them room and board to raise a farm daughter whom they could never produce for themselves. The Lord had called them to live in seclusion on their farm to protect them from a corrupted world. Vera was in need of separation and protection, just the same as them. They agreed as well that they could use an extra hand with the chores and eventually would need an offspring to carry on a reasonably profitable farm that they started from scratch over fifty years ago. Besides, they had prayed on the decision, and the Lord had given them the go-ahead to adopt this young girl awash in a life of sin. They dutifully feared and obeyed the word of the Lord by reading the Good Book when they arose long before dawn and after they turned in at dusk. The rest of their day was spent tending the crops, caring for the livestock, and maintaining the farm.

"Well, I'm sure the three of you will have plenty of time to talk later," Slaughter suggested, breaking a prolonged silence as he handed the government's copy file to Ezekiel. "Better read over this as it contains a lot of pertinent information. Now, Victoria and I have to keep one more appointment downtown, and I will ride her out to your farm late this afternoon."

Grasping Victoria's left hand in her left and without another word, except for Lucinda's faint utterance, "Welcome, daughter," the Pierces abruptly left through the same door that they had just entered.

* * *

Slaughter drove his green government truck into a blinding sunset with the driver's-side visor down and his left hand shielding the sun from eyes already protected behind dark black sunglasses. Slaughter's rolled-up sleeve revealed his forearm tattoo, in the shape of a heart, shot through by a feathered arrow and inscribed with the single word, "Mother." Victoria sat motionless in the passenger's seat except when Slaughter bounced the truck into the bottom of a cavernous mud hole along the dusty road that led to the Pierce Farm and jostled his plug of tobacco centered in his bulging right cheek.

Acres of corn, turning from beige to brown, lined each side of the road as streams of dust kicked up by the rear spinning radial tires left a trail like rocket vapor almost a mile behind the truck. Anyone in the Pierce farmhouse, gazing east, could not help but notice that visitors were on the way. Victoria rubbed her bandaged neck underneath her hair from her earlier appointment at the tattoo parlor.

Parked in front of the opened front gate was a classic Farmall tractor, vintage 1945. The two rode through the gate past a dairy barn, henhouse, and horse corral to the front steps of a modest two-story white farmhouse. Slaughter tapped the horn as he exited the cab and slammed his door with extra force to announce their arrival.

Victoria remained in her seat thinking to herself that if she exited the cab she would likely fall right off the face of the earth. Never had she seen a real farmhouse, much less visited one, and now she was about to take up permanent residence in this farmhouse that was framed right through the passenger's window.

"Hello inside," Slaughter called out as he climbed the porch steps. "Anyone at home? Mr. and Mrs. Pierce, are you there?" Slaughter knew from experience that doorbells did not exist in farmhouses and that the safest way to announce a visitor's arrival was by making an abundance of noise. Besides, most farmhouses were protected by an alarm system in the form of a large canine. You wanted to be sure that both the dog and occupants inside were aware of your presence so as not to startle either, particularly the dog. From the bottom of the front porch screen door, a quite mature German Shepherd, named Sergeant, erupted into ferocious barking, daring Slaughter to take another step across the front porch. Fortunately, the screen door was securely latched, but Slaughter unsnapped his holstered .45 service revolver just in case.

Lucinda Pierce unlatched the screen and stepped onto the porch as Sergeant leaped at full speed toward Slaughter, striking his left pants leg a glancing blow as he bolted down the steps and jumped up onto the side of the cab with his two front paws planted right beneath Victoria's closed window, greeting her with the ferocity of a hound baying at a treed bear. Sergeant stopped barking long enough to turn his head around, whining to make sure that Lucinda knew there was another intruder in the cab.

"Don't let Sarge frighten you, Daughter. He's harmless," Lucinda called out. She slapped the side of her dress with her hand as Sergeant returned immediately to the porch. In the Pierce household, animals, both farm and domesticated, were the only other creatures, outside of themselves, with whom they regularly communicated and mostly by gesture and intonation instead of words.

"Victoria, it's safe to get out of the truck now, and I'll help you with your suitcases." Slaughter turned around from the porch and spoke to the motionless figure in the front seat of the cab. Then, after a moment with no acknowledgment, he stepped back to the truck, courteously swung open the door, walked behind to the bed of the truck, dusted off her two suitcases, and dropped them to the ground. Slaughter thought to himself that if he did not soon coax Victoria inside the house, he might have to pry his frozen passenger out of the front seat by resort to threats and intimidation.

"Come on now, Miss Victoria, please step out of the truck. Besides, as I understand it, this whole idea was yourn's in the first place. Believe me, not a single member of that gang of hoodlums back east will ever follow you way out here. You're completely safe to live out your life on this farm."

Victoria remained as lifeless as a mannequin in a storefront window. The idea of living out the remainder of her life on this farm was worse than death.

Drooling slightly from his leaking plug of tobacco, Slaughter spat outside and then leaned closer to Victoria's right ear as he whispered, "Besides, you are free to leave according to that contract that you signed this morning as soon as you pass your high school equivalency exam." Life slowly returned to Victoria's face as a faint hope for a return to a more urban existence welled up from inside, and in an instant she landed both feet on the ground aided by Slaughter's downward tug on her arm. Now that Victoria was in motion up the steps toward the front door, Slaughter pulled her along by fastening his hand to her upper arm to maintain a forward speed at his pace, not hers, straight up the stairs and across the porch into Lucinda's embrace, which was more like that of a wrestler turning an opponent than a mother embracing her daughter. Soon, both women, still entwined, disappeared inside the screen door.

Slaughter, knowing his day's work was near completion, stepped backward over Sergeant, now resting his docile head between his front paws and staring aimlessly into the cornfield out front. The marshal hurriedly retreated to the truck long enough to retrieve Victoria's suitcases and return them to the porch, strategically positioning both just outside the front screen door. Slaughter tiptoed back again over Sergeant, down the front steps into the driver's seat of the cab, fired up the engine, kicked up gravel as first gear engaged, and raced the truck past the horse corral, waving his tattooed arm backward outside the window before he ground the transmission into second gear. The truck quickly disappeared into a plume of dust, leaving behind only the distant sound of the transmission protesting Slaughter's entry into third gear.

* * *

As the afternoon sun sank into twilight, Victoria sat on the elongated side of the supper table, glancing alternately to Ezekiel and Lucinda, who were seated across from each other eating an array of mysterious-looking food off matching tin plates and flatware, without a word of conversation between the two. Victoria had a sudden urge for Manhattan pizza instead of what was portioned and resting in her tin plate. Sergeant was curled up on the floor beside Ezekiel's chair, periodically glancing upward from the floor at the stranger sitting at the table. Thinking she might be better able to identify what's on her tin plate, Victoria asked if she might turn on a light.

"Ain't got no electric lights or indoor plumbing for that matter," Lucinda responded, pointing her fork at Victoria. "Now, listen carefully, Daughter, this is how it is out here on the prairie. The outhouse and well are in the backyard. Snakes are a problem this time of year, so you best do your business in the daylight. Bedtime is one hour after supper. You're out of bed two hours before sunup to read the Good Book, clean your room, and start your chores. Before breakfast, I'll show you how to fetch the eggs, milk the cows, and slop the hogs. You'll help me with the breakfast, and after cleaning up, you'll have one hour to study your lessons before spending the rest of the day helping barn the corn or whatever you're told to do around here. That's pretty much every day, seven days a week."

Victoria could not imagine living her life under such conditions. She could feel a burn rising within her that signaled that tears were on the way. *No*, she said to herself, *they're not going to see me cry!* Under the weight of disillusionment, she slumped down in her chair. But soon a self-willed determination took over her emotions so she could think rationally. *How do I escape?* she thought. Marshal Slaughter had given her the answer. She conformed to the supper table silence and mentally calculated how long it might take to prepare and pass the high school equivalency test with only one hour of study per day. This could take months.

In her austere bedroom, dimly lit by a single oil lamp that filled the room with a cloud of fine smoke and a strong odor of kerosene, Victoria flipped through the papers in her folder filled with her fictional but meticulously alphabetized documents, stopping at the instructional manual labeled "Oklahoma Department of Education, High School Equivalency Course of Study." She opened the manual and began to read the section titled "Geometry" until Lucinda interrupted in a loud voice from the other side of the door. "Turn your lamp out and go to sleep."

In her new bed, a troubled sleep enveloped Victoria throughout her first night on the Pierce Farm, punctuated by momentary awakenings caused by the deafening prairie silence in her mind's search for the accustomed familiarity of the droning noise of the big-city night. The springs supporting the single-bed mattress creaked at her body's slightest movement. Her dreams were dull, muted, and unrecallable.

A bang at the door accompanied Lucinda's voice from the other side. "It's three-thirty, Victoria. Time to begin reading from the Good Book. You'll find the Bible in the top drawer." A simple instruction, easy to follow, given the chest was the only other item of furniture in the room. "Might as well start at the beginning. Light your lamp, and I'll be back in an hour. Be dressed and ready for a day of hard work under a hot September sun." Victoria illuminated her lamp and began at the beginning, except her first chapter was not Genesis but Geometry.

In the dairy barn, Victoria observed Lucinda and Ezekiel milking the herd of about twenty-five cows all nervously waiting their turn to be next in the stall to drain the contents of their bloated udders into the milking buckets below. She thought, *How could anyone possibly tolerate the huge creatures bellowing their discomfort in the morning darkness and withstand the stench of a barn filled with discolored straw saturated in cow urine and manure?* This was her first chore for the morning, shoveling the contaminated straw with a pitchfork and replacing it with fresh straw from the loft.

She would have gladly remained in the stench of the milking stalls compared to the mud pen, where the hogs lived in a filthy squalor. Ezekiel dumped slop from a barrel into the troughs crowded with rude and squealing swine, each trying to inch in front of the other to gain better access to their one meal for the day. Victoria was close to heaving up the contents of her stomach from the unbearable penetrating smell of the hogs. Had she not filtered the odor with a handkerchief quickly retrieved from her pocket, the hogs might have enjoyed a bonus meal consisting of the contents hurled up from Victoria's stomach. She kept the handkerchief with her since her earlier visit to the outhouse. Until she came upon the unpleasantness of the hog parlor, she had not encountered in her young life an odor more offensive than the outhouse.

The chicken house was a more hospitable location, occupied by the clucking red hens atop their nests. All that was required was to collect the brown eggs from the roost of the Rhode Island laying hens. Some of the red feathered "ladies" had to be coaxed from their perch before parting with their night's labor. They flew down off the nest cackling in protest. The others yielded their perch voluntarily to peck at the corn scattered on the earthen floor. Victoria followed Lucinda from roost to roost, collecting the eggs into a brown wicker basket and thinking to herself she might be able to manage this chore.

Victoria mused that she would be doing a lot of thinking to herself as perhaps three complete sentences had been spoken to her since awakening three hours before dawn. The henhouse was not an altogether unpleasant location compared to the other venues she labored in that morning. When the two exited the henhouse, faint slivers of dawn greeted them, marking the official beginning of daytime. Victoria had seen the dawn on rare occasions before, but could never remember arising at the ungodly hour of 3:30 a.m. She was exhausted now long before her normal day would have even begun back in Brooklyn with the simple task of brushing her teeth. Her mental retreat back to her upstairs bedroom was interrupted with Lucinda's fourth completed sentence of the day. "Time to rustle up some breakfast."

Much of the breakfast preparation had been readied the night before. What came from the kitchen to the breakfast table in short order was country ham, fried eggs, stewed apples, scratch biscuits, and black coffee. Breakfast and lunch were the big meals of the day, cooked before the afternoon sun could broil the kitchen and its occupants in an unbearable heat. Mostly, besides setting the table, Victoria just stood by Lucinda's hand to observe the details of the breakfast preparation, but she surmised that Lucinda would remain in the kitchen in the wee morning hours while Victoria became her replacement for the more rigorous and unpleasant outside chores. Once again the meal was partaken in silence, with Sergeant's curious eyes observing her from the floor. Victoria was surprised at her morning appetite for a meal so often rejected in the past amid the frantic rush for school.

After cleansing the tinware in boiled well water and lye soap, Victoria returned to her room even more exhausted than before breakfast to focus on her one hour of unsupervised study. *How can I possibly study now?* Victoria thought from the confines of her bedroom, resting horizontally on her bed. "I cannot even keep my eyes open." Without notice, the Geometry chapter collapsed onto her chest right before she dropped off into a deep and tranquil sleep. Victoria's dream drifted her back to her Brooklyn bedroom in the hallway at the top of the stairs where she would soon awaken to resume her city life by merely shaking out the nightmare of the Pierce Farm. Victoria tried subconsciously to reconcile Lucinda's knocking at the door with her father's knocking in her dream. "OK, Pops. Just a few more minutes. I'll be down," Vera mumbled aloud from her hypnotic trance. But she could not remain in her trance-induced Brooklyn bedroom and conform it to the reality unfolding in the anguish emerging in the starkness of her bedroom. Victoria suddenly rocketed back to the Pierce Farm, her despair now overwhelming. "Life imprisonment would be better than this," she muttered. "OK, OK, I'm up. Give me a sec."

Victoria's lost hour of study would have to be made up secretly sometime later in the day. If she had taken Geometry in her junior year, this would have been a simple review and not active learning. She regretted postponing Geometry to her senior year. Mastery of the puzzling geometric figures might not come to her as easily as the other subjects, which were a snap when she concentrated. Victoria concealed her Geometry chapter in her blouse and awaited her opportunity to make up for lost time. Later that morning, in the barn hayloft where she pitched down hay into the horse stalls below, she retrieved her Geometry lesson from the center section of her bra and began studying in earnest. Lying in the hay, she memorized the theorems of the isosceles triangle before sleep once again overcame her.

"Daughter, are you asleep?" Undetected, Lucinda had climbed the handmade ladder up to the loft. The chapter on Geometry lay resting on her chest. "There's no time for naps on the farm. You have plenty of time for study in the morning after breakfast." Lucinda grabbed the lesson from Victoria and scolded, "I'll hold onto this for you and give it back in the morning so you won't be tempted to let it interfere with your chores. If I see it outside of your room again, it will become mine permanently. You're way behind in your chores by now. You'll remember this little rule of ours better if we add a few extra chores to your day. The corn crib will be hot this afternoon, but removing the corn from the ears with our new machine is a lot easier than doing it by hand. Start first by picking up the mail, and you can finish up in the barn after supper before dark."

Picking up the mail meant walking the mile and a half down the dusty road in front of the farmhouse to the stand-up aluminum mailbox that sat atop a wooden post just off the highway right-of-way. Besides being the only mailbox within miles, it was also easily identifiable with the Pierce name hand-lettered in black paint on the side. Victoria's chore was to retrieve the contents of the box and reverse direction back the mile and a half to the farmhouse. All told, it would take more than an hour each day. Lucinda pointed Victoria in an easterly direction as she stepped off on foot with Sergeant as her guard. This chore would reoccur daily after lunch at exactly one half hour past high noon. Victoria had no experience with such a dirt road walk underneath a hot Oklahoma sun, but was quite accustomed to traversing the paved city blocks of the Manhattan Business District. Except for Sergeant hauling off into the cornstalks giving chase after a jumped prairie rabbit or an occasional glance upward at a hawk gliding on a west wind, or stopping dead in her tracks to yield the right-of-way to a sidewinder meandering across the road, the walk to the mailbox was otherwise uneventful. About halfway to her destination Victoria stopped to rub her blistering feet and mop the sweat pouring profusely from her forehead down her cheeks, almost as if she were crying. For her next trip, she would have to find better walking shoes and definitely wear less clothing. Pain emerged but abated as her feet traipsed on automatic pilot to their destination, freeing her mind to escape into distant dreams. She dwelled first on what might have been with Felipe Sanchez, wondering which prison he landed in for his twenty-year stretch, regretting the mindless events that forced her betrayal, and finally appreciating that, just like Sanchez, she, too, was locked up in a prison without bars in the isolation of the Pierce farm. Before her thoughts could lament her father's death, her dreaming ended abruptly as she recognized the intersection of the road and the highway.

While she rested at a standstill, her rapid breathing gradually returned to normal. Victoria decided there would plenty of time to grieve for her father on the long walk back. As she turned to grasp the handle of the mailbox and retrieve its contents, a white ten-year-old Ford Falcon pulled off the road behind her and slid on the grass to a halt with the amber emergency lights brightly flashing. Janet Flowers was sitting in the right passenger seat, oddly driving the car with her left foot moving from the gas pedal to brake and her left hand lightly attached to the right side of the steering wheel. Janet served a dual function in the community. In the morning she was a typical farm girl like any other, and a contract mail carrier for the U.S. Postal Service in the afternoon. Her bulging bicep extended through a red short-sleeve plaid shirt, with her elbow bent slightly out the window.

"Hi, there. You must be Victoria. Nice to know someone new way out here. Just call me 'Jan.'" As she extended her right hand full of mail out the window in the direction of Victoria's hands, she also flipped Sergeant a dog biscuit.

Victoria was not only stunned that Jan spoke her new name out loud like she knew this fictitious person named Victoria, but there might be someone around who could actually speak more than one sentence to her at a time.

"How do you know my name?"

"I guessed you must be the Pierces' new adopted daughter. Lots of government mail has been coming in with your name on it so I just guessed you must be her. Lucinda's probably gotten tired of the long walk down to the box, and Zeke could use a younger set of hands around for the chores. Welcome now. Look forward to another visit soon, but got to go and catch up before someone complains."

With that, Jan pulled the old Falcon back onto the highway, steering with her left hand en route to her next appointed farm five miles down the highway. Victoria watched the Falcon disappear with its passenger-seat driver, amber lights flashing, and big printed sign across the back that read, "Caution, Frequent Stops."

She sorted through the mail before trudging the long walk back to the farmhouse with Sergeant walking in the lead. Victoria, as she quickened her pace west, held one brown government envelope up to eclipse the bright sunlight and saw clearly the joint names of Ezekiel and Lucinda Pierce on a brown voucher beside the printed figure, "Three Thousand, Four Hundred Dollars. Monthly subsistence. Victoria Pierce."

"Holy shit, Sarge, no damn wonder they want me to stay!"

CHAPTER TWELVE

August 2008

"The O'Connor family extends to all Americans our sincere thanks and gratitude for the outpouring of goodwill we have received from so many in the last twenty-four hours."

Standing at a podium in front of the entrance to St. Vincent's Hospital, Larry O'Connor read from a prepared statement to an audience of television cameras and assembled press.

"The Speaker of the House," O'Connor paused and then departed from his prepared text to insert a personal aside— "and, of course, the Speaker of the House *is* my beloved wife"—"remains in stable condition after a fall in a New York City hotel stairwell yesterday. She suffered numerous contusions, a concussion, and a compound fracture that required a three-hour surgical procedure last night under general anesthesia to insert pins to reconnect and mend her left tibia. The extent of injury, if any, to her cranium and spinal column have yet to be fully determined, but the results of the MRI imaging testing are normal, indicating that, although there was major trauma to both her head and spine, there appears to be no permanent injury. Because of a severely sprained back, the Speaker is not expected to be ambulatory for several weeks. We anticipate at a minimum a two-month convalescence period before she will be able to return to our home and at least another month before her return to her official duties as the Speaker of the House."

O'Connor looked up and then immediately back down at his text. "Next, our family wishes to gratefully acknowledge and thank Brigadier General Victoria Pierce for literally saving Maggie's life by rendering emergency medical care before the arrival of the first responders. All of her medical team agrees that Maggie could well have been lost to her injuries without General Pierce's rapid intercession in the stairwell, administering first aid to stop the hemorrhaging around her fractured tibia, her treatment for shock, not to mention her calming reassurance given to my wife as they waited for the arrival of emergency personnel. Our family cannot thank General Pierce enough, and we will be eternally grateful to her."

Larry O'Connor again looked up, paused to indicate that a transition was ahead, and then glanced immediately back down at his text. "Lastly, you must know that Speaker O'Connor was visiting the campaign headquarters of United States Senator and presidential candidate Sam Eagan yesterday. As has been widely speculated in the press for months, we now confirm that Senator Eagan had been courting the Speaker as his vice presidential running mate. Although flattered to be considered, Maggie has steadfastly declined and again declined this offer yesterday. She would rather be the Speaker of the House of Representatives than vice president of the United States, a point she has repeatedly made to the senator's campaign staff. She was there in the senator's campaign headquarters to politely listen to Senator Eagan's final overture."

For the first time, Larry O'Connor appeared confused as to his next move as he looked around for a cue. Someone pointed to a man wearing a stethoscope around his neck. "I will now turn the podium over to Maggie's lead surgeon to answer any further questions as to her medical condition."

After watching Larry O'Connor's remarks from the plasma-screen TV inside the campaign suite, Tom Pearsall stood up, walked over to the picture window, and after taking several long drags from his cigarette in rapid succession, shook his head, saying, "Well, at least the good news is we're not responsible for the death of the legendary Speaker of the House. The bad news is the lying bitch has made me look like idiots for not having a clue as to who potentially will be the vice president of the United States, or potentially the president for that matter, three days before the nomination."

"Don't be too hard on yourself, Tom. There's still time," said Sam, the eternal optimist. "So many events affecting the political life of officeholders happen outside their sphere of control. Tom, this is such a time. Let's be like the good officeholders and recognize these events as fortuitous circumstances and fashion our responses accordingly. We do not have to claim responsibility for the occurrence."

Sam's long political life taught him this lesson. The resolution was apparent. But Tom was a worrier, and he saw the consequences of Maggie's accident as somehow a product of his own creation because it adversely affected him.

Watching Tom pace and smoke, trying to solve a problem that he did not create, Sam continued. "If this was August of 1960, none of this would matter. I remember back in the days when the convention meant something. The vice presidential nominee was a presidential nominee who fell just a few votes short, and the second spot was his, automatically. More deals were being cut this day, forty-eight years ago, than trades on Wall Street. The political excitement of the convention was almost unbearable. Uncommitted state delegations deciding in huddled caucuses who would be the best candidate for president and announcing the count on the floor in front of a national TV audience. 'The Great State of . . .'"

Tom continued his extended gaze out the window, not hearing much of Sam's talk about the 1960 political convention. But Victoria, who on the other hand had a direct stake in how Tom solved his problem, tried unsuccessfully to interrupt, "Not now, Sam."

"And those conventions produced real candidates . . . not the robots we have today."

Tom, cognizant now of Sam's last sentence, said, "Will you please just shut up, Mr. Robot, and let me think?"

Victoria, realizing that Tom was not recommending the obvious choice for vice president, tried to reassure him that the results of the fortuitous event were favorable. "It was really the best thing to happen to this campaign, Tom. Maggie O'Connor just showed you her real colors. She only agreed to move from three to two on the presidential list so she could eventually get to number one. Even in her battered condition, broken leg and all, she's still trying to land on her political feet."

"That doesn't sound like the Maggie O'Connor I know. Maybe Larry O'Connor, but not Maggie," Sam responded.

"Officially, according to Larry O'Connor," Victoria stated, "the Speaker declined to be your running mate, but we all know that she accepted it in this very room, less than twenty-four hours ago. But my real point, Sam, is that she was not good for you or the ticket. Call it a woman's intuition or whatever, but the best thing to happen to this campaign is that she has removed herself from a nomination she really never wanted. She was going to finish no less than third in presidential succession no matter how this election turned out. This was all about her, Sam—not about this nation and certainly not about you."

Tom woke up again from his Manhattan trance, walked over to his laptop, and after a minute pulled up a file. "In June, we had several congresswomen left under consideration out there, all pretty far down on the original list. There were also three governors and two senators. Calls are coming in right now from everywhere in the country wanting a shot at the number-two slot. We will have to make this decision today."

"What kind of background clearance do we have?" Sam inquired. "I bet we don't have a single one, do we, Tom?"

Finally, Victoria had enough of Tom avoiding the obvious remaining choice. "It's quite simple, gentlemen. You're down to your last trump card. Fortunately for you, I'm your Queen of Spades. Now, do I have to go over the polling issues again?"

"You don't have a clearance, either, do you, Victoria?" Tom desperately rejoined before Sam could side with Victoria.

"Oh, yes, she does," Sam replied and walked toward her, holding his jacket lapel with his left hand while pointing to the ceiling with his right, a gesture he often made during debates on the Senate floor. "I've personally known Victoria for the last twenty-five years. I can vouch for her. Besides, Tom, do you think you can become a brigadier general in the United States Marine Corps without a top security clearance?"

"Look, Sam, let's get this thing out on the table right now. There's a bomb planted here that everyone seems to be overlooking."

"And what exactly would that be?" Sam asked.

"How about a twenty-five-year affair with your running mate?"

Sam instantly replied, "An absurd insinuation that we would adamantly deny. I'm offended you would even suggest such a thing. Besides, if it was an affair, it was a very discrete affair, my friend, and at most mere speculation to impugn my fidelity to Betty Belvedere in our forty-year marriage."

"Well, don't think for a minute that it won't come up," Tom said without looking up.

"No one with any credibility can confirm such a relationship. Besides even you, Tom, my closest friend and confidant, cannot confirm it yourself, nor can you refer me to anyone who can verify such an accusation. I'll wager you that even if it were to reach the level of gossip, which the campaign would categorically deny, the most it would do is to enhance by implication the reputation of a man my age among a certain category of voters. Besides, what other choice do we really have? For once, Tom, go with your gut."

Tom, knowing he would have to respond to Victoria's twin significant negatives, inexperience and infidelity, addressed her by a nickname, baiting her as well to turn bitchlike. "I will treat Miss Vicky here the same as any other potential nominee, Sam. Give me twenty-four hours to run the numbers, and you will have a scientific answer. And, Sam, never ask your pollster to go with his gut."

Tom's ploy partially worked. "You're out of time, you gutless pollster. You don't have twenty-four hours!" Victoria, intentionally restrained, bristled nevertheless, staring directly at Tom.

Before the name calling could escalate further, Sam confirmed Victoria's point. "We'll keep this under wraps for twenty-four hours. But as I see it right now, Victoria is the only viable choice, and it's a good thing that we have her as such a viable alternative at this late date. It's also a good thing that we've known the outcome of the delegate count for almost two months. The first two and a half days of this convention are planned, in the can, scripted, and even choreographed, which allows for some breathing room. But you are both right, we are out of time."

The three reentered the campaign suite, where staffers besieged each one, pulling them in separate directions with demands for immediate answers to long-overdue convention decisions, all shouting above the rest, until the roar was deafening.

Victoria knew she was vulnerable. Tom was trying to buy precious time to expose Victoria's considerable political weaknesses, multilateral weaknesses, across-the-board weaknesses—ranging from foreign policy to tax policy and almost everything inbetween—except for her natural competence on women's issues and her acquired knowledge of military issues.

Victoria's principal aide, a college-aged volunteer, shoved her cell phone directly in her face. "It's Grace Brandon. She's been trying to reach you on this phone for hours, even before the story on Maggie O'Connor broke."

Victoria took the phone—trying desperately to think how to stop Tom—looked at it, and shrugged absentmindedly.

"Sorry," the aide said, "just following instructions. You did say she was a top priority."

"There's not time not right now." Victoria's voice faded and fell almost silent before she finished her reply, trying desperately to crystallize an inspiration in the midst of the clamoring chaos in the room. She stared blankly at the cell phone.

The aide, motioning for the return of the cell phone, said, "Fine, forget Ace. I'll just return her call myself and put her off until you can get back to her. There are a lot of important calls. Do you want the major dailies first? Most are looking for a comment before press time about your saving O'Connor's life in the stairwell. Shouldn't Mr. Pearsall have a campaign press release on this?"

Victoria heard practically nothing of her aide's peppered questions, finally seeing her cell phone in her hand for the first time as a telephone. "Grace Brandon? Why, of course, of course, of course. That's it, I'll take Grace Brandon's phone call. That's exactly what I'll do."

Victoria's aide, confused because they had returned to an issue already resolved, greeted Victoria's resolution with a hint of sarcasm. "Now there's a real plan. Yeah, of course, return Ms. Brandon's call, good plan."

Not to clarify her aide's questions but to clarify her own thoughts, Victoria spoke confidently aloud. "You're damned right I'll return Grace Brandon's call," she said with a gradually escalating pitch and projection while retreating out the door, punching in Grace's direct line at the *Times*, and then racing down the hall to the privacy of her smaller suite on the same floor. Victoria slipped her card key into the device above the door handle, gaining entrance into the privacy of her suite.

"Grace, hi. Victoria here. Sorry I've been so delayed getting back to you. Look, can we talk in private, meet somewhere, as crazy as that might sound? . . . Yeah . . . Will tell you all the details about Maggie O'Connor." Dropping her voice, Victoria said, "But there's a bigger exclusive out there, but I can't give it to you over the phone. . . . Yeah, even bigger than saving the life of the Speaker of the House. I'm famished . . . haven't had anything to eat all day and would love to split one of Mr. Margolis's takeout lobster and shrimp salads. Right, the seafood deli on Seventh Avenue. I'll buy, if you'll pick it up. Meet you in Central Park in two hours. . . . How about the bench near the famous bust? Look for a tall general in civilian clothes wearing a beige raincoat, burgundy scarf, and black sunglasses."

* * *

A few disinterested pedestrians walked past the women sharing a salad on the isolated park bench just as the sun dropped below the park's northwestern tree line. Grace, with her mouth half full, stuffed her white plastic deli fork through lettuce and a large combination of shrimp and lobster. "This is really good." As she chewed, her next question surprised Victoria. "You know, I've been meaning to ask you how you knew Mr. Margolis."

"What?"

"Yeah, Mr. Margolis. The owner. Nice man. How did you know him?"

There was an uncharacteristic pause as Victoria stopped eating and stared at her companion.

"His name appears nowhere in his deli, just his photograph on the wall. I've been meaning to ask you how you knew who he was?"

Victoria glided into her answer. "Simple, Grace. I just put two and two together. His name is on the outside of his deli. His picture is right behind the cash register. The man serving his customers in the deli was an older version of the same man centered as the patriarch in the family photograph. I never knew Mr. Margolis. I just guessed his name, as would any good campaigning politician entering a proprietor's establishment."

The answer satisfied Grace's curiosity. But what Victoria could not tell Grace was that Vera Ochman had frequented this deli on numerous occasions as both a child and a teenager with her mother. It had been one of their favorites. Mr. Margolis bought the deli as a young man shortly after emigrating from Italy. His deli had been one of their stops, almost weekly, when visiting the Fashion District. She remembered Mr. Margolis immediately, greeted him spontaneously just as she did when she was a child, and now was greatly relieved that he had not recognized his young patron turned brigadier general.

"So, what happened in the stairwell?" Grace moved ahead to the next issue.

"Nothing, more or less, than any Marine trained in combat emergency medicine would not have done in the same situation. It was an automatic reflex. After the fall down the steps, she was badly injured. So, first, I stopped the bleeding. Second, I treated her for shock. And third, I secured medical help by using her cell phone. On the battlefield I would have called a corpsman. But we can get back to those details. Let's get to the good part, Grace. Now, just like the statement Larry O'Connor issued at the hospital, it's true Maggie O'Connor had been offered the second spot on the ticket. But now get this, unlike the statement issued at the hospital, Maggie O'Connor had accepted the offer of the number-two spot."

"You're kidding. Why would she deny accepting it?" Grace dropped her plastic fork into her half of the salad and prepared to scribble on her pad.

"My guess is, after the accident, she must have taken a good look at herself, decided she was in no condition to appear before any political convention for any reason—much less to accept the nomination for vice president of the United States—and then at week's end start on an endless campaign trail hobbling all over the country on a severely fractured leg. So I suspect it was just easier to have said that she declined the offer. Besides, if you ask me, she never wanted it in the first place. Maybe she didn't think Sam could win. Maybe she liked being Speaker more. I really don't know why she did it, but it was just too easy for her to wave it off."

"So, who's going to be the vice presidential nominee?" Grace asked her next question in natural progression.

This was the question that Victoria waited and hoped would emerge, without prompting—the same question she had contemplated while staring into her cell phone. Victoria would leak to Grace what Sam had already decided; Grace, acting on the leak, would have to seek comment from the campaign before publishing the identity of the leaked vice presidential nominee; and Sam, without resorting to fabrication, reluctantly would have to tell the truth, preempting Tom's last-minute challenges.

"Officially, Grace, it has not been decided." Then, after a long pause, Victoria forked a large piece of lobster, elbowed her younger friend, and said, "Unofficially, Sam offered the position to me this afternoon."

Grace screamed, "You are kidding!" Victoria put her hand over Grace's mouth. Grace whispered, "That's great, congratulations!"

The execution of the planned leak was flawless. The Victoria-Grace, politician-press duet was the precisely needed combination to confirm General Pierce as the vice presidential nominee and allow Grace Brandon to scoop the national press with a sensational story. Responding to Grace's official call for comment later that same evening, Sam, as anticipated, confirmed that Victoria would be his vice presidential nominee. The following morning, Grace's brilliant front-page story provided the exclusive details of both Victoria's stairwell heroics and the campaign's confirmation that she would be the announced candidate for vice president. But neither Larry O'Connor nor Tom Pearsall would confirm that Maggie O'Connor had first accepted and later declined the offer of the number-two spot.

The entire nation went agog with the announcement. Political pundits and bloggers alike roared their approval of the farm-girl-turned-general as the vice presidential nominee. The morning show hosts and evening news anchors demanded time with the nominee. Every channel, every hour, trumpeted the news. Even Tom was aghast at just how popular the decision was across all polling profiles, but particularly among likely voters. Within hours, the campaign easily exhausted every shred of literature available on General Pierce. Some in the foreign press corps, previously expressing little interest in the American election, ran front-page stories throughout the world from Calcutta to Brussels. Tom Pearsall could not believe the political tidal wave that the campaign was riding—one not even close to cresting—so much so that he suggested, tongue in cheek, that Sam and Victoria switch positions on the ballot and that Sam would make a great "titular" vice president.

The suspense that Tom supposed would be generated by being coy with the announcement until late in the week was overshadowed by the clamor to see and speak with the soon-to-be vice presidential nominee. Tom did insist that the "couple" appear together at every possible opportunity, so much so that Betty Belvedere Eagan, the senator's cultured society wife, almost disappeared from view. She did not mind. She wanted her husband to win the election and for her to take her place in history at his dutiful First Lady.

Convention week took on a life of its own. When it was time for the vice presidential speeches, slotted now for the last night of the convention, barely any time remained for them as Tom had reengineered the early week schedule to frontload all of the partisan-oriented speakers in the prime-time slots, knowing viewers would remain glued to the end to watch Victoria. There remained only one primetime slot, reserved for Victoria's hour-long acceptance speech, preceded by her one personal seconding speaker.

The seconding speech came from former Marine Corps Major Walter Clarke, now a highly decorated four-star general, who first witnessed young Victoria's people skills in the marketplaces of Bogotá, and who could attest, as well, to her battlefield bravery in accomplishing her undercover mission of dispatching a Colombian drug lord on her way to winning the Marine Corps' highest medal. Clarke, an American citizen of British origin, was both charming and convincing. He congratulated the party delegates and all America for the wisdom to nominate General Pierce, a nonpolitical, national hero, to be a Vice President of the United Sates, recognizing what he had first observed in her when she was fresh out of boot camp. Victoria remembered her Sunday afternoon encounter with Clarke in the Bogotá marketplace.

> I was dressed in revealing civilian attire, consisting of yellow shorts and a white blouse, and bargaining in Spanish with an inner-city street vendor over the price of Aztec jewelry. The entire Bogotá market bustled with vendors calling loudly to buy everything from slaughtered chickens, hanging upside down by their feet, to freshly cut flowers to decorate the homes of rich Americans, to precious stones fashioned into fine Aztec jewelry.
>
> "¿Por favor, cuánto por esto?" (Please, how much money for this?) I held up a spectacular silver and gold necklace richly adorned with rubies and emeralds. The market vendor immediately recognized American dollars as an excuse to jack the price to almost double for the Americano. Every time I leaned over in my low-cut blouse, I dangled my dog tags for the vendor to see. I recognized a ripoff when I saw one. I knew, as a child pulled along by my streetwise mother in the inner-city markets of New York, that the asking price was just that, the opening salvo in a protracted round of negotiations. I remembered my mother angrily pretending to stomp away

at such an insulting opening offer to see if the merchant would make a counteroffer before she would disappear forever in the crowded city market. I learned that pity by the American for the poverty of the merchant must have nothing to do with the negotiation and actually could be used to my advantage, knowing the vendor might not make enough that day to feed his children that night.

The vendor responded, "Ciento y cinco dólares." ($105).

I responded, "Veinte dolares." ($20.)

The vendor rolled his eyes and took back the beautiful necklace from my hand to examine it closer and potentially to signal the end of the negotiation. I pointed to a perceived flaw in one of the stones and shook my head.

The vendor said, "Setenta y cinco dólares." ($75.)

I said, "No, yo tengo solamente treinta dólares, es todo." (No, I don't have but $30.)

The vendor took the necklace and put it away.

I located my purse and handed the vendor two crisp twenty-dollar bills.

"Esto es todo que tengo." (That's all that I have.)

The vendor rejected my offer and said, "Lo siento mucho, no es suficiente." (I'm sorry, that's not good enough.)

"No gracias" (No, thank you), and I walked away toward another vendor who was also selling similar jewelry and picked up an almost identical necklace and then walked back when the first vendor yelled, "Cinquenta dólares." ($50.)

I knew that I was about to close the deal as I searched through my purse for another five-dollar bill. I added the five to the two twenties and held them up to the vendor. "Fine!"

He smiled and replied, "OK, OK, no más, linda senorita." (No more, my pretty girl.) He placed the necklace in a white gift box and handed it to me as I released the forty-five American dollars to the vendor.

An Englishman with thinning hair and a British sense of humor stood in civilian khaki pants and a light safari shirt next to me admiring my negotiation skills in the just-completed transaction. From his black-stemmed pipe, he radiated a faint aroma of cherry tobacco as he exhaled the smoke without removing the pipe, musing aloud to me and himself simultaneously, "In Spanish no less."

Surprised at the English comment, I turned to see the man and said, "Excuse me, were you talking to me?

"Yes, by all means. I'm sorry. Please forgive me, but I was just admiring your skill. Normally he does not yield to that degree," pointing with his pipe to the vendor as if he knew him. "Your necklace is quite beautiful and worth far more in the States than what you just paid. I am trying to buy a piece of furniture for my flat and cannot seem to budge the old man down there," pointing again with his pipe in the direction of a man about fifty yards away, who was surrounded by hand-made bamboo furniture. "Do you think you could assist me with my broken Spanish and, perhaps, a little of your considerable negotiating skill?"

I immediately sized up this Englishman as harmless. He turned to leave, assuming I would just blindly follow, which is exactly what I did, and we made our way past hawking vendors back to the bamboo furniture.

Walking now side by side, he said, "My name is Walter Clarke. That's Clarke with an 'e.' My friends call me 'Walt.' You're American. What is your name?

"Victoria."

"Well, that's British enough! Are you of British ancestry? Please don't tell me they call you, 'Vicky.'"

Besides the one insulting reference made by Sergeant Goodheart, a man I detested who called me "Miss Vicky," I had never heard my name as "Vicky," and didn't particularly care for the name then, coming from someone I thoroughly detested. I was certain that Mr. Clarke would not like the nickname either, so I said. "No, sir, Mr. Clarke. It's Victoria Pierce. I'm a private in the United States Marine Corps, sir."

"Please don't age me beyond my years by calling me 'sir.' It's 'Walt.' How do you do, Victoria?" We shook hands just as we arrived at the bamboo furniture. "I've offered twenty-five pounds for those two chairs and table, and the rascal will not budge for less than sixty-five. I'm willing to go higher, but it's not worth that!"

"How much is twenty-five pounds in American dollars?" I had no clue as to even what an English pound was, much less the exchange rate in dollars.

Before Clarke could answer, I asked, "You don't mind if I just deal with him in dollars, do you?"

"Fine."

"I'm sorry, Mr. Clarke—excuse me, Walt. As long as you are standing here, he won't budge. Just step down the market, do a little shopping, and come back in about ten minutes, and I'll let you know his bottom line."

Clarke stepped away and observed my negotiations from a distance. The furniture vendor and I started peacefully enough, but it soon turned into bargaining warfare. At one point I walked away holding cash above my head, turned around, and restarted the negotiation. Finally the finger pointing and arm waving stopped, peace was at hand, and the negotiation was over. Clarke returned.

"How much?"

"Forty dollars, sir, but that includes the mirror. He will not sell the set without the mirror. That was your problem."

Walt handed the vendor two twenties pulled from one of his many side pockets. I then assisted Walt with loading the pieces into the back of his dark green Land Rover.

"Thank you very much, Victoria. I really needed these items for my flat. May I give you a ride back to your quarters?"

"Thank you. That would be a big help. My orders are to report back to the sergeant's desk by eight o'clock."

Clarke nominated Victoria with British humor and flare, perhaps overworking a bit the Marine Corps slogan, *Semper Fi*, but nevertheless wowed the wildly approving delegation. Besides Clarke's glowing accounts of Victoria, there would be no shortage of other testimonials to her bravery. Busting the gang in Central Park or saving the life of the Speaker in the stairwell was either singularly or collectively the stuff of bona fide heroes. Besides her valor, Victoria was also an outstanding honors graduate of an excellent university; a pioneer feminist, the first of her gender to achieve the rank of Marine Corps brigadier general; and, coupled with those accomplishments, a top military advisor to one of the most politically powerful United States Senators in the country... all combined, it simply made Victoria look perfectly vice presidential, and Sam look flawlessly presidential.

Victoria, in the words of General Clarke, was still "drop-dead gorgeous" at age forty-five, which made it practically impossible for her to deliver her acceptance speech for the constant and persistent interruptions of the delegates, so much so that at one point she had to leave the podium and simply step forward with both arms outstretched to acknowledge her admirers, which only made the convention hall shake to its foundation under stampeding waves of thunderous applause. Delegates thrust campaign placards, carrying the name of the Eagan-Pierce ticket, high in the air as they marched around the floor.

Victoria repeated many phrases in her speech in polished Spanish, not the Spanish of an American trying to imitate her high school teacher, but the flawless Spanish of natives in conversation. Finally, she concluded on a patriotic theme. "The American way of life was won by the sacrifices of Americans in uniform on battlefields all over the world. I intend never, never, on my watch—in the new administration that will surely come—to permit their sacrifices to be forgotten!" Strangely, the last phrase was added by Tom, minutes before Victoria went on stage, based upon overnight polling numbers that proved Victoria's role as the legitimate defender of the combat soldier. A mesmerizing silence preceded the echoes of her final sentence in a hall about to erupt in euphoria as Victoria walked back and clasped Sam's hand in hers. The speechmaking was over. Sam and Victoria were accustomed to holding hands entangled as lovers, but now they held hands extended upward as a sign of the coming political campaign, as running mates sharing a ticket for the leadership of the free world.

By three the following morning, the political revelers had finally turned in, as well as the campaign staffers in the hotel suite. But this time, Victoria, not Tom, was musing beyond the confines of the window over Lower Manhattan. Victoria looked down at the lighted sidewalks where she and her mother walked and shopped. She saw her mother in the window's reflection, beaming with pride for a daughter who accomplished so much.

Tom's secure cell phone rang to break the silence. Instinctively, Victoria picked up the receiver. "Hello. Why, yes, yes it is. This is Victoria Pierce."

She expected to acknowledge a perfunctory congratulatory message. Instead the voice on the other end of the line declared, "I know who you are!"

CHAPTER THIRTEEN

August 2008

"Well, who might that be? I've been trying to figure that out myself," Victoria joked.

"You're the woman I saw standing in the stairwell."

"Who is this?"

"Never mind who this is. Would you like to know what I saw and recorded in the stairwell as you watched O'Connor dying at the bottom of the flight of stairs?"

"How did you get this number?"

"Very clever, my dear, but you will not be able to change the subject or talk your way out of this one, so you better just listen. Lucky for you, I'm just like you. Really, now, pushing the Speaker down the steps just to become vice president of the United States. How will your friend, Ace, respond to that side of you?"

"That's a lie. I saved her life."

"That's not the way I saw it. But it really doesn't matter. Why did you wait a full three minutes before you rushed down to her side?"

Victoria stumbled. "Not true." She tried to recover. "But if it were true and you were there as you actually say, then why didn't you do anything?"

"Oh, you are quick, aren't you? That's why I've grown to admire you so much. Look, I've got the cell phone pictures to prove it."

"Cell phone pictures?"

"Yes, of course, each one taken of you while you just stood there, time and date imprinted on each one. What's your e-mail? I'll send them to you, or perhaps, your friend, Ace."

"What do you want?"

"I want nothing more than for you to become president of the United States. And I am going to help you. But please, stop doing your own dirty work."

"Well, then, you must tell me who you are."

"In time, my dear, in time."

"Well, how will I know it's you?"

"Oh, you'll know! So please, for the time being, stop trying to do your own work. Frankly, you're not very good at it. Just leave it to me."

"Blackmail is a crime, you know."

"Lucky for you, this is not a call for money to avoid political embarrassment. No, I'm not going to the press, at least not right now. In fact, you will not hear from me again for a long while. Disappointed? But at just the right moment, I'll let you know who I am, and you can thank me personally for making you president. You'll be so grateful, you'll want to marry me."

"I've regrettably turned down a lot of marriage proposals from a lot of good men, but I'll relish the opportunity of turning down a creep like you!"

"Oh, could it be you're in love with someone else? That will all change, but you'll accept my proposal once you've gotten to know me, and you will get to know me. Besides, you really have no alternative, do you? Now, anything that you would like to ask me before we hang up? By the way, your blouse fits you perfectly. Why don't you take it off while

I watch? No, wait, that's not a good idea. Someone else might see you. Let's reserve that for a more private time. It's late. Perhaps you should just step away from the window?"

Victoria gasps, pulls the blinds, and backs away from the window.

"That's better. Oh, I thought you'd never ask: all I'm wearing are my tennis shoes." Laughter preceded the dial tone. The line went dead.

Victoria immediately punched in the number of the Secret Service to report her night stalker, but before reaching the final number she stopped, reconsidered, and decided she could declare the caller a perverted prankster, if ever he went to the press with his theory.

Exhausted now, she walked over to the couch, lay down, and dozed awkwardly for several hours. She awakened early, showered quickly, and dressed fashionably. Victoria contemplated again her conversation with her enigmatic night caller and concluded again that she could defend her inaction in the stairwell by asking the press to imagine her shock at witnessing Maggie's devastating fall, followed by the not-inconsequential fact of actually saving her life.

Sleepy, nervous, but reenergized with her victory over Tom, Victoria reveled in beating the odds of becoming Sam's running mate with a perfectly executed strategy, devised by the mind of the brilliant general that she was, thinking politically for the first time in her life. She defeated Tom by taking a play right out of his own book of dirty tricks, to claim her rightful place beside the man she loved, united in politics if not by marriage, where she could protect Sam from women like Maggie O'Connor. Besides, Victoria was warming to the wars of politics and the spoils of victory that would certainly follow.

Above all, she enjoyed misbehaving at Tom's expense. She knew Tom would sleep late this morning. Deciding now was a good time to misbehave, Victoria sprang down Seventh Avenue alone to Lincoln Center, without notice to either Tom, the Secret Service, or anyone on the campaign staff, two hours in advance of her scheduled appearance there. Later, the general would defend her impulsivity as a "necessary command decision," a military term familiar only to those who had answered their country's call to duty, excluding, by definition, such an unpatriotic civilian as Tom Pearsall.

Along the way to Lincoln Center, Victoria responded to questions from reporters who quickly gathered as she sauntered along the sidewalks, reminiscent of her solo walk with Grace the previous March, except this time throngs of admirers gathered to follow her every step, as if she were visiting royalty. General Pierce spoke bluntly about the lack of military funding and the need to maintain a strong militia.

Out of breath from chain smoking, but finally catching up to Victoria's entourage, Tom winced at each of Victoria's one-liners. Fortunately, she uttered not a single word about her nuclear first-strike philosophy. Tom knew too well that his clogged arteries could not take this kind of stress, but he had to be prepared to intercede for the good of the ticket. How quickly the press could seize on a politically incorrect sentence and pull public opinion away from his candidate's targeted message, no matter how skillfully he later spun the correction. But Tom's apprehension was misplaced. Victoria could do no wrong. If she committed murder in front of the Metropolitan Opera, the press would applaud. America was in love with General Pierce.

Grace could not compete with the crush of the bigger bodies and even bigger hand-held television cameras, so she gradually filtered backward through the crowd. Caught herself off-guard by Victoria's early morning foray, Grace did not expect Victoria to hem and haw her way up Seventh

Avenue at such a dawdle, so Grace ducked into Mr. Margolis's Seafood Deli for a short break to munch a bagel with lox and cream cheese. She calculated that this quick stop should still leave ample time to catch up to her candidate and cover her official remarks. Besides, she had been alerted already to the theme of the military message and actually possessed Victoria's original handwritten notes, securely hidden behind her reporter's pad. Grace knew the exact time that Victoria would deliver her message and had all but written her story, at least in her own mind.

Competing with the press of numerous other patrons inside such a small eating space, Grace hoped Mr. Margolis would finish with her order before someone took the open chair at the small table beside the window. As she stood waiting impatiently at the counter, she noticed, even with his gray mustache and thinning hair, how much Mr. Margolis reflected the image of the clean-shaven man in the photograph with his arm around his oldest son's shoulder.

Grace literally snatched her order from Mr. Margolis, handed him the only bill in her purse, a twenty, and observed that the table next to the window was still open, but then she unexpectedly paused to ask a question. She points up at the black-and-white photograph behind the register. "Mr. Margolis, tell me just how long ago that photograph was taken?"

"Years ago, honey."

"But how long?"

Mr. Margolis stopped in the middle of making change for Grace's twenty-dollar bill, turned around, and rubbed his chin. "That photograph was taken by my wife on September 1, 1970, when Frankie, my son over there, joined me in the deli business. One of the proudest days of my life . . . week after next will be thirty-eight years. Now, Ace, that would make a good story, my retirement after thirty-eight years in the deli business together, don't you think? Or are you too busy covering that good-looking general, running for president with my good Catholic boy? I've been watching her on television all week."

"Think they'll win, Mr. Margolis?"

Gus Margolis ignored the question and, instead, reminisced. "Something about her reminds me of a customer that used to come in here, years ago, with her daughter. I never forget a regular customer's face. Not good for business."

"What do you mean, she reminds you?"

"Yeah, a woman, long time ago, maybe thirty years?"

"But how do you remember someone from so long ago?"

A hurried and impatient New Yorker, waiting in line behind Grace, realized this discussion was drifting far beyond delivering change for a bagel, so she elbowed her way around Grace to the front of the counter.

"Two pounds of crab salad, or I'm walkin' right now."

"Frankie, need two pounds of crab salad!" Gus's voice boomed and pointed the irate customer in the direction of his son's cash register at the opposite end of the counter, and then looked back at Grace.

"Maybe when you get a little older, you'll understand how men remember women. Well, as I said, never forget a regular customer's face. She came in about twice a week." Gus leaned slightly over his side of the counter. "Don't tell my wife, but *this* woman was one of the most gorgeous women God ever made to walk the streets of New York. A face you could never forget, and your general friend reminds me of her. Matter of fact, it's eerie. Just like her."

"What was her name?"

"I remember faces, but terrible with names. Who knows, maybe I can remember hers, but not today!"

"But General Pierce is from Oklahoma . . . can't be the same."

"Guess it couldn't be, honey," said Mr. Margolis as he handed the change back to Grace. "Next, who's next?" his voice boomed.

Grace pocketed her change and raced to the seat once open beside the window, now taken by the women with the crab salad, who sat with her unopened deli bag in front of her, albeit no longer in any hurry, staring aimlessly out the window. Grace shifted uncomfortably in her chair at the last seat in the deli as she sipped mineral water from a plastic bottle, oblivious to anything but her gourmet bagel, but contemplating what Mr. Margolis just said.

"Maybe it was Victoria, once a little girl shopping with her mother, who immediately recognized Gus Margolis," Grace mused as she resentfully stared into the hand-carved graffiti on the back wall, certainly not her preferred view of Seventh Avenue. She was completely wrapped up in her daydream until she glanced down at her watch, realizing she was late. She retrieved the remnants of the quilted silver aluminum foil, covered the remainder of her bagel in its cardboard dish, shoved it into her black reporter's bag, slung it over her arm, and sailed out the door, frowning as she went at the woman with her bag of crab salad, still unopened.

Tardiness is a reporter's biggest sin, thus causing Grace's exile to the back edge of the unexpectedly massive crowd. Grace lacked the physical stature to muscle her way through to the front of or even to skirt the perimeter of such a massive oval. Finally, Victoria began to read her prepared statement through a portable microphone, but she was barely audible to those, like Grace, at the crowd's edge. The only thing worse for Grace than the faintness of Victoria's audio was her obliterated visibility. Grace could see nothing but the impenetrable shoulder blades of the T-shirted gargantuan standing right in front of her, so without any other option, Grace glanced downward, with perfect clarity, at her shoes.

There she found that her shoes were planted squarely on Tom Pearsall's circulated press release. In bold and large print are the words, "Oklahoma City."

"Oklahoma City? She didn't say anything about Oklahoma City." Grace lifted the circular, muddied slightly with her shoe print, stumbled forward from the nudge of another large man trying to gain better advantage, and reversed direction to the security of a concrete planter holding a crimson Japanese maple.

> Presidential nominee, Senator Sam Eagan, and vice presidential nominee, General Victoria Pierce, will appear jointly tomorrow in Oklahoma City to address the significant issue of health-care cost and containment for the elderly. This will be the first in a series of policy initiatives on major issues that are important to the American people. Oklahoma City is home to the vice presidential candidate's mother, Lucinda Pierce, who suffers from advanced and incurable Alzheimer's disease, and is confined in the hospital section of the Sunset Rest Home, a skilled nursing and assisted living center.
>
> Senator Eagan will fly later that evening to San Diego. The next day he will observe a U.S. Border Patrol checkpoint and issue a position statement on immigration policy. General Pierce, after spending the evening with her mother, will fly back to Fort Leavenworth, Kansas, to meet with the post commander there and issue a position statement on U.S. military preparedness.

Oklahoma City! How am I going to rearrange my schedule to get to Oklahoma City by tomorrow? Book a flight to nowhere. . . . Wonder why Victoria didn't let me in on her plan? OK, must be Tom's plan . . . sounds like Tom. . . . Maybe he's trying to counter the hype sure to surround next week's convention in Miami. Grace looked up as she thought, finally seeing her subject, clearly for the first time, finishing her remarks as Sam stepped up to the microphone.

Listening with one ear to what Sam might have to say, Grace, with her other ear stuck in her cell phone, called to ensure that her editor at the *Times* was aware of Victoria's surprise Oklahoma visit and to ask for perfunctory permission to rearrange her schedule to join the presidential press corps in Oklahoma City and then at Fort Leavenworth. Her editor, surprised that Grace was unaware of her subject's campaign schedule, had already confirmed Grace's travel arrangements through staff the moment the *Times* received the press release, ensuring that their "Ace" presidential reporter would cover the events in Oklahoma and Kansas.

Grace's only comment by way of defense was, "Can't you please stop calling me 'Ace'?"

The voice on the cell phone replied, "Sorry, Ms. Brandon, but that's what everyone calls you!"

Grace hung up and caught the subway at the Lincoln Center station to ride the forty blocks down to her apartment.

"Damn, I don't even know how to open this thing!" Grace dumped everything she owned into her brand-new, never-before-used, travel suitcase, a Christmas gift from her father who, in his retirement boredom, took it upon himself to inventory, organize, and repair everything in Grace's apartment to his satisfaction, tossing out her old bag, completely without permission. It mattered not that her father made the correct decision. What mattered was that her father was still treating her as his little girl. The search for her old luggage lost her thirty minutes in her race to LaGuardia, but, more important, she was perfectly capable of deciding when to discard her things.

Checking the campaign's website from her home computer, Grace read the details for the first time. The candidates would jointly appear and issue a health-care policy statement in front of the Sunset Rest Home, an obscure medical facility somewhere on the west side of Oklahoma City where Victoria's mother was receiving long-term care.

Grace stopped packing and reached Victoria on her private cell phone at her hotel suite and confirmed the itinerary. Grace was still mulling over her conversation with Mr. Margolis about the similarities of the beautiful mother with the small child as she listened to Victoria explain how Tom conceived his "bright idea" during the last days of convention week. "He should have said something to me way before now, Ace!" Tom explained to Victoria that he planned to go over the details of her Oklahoma and Kansas schedule fully earlier that morning, but she had childishly bolted from the hotel two hours ahead of schedule.

"'Why did you leave so far ahead of schedule this morning?'" Victoria mimicked Tom's voice sarcastically. "'It was your own damned fault! Had you stayed where you were supposed to stay, you would have been briefed just like everyone else.'"

"So that's why you didn't tell me."

"I screwed up. Tom handed me the release right before speaking at Lincoln Center, probably about the same time that you were reading the same release."

"Yeah, I was surprised and late, too, way in the back of the crowd, beneath the shade of one of those Japanese maples."

Victoria, carping further to Grace, began to complain legitimately. "I not only have to deliver a speech on a subject I know practically nothing about, but my wheelchair-bound mother, whom I have not seen in years because of our estrangement, is going to be the visual centerpiece of the announcement, something like announcing military policy in front of the Tomb of the Unknown Soldier."

Grace had heard Victoria speak before in callous military terms, but the analogy between her own mother and the Tomb of the Unknown Soldier was out of place even in the salty language of a combat-tested Marine. Grace reminded herself that this whole idea belonged to Tom Pearsall, not Victoria Pierce. The unaccustomed nervousness and irritation in Victoria's voice seemed to verify the truth of her protestation that these lately scheduled events had, indeed, caught her off-guard, ridding Grace of a nagging, intuitive suspicion that Victoria was concealing something. Besides, had Victoria known all along, wouldn't she have stopped momentarily to give Grace the heads-up, as she had done so often before, alerting Grace to such an important campaign event in the hotel's back hallway on the way to last night's convention, when she surreptitiously passed her press notes to Grace with the ease of a track star passing a baton in a four-hundred-meter medley relay? No, at least for this time, Victoria told the truth, or so Grace surmised.

* * *

The twenty-seven-year absence from last seeing Lucinda Pierce atop the Farmall tractor in her last-ditch attempt to block Victoria's escape from the Pierce Farm had not changed her leathered expression.

> Sarge was sitting obediently at my feet as I stood by the highway, striking a hitchhiker pose, right arm and thumb extended, waiting for a ride from a passer-by, any passer-by, who was going anywhere but back to the Pierce Farm. April

22, 1981, was to be the luckiest day of my life, but I first had to land a ride. I thought that hitchhiking along a county road, like the one in front of the Pierce Farm, was a simple matter of flagging down a passing vehicle.

A car moving less than the speed limit was a mile in the distance, but it took what seemed to be an eternity to arrive. I gave the driver my best smile and pushed out my arm, right thumb clearly extended. An elderly man clutching the wheel of a white Plymouth Fury swerved into the opposite lane, avoided looking at me and Sarge, and then accelerated past us as if we were not there. Taillights were all that was left of freedom. "Damn, Sarge, so much for friendly country neighbors. Next time you're going to have to hide in the ditch!"

I turned back to the highway and surveyed the roadscape for potential vehicles. There were none. I looked back to the farm and with dreadful astonishment spied Lucinda, a mile down the road, riding atop the Farmall tractor, making all due haste in my direction at the maximum speed of twenty miles per hour. The Farmall had been turning the fields for the last month, but that was not Lucinda's intention today. I quickly contemplated escape at a full sprint but concluded I could not outpace the Farmall tractor either on the road or in the fields. There was no place to run or hide on the treeless Oklahoma prairie. All I could see in every direction for miles were cleared fields, all neatly plowed for spring planting. Not a hint of help was in sight, including Jan, who had left almost an hour earlier. Lucinda quite probably had either the 12-gauge shotgun or the World War I army pistol. Both had been propped fully loaded in the corner wall beside the front door to blast intruders in the night whom Sarge could not dissuade.

As Lucinda approached within less than fifty yards, she brandished the army pistol with one hand and beeped the tractor horn with the other. But she would have to stop and dismount long enough to unlock the gate. My desperation turned to hope at the distant sound and then sight of a tractor-trailer loaded with farm supplies lumbering along the highway at a rate far in excess of the fifty-five-mile-per-hour posted speed limit, rolling in my direction. I glanced back at Lucinda, instantly calculated the time it would take for me to intercept the truck, and erupted in a full sprint down the highway with Sarge barking along beside me. Like a mother protecting her baby, I clutched in my right arm Marshal Slaughter's file folder full of my counterfeited documents.

Lucinda reached the Pierce mailbox, hopped off the tractor to unlock the gate, remounted, turned the tractor sharply to the left, and notched the metal accelerator, located below the steering wheel, up to full throttle. Lucinda apparently did not see the rapidly approaching truck and thought all she had to do was outlast a soon-to-be-fatigued highway jogger. As a warning, Lucinda fired her pistol into the air. I thought to myself, *She will just have to shoot me.* There would be no turning back. Fifty yards separated us, but Lucinda was closing in on me faster than expected. Soon she was to be within pistol range.

I stopped running, crossed the highway, and tried to regain both my breath and composure as the tractor-trailer approached within a hundred yards. It was now or never.

I assumed my most feminine hitchhiking posture, except this time my hand went to the hem of my skirt, soon to be pulled almost to the top of my thigh. The tractor-trailer flew past at an undiminished speed. I supposed all was lost, but suddenly the brake lights flashed at maximum radiance as eighteen recapped tires locked up, screeching to a stop, filling the air with the acrid smell of burned rubber. The right cab door flung open as I raced through the fog of burning tires to reach the door before Lucinda could get fully into range. In a flash, I was in the cab.

"Get the hell out of here, mister!" I turned to the young driver.

"What's the hurry? Where you going to, pretty-lil' farm girl?"

"Same place as you!"

"That would be San Francisco."

The big rig rumbled slowly at first down the highway as the driver ground through the lower forward gears while I expected to hear shots ring out at any time. The truck driver did not observe Lucinda's irate arm-waving tirade that I could clearly see out of the passenger-side rearview mirror. But there, halting the Farmall in its tracks was my friend, Sarge, barking menacingly in front of the tractor at Lucinda and preventing her pursuit. The truck driver failed to notice anything on the road as both his eyes were now fastened squarely on my legs, which were strategically curled and pointing in his direction.

Lucinda Pierce had the same hardened face at age ninety-seven that Vera remembered at age seventy. She survived Ezekiel by ten years, just before she slipped into the early stages of Alzheimer's. Ezekiel died of cardiac arrest. His heart exploded one afternoon on the front porch of the same rest home, the very spot where the national press was now gathering. On his last day, Lucinda, with her usual economy of words, directed Ezekiel to "pack up" as they would be leaving the rest home that afternoon to return to the farm. She didn't say why, but apparently Lucinda's early stage of Alzheimer's robbed her of one very important memory, a fact that Ezekiel remembered all too well. They had sold their farm to a young couple to provide the funds for their final care. At his memorial service at the Sunset Rest Home, the preacher said that Ezekiel had found a better place—and no one disagreed that any place without Lucinda would have been a better place for Ezekiel.

Today, Lucinda was a little too feisty for Tom's comfort, periodically spewing out unconscious words that Tom often employed himself, but words that would not be appropriate to hear in the background of a presidential press conference. He asked the rest home manager if he might not have a little something to "calm her down a bit" to let his candidates get through the event without interruption. The medication, slipped into Lucinda's apple sauce, produced the desired result. Except for a slightly audible snore, Lucinda rested asleep in her wheelchair, with her head slumped downwardly, as a perfect backdrop for the press conference, exactly as Tom envisioned an advanced Alzheimer's patient should look.

It mattered little to Tom how such patients actually lived or looked on a daily basis. It was the image of Lucinda, the patient/mother contrasted with Victoria, the daughter/caregiver, that would personalize the event and provide an emotional connection between this visual human suffering and the Eagan campaign's policy solution for taking care of such patients. This visually enhanced emotional connection between problem and solution, if it could be pulled off, would heighten the likelihood of persuading the expanding segment of voters already concerned about long-term health-care costs, coupled with an even larger segment of untapped voters that could be alarmed or frightened into being concerned about these issues, to cast their ballots for the Eagan/Pierce ticket, in three months on Election Day. Tom's dissatisfaction with this press conference, as with all others, was that not enough of the targeted potential voters would see the contrived message, but he also knew, if the staged event was successful, that these numbers could be reached and even saturated, if necessary, with tailor-made television spots, produced from today's news conference video footage, in order to reach the maximum number of potential voters, aged fifty-five to seventy-five, particularly in the retirement-laden southern regional markets. The added benefit for today's portrayal was that his team would be engaging the press on serious policy questions while his competitors would be engaging the press on the early-week frivolity of their party's convention.

Right before Victoria was to deliver her prepared remarks, Tom—ahead of her scheduled speech—explained the objectives of this strategy to Victoria, who consistently in the past spurned such pretense. Tom reinforced his directive by placing exactly what he wanted her to do in bold type, within brackets, in the printed copy of her speech: "Pause, turn around, and slowly walk back to embrace your mother in her wheelchair before beginning your delivery."

Victoria knew in advance that she would have to feign any genuine emotion, except resentment, toward her supposed mother, so she focused instead on the devastating loss of her real mother, which seemed to produce at least an emotional balance between ambivalence and grief that would ease her through her short introduction until Sam could issue his policy statement. Then she would be on her way to Fort Leavenworth, and Lucinda Pierce could die in the wheelchair behind her for all she really cared. Her objective was to end the encounter as quickly as possible, clumsily following Tom's absurd directive by awkwardly hugging her mother while reaching around her snoring head, which drooped down and listed sharply to the right as she slumbered in her wheelchair. This awkward embrace did not achieve its desired effect. Instead, the gesture roused her mother from her comatose-like stupor just as Victoria returned to the podium.

"Ladies and gentlemen," Victoria began, "my purpose here today is to introduce to you the next president of the United States, Sam Eagan, the senior senator from the state of Virginia. I am honored to share the ticket with Senator Eagan as his vice presidential candidate, and I wish now to say only a few words about the issue of health-care costs before introducing Senator Eagan, whose destiny is to be the next president of the United States."

As Victoria concentrated on her mission, she read the words of her prepared speech, words as superficial to her as her feelings for Lucinda Pierce—a crabapple of a woman, the fictional mother of a fictional daughter—and remembered her real mother, who rested next to her real father in a Long Island cemetery, a place Victoria could not visit for fear that someone would learn her identity. Victoria fought back a smile that reflected her true feelings for Lucinda's dementia, a smile of revenge that only a Marine Corps general could feel at the defeat of an old enemy. Clearly for Victoria, the dementia represented justice for Lucinda's cold life that would soon terminate in a cold grave. Ambivalent, Victoria continued to read the words printed on the page.

"We are here at the Sunset Rest Home in Oklahoma City to make a major policy statement concerning health care in this country and its spiraling costs, costs that we project will close the door to most Americans for assisted living in their retirement years, particularly for the aging baby boomers, because of the extraordinary expenses associated with medical care for such diseases as Alzheimer's and related dementia. Medicare, Medicaid, and Social Security Disability simply cannot and will not pay enough for the number of Americans who will some day face these diseases in their retirement years. In just a few moments, I will ask that all Americans listen carefully to Senator Eagan's solution to this problematic issue and his plan to ensure the necessary federal funding to provide coverage for such extended treatments, together with containment measures that will reduce the costs for all Americans. But first I want to make you aware of my personal dilemma that I share with so many other adult children who have parents in assisted living. My mother, Lucinda Pierce, sitting behind me suffers from advanced Alzheimer's Disease. . . ."

At the mention of her name, Lucinda, through glazed eyes, stared out at the unaccustomed assembly on her front porch and shouted, "Here, Sarge. Come on, boy!"

Victoria remembered Sarge, the only friend she ever had on the Pierce Farm, who faithfully guarded her and the front porch. Smiling at the press, Victoria turned to face Lucinda.

"Sarge was our beloved German shepherd guard dog, who died some twenty years ago."

Now fully awake and making matters worse for Victoria, Lucinda shouted, "Help me get out of here. Damn it, Ezekiel, get me out of here."

Victoria picked up on this dilemma, which forced her off text. "You can see for yourself, my personal difficulty . . . and I, fortunately, am in a better position than most to cope with this problem and financially manage my mother's care, thanks to the Marine Corps' outstanding disability family coverage."

Victoria looked down again to her prepared text and slightly modified the next sentence by adding "so" at the beginning: "So many other Americans are trapped in despair, financially unprepared to deal with the plight of a parent caught in dementia."

Lucinda shouted again, "Wait a damned minute. Don't I know you?"

This last question caused Victoria to stop, hand the microphone to Sam, and without missing a beat, announce, "It's time, right now, for me to care for my mother."

Victoria stepped back to her mother's wheelchair and began to roll her inside the hospital wing, freeing herself from Lucinda's troubling question and allowing Sam to continue the press conference without introduction or interruption.

Tom Pearsall checked to ensure that the campaign's paid video cameraman captured the treasure trove of Victoria's unrehearsed performance. His own exuberance for this good fortune overtook him as he broke out in applause that soon became infectious. Applause thundered as the camera panned and recorded the clapping hands of the audience and press.

Grace rose from her seat, carefully placing her tape recorder in the chair beside Lennie. She rushed to comfort her friend, trying desperately to catch up with Victoria, who was now rolling her mother at breakneck speed down a remote hallway to her private room beside the rear exit, a room far from the earshot of the press.

Lucinda strained to see who had rescued her from the front porch. "You're that damned hoodlum. Thought I recognized you from the TV!"

Grace arrived and eavesdropped unobserved on this conversation between mother and daughter. Victoria, without a glint of care or word of comfort for her mother, released the wheelchair with a push toward an orderly, turned to the other white-clad person in the room, and explained, "She's really lost it—cannot even recognize her own daughter."

With that, Victoria silently shoved her way through the fire exit door, disregarding the warning marked in large, bright red letters, "Alarm Will Sound"; stopped a moment in the large asphalt parking lot; and checked her lipstick before returning to rejoin Sam at the podium.

Grace, trying to resolve what she just observed between mother and daughter, walked into the room as Lucinda said, "Damned hoodlum, that's all she is!"

"But that's your daughter, Mrs. Pierce."

"Miss, it would be better for you to leave right now," said an older orderly. "She's likely goin' to slip right out of her chair, certain to hurt herself, if she don't stop flailing 'round." The orderly cinches Lucinda's wheelchair strap. "She'll break a hip if she falls out, and that might spell the end."

Grace retreated through the same fire exit door, again with no warning alarm sounding, listening on her way out to the rantings of an elderly Alzheimer's patient. "This time, I'll break her neck in half."

Grace overtook Victoria in the parking lot. "Someone needs to report that the door is malfunctioning."

Victoria looked backward at the closing exit door and realized that Grace had followed her. Grace said, "This just has to be tough on you."

Victoria replied, "More than you can possibly know. This whole place is just filled with so many bad memories, but mostly resentment."

"But why so much resentment?"

"Grace, I hate Oklahoma!"

"I've got it, General, let's do a feature on your life here. Go back to that farm where you grew up, relive your childhood, and tell our readers what it was like for you there."

"Don't need to waste our time doing that, Grace. I'll tell you what it is was like out there on that farm, living in total isolation. It was hell on earth! And you want me to go back there? Never again will I step foot on that farm, *never*!"

"What about your mother?"

"I'll tell you all about her sometime, but right now I'm in the middle of a press conference. Soon as I am finished here, I'm going to a real home, a military base. This one just so happens to be in Fort Leavenworth, Kansas."

Victoria left Grace standing in the middle of the asphalt parking lot. Grace paused, thinking to herself that what she had just witnessed was out of character for Victoria— overdramatized, especially for the normally objective General Pierce. Grace thinks, *It is her mother and there is a lot of pain associated with her relationship. But something doesn't feel right about all this.*

A reporter's unanswered question needed answering, particularly when covering a potential president of the United States. Grace determined to resolve her dissonance. She would search for the answers at the Pierce Farm. But she did not know where it was or how to get there.

The Sunset Rest Home resident manager was thin, busy, and annoyed. "Look, for the third time, miss, I cannot give you a patient's home address. All the information contained in Lucinda Pierce's medical file is subject to the Patient's Medical Privacy Act," the manager rebuked Grace in response to her repeated questions, each time framed slightly differently.

But Grace was persistent. "Look, I just don't agree. Mrs. Pierce is now a public figure, and her address is a matter of public record. You can give it to me or—you really don't want to be talking to my editors about this and have some New York lawyer calling us now, do you? The lawyer's answer is always the same. It's always public information. So let's stop wasting time."

"The answer is still *no*! And my answer will be the same tomorrow, but I'll call my lawyer later to be sure. Come back at 8:00 a.m. Good afternoon, miss. I have work to do."

The manager closed Lucinda's file, walked to the other side of the room, and made a telephone call, but left Lucinda's file within reach. Grace picked up the file, opened it, jotted down the address, closed the file, and departed before the manager hung up.

Driving well over the posted speed limit west on the interstate to Lawton, Grace pleaded with Lennie, "Look, the last time I had a hunch like this, you took the best damned photographs of your entire professional career, right?" Grace searched her friend's face for his agreement to stay with her one more day to photograph her contemplated feature story and not to rush out a day ahead just to cover Victoria's arrival in Fort Leavenworth, Kansas.

"I'll ask a few questions on the farm, you'll take a few pictures, and then we're out of here in plenty of time to drive tomorrow to get to Fort Leavenworth. If we wait for permission, it will be too late."

Before Lennie could respond in the negative, Grace begged, "Promise me that you will at least think about it. For once, climb out on the limb with me."

After asking for directions at a local feed store and hailing several farmers on tractors, Grace and Lennie turned into the same potholed dirt road that Victoria rode for the first time with Marshal Slaughter over twenty-five years earlier. A young mother with two small children giggling and coiling in and around her feet answered the front door and said through the latched screen door, "May I help you?"

Grace responds, "Yes, we are here from the *New York Times* to do a story and want to ask you or your husband about Victoria Pierce."

"Sorry, I don't know anyone by that name, and my husband is not here."

"Well, Victoria Pierce is Sam Eagan's vice presidential running mate." No answer, total silence. Grace surmised that this overburdened mother had not a clue who the candidates were running for president or vice president.

"You are aware that Senator Eagan is running for president of the United States? General Pierce, his vice presidential candidate, grew up here on this farm."

"That would be news to me. Don't mean a thing. We bought the farm from Mr. and Mrs. Pierce, but they had no children that they ever talked about."

One of the little ones pressed her face against the screen and then fell backward to the floor, hitting her head and pausing just long enough to gulp down enough breath for a wail that could be heard in the next county and a flood of tears to go with it. Grace knew the interview had ended even before the mother, picking up her crying child, said, "Wait for my husband. He will be back from the hardware store in about an hour. Ask him."

"We really don't have that much time. Do you mind if we snap a few photographs and look around out back?"

"Sure, go right ahead." She closed the door, trying to comfort a screaming child who could not be quieted. "It will stop hurting in a minute, dumplin'."

Grace walked around the back to the barn while Lennie remained to shoot the front of the house. Grace entered the barn and, finding nothing of interest below, climbed up the nailed wooden ladder into the loft, where she discovered a very old tin trunk with decorative leather sewed into the lid. Grace slowly lifted the lid, long unopened, to a creaking protest that seemed to say to her, "Don't open me." She quickly sorted through reams of mildewed farm journals, some going back as far as 1943, presumably in Ezekiel's handwriting. Grace bypassed the journals once she determined that they contained the recorded poundage for each crop harvested, deriving the gross profits by subtracting from the market price the associated fertilizer expenses and related costs in neatly blue-lined columns with a final figure listed at the bottom of each page in faded numerals, above a date and an unreadable cursive signature. Reaching further down into the contents of the trunk, Grace found a single white discolored page with a multitude of what appeared to be pin holes, the aftermath of which had been eaten through by tiny insects that dined on the paper's chemicals, that, much to Grace's alarm, partially disintegrated at her touch. The fractured remnants revealed a jagged and torn isosceles triangle above a partially obliterated typed test question. The more Grace tried to repair the damage she had done, the more the page disintegrated until there was nothing left to hold.

"Damn it!"

Discarding the Geometry figure, Grace looked further into the contents of the trunk. Stuck fast to the left interior side of the trunk by its glue, practically unnoticeable, was a faded brown envelope, the type the U.S. government might use to send a tax refund check. Grace, fearing she might again destroy another document from the trunk, turned 180 degrees in each direction to look for anyone who might have climbed the ladder, without notice, to observe her investigative reporting. She then realized that no intruder in her right mind would be up there with her in an abandoned loft unless it was some other dizzy reporter looking for a story that likely did not exist. Carefully this time, Grace leaned inside the chest to examine, without touching, the envelope's return address. "Marshal William S. Slaughter, United States Marshal, Federal Marshal's Office, Murrah Federal Court Building, Oklahoma City, Oklahoma." The envelope was addressed to "Mr. and Mrs. Ezekiel Pierce."

Grace, coughing from the dust and mites that she had dislodged in her rummaging, carefully peeled the envelope off the side.

"Must have something to do with taxes," Grace surmised. She opened the envelope to confirm her suspicion.

"Nothing. That can't be. There must be a letter . . . something."

Desperately, she opened wide the envelope, turned it upside down, and shook it as if this might free some letter stuck to the bottom.

"Grace, are you up there? I've taken all the photographs we need. We've got to go. I've got a plane to catch. What did you find?"

"Oh, nothing really," Grace replied, not sure exactly why she could not be more candid with her colleague. Perhaps it's because she slipped Marshal Slaughter's envelope inside her reporter's bag, completely without permission.

Bumping again along the potholed dirt road leading off the Pierce Farm and then getting back on the interstate to Oklahoma City, a sharp disagreement erupted and escalated between the two passengers concerning their departure time for Fort Leavenworth. Grace's inartful arguments proved unpersuasive to her companion, as she could not reveal her real reason for wanting to wait until tomorrow to leave— that reason being to somehow locate one Marshal William

S. Slaughter. After a twenty-minute break to respond to the Oklahoma State Highway Patrol, a traffic offense with a minimum fine of five hundred dollars to be doubled for speeding eighty five miles per hour in a fifty-five-mile-per-hour work zone, the two arrived back in Oklahoma City in an angry silence, parting ways at the airport. Grace screeched to a halt outside the departure terminal and all but shoved Lennie out the door, with a demeaning characterization of his courage and blurted out as she slammed the door, "Lennie, you're such a wus!"

Irritated and sleepless at ten o'clock that night in her motel room, where the thin curtains let in the bright red lights flashing from the cowboy marquee outside her window, Grace, tortured long enough by an empty envelope from law enforcement and a criminal epithet from Victoria's mother, all in the same day, left her room for one final attempt to get Lucinda to answer what she meant by "hoodlum girl."

Parking behind the Sunset Rest Home, Grace knew with certainty that she would not be able to ask the manager for permission to see Lucinda, but had the side entrance fire exit remained unlocked and disarmed as it had been earlier that day, Grace could have entered easily undetected, and walked straight into the interior of Lucinda's darkened room.

"Who's there? That you, Ezekiel?"

"No, Mrs. Pierce, it's Grace Brandon, the reporter that you met this afternoon from the *New York Times*."

"Well, have you seen Ezekiel?"

"I wanted to ask you if you are not proud of your daughter?"

"Daughter? What daughter?"

Grace stepped over to the bed, nervous that she would be detected, thrown out, and then prosecuted on a criminal trespass warrant. She decided to quickly turn on the bedside light to show Lucinda a large color photograph of Victoria. Immediately afterward, she turned off the light.

"That ain't my daughter. Me and Ezekiel never had no children. That's that hoodlum girl."

That was the description that Grace wanted to hear again. Even the cops could not drag her out of the room before she could hear the answer to her next question.

"What do you mean, Mrs. Pierce, when you call her that 'hoodlum girl'?" Grace knew she could not ethically quote any source with advanced Alzheimer's disease, but she had to know why Lucinda continued to refer to Victoria as "that hoodlum girl."

"If Victoria Pierce is not your daughter, then tell me who the 'hoodlum girl' is."

Lucinda became agitated but could not seem to remember Victoria's real name or even to comprehend the question or the means to answer it.

"What's the hoodlum girl's real name, Mrs. Pierce?"

Lucinda moaned like she was in acute pain. Her groans and agitation escalated uncontrollably. Grace heard the sound of tennis shoes coming down the hallway, squeaking on the polished linoleum. She backed away slowly behind a movable privacy screen, temporarily placed next to the doorway. A man in white tennis shoes and a medical uniform, with syringe in hand, burst through the door as Grace remained in shrouded silence behind the privacy screen.

"That you, Ezekiel?"

Seconds later, as Lucinda's life was draining away from the effects of the poison in the syringe, her once-sharp memory resurrected the forgotten name. Lucinda screamed, "Vera!"

CHAPTER FOURTEEN

September 2008

"Candidate's Mother Succumbs to Alzheimer's"

Grace was startled by the headline as she removed the Oklahoma City newspaper, late edition, from the rack inside the motel's dining room.

"Dead?"

She sat down in a booth, fidgeting nervously with the top right corner of the front page as she read and talked to the story.

"But how? Reaction to the drug?"

The breakfast waitress, carrying a glass coffee urn, half full and marked on one side in partially obliterated white letters, "Cory," filled Grace's white ceramic mug and interrupted, "Anything for you, hon, besides coffee?"

Grace answers without looking up, "A bagel with cream cheese."

"Sorry, hon, no bagels. How about the country ham special?"

"Cereal. Corn flakes."

"Corn flakes we got. Be right back."

Grace did not hear or see the waitress return with her order. She speed read the article: three short paragraphs, without byline. "Lucinda Pierce was found dead in her bedroom at the Sunset Rest Home at about 2 o'clock this morning. Coroner ruled she died in her sleep from natural causes, resulting from advanced Alzheimer's disease. . . . No autopsy. . . . Attempts early this morning to contact vice presidential candidate, Brigadier General Victoria Pierce, for comment . . . unsuccessful . . . funeral arrangements . . . incomplete."

Grace put the paper down and looked around the room, and then back down at her cereal. She hid behind the newspaper, continuing to talk to herself.

"I was one of the last people on earth to see Lucinda Pierce alive? Did the orderly administer too great of a sedative for Lucinda's agitation . . . agitation likely created by an unknown or unidentified late-night visitor? Or was it just Lucinda's time to check out of this world? No report of foul play. Coroner decided she died of 'natural causes.' So what about the cops? No, whatever happened in that room happened after I left. I'll be covering her funeral. If anything comes up indicating foul play I'll go to the cops. Problem solved!"

Grace chuckled to herself as she now realized that she had won the battle with Lennie to even the score, as it were, because he certainly would have to scamper back to Oklahoma City to cover the funeral while she had the good sense to remain to follow up on some leads that other reporters, once again, had carelessly abandoned. She was, in fact, Grace Brandon, ace presidential reporter for the *New York Times*, about to uncover one of the biggest political stories in presidential history—if Victoria somehow turns out to be the enigmatic Vera, a quite unsubstantiated long shot.

"Oh, God, please tell me I didn't just refer to myself as 'Ace.' Did I? What about Victoria? Victoria, the only child, is bound to grieve the loss of her mother. But this

Vera, whoever she is, definitely a daughter disavowed, will not grieve for a mother she never had. But damn, it will be hard to know what she will do because Tom—oh, yes, Tom, ever the spinmeister—will tell her how to play it to maximize coverage."

Grace glanced at her watch and realized she had but a few hours this morning to track down William S. Slaughter before Victoria hopped a jet back to Oklahoma City from Fort Leavenworth to make the final arrangements for her mother's funeral.

Grace overtipped the waitress with a dollar, the absolute minimum by New York City standards, leaving flattened on the table three new dollar bills with two quarters stacked atop her green and white restaurant check that itemized the total of $2.47 in looping blue cursive, for "cereal and cafee," the word "coffee" either intentionally abbreviated or misspelled. Then Grace saw there was no one at the front desk, so she made a beeline to check out, paying for her night's stay with a *New York Times* credit card, and bounced out the front door, all in less than five minutes.

Inside the clerk's office on the fourth floor of the new federal building in Oklahoma City, Grace typed the search word "Vera" into the public records computer, which sat on a small desk under a sign marked "For Public Use Only," next to a bank of windows and right across from a woman wearing a federal identification badge that dangled back and forth as she flitted from one end of her workstation to the other. Moments later the words "No entries" popped up on the screen. Next, Grace, anticipating the same results, typed in the search words, "Victoria Pierce." Almost immediately, the computer screen responds with "Unavailable, File Destroyed."

"Whoa, what does that mean?"

After entering many variations of her search words with the same results, Grace, frustrated, asked the woman with the unreadable name on her identification badge for some clarification.

"What does 'File Destroyed' mean?"

The women appeared to have either not heard Grace's question or has become desensitized to this particular inquiry from someone she believed should know the answer before asking such a stupid question.

Exhaling with displeasure, the woman responded, "It means the file was destroyed in the Murrah Building explosion."

Grace vaguely remembered the fertilizer blast that destroyed the courthouse in Oklahoma City. But, then, she was a naïve adolescent at the time.

"Oh, yes, of course. Can you get a copy of a file like that, somewhere else, perhaps a microfiche file or something like that?"

"No."

"Well, let me ask you another question on another topic. Do you happen to know a federal marshal by the name of William S. Slaughter?"

"No. Check with someone down the hall at the marshals' office." As she replied, the woman, ID dangling more pronounced now than before, escaped to the other side of her workstation to avoid any more of Grace's questions.

An older man in a neatly pressed uniform strode in between Grace and this less than helpful woman, and interrupted with a smile, "Did you say, 'William Slaughter'?"

The man proceeds before Grace can reaffirm her question. "I remember Bill Slaughter. Had just a great reputation around here as a marshal, kinda like a folk hero, you might say. Retired now about twenty-five years. Remember he used to come back for some of his buddies' retirement parties. Guess all of them must be gone, too, cause haven't seen Bill around here in quite a while. He must be damned near ninety years old by now."

"Do you know how I might reach him?"

"Not for sure, but everyone around here knows he hangs out mornings in a saloon not far from here. I even joined him there a time or two. Bill loves a draft beer better than almost anyone, but he's probably too old for that now."

"What's the name of this saloon?"

"Let's see . . . see if I can remember. Oh yeah, the Crazy Horse, a cowboy bar about three blocks out the front door, down Main Street. Take a right on . . . damn, what's the name of that street? Then one block . . . can't remember that little street. Here, I'll show you out the window."

Grace and the marshal looked out and down from the bank of windows over the Oklahoma City skyline. Pointing with his finger mashed against the window, "See that tall, adobe-brick-looking building? It's right next to it . . . can't miss it. Oh, Bill's got a big ol' tattoo about right here." The man then pointed to a place on his own forearm.

Grace had no real expectation of finding retired ninety-year-old William S. Slaughter right before high noon in the Crazy Horse Saloon, sipping his favorite draft beer, but Grace had learned to never give up on either a lead or her intuition. Besides, she might have found someone there who knew where he lived, so she thanked the kind man in the crisply pressed uniform who helped her, but offered not a word of thanks to the woman with the dangling ID, who did not. Grace dashed out the front entrance of the courthouse for the short walk down Main Street, three blocks, to the cowboy bar next to the tall adobe-brick-looking building, where she found inside a white-haired man, sitting on a bar stool, matching perfectly the description of Marshal Slaughter.

I hit the jackpot, yesiree, hit the damn jackpot, Grace exclaimed to herself as she approached the man sitting at the bar. "You wouldn't be retired federal marshal Bill Slaughter, would you?"

As he lifted his right hand to cup his ear, Grace unmistakably noticed his forearm inscribed with the word, "Mother," in the middle of a faded tattoo with a heart shot through by a feathered arrow. "I'm sorry, Little Filly, didn't hear a damned word. If you're talkin' to me, you'll have to speak up."

Already knowing the answer to her question before she asked it again, Grace, excited, leaned over to Marshal Slaughter's cupped ear and yelled, "Are you Marshal Slaughter?"

"Good Lord, I ain't that deaf!" Bill Slaughter pulled back, reached into his pocket, dragged out his hearing aid from his upper shirt pocket, and slid it into his ear. "Who wants to know?"

"Marshal Slaughter, I'm Grace Brandon, a reporter from the *New York Times*, here doing a feature article on the life of Victoria Pierce." She extended a handshake into the thin air between the two, which was rebuffed with the revelation that she was both a reporter and someone from New York.

"Know who?"

"Victoria Pierce. She's a brigadier general in the Marine Corps, but grew up in Iowa County north of Lawton. Do you know her?"

"Can't say that I do. Why would I know her?" Slaughter turned back to the bar, held up his thick glass mug, and pointed it at the bartender before sliding it the exact length separating the two, a routine learned from years of experience. "Do you drink beer?"

Grace drank beer but never at this time of day, so she just shook her head, waiting for her answer.

"Sometimes I put egg in my beer in the morning and call it breakfast," he chuckled. The bartender jerked a draft beer into a clean mug, perfectly sliding it down the bar in front of his old customer, some of the head spilling down the side of the glass along its short journey.

"I'll get right to the point, Marshal Slaughter. I found an envelope, postmarked September 30, 1980, with your return address on it."

"Let's see, that would be twenty-eight years ago? You're asking me about a letter I mailed to someone twenty-eight years ago? Mailed a heck of a lot of letters in my time with the government, Little Filly. Got the letter?"

"Well, not exactly." Grace pulled the envelope from her purse. For the first time, she saw the words on the envelope marked, "Official Business, Addressee Only, Open Under Penalty of Law" and handed it to Slaughter.

Slaughter reached into his other pocket, lifted out his bifocals, put them on, and looked at the envelope. Grace observed a faint glint of recognition in the retired marshal's eyes when he read the name, "Ezekiel Pierce."

"What do you mean, 'not exactly'? Either you got a letter or you don't." Slaughter then mused out loud, "I'll be damned, a Marine Corps general . . . bound to be a pretty damned ornery woman."

"Does the name 'Vera' mean anything to you?"

"Don't recognize the name, Vera Pierce." Slaughter turned his mug up and gulped down about half of its contents.

"No, not Vera, Victoria. Her name is Victoria Pierce."

"Well, this is already confusing enough for a man almost ninety years old. Which is it, Victoria or Vera?"

"Look, here's a picture of her as she looks today." Grace unfolded a glossy campaign photograph that she pulled from her purse and handed it to Slaughter. Instantly now, Slaughter recognized Victoria as the eighteen-year-old Vera and all the work he had done to conceal her identity under the U.S. Witness Protection Program. Yes, he remembered. How could he forget? Just like Mr. Margolis, Slaughter also never forgot the face of a pretty woman. Slaughter had never worked a more confidential or sensitive case and would also never—even under the threat of death—compromise the identity of anyone in the Witness Protection Program and, for sure, never casually discuss such a topic in a saloon with a total stranger from New York, a reporter no less.

"Don't know her," Slaughter lied, as his beer glass shook, slightly, as he tried to drain its contents.

"Brigadier General Pierce is about to become the vice president of the United States. Do you want that to happen, Marshal Slaughter?"

Slaughter's nervousness turned to anger. "I don't give a rat's ass about politics. She can become president of the United States, the United Nations, or the whole damned world, for all I care. What I'm not going to do is talk to you any longer, so you can just skedaddle."

"You know something. Tell me what you know, Marshal. It's important to your country."

"I fought for this country as a Marine in both WWII and Korea. Don't preach to me about what I owe my country." Slaughter's voice rose and caught the attention of the bartender.

"Another draft, Bill?"

"Sure thing." Slaughter slammed his empty mug on the bar and slid it toward the bartender, who filled up another clean mug and slid it back.

"Don't you agree, Marshal, that your country needs to know who the real Victoria Pierce is before she becomes vice president of the United States?"

"Look, if the Nazi SS couldn't pry secret information out of me," he lifted and pointed to a deformed left index finger and nail, "a Little Filly reporter, the likes of you, for damned sure is not going to get me to talk about something I don't want to talk about, especially from a man who, practically speaking, is all but ninety years old, and I got very little to lose, so you better just head on out of here the way you came in." Slaughter pointed to the double swinging doors in the front of the saloon.

"Look, Marshal Slaughter, obviously there's some big secret here that you won't tell me about, but you fought in those wars to protect my right, the right of a free press, to ask you these questions."

Slaughter did not expect the truth to be so tightly wrapped up in Grace's answer. He calmed down a bit. "Look, Miss—you did say 'Brandon'?"

"Yes, Grace Brandon."

Slaughter paused, rubbing his temple. "We've both said quite enough already, probably too much. I'm going to walk to the bathroom, and after finishing my business, out the back door. I've still got a wife who loves me, a slew of grown children, a passel of grandchildren, and the cutest great-grandbaby you've ever seen. Who knows, some day, I might even have a great-great-grandchild before the Lord's finished with me. I'm done with my duty to this country. My country now owes it to me to live out my last days in peace. If you won't go away, then I will."

With that, Marshal Slaughter guzzled down his last draft beer of the day, slid off his stool, raised up to his full length, threw out his chest, peeled off a ten-dollar bill, placed it under his glass of beer, pointed to make sure the bartender saw it, and wobbled as he walked back to the bathroom. Without looking back, he thought to himself, *Just can't be the same.* And then he said out loud, "Go back to the bright lights, where you came from, Little Filly. The answer's right under your prying nose, but it ain't here in Oklahoma City.

And by the way, if I ever see you here again, I'll have you locked up for tampering with official U.S. government mail!"

Before driving away to the Sunset Rest Home, Victoria meticulously recorded everything Slaughter said in her reporter's notebook just in case she broke this story.

* * *

Victoria would have preferred to bury Lucinda in a pine box behind the Sunset Rest Home, but Tom had different plans because the campaign needed the publicity and not just because it was free. He would have given Lucinda a twenty-one-gun salute in Arlington Cemetery with military planes flying over in formation, but Lucinda did not qualify. Tom could never be accused of staging the death of his vice presidential candidate's mother the day after the press conference in Oklahoma City, but he knew how to milk a political funeral for all its worth. The unfabricated good fortune of Lucinda's timely demise presented the perfect opportunity to drive home his candidate's message from yesterday's press conference.

Tom had his back turned on the manager inside his office at the Sunset Rest Home, talking to Sam on his cell phone and explaining the good news.

"Believe me, Sam, the media will seize on the connection between Lucinda's death and the campaign's health-care message, reinforcing why, only yesterday, you visited Oklahoma City in the first place. Look, the press conference was effective, but has, as we expected, not reached a large audience because it was too short-lived to saturate the targeted market in any significant way." Tom stopped talking and listened.

"No, you don't have to be here. Lucinda's funeral will visually link the health-care message with her death in a very personal way, expand the coverage to further reach the targeted group, and legitimately permit Victoria, while dabbing her tearful eyes with her handkerchief, to tie in her mother's funeral with the health-care issue."

"Can't say I've ever heard Victoria cry," Sam's muffled voice could be heard through the receiver.

Tom said to the manager who was too close to the conversation, "Please excuse us for a minute?" The manager nodded and left his office.

"Listen, Sam, to maximize the press coverage, all free to the campaign, Victoria's grief for her mother, practiced in front of a mirror if she has to, will begin tonight at the visitation inside the Sunset Rest Home. I can fill up the rest home with employees, paid overtime if necessary, roll the residents out in their wheelchairs, and summon all our available campaign staffers to serve as mourners. I can draw it out all day, Sam, long enough to keep the cable markets tuned in from early morning to early evening."

Tom listened again, then replied, "I know it's going to be hot as hell tomorrow, but from what I've learned from this file, looks like the ol' bitch is heading down instead of up, if you ask me."

Victoria walked in on the conversation. Tom turned around and said, "Victoria, the funeral is legitimate news, fortuitous but not fabricated." Tom struck preemptively to avoid Victoria's normal aversion to his contrived pretensions. "Lucinda's funeral can help draw coverage away from our opponents' convention in Miami, the very day they are rolling out their heavy entertainment guns to make their most important policy speeches."

"Tom, is anything sacred to you?" Victoria questioned.

"Yeah, winning is sacred to me! And you better get on board with this funeral just the way I am going to script it."

Tom would have nothing to do with quietly burying Lucinda in a pine box behind the Sunset Rest Home. No,

Lucinda would be buried with the flare of royalty or as close as Tom could get to it, given what they had to work with in Oklahoma City on such short notice.

Standing beside Lucinda's open casket inside the rest home surrounded by mountains of flowers the night before and at the graveside burial late the next afternoon, Victoria believably grieved for the cameras. She spoke passionately about her mother's courageous battle with Alzheimer's disease in interview after interview, always dabbing her eyes with a laced monogrammed handkerchief, supplied for that purpose by Tom. Grace was not sure how the redness around Victoria's green eyes spontaneously appeared. Perhaps it was professionally applied makeup or the aftereffects of a harsh mouthwash gargled intentionally too long from the travel-sized bottle tucked neatly in Victoria's purse, because up close Grace detected a counterfeited grief. The one-hour graveside service was preceded by an hour-and-a-half-long church service, complete with a eulogy delivered by Victoria, in spite of her breaking down, overwhelmed emotionally at several junctures during the delivery of prepared remarks that were laced with whimsical irony. "Yes, my mother died last night in the very place that Senator Eagan spoke so passionately about the need for Americans to face the challenges of these protracted end-of-life diseases." Victoria employed the same campaign rhetoric that she used two days before, except this time she mastered the technique of speaking directly to a greatly expanded television audience. How could Victoria feign such grief? Grace surmised that Victoria, the general, was a master at diversion, because Tom's objectives were met through Lucinda's choreographed funeral. America tuned into Lucinda's funeral and tuned out their opponent's Miami convention.

Grace watched Victoria's Academy Award–winning performance, acting perfectly the part of the grieving daughter, and concluded that Victoria's heartless pretension to mourn a mother whom she never had was a despicable campaign ploy.

At that moment, Grace realized that her personal attachment to Victoria no longer mattered. For weeks, her intuition called into question Victoria's authenticity. Now it was more than intuition. But the hard evidence was lodged in a past obliterated in a file blown to kingdom come by a massive fertilizer bomb with only a trace of a clue left behind in a public computer and in the memory of a man approaching ninety years old, whose only tangible connection to Victoria was preserved in the bold print of a return address on a government envelope. Grace's intuition told her that Victoria had something to hide, but her intuition was not enough to discredit a brigadier general who heroically rose through the enlisted ranks to commander, and then to her party's vice presidential nomination, not to mention a woman whom she called "friend" who had swept Grace from journalism purgatory to journalism stardom and whom Grace greatly admired for her persistence, right from their first encounter the day they walked together up Seventh Avenue to Central Park. Even if her intuition was true, Grace would barely have enough facts to convince her editors to pursue an investigative story. What she did not want to have to explain was why she was in Lucinda's bedroom listening to her dying exclamation minutes before her death. She would have to have more, but if her suspicions could be substantiated, friend or no friend, it was her duty to see that the truth was published despite the dire consequences for Sam Eagan's long-awaited run for president that would all but coronate his challenger, if his vice presidential nominee proved to be a fictitious person.

* * *

"What did Slaughter say?"

Sitting beside Grace in the middle seat—not his choice but hers—at twenty thousand feet over farmland as far below as the eye could see on their flight back to LaGuardia, Lennie said, "Are you asking me a question?"

Grace said, "Of course not. That would mean that I would be talking to you, which I am not and probably will never again. It was like a Shakespearean-like rhetorical question. I'm not sure that a photojournalist like you would know the meaning of 'rhetorical.' It means I'm not looking for an an—"

"—answer." Lennie finished Grace's sentence. "I know what it means."

Flipping open her reporter's pad and checking her unconventional shorthand that looked something like primitive stick drawings on a cave wall, Grace tried to figure out exactly what Slaughter had said.

"'Go back to the bright lights, where you came from, Little Filly. The answer's right under your prying nose, but it ain't here in Oklahoma City.'"

"Are you 'Little Filly'?"

"Shut up. Do you have Victoria's campaign schedule next week?"

"You can't have it both ways—ignoring and talking to me at the same time."

Lennie handed Grace the itinerary, produced from his carry-on luggage secured underneath the seat in front of him.

Grace silently reviewed Victoria's schedule. Next week, Victoria returned to the Empire State for a series of chicken luncheon speeches stretching from Albany to New York City. It was Grace's perfect opportunity to follow up and supplement her one verifiable source. Mr. Margolis, by now, might have remembered the last name of the beautiful mother tugging along a pretty little girl with the first name of Vera.

* * *

"I have a hunch, Mr. Margolis, and I need to talk with you."

"What will it be this morning, Ace?"

Grace sighed, frowned, and ignored the shortened reference to her real name, but realized that this nickname would stick with her for the rest of her natural life, so she might as well get used to it.

"Nothing but a little conversation in private, Mr. Margolis. I need to speak with you not as a customer but as a reporter."

Gus Margolis looked across his deli shop at all the customers lined up trying to snap up something to eat before crowding into their skyscrapers. Mr. Margolis thought that this was not the time to discuss a reporter's hunch, unless, of course, Grace was working on his retirement story.

"Frankie, take over for a minute. I'll be right back."

"Hurry back, Papa. It's a zoo in here this morning!"

Mr. Margolis motioned to Grace to follow him back into his small office. They walked down a narrow hallway filled with white corrugated produce boxes through a kitchen saturated with the pungent odor of seafood cooking, where Latino workers wearing white aprons furiously scurried back and forth between preparation areas and the walk-in coolers, trying to keep ahead of this morning's specialty orders. Finally, the two passed through the kitchen, littered with obstacles in cluttered disarray, down another narrow hallway, similar to the first, back into an office overflowing with stacks of invoices scattered across a metal desk. Mr. Margolis walked behind his desk and sat down on a wooden chair that allowed him to tilt backward, aided by a squeaking spring. Grace sat in a straight-backed chair in front of the desk. But before Ace could ask her question, Mr. Margolis said, "Been almost sixty years in this business. We've made a decent living here for me and my family, but it's time for me to move on." It took Grace a minute to realize that Gus was not making small talk as she recalled his suggestion that she should feature him in a retirement piece. "Oh, my God, your retirement, of course."

Grace went along, pretending to take notes on her pad and asking a few perfunctory questions, like, "What led you to leave Italy and come to America?"

"I was but a bambino. My family had to flee Mussolini and the fascist government."

Grace was barely listening to or recording his answers on her pad because she wanted to conclude the charade and move Gus along to her real question. Her interviewee, however, was going on in endless detail.

"If it were not for Frankie coming into the business at such a young age, I would have never survived here."

Grace scribbled and daydreamed.

"The recipe for the crab and lobster seafood salad came from my blessed mother." Gus crossed himself because he still grieved for her, thirty years after her death. "Not real sure where she got it . . ."

Grace faded further into the design of her question. "Mr. Margolis, I know your time is valuable this morning, and you need to get back to your customers, so let's break our story into two interviews, and I'll come back in when you're not so busy."

Grace pretended to get up, sat back down, and sprang her question as she rose again. "Oh, that pretty woman who used to come in years ago, that looks so much like General Pierce. Did you ever remember her last name?"

Slightly startled at the change of subject, Mr. Margolis responded without hesitation. "I have tried to remember that woman but just cannot. Sometimes her name is almost there."

"Was the little girl's name Vera?"

"Vera . . . Vera . . . let's see. You know, I think it was. How would you know that?"

"Can you be sure?"

"Not really. It was such a long time ago, but she used to ask for specialty orders. Always wanted to negotiate my prices, and I always gave in. I had a real soft spot for that woman. Maybe her last name will come to me now. You know, better yet, let me check my old invoices. You know, I got audited years ago by those bastards at the IRS. Didn't have all of my invoices, so they tagged me with back taxes. Never threw anything away since. I've got thousands of receipts in storage boxes at the house. Maybe I can check there, if it's important to our story, and get back to you when we go on . . . you know, go on with my life's story. OK?

"I'll be back Tuesday morning."

"No, make it Tuesday afternoon, around six. We can avoid the morning rush."

* * *

Late Tuesday morning in a hotel parking lot, visible from the interstate outside of Albany, cars lined up, double parked for miles, to glimpse political heroine and celebrity General Pierce on her way inside to make a luncheon speech that cost a five-hundred-dollar minimum, a bargain in comparison to the five-thousand-dollar dinner speeches that Sam routinely commanded. For five hundred dollars, the patron received a barely palatable luncheon, consisting of a limp lettuce salad appetizer, a chicken-vegetable casserole entrée, and white pudding-dessert-cake, followed by a canned political speech designed to infuriate supporters with an exposé of their opponents' ill-conceived and weak policies. Then came a postluncheon photo with the candidate, later mailed for an additional credit card charge of one hundred dollars, designated as a "shipping and handling fee," well worth the coffee table memento, commemorating the patron's wisdom as an early campaign supporter in case of victory, but likely never to be seen outside of an attic trunk in the event of defeat. The campaign collected the contributor's name for an e-mail list of supporters, for a last-minute desperation plea for additional contributions in the weeks before Election Day to carry the team to victory and an e-mail list later to be sold and resold to philosophically related political action committees, a source of junk e-mail for years to come. Unsuspecting contributors had little idea of the extent their names were collected and resold based upon a one-time emotional response to their candidate.

Grace was thunderstruck at the sheer number of candidate gawkers who lined the sidewalks, sometimes five deep, over a half-mile path leading to the hotel. They were not even sure that General Pierce's limo would pass along this route on the way to the hotel's entrance.

Her black limo arrived and rolled along to cheers, waves, and whistles. Finally, the candidate stepped out well in advance of her destination to mingle among and shake hands with her admirers.

Grace blended, camouflaged, into the sidewalk crowd, concealed behind Lennie, her, once again, jaded photographer. As had become her standard practice, Grace grasped his sleeve with her left hand, knowing his uncanny ability to absent himself at the most inopportune times. Victoria approached a forty-something woman right in front of Grace.

"Good morning. Thank you for coming out today. This is an important election and we need your vote and the vote of your friends. . . ."

As she turned to extend her hand to the next well-wisher, Grace summoned all the courage she could muster and proclaimed in her best Brooklyn accent, "Vera, is that really you?"

Victoria stopped frozen, turned to verify the source of the inquiry as if she were responding to an ambush by an enemy combatant. She recognized Grace and smiled.

"What did you say?"

Grace knew she had crossed a line. There was no turning back now, so she went straight to her trump card.

"General Pierce, last week in an interview with your mother in Oklahoma City, she referred to you as 'Vera'? Why would she do that?"

Victoria's visage drained to white as if she had all of the blood drawn from her face, but then the color returned to a flushed red.

"You mean to tell me that you interviewed my mother, a dying Alzheimer's patient, without my permission? For what purpose? To torture her memory, a memory long since disintegrated? How dare you!"

Victoria turned to her campaign aide.

"Her name is Grace Brandon. She's a reporter for the *New York Times* and a former friend. File a formal complaint with her editors for violating the federal HIPAA Act and violating my dying mother's right to privacy. I want a full report by tonight! I'll accept nothing less than a complete apology, or tell them at the *Times* they can expect an immediate lawsuit!"

Grace recoiled first from the blistering speed of Victoria's counterattack, placing a wet-behind-the-ears reporter, masking as a seasoned one, completely on the defensive, while simultaneously avoiding a response to her direct question. Next, Grace recoiled from the second prong of the counterattack, Victoria's characterization of Grace as her "former friend." Grace immediately realized her high-stakes gamble had forever lost a coveted friendship, not to mention that by press time, at the very latest, she would be called on the carpet by her editors. There she would try to explain her unverifiable hunch about Victoria's false identity that inevitably would force Grace to reveal exactly what she was doing in Lucinda's room, seconds before her death, asking this advanced Alzheimer's patient—by definition, one who has no memory—about the adolescent history of her only daughter, which ended in a one-word dying exclamation, "Vera."

In the face of Victoria's blistering counter attack, Grace retreated or at least tried to, but she could not get Lennie to budge. This time he was going to earn his title of photographer. Lennie obsessively memorialized every imaginable detail of Grace's defeat. Grace finally grabbed Lennie from behind by his camera straps and dragged him backward off the sidewalk like a wounded soldier.

Secure in the front seat of the car, Grace said, "I want all of those pictures."

"Well, you can't have them!"

"I'm dead meat already, so if I have to kill you to get those pictures, it will matter little to me right now!" Grace thought aloud as she spoke to Lennie. "My only way out is to establish by an independent, competent, and reliable source that Victoria Pierce is in fact Vera 'Somebody.' Seven p.m. is my drop-dead deadline conference with my editors. My one hope for stopping the change of my new nickname from 'Ace' to 'Disgrace' is to keep my late-afternoon appointment with Gus Margolis."

"You know, Ace, I like the sound of 'Disgrace.' Sounds more like you," Lennie chided.

"Margolis all but told me he remembered Vera as the daughter of the beautiful woman whose face he could never forget, but her name escapes him. He's got the answer. It's just a question of prying the name out of his fading memory and preserving my journalistic reputation by publishing Victoria's true identity."

"How are you going to get the ol' guy to cough up the name before seven o'clock?"

"Don't know, but he's all I got."

"Well, I have some film to develop. Maybe I'll accidentally turn on the overhead light while I'm developing. Good luck with Margolis."

* * *

At five minutes to six, Grace approached the Seventh Avenue seafood deli, ready for her answer and a seafood salad, but the lights were off and the door was locked. A torn-square white corrugated sign hung inside the window. "Deli closed for owner's funeral." Grace began to read the long obituary that traced Mr. Margolis's roots back to Italy. He died at the hands of a hit-and-run driver near his Brooklyn home, a mere two hours after their interview. The time to ask questions of the living is when they are alive.

Grace forgot herself for the moment and mourned the man who had such a spirit for life. But she knew, too, that with his death, her journalistic career was all but finished. Grace continued to read as if in a daydream. Gus Margolis got his retirement story, pretty much written how he wanted, but lamentably not through the well-chosen words of Grace's nostalgic feature about a first-generation father passing his established deli business onto his second-generation son, but rather preserved in the inartful words of an Italian funeral home director printed in a paid obituary.

Somewhere between the pit of her stomach and the lump in her throat, the phrase, "Shit, what now?" was the only expression that Grace, a professional journalist, could articulate to describe her present reality. Grace stood as motionless as a bronze statue staring into the window, reading, rereading, yet not believing the enlarged printer's ink of Augustus Aristarchus Margolis Sr.'s obituary.

About three hours later, Victoria, Grace's former friend, stared also into a glass, but this was the reflective glass of her bathroom mirror at campaign headquarters in Lower Manhattan. Her open tube of lipstick beside the sink had been used like a Magic Marker to write a bright red message on the mirror.

"Two down, VERA! How many more?"

CHAPTER FIFTEEN

April 1981

Victoria felt incrementally liberated, measured by each mile that the big rig put between herself and the Pierce Farm. After her escape from Lucinda, with a good deal of help from Sarge, Victoria's intelligence and resourcefulness would have to devise a second escape from her newly acquired truck-driving companion, who apparently had a misimpression about her promiscuity. After perfunctory conversation with the thin young man, who had a pack of cigarettes curled tightly up in the right sleeve of his white T-shirt, Victoria pretended to doze in the front seat of the cab. But before planning the fine points of her second escape of the day, she first wanted to revel in the precisioned execution of her first escape that won her freedom from permanent confinement on the Pierce Farm.

Involuntary servitude fueled a desperation to escape, and the linchpin for escape demanded mastery of the Oklahoma High School Equivalency Exam. At first, it was a simple matter of studying for the allotted hour before breakfast in her bedroom and surreptitiously at other times throughout the day when she could slip the materials past Lucinda's prying eyes. Extra study time became progressively more difficult. Victoria desperately wanted to leave the farm, and this desperation led to a carelessness that played right into Lucinda's well-laid traps.

It was a game of cat and mouse, and Lucinda, the cat, knew the game better than Victoria, the mouse. The stakes were high for the cat. The mouse provided free farm labor at a minimum of twelve hours per day at a thirty-four-hundred-dollar monthly stipend. Installments deposited at a 10 percent annual compounded interest rate would mature into a half million dollars in a little over ten years, but only if Victoria remained a captive. To lose such a bankroll to a high school equivalency test was senseless. Besides, to Lucinda's way of thinking, what was the use of a high school diploma when "Daughter" and her future husband would jointly inherit the profitable Pierce Farm at the death of her adopted parents, an eventuality preceded by a husband to be ensnared through an arranged marriage, just as Lucinda's parents had ensnared Ezekiel and claimed a sizeable dowry in the deal? Victoria over time would come to realize the wisdom of living out her life in purity on the farm, but until such wisdom arrived at the terminus of a natural and mature progression, she simply would have to remain a captive.

The obviousness of Victoria's plan to escape through high school graduation led Lucinda to confiscate all her study materials—everything from Geometry to American History—eliminate the one hour of morning study, and extend Victoria's workday into the late evening for canning vegetables and curing hams as punishment for her direct disobedience. All that remained of Victoria's contact with the outside world, besides thumbing through the mail-order catalogs in the outhouse, was her daily conversations with Jan Flowers.

Lucinda underestimated two things about Victoria, however: her intelligence and her resourcefulness. Early on, Victoria's intelligence unraveled Lucinda's scheme to block her one avenue of escape, so she memorized the address for the Oklahoma Department of Education right before her materials were stolen. Victoria's resourcefulness spawned a well-crafted plan that involved her one independent variable, Jan Flowers. Jan sold stamped envelopes out of her mailbag, to which Victoria simply inscribed the correctly memorized address. In the short course of four business days, by return mail, Victoria possessed the complete Oklahoma High School Equivalency Exam. What she did not possess was the confidence to take the exam without reference to the preparatory study materials.

It was only a matter of time before Lucinda inevitably would root through every nook and cranny of Victoria's bedroom, discovering the standardized test and then raiding the contents of her most obscure hiding places. Victoria had to find a foolproof hiding place and create a diversion. She began by convincing Lucinda of a dual epiphany, the first, a come-to-Jesus religious conversion, and the other, a discovery of the real meaning of life found only in the daily routine on the farm, the latter discovery delayed only by her slowness to embrace a fourteen-hour workday. This was a tough act for Victoria because no matter how hard she tried, Victoria's face revealed just how much she really detested work on the farm. Nevertheless, she cooperated with her captors in their every directive.

In the meantime, Victoria settled on a hiding place. She secreted the exam in the dark rafters of the outhouse, far above and out of Lucinda's sight and reach. She cautiously answered the test questions each day on her fifteen-minute twice-daily bathroom break. She dared not extend beyond fifteen minutes per visit, as it would inevitably draw Lucinda's attention to her routine. Just enough light filtered through the slit left by the half moon carved through the outhouse door to quickly pencil in the answers to the multiple-choice questions and to write in cursive her response to the English Literature essay question. She watched for Lucinda by peeping out through the half moon, knowing that Lucinda avoided the outhouse out of an acute phobia for snakes, a few actual bites, all of which strictly limited Lucinda's visits to normally one per day with a hurried exit. Ezekiel's business occupied even less time than Lucinda's. Victoria's only time for complete solitude was there amid the stifling smell of the outhouse. As fall turned to winter and winter to spring, the exam was finally completed to Victoria's satisfaction. Besides, Lucinda was becoming suspicious of her lengthening visits to the outhouse to complete the final segments of the exam. Victoria had no confidence that she would pass, particularly Geometry, but she would not return the exam for grading until she had given it her best shot—in fact, her only shot. Pass the test and legally escape, as discovery was a certainty, or live out Lucinda's self-fulfilling prophecy on the Pierce Farm.

On April Fools Day, 1981, Victoria summoned the courage to hand the test back to Jan in the return envelope, but addressed in care of Marshal William S. Slaughter, United States Marshal, Murrah Federal Court Building, Oklahoma City, Oklahoma, with a note to Marshal Slaughter that she had taken the test honestly, according to instructions, and that he would have to see to it that it was properly delivered. She also extracted from Jan an oath to tell no one about her experiment and more importantly making her swear to the sufficiency of the return postage. Jan swore to both. In three weeks, again by return mail, Jan handed Victoria a brown envelope marked, "State of Oklahoma Equivalency Test Results," in bright red letters. A full day passed before Victoria could muster the courage to open the letter, but finally she could wait no longer.

"Yee-ha and whoopdeedamneddo!" Victoria could not repress the spontaneous eruption of her newly acquired country vernacular screamed at midday through the outhouse half-moon. Sarge, resting on the front porch, was the only one to seem to notice as his ears rose up and curved slightly toward the direction of the outhouse. Victoria passed the Oklahoma Equivalency Test at the ninety-ninth percentile, an astounding accomplishment given that she had not a shred of study materials.

The time had come to permanently depart the Pierce Farm, but how? Victoria contemplated the break for days, but rejected any attempt at an in-person and honest disclosure in a sit-down with the Pierces. She decided upon a note hidden under her pillow and a breakaway at the midday mail chore. She would leave her suitcases behind and carry only the file full of documents that Marshal Slaughter had meticulously prepared. She gladly exchanged her worldly possessions for permanent freedom.

The difficulty for her came in her farewell to her one genuine friend on the farm: Sarge. Victoria did not realize the depth of her feelings for her canine companion that grew from the hourlong daily trek for the mail. Sarge listened, much like a therapist, to Victoria's angry feelings about herself and the farm. Often, Victoria would say to Sarge, "Can you really believe that?" and then add, "Well, neither can I." Sarge, along the way, also became quite protective of Victoria, a characteristic made more difficult in Sarge's absolute refusal to stay at the house on Victoria's final escape to freedom.

One flaw in Victoria's plan on the day of her escape led to a near disaster. On the outhouse floor, Lucinda had discovered the carelessly dropped pencil that Victoria had used to complete her test. Lucinda's calculating mind could not determine its origin. A quick exit from the outhouse to

Victoria's bedroom produced Victoria's note and the answer to her question. Lucinda's worst financial fear came to full realization, exacerbated by Victoria's candor at her expression of genuine displeasure for life on the farm, moderated only slightly by a feigned gratitude for the sacrifices of her adopted parents. One point was made abundantly clear: Victoria had earned Oklahoma's GED and had now fulfilled the contractual requirements for her release from her mandatory confinement. If the Pierces wished to verify the results, they could contact the Oklahoma Department of Education and then check with Marshal Slaughter about the details for the discharge of her contractual obligations.

A dip in the road brought Victoria back to her present dilemma, but in her silence she also had time to devise a second plan of escape. She would spellbind her driver with a protracted yarn of her tortured youth, growing up into a young woman on the Pierce farm amid the horrific abuses that she suffered at the hands of her adopted uncle.

"Well, before you sleep all the way to San Francisco, might want to tell me your name. Got a name, don't you?"

"Yeah, I got a name. But tell me yours first."

"OK, I'm Charlie Sorrell." Charlie extended his right arm sideways, and Victoria shook his hand. At the bottom of the handshake, Victoria said, "My name's Victoria . . . Pierce."

"What's a pretty girl like you doing out hitchhiking?"

"Runnin' away."

"From what?"

"My uncle Joe, the meanest man alive."

"What makes him so mean?"

"Can't tell you. Ain't safe for you to know too much . . . but I am lookin' for a boyfriend or a husband."

"Well, a pretty girl like you won't have any trouble." Charlie liked the direction the conversation was going.

"You see, my Uncle Joe—really he was my step-uncle, my momma's older brother, but they weren't kin or nothin' like that because Uncle Joe belonged to my stepfather. Anyway he took Momma, me, and my sister to raise after we had to run away from my stepfather. Momma's gone now."

"How old were you . . . ?"

"When Momma died? Can't just say she died, but she was shot when I was thirteen. My older sister, Jess, was fourteen."

"What happened?"

"Momma wouldn't marry Uncle Joe after we ran away from my stepfather to live on Uncle Joe's farm. That's where you picked me up back there. After we had all been with Uncle Joe for 'bout a year, Momma tried to move us all out so Uncle Joe shot Momma dead just before we could get away."

"Did he go to prison?"

"No one seemed to notice that Momma had died. But after that Jess became, let's say, his girlfriend, but she really hated Uncle Joe. We all did, really, so when Jess became legally old enough to get married, she ran away with her boyfriend. Last year it was."

"Why don't you go live with her?"

"She's dead. Uncle Joe shot her and her husband. Took him almost a week to find 'em. Said he shot 'em both in bed while they was sleepin'. Weren't long after that Uncle Joe started lookin' to me to be his girlfriend. So I had to run away but knowed he'd just chase after me like he did Jess. Thought I better shoot him before he shot me."

"Did you kill him?"

"No, couldn't do that. Good Book said that would be a sin. So I shot him in the foot this morning. Slowed him down quite a bit. He was pretty mad at me about doing that. Said he'd get me. By the way, you ain't married or got a girlfriend or nothin' like that, do you?"

The young truck driver never answered that question. Silence blanketed the inside of the cab. Charlie Sorrell drove well beyond the posted speed limit and arrived in San Francisco three hours ahead of schedule.

By the time Victoria stepped down from the big rig, with her full farm-girl figure silhouetted in the background of San Francisco's skyscrapers, the driver hardly knew what to say, so he peeled off a twenty from a roll of bills in his T-shirt pocket and threw it out of the cab, where it landed on the ground beside Victoria. Victoria picked up the bill before it could blow away in the wind from off the Bay.

"Promise me you won't ever tell your Uncle Joe that I picked you up?" But by the time Victoria winked and pantomimed her promise, Charlie Sorrell had slammed the door and strained his Peterbilt diesel engine so quickly through its lower gears that Victoria doubted that he ever heard her make that promise.

After congratulating herself on successfully accomplishing her second escape within a twenty-four-hour day, Victoria turned her immediate attention more seriously to the matter at hand: survival in the big city of San Francisco.

Soon finding her way to Chinatown, Victoria landed the first honest paying job of her life as a dishwasher in a Cantonese restaurant. The wage was far below minimum but provided the immediate benefit of unlimited trips through the buffet line after closing hours. Victoria delighted in this cuisine when she dined with her father in New York City's best Chinese restaurants. She had all but forgotten about Cantonese entrees, totally absent from the menu at the Pierce Farm.

Victoria could not recall ever tasting anything better than the remnants of the hot and sour duck left behind on the buffet after midnight when the restaurant closed. Fortunately, life on the Pierce Farm trained her for long hours and hard work. What proved to be worse than the back sink was her first night alone on the streets of San Francisco after midnight.

To combat the fatigue and cold of her maiden walk along the streets above the Bay, filled with drunken voices propositioning her from the dark of foggy shadows, Victoria took refuge in an all-too-familiar setting: a motorcycle bar, located at a corner intersection in the Embarcadero, next door to a military recruiting office.

But the game for Victoria was survival, and her mentor, Felipe Sanchez, taught her well how to survive on the dark side of a big city. She knew pool tables, biker chains, and illicit drugs. She spoke the biker language, won more than beer change by running successive racks of eight ball, and convinced the gray-haired bartender, somewhat of a father figure with his belly button displayed beneath a bulging beer gut, to allow her to rest the night in a tall pool-hall chair next to the bar.

Spending several nights in the same chair, Victoria was quick to make friends among the patrons, fend off crude biker advances, and participate in the customary drug deals going down inside the premise's bathrooms. Victoria returned night after night to the bar and, after her first cash advance from the restaurant, exchanged her farm clothes for biker leather as well as the hard money of the Cantonese restaurant for the easy money of drug deals. Sleeping during the day in flop motels, she plied her street trade at night mostly through the passenger windows of automobiles owned by rich kids, who stopped momentarily at street corners long enough to exchange money for illegal drugs. Victoria sold quality hashish by the ounce supplied by dealers in the bar who trafficked in pounds of hashish sold to them by the city's major drug cartels.

Four o'clock p.m. was the normal start of business for Victoria. She daily reminded herself of the perils of what she was doing on her late afternoon walks from the filthy motel to the filthy bar to purchase her stock-in-trade for the night. Vera's downfall began at the Wicked Whiskey Bar, followed by a trip through the Manhattan Federal District Court, and ended with incarceration at the Pierce farm. Victoria's spiral downward could end at the bottom if she continued her present profession. She would have to finance, on her own, a major change in direction, but she needed a few more weeks of drug profits to make a financial stake in an honest career. What exactly that was to be, she could not imagine. She had absolutely no qualifications to support a respectable professional career.

Victoria rounded the final corner on her walk down the crowded sidewalk to the corner motorcycle bar. She stopped momentarily in front of the Marine recruiting office and stared through a converted storefront window at a new poster of an attractive woman dressed in green fatigues under the caption, "Join me in the Marine Corps." Victoria saw this woman as out of place in a military uniform, so she turned to continue her walk to her final destination, the bar next door. As she was just about to step away, a SWAT team of San Francisco's finest riot-helmeted cops launched themselves from squad cars with flashing lights and screaming sirens and converged on the bar, each cop blaring commands for patrons to drop to the floor and cracking resisters across the head with foot-long billysticks. Victoria turned back to the face of the woman Marine in the poster and decided this might be the right time to check out her invitation to join the Marine Corps. She disappeared inside and encountered a ruggedly handsome and finely chiseled Marine with a slightly darkened face, reflecting a trace of Cherokee ancestry, who stood up immediately, attention-like, in crisply starched and pressed green fatigues."

"May I help you with some literature on the Marine Corps or answer any questions that you may have?" inquired the Marine, displaying a brightly polished brass name tag just above his shirt pocket, inscribed "First Sergeant Goodheart." Through the storefront window, the sergeant observed cops swarming over the sidewalked street, searching pedestrians with drug-sniffing police dogs. Victoria pretended not to notice the commotion outside and then responded, "I have always been fascinated by men in uniform, but was surprised to see that women can join the Marine Corps."

The first sergeant inspected Victoria's leather attire from head to foot and suspected that there may well be some unresolved issues with the cops outside. "Why yes, the Corps has quite a long tradition of recruiting women Marines or 'WMs' as we call them . . . been going on for years. Why, are you interested in joining up?"

"Not really. What I'm truly interested in is the back door. My car is parked in back," she lied. "Do you have an exit to the back parking lot?"

"I'm sorry," Sergeant Goodheart replied, "I don't believe I caught your name, Miss . . . ?"

"Look, sir, the name's Victoria, but I'm not the Marine Corps type, really. Now if you could just show me the back door, I'll be right out of here and out of your way."

"First, uh, Miss Vicky, don't call me 'sir.' That's reserved for officers. I'm enlisted, just like you're going to be soon. Of course, I could show you out the front door, Miss Vicky. We do not have a back door open to the public. Perhaps you would like to meet one of those cute drug-sniffing dogs and his uniformed trainer?"

Victoria stared blankly at the sergeant, at first not recognizing her name as "Miss Vicky," and then she realized that her time over the next half hour or so would have to center on Marine Corps business inside the recruiting office in order to avoid arrest by dogs sniffing the hashish inside her clothing.

"You know, Sergeant, come to think about it, I do like the image of the new woman in military dress—a certain toughness and respect for the weaker sex." Victoria approached the sergeant, violating the accustomed space separating men and women. "You know how women can be vulnerable to men, don't you, Sergeant?"

The sergeant in a monotone reply completely ignored Victoria's provocation. "Now, we have your first name. Let's see if we can put the first name together with a last name?"

"It's Pierce."

"Let's run your name through our computer for a quick criminal check. No need to go further if it comes up positive for a felony conviction. Give me your Social Security number."

Victoria searched through her purse, attached to her leather pants, pulled out her wallet, and read the number from the card. She remembered how assured Marshal Slaughter was of the authenticity of all of his counterfeit documents. If the check came back "unknown"—or worse, revealed even a felony arrest in Manhattan—jail time in San Francisco was a certainty. A felony arrest for gang-related activities in less than a year after a merciful release into the federal Witness Protection Program from charges stemming from murder and drugs just would not have looked all that good to a sentencing judge.

Sergeant Goodheart stepped away from Victoria into the back room and ran the check on the small green screen government computer, state of the art for 1981. "No Known Criminal Record" popped up on the screen after a ten-minute wait.

Victoria's tanned face turned pale white as the sergeant reentered the reception room and said, "Now, Miss Vicky, your criminal record was clean as a whistle. All we need is a copy of your high school diploma, verification of date of birth, and we can complete the paperwork today. You can walk out of here on the way to Marine Corps basic training."

Victoria exhaled, "Thank God," under her breath, relieved to hear that her criminal record was as clear as Marshal Slaughter expected, but she still balked at the thought of joining the Marine Corps. Victoria checked the front window and decided if she could just make it across the street and down the alley, she would be free of both the cops and this impetuous recruiter. But she needed just a few more minutes.

"It so happens that I have both right here. Drivers license and proof of GED, both official documents issued by the state of Oklahoma." She handed them to the sergeant. He sat down beside Victoria at his desk, reviewed the documents, and began to type out the enlistment forms on a green Selectric typewriter. He stopped periodically to ask clarifying questions. The answers fit nicely in the blank spaces, such as physical dimensions, eye color, and vaccination history. Victoria absentmindedly responded at first that her eye color was "blue," but the sergeant could plainly see her eyes were "green." Victoria corrected herself, "I mean green," in a tone equally disassociated as the sergeant, now more than mildly irritated, continued his questions, each time interrupting Victoria's preoccupation with the spectacle out front. Victoria was monitoring the sidewalk, waiting for any opportunity to bolt. She was still obstructed by squad cars holding her arrested suppliers seated uncomfortably in the backseat with hands cuffed behind them. Victoria paced back and forth like a leopard in a cage.

"Sign here, Miss Vicky, unless you want me to invite inside our canine friends on the sidewalk who appear to still be looking for someone."

Startled in disbelief, Victoria watched Sergeant Goodheart get up from his typewriter and step outside the front door to engage a cop in conversation who appeared to be about to follow his canine through the front door. Victoria thought that her handsome Marine recruiter was going to give her up on the spot. Instead, Victoria watched the recruiter point in the direction of the alley across the street. The cop summoned several of his helmeted comrades, and all of them raced across the street and down the alley in hot pursuit of no one. The sergeant returned.

"That should occupy them for about ten minutes, just long enough for the ink to dry on these enlistment papers and for you to take the oath of allegiance to the United States Constitution and the Marine Corps. If you have not signed by the time they return, I will be forced to introduce you to my new uniformed friends outside."

"Isn't this some sort of blackmail, Sergeant?"

"Call it what you want. Either sign or be arrested."

Victoria, left with zero options, made a four-year commitment to the United States Marine Corps with the stroke of the sergeant's pen, followed swiftly by the administration of the oath while both stood at attention with Victoria holding a black leather Bible.

"You better leave by the back door to the parking lot."

"What back door? I thought you said there was no back door. You know, Sergeant Goodheart—by the way, just how did you get such a name anyway, 'Goodheart,' for God's sake?—I'm beginning to think you're the damned criminal."

"Remember, if you don't show back up here tomorrow I'll have the military police out combing the district for an AWOL recruit. They'll find you, too. May take a few days, a week at the most, and then lock you away in the brig for six months before shipping you off to basic training anyway, so you might as well come back voluntarily tomorrow. Besides, Miss Vicky, what were you saying about how women are vulnerable to men? Dine with me tonight. We'll begin your Marine Corps basic training tonight at my apartment with moves you'll never forget."

Sergeant Goodheart penetrated the vacant space next to Victoria, grabbed her by the waist, and pulled her to him with one arm. Victoria bristled, instantly punched First Sergeant Goodheart squarely in the nose, and removed his arm in the same motion.

Surprised by the ferocity of the blow, while deciding the better course was to leave well enough alone, Sergeant Goodheart replied, "A word of advice, 'Recruit,' you better learn to be a bit more cooperative with the Marines at basic. They have a way of getting what they want."

Victoria slammed the back door so hard on the way down the back steps, it sounded like the blast of an eight-inch howitzer. As she stormed across the rear parking lot as if it were the sands of Iwo Jima, Special Marine Corps Trainee Victoria Pierce could be heard in the distance sounding off in a voice that would make any Marine proud, "Screw yourself, Sergeant Goodheart!"

CHAPTER SIXTEEN

Spring/Summer 1981

Three days later, Victoria watched her dirty blonde hair drop in long strands to the floor of the military barber shop at Parris Island, South Carolina. Female recruits all lined up in single file and dressed in freshly issued military fatigues watched in astonished silence at the speed of the electric trimmer that reduced Victoria's shoulder-length hair to the uniform stubble of a Marine Corps jarhead in less than a full minute. All that could be heard in the barber shop, besides the electric trimmers buzzing in unison, was the voice of Victoria's drill instructor—"Judy something," who introduced herself abruptly five minutes earlier with an unpronounceable last name sounding like "Wiener"—who was now barking insults at the recruits as they waited in line for their turn with the barber.

"You maggots better not make me late to our next station," blasted the shrill voice of Sergeant Judy, whose face was half hidden beneath the brim of her circular Smokey the Bear hat, pulled down to less than an inch above her dark eyebrows. Her muscular frame stood almost five feet four inches and invited the slightest challenge to her unquestioned authority. Victoria thought that her accent hinted at a country upbringing, something like that of Jan Flowers.

The barber, as he razored the back of Victoria's neck, noticed the outline of the lightning-bolt tattoo and commented, "What in the hell is this thing? Never seen a tattoo on a women's neck, or what's left of it," as he pointed out the remnants to the barber in the next chair.

Victoria, not realizing the question was directed to the barber in the next chair, sighed, "Just something left over from bygone days in the big city." As the last syllable of her reply escaped upward to the barber's ear, Sergeant Judy's face was suddenly less than an inch from Victoria's nose.

She screamed, "Who gave you permission to sound off in *my* barber shop, you slimeball? If you make me late to the next station, I'll promise you, I'll make this the worst day of your short young life."

Fortunately for Victoria, the platoon was not late to its next station, which was the photography station, and she avoided the worst day of her life, at least as of 9:30 a.m. of a morning that started before dawn. The photographer snapped Victoria's picture in front of a drab green pull-down screen that was to provide the background for Victoria's military ID. She endured the humiliation of having her picture made with a shaved head, a photographic portrait completed in less than five seconds. "Were my eyes closed?" Victoria wondered. The rest of the platoon followed hastily along in total silence, all realizing that idle chatter would be met with dire, life-threatening consequences from Sergeant Judy. Inoculation from both domestic and foreign diseases was shot by pneumatic gun into Victoria's left upper arm at the next-to-last station.

At the last station, Victoria was issued her bedroll and pillow. In a matter of a few hours, everything brought with her from civilian life had been taken away and replaced with everything she needed to sustain life in Marine Corps basic training. Standing beside the top bunk of her bed, nestled on the far back left side of the interior of a colorless curved aluminum and steel barracks, Victoria was trying to make her bottom sheet fit the tightly sewn cotton mattress.

Victoria reflected again on yet another major mistake in her short life, but this one had the potential of being the most regrettable of them all. How could she have let such a thing happen again? She would just have to devise a strategy to undo this last mistake. The structure of military life was not for a New Yorker from Brooklyn, the daughter of an urban architect, no matter how her subsequent legal entanglements unfolded over the last year. Her fellow recruits were largely rough farm girls from rural America. *Haven't I just escaped from life on the farm?* she thought. Besides, someone had to report Sergeant Goodheart's unethical recruiting techniques in San Francisco. He was giving the Marine Corps a bad name.

Victoria tugged at her top sheet and then her blanket, forcing both to fit the oversized mattress, when the simplicity of an exit strategy hit her. "Why haven't I thought of this before?" she said out loud. At the first opportunity, Victoria was going to speak to Platoon Sergeant Judy and ask her to identify the officer in charge of reversing such mistakes. Victoria could not have been the first to be a bad fit for the Marine Corps. Obviously, there must be a relatively simple procedure to reverse course at such an early stage. The Marine Corps could save tons of money wasted on her training. It was a good deal for both the Marine Corps and her.

As the final thoughts of this half-baked plan coalesced, Platoon Sergeant Judy burst through the swinging barracks door and announced that everyone had less than one minute to complete making their bunk and fall out in formation in front of the barracks.

"This moment could be the right time for me to request the identity of this officer in charge of rectifying such mistakes," Victoria spoke in a whisper. Victoria walked to the front of the barracks swaying from side to side in her most cosmopolitan style to add credence to a city girl so badly misplaced among country girls in such a rude environment and asked Sergeant Judy a polite introductory question.

"Hi, Judy, seems to me you're having a bad day?"

"I know, Scum Maggot, you're not talking to me, 'cause no recruit ever addresses her D.I. by first name. If you want to keep those pearly white front teeth of yours, I suggest you be out of my face in the very next second!"

Ignoring this warning, Victoria continued, "Look, Judy, I need to talk to the officer who is in charge of mistaken enlistment."

Sergeant Judy ominously removed her Smokey the Bear hat with both hands, revealing the stubble of an identically dark shaved head, and carefully placed her hat on the top bunk nearest her. She walked within about a half-inch of Victoria, her face slightly closer than it had been in the barber shop, and with the speed of lightning, launched both her arms outward and upward into Victoria's chest area, ejecting Victoria into a backward blur down the barracks middle aisle with such force that she landed on the bottom bunk three rows down. Sergeant Judy stalked Victoria down to her landing area and leaned over, taunting her to get up. When Victoria did not respond immediately, the sergeant turned to walk back down the center aisle. "Anyone else want to ask their D.I. a question?"

Victoria thought aloud, "Enough of this rude behavior." She had survived a motorcycle gang, a slugfest with Amber, a shootout at the Wicked Whiskey Bar, forced confinement on the Pierce farm, and an altercation with Sergeant Goodheart. She needed a simple answer to a simple question and an end to this military rudeness. With an anger pent up from a series of events lasting almost a year, Victoria sprung forward from her position on the lower bunk, raced toward Sergeant Judy, and as the sergeant was just about to turn, Victoria struck out to punch Sergeant Judy's face.

That punch was just about the last thing Victoria could remember about the fight as she woke up from an unconscious dream a few seconds later being lifted up from the barracks floor with the assistance of several other recruits who had been ordered to lend a hand to the trainee who had so clumsily tripped and fallen to the floor. What Victoria remembered was Sergeant Judy instantly grabbing her fist at the end of her extended right arm and flipping her over her shoulder with the ease of a figure skater's pirouette and landing her head-first on a floor as hard as ice. Victoria immediately felt the pain of bruised ribs on her left side, possibly from the point of Sergeant Judy's boot, and a swollen sore jaw that turned slightly blue. None of the other details could honestly be remembered in the aftermath of such a misguided punch. She survived the encounter and knew with absolute certainty that from that time forward she would never again refer to Sergeant Judy as "Judy" and never again ask her even the most rudimentary question. Sergeant Judy pulled Victoria up by the shirt to an inch of her face, and said, "Welcome to the Marine Corps!"

Victoria correctly assumed that the Marine Corps could be the most personally regrettable decision of her young life. It was, in a word, hell. She would have given anything to return to the cakewalk of the first day's muster at Parris Island as compared to the daily physical and mental torment lavished upon all Marine Corps recruits. The workday was anything but a routine nine-to-five. It began before 4 a.m. and ended, if lucky, in total collapse at lights out at 10 p.m., that is, if there had been time to polish her military boots into a razor shine and her military brass into a copper mirror. Otherwise, Victoria performed this last assignment in total darkness.

Special duty could extend the eighteen-hour day by as much as four additional hours for kitchen patrol, abbreviated K.P., scrubbing the black off of pots at the back sinks of the chow hall until her arms were about to fall off. Fortunately, her time at the Chinese restaurant and long hours on the Pierce Farm prepared her for K.P. and the excruciating training under a broiling South Carolina sun.

Many recruits left the field, as they called it, because they could not hack the training. This euphemism meant they were discharged from the Marine Corps because they did not have the mettle to be Marines. Victoria would have jumped at the opportunity to voluntarily exit military life on her first day, but she, for damned sure, was not going to be kicked out. Sergeant Judy dished it out and Victoria took it, no matter how hard or much she wanted to quit. A determination welled up from within that Victoria had not before recognized. Victoria learned that she was not the slacker that she had been in civilian life. She was not in love with the Marine Corps, but the Marine Corps might be her best opportunity to make an honest living, at least while she tried to figure out what she was going to do with the rest of her life. She had been tested over the last year, and this testing had sharpened her determination into a fierce will to survive an unbelievable series of events that would have defeated any ordinary woman her age. She was hardened to life by the death of her father and mother, not to mention Vera's "death" on the steps of the Manhattan Courthouse.

What's more, she was better than the rest. She mustered into the Marine Corps familiar with firearms, trained in marksmanship by picking off wharf rats at fifty yards in the city's largest garbage dump, and combat tested in the blazing battle of ricocheting bullets at the Wicked Whiskey Bar. Her marksmanship on the rifle range, firing at concentric circles with her M-16 at a hundred yards, surprised even

Sergeant Judy when the bull's-eye revealed a tight circular pattern of rounds in the center of the target, a remarkable accomplishment in comparison to her gun-shy peers and even more remarkable given that this was her first practice at the firing range.

After that accomplishment, Sergeant Judy kept a sharp eye on Victoria because she knew she had the mettle to be an outstanding Marine, but who for now was just a raw recruit who could be lost to failure through a desire to return to civilian life. Sergeant Judy became a strict monitor and tough taskmaster, but not as monitoring and tough as Lucinda had been in the early hours before daylight on the farm. To Victoria's surprise and annoyance, Sergeant Judy paid far more attention to her than she did to any other recruit in the platoon. It started by calling her out of formation at every opportunity whether as a model for good performance or a model for poor performance. The former conduct was rewarded with front-and-center praise, and the latter was punished with a front-and-center blistering dress down, followed closely by more push-ups than any human could do. Victoria felt uncomfortable at the loss of her anonymity, but there was really nothing that she could do about the attention except to deal with the reality of it. The platoon recognized that often Victoria took the punishment that they all deserved.

The attention finally culminated with Sergeant Judy's announcement in early-morning formation that Victoria was selected to be the platoon leader, a type of communications' liaison which meant that Victoria was caught in the perpetual middle between trainer and trainee. If done well, Victoria would earn the respect of both, and if done poorly she would earn the respect of neither.

What Victoria lost in physical fitness in transition from the toughness of the Pierce Farm life to the slacker's life of a hashish dealer on the streets of San Francisco, she soon regained through the excruciating pain of predawn calisthenics, called, innocently enough, "P.T.," performed in place at the day's first formation, followed by a two-mile running march in full gear before breakfast, and followed after breakfast by a forced march through the scrubs of Parris Island to various training stations. Each station taught the new recruit survival techniques through bayonet practice, weaponry fire, grenade throw, and self-defense.

The platoon marched from station to station to military ditties droned in Sergeant's Judy's perfect cadence call, her pitch morphing into a sound something like a duck hunter calling to a flock of Mallards. "Your left . . . your left . . . your left-right-left," and as the recruits landed in unison on their right foot, Sergeant Judy called in a higher pitch for them to "sound off." The platoon responded immediately in unison: "One-two." Sergeant Judy called again for them to "sound off." The platoon responded again in unison: "Three-four." Sergeant Judy lowered her pitch slightly and called for them to "bring it on down." And the platoon responded in chorus, "One-two, *three-four*," projecting forcefully on "three-four." The cadence call-and-response served to break the monotony of the long morning marches, but also reminded the platoon that it functioned as a unit.

Victoria needed no tutoring for mental testing. She hastily completed the Wechsler Standard Intelligence Test way ahead of the rest of her platoon. Her IQ was measured in the genius range, exceeding that of everyone on the post, including the post commander, but no one seemed to care or notice. She was not being trained as a thinker but as a Marine who blindly followed orders to do battle with the enemy and to die if necessary, all without the slightest hesitation or questioning. Even Victoria did not pay much attention to her score.

Her goal was to survive basic training and move onto a station where she could enjoy life to the greatest degree possible as a Marine. She listened intently in the night, after lights out, to her bunkmates' tawdry barracks talk peppered with language that would have shamed even Amber and the other women in the motorcycle gang. But, tiring of this chatter, the conversation turned more seriously to duty stations and desirable base locations. Some of the gung-ho women would have settled for nothing less than a war zone. Clearly, that held little interest for Victoria. She was looking for a beach and light desk duty somewhere in a tropical climate—like some of the locations depicted on the posters inside Sergeant Goodheart's recruiting station. Certain destinations were a living hell and, what was worse, whether or not a private landed in one of these hell holes seemed to depend entirely on the luck of the draw.

Landing in a cushy destination was like winning the lottery, she thought. *How do you increase your odds of winning the lottery?* Victoria occasionally wondered and sometimes asked outright, but no one could answer the mystery of how or why the Marine Corps made an assignment. There had to be a way of increasing the odds of winning a desirable duty station. The answer to this troublesome question required further study and analysis as Victoria fell asleep puzzling on the question and dreaming up a séance with the attractive Marine who sprung to life from Sergeant Goodheart's storefront poster. "Wasn't this temptress, after all, responsible for my predicament? Wasn't she standing on sand?" Victoria confronted her with clear and precise questions. "Where is the sand? Where is the beach? How do I get there?" The Marine smiled, beckoned, and vanished suddenly into the shadows of her dream without answering.

"Ain't no use in looking down. Ain't no discharge on the ground." Sergeant's Judy's marching cadence turned humorous to divert the platoon's attention from the long three-mile march to the Combat Self-Defense Duty Station. Inside a metal building about the size of a basketball court, the platoon stood at rest in formation to learn and practice a method of self-defense known as the "Counter to the Rear Take Down." The training sergeant at this station demonstrated, hypothetically, an enemy combatant approaching unnoticed from the rear and grabbing the unsuspecting Marine with one arm around her neck and the other about to impale her with his knife. In the blink of an eye, the captured Marine would be dead unless she could free herself from her enemy combatant's restraint.

The sergeant asked collectively of the platoon, "What would you do?" The troops knew better than to take the bait offered by the sergeant's question. Anyone so stupid to volunteer an answer would soon be the sergeant's guinea pig.

"Platoon Leader Pierce, since none of your troops is brave enough to offer a simple answer and instead chooses to die in ignorance, please step forward so you can sacrifice your life for the rest." Victoria, accustomed by now to volunteering by default, approached the sergeant's elevated platform covered in wrestler's matting. Victoria knew that soon she would be laid flat on this mat because she was yet to be trained on the Counter to the Rear Take Down. The sergeant positioned Victoria immediately behind as she grasped the sergeant with one of her arms wrapped tightly around his neck.

The sergeant inquired of Victoria, "Have you got me tightly bound in preparation for the kill?"

Before Victoria could answer, the sergeant launched his right arm upward and then, fist first, backward, landing perilously close to Victoria's groin, an area certain to incapacitate any male combatant, simultaneously grasping Victoria's right extended arm above the elbow and at her wrist. He flipped her rapidly over his shoulder, slamming her to the mat, while pretending to kick Victoria in the ribs and face with his boot. Victoria, reeling from her perspective on the mat, understood immediately what happened to her in the segment of her barracks brawl with Sergeant Judy when she lost consciousness. Did not Sergeant Judy perform the same maneuver after flipping her over her shoulder and then holding her fist at the tip of her extended right arm, while the good sergeant stomped her face and kicked her ribs with her boot? Victoria glanced over to Sergeant Judy, who confirmed in the communication of a silent nod that that was precisely what happened. The visual confirmation occurred while the training sergeant completed the feigned process of breaking Victoria's neck with another slam of his boot to her face less than a millimeter from her chin.

Without in any way assisting Victoria up from her prone position on the mat, the sergeant turned to the assembled. "Are there any questions, or would you like to see the demonstration again?" Victoria resurrected herself from the mat and stared from behind the sergeant into the platoon, daring anyone to suggest that they would like to see the demonstration again. Out of fear and deference for their fallen leader, no one recommended a repeat of the demonstration. The rest of the one-hour block of instruction paired recruits together to practice the maneuver. One was the aggressor and the other the defender. Then they switched roles and repeated the trial. The two sergeants observed the trainees, sometimes loudly correcting a misdirected or misguided maneuver. Each pair went through about thirty trials until they had perfected killing their adversary to the standards required by the Marine Corps. By the end of the one-hour block of instruction, the training sergeant and first sergeant had observed that each troop had mastered the Counter to the Rear Take Down. Victoria was now more convinced than ever that she would never volunteer for combat duty.

The normal Marine Corps basic training cycle lasted about two months, unless a sadsack troop was recycled, meaning starting back over from day one, a common threat made by all sergeants to leverage more effort out of trainees. Victoria's status as platoon leader all but guaranteed her timely graduation and promotion from private to lance corporal, save for a serious injury or another confrontation with Sergeant Judy.

Actually, Sergeant Judy was becoming almost a human being by the end of the cycle, not just to Victoria but to the whole platoon, more like a Girl Scout leader than a D.I. Most recruits transformed themselves into Marines with a new self-confidence and realized it was their D.I. who led the way, so there was little chance that Victoria would have again challenged Sergeant Judy's valor. Besides, there was no officer in charge of mistaken enlistment, and Sergeant Judy definitely had eased up on her singular focus on Platoon Leader Pierce.

Subtle change came over the platoon to make life bearable at the end of the cycle. For example, troops actually strolled into and out of the chow hall, instead of the previous routine of charging in from the outside, screaming unintelligibly their name, rank, and serial number, ending with, "Sir, yes, sir," and once inside, shoveling down a full, unmasticated meal in less than fifteen seconds. Contrasted with the previous drill, the troops strolled in, sat themselves comfortably at a table for four, chewed their food slowly, and conversed leisurely with their companions. The postmeal mandatory formations were gone now, replaced with a leisurely walk back to the barracks. Some were allowed to wander off into off-limits areas like the barracks bulletin board in front of Sergeant Judy's office. There Victoria stopped to read in big letters words she had never seen before: "Report Sexual Harassment." "What does that mean?" she whispered to herself. Quickly, her attention narrowed to more timely information printed in faint computer type, listing the names of the troops from Sergeant Judy's last training cycle and their duty stations: Oregon, Texas, Oklahoma.

"Oklahoma, God, no!"

"Alaska, Germany—Germany, that's more like it."

"Puerto Rico, San Juan—San Juan, that's it. How do you get there?"

"Bogotá. Where's that?"

Her same confusion ran back to the early barracks conversations. "How does the Marine Corps decide who goes where?" At the bottom of the computer printout, barely legible, was the name of Warrant Officer Enrique Rodriguez. "Who is Rodriguez?" At that moment, from the office beside Sergeant Judy, a tall, handsome Marine popped out, wearing a soft cap pulled down over his eyes and the name tag, "Rodriguez." Before Victoria could clear her throat to interrupt, Rodriguez was gone, but Victoria had made the connection. Rodriguez was linked to desirable destinations. "Get to Rodriguez, get to San Juan!"

Victoria forced down every meal in the chow hall in double time over the next several days to give herself extra face time in front of the barracks' bulletin board, where she pretended to be interested in the posted material when actually she was waiting for the tall, dark Rodriguez to resurface in the hallway. But to no avail. So while continuing to wait on the phantom Rodriguez, Victoria actually memorized every detail on the bulletin board. She could recite every Marine Corps base location throughout the world. The fine print of pages and pages of newly posted Marine Corps regulations titled "Sexual Harassment" held Victoria's interest more than the new uniform specifications and length of a Marine's haircut. The contrived perusal of the postings could mask this pretext, but only for so long. What if someone was watching her? Where was this Rodriguez? The next segment of Victoria's life could not flow from the same channel of mistakes that she had repeatedly made over the last year. It was time to exert some control over her future—a future that did not include a faraway dusty war zone full of combatants trying to painfully end her young life. Her goal was to land a light-duty station somewhere in a balmy climate near a beach, and Warrant Officer Rodriguez held the keys to the beach and all the other cushy destinations.

At last, without the slightest reason, he reappeared, making long strides down the hallway like a drill instructor on a field mission, oblivious to everything and everyone in his immediate environment. Victoria waited until Rodriguez approached to about two strides of his office door when she stepped out right in his path. The encounter produced a catastrophic collision in the hallway with Victoria reeling backward and landing squarely on the floor face up. She propped herself up on her elbows from the floor as Rodriguez extended his long arm down to assist Victoria back to her feet.

Victoria said, "señor, nosotros no poníamos mucha atención adonde íbamos, parece qué siempre me empujan a una contidad de Marines aquí, la realidad es qué estoy acostumbrada a eso." (Sir, we both must not have been paying much attention to where we were going . . . Seems like I'm getting pushed down a lot by large Marines around here. . . really I'm kind of used to it.)

"¿Usted habla español?" (You speak Spanish?)

"Sí." (Yes.)

"Lo siento mucho." (I'm very sorry.)

"Gracias," Victoria replied as she dusted off her fatigues and stared up into the brown-eyed Rodriguez's face, trying to think how to extend the conversation.

"My mother was from Puerto Rico." Victoria caught her error immediately and wondered to herself if somehow Rodriguez would check her enlistment file that would reveal her mother's identity as a woman named Lucinda Pierce from Lawton, Oklahoma. Too late for such a distraction, Victoria would have to continue on the theme of conversational Spanish before Rodriguez and San Juan disappeared permanently behind his closed and locked office door.

"Do you have a moment, Señor Rodriguez, to explain this posting to me? Look, right here. Isn't that your name?" Victoria stepped back to the faint computer printout and pointed to his name. Rodriguez quickly approached the papers and yanked them off the bulletin board.

Rodriguez checked Victoria out from top to bottom and focused on her name tag. He glanced down at his wristwatch. "Forgot to take these down after the last cycle. This is an old posting and has no current value. And actually, I don't, right now, have time to explain this to you . . . uh . . . it's Pierce? I have to be in the post commander's office at fourteen hundred hours, and that's about ten minutes from now."

"Well, is there another time that I could come back?"

"Look, Pierce, this subject is really off-limits. Better to leave well enough alone. But if you are really interested, you can meet me at the NCO Club at 1800 hours to discuss a special assignment. I'll clear it with your D.I. We will be talking about classified subjects, including some general information about this posting, and your special mission may require overnight medical leave, which I will also authorize."

Rodriguez winked and stepped away as Victoria said, "Eighteen hundred hours it is, sir, at the NCO Club!"

For the entire basic training cycle, recruits were not granted leave away from even their barracks, much less an overnight departure through the gates of Parris Island. The temptation to go AWOL and return to the comfort of home and flee the brutality of combat training was just too great. Near the end of the cycle, this risk diminished, but such a Saturday night was never voluntarily permitted. Victoria would have to make roll call formation on Sunday.

Victoria picked up her medical leave slip from the first sergeant's desk for her Saturday night "date" with the tall, handsome Rodriguez. She scoured the barracks for makeup and lipstick, brushed the short stubble of her natural locks grown out almost an eighth of an inch since her last mandatory buzz at the base barber shop, and squeezed into her dress uniform. Basic training had done wonders for her figure and complexion. Glancing into the small bathroom mirror above the latrine sink, she checked out her image in the mirror with approval and blurted out, "San Juan, here I come."

Walking with temerity through the front door of the NCO Club, a place filled with Marines clustered at the bar downing mixed drinks amid a scattering of women whom Victoria believed to be either NCO officers, wives, or dates, Victoria searched for Rodriguez through a cloud of cigarette smoke and a permanent odor of stale beer. The NCO Club was off-limits to all recruits and enlisted personnel. Victoria knew she would soon be bounced out unless her NCO escort arrived. It was exactly 1800 hours. Several of the Marines at the bar noticed Victoria at the door. She was dynamite with a short dark fuse, looking like she just stepped out of one of Sergeant Goodheart's recruiting posters. Elbows and nudges were exchanged among the Marines at the bar, and Victoria saw fingers pointing in her direction. One stumplike Marine with a neck the width of his shoulders slipped off his bar stool and headed toward her at the door. Victoria decided the best course for her was to leave now, and as she turned, banged right into Enrique Rodriguez for the second time in less than four hours, but this encounter, unlike the last, was completely unintentional. Rodriguez brushed past Victoria, stepping in front of her to confront the approaching Marine. Knowing Victoria was the "property" of Warrant Officer Rodriguez for the night, the stump made a 180-degree turn and returned to his companions seated at the bar.

"Don't let any of those jarheads bother you. You're safe with me!"

Victoria breathed a sigh of relief and masked her nervousness. "I can handle myself both on and off the field, sir, without your help, but let's just say I am really glad you made it when you did, even if you're five minutes to the tardy side of 1800 hours."

Victoria smiled up at Rodriguez, but she could not and would not be distracted from her evening mission by his good looks. Seated at a small table for two in the club's noisy dining section, the pair made small talk, alternatively in English and Spanish, along several introductory conversational paths while each enjoyed frozen margaritas from the bar. Rodriguez observed his peers circling like vultures and closing in for introductions and banter. This picture did not at all fit the Rodriguez plan for his evening with Victoria. To make matters worse, Victoria began peppering Rodriguez immediately with questions about exotic destinations. Rodriguez whispered answers that were intentionally inaudible and impossible for Victoria to hear above the noise of the club.

They mutually decided to leave, each to advance a separate evening agenda in a more tranquil location. Rodriguez drove his candy-apple red high-performance sports car out the front gate in the direction of a local bar and grill. Once past the gate, Rodriguez turned himself and his vehicle into a Mario Andretti Formula One race car to either frighten or impress Victoria. Normally, Victoria would be more frightened than impressed, but what captured her fascination was the all-but-forgotten civilian life parading around outside the front gate.

Crammed in beside Victoria in a corner booth that would comfortably seat four, Rodriguez plied Victoria with the house specialty drinks from the bar at the Palmettos Motel and Restaurant. Victoria declined the Long Island Ice Tea that Rodriguez ordered for himself. These potent drinks produced for Rodriguez the unintended consequence of rapid inebriation. Victoria remained in her comfort zone and formulated in her mind another plan as she pressed Rodriguez for a destination. After two Long Island Ice Teas, Rodriguez, emboldened, bragged to Victoria in slurred Spanish that he could secure almost any destination she desired, but it would come at a price, a quid pro quo. Finally, in response to Victoria's inquiry as to what exactly he meant by "quid pro quo," Rodriguez blurted out a drunken invitation to join him for the night in the upstairs motel to consummate the bargained-for destination. Victoria accepted her officer's kind invitation for an overnight tryst, but only if they could have more drinks on the way to the room to put her at ease in order to fulfill her side of the bargain. Rodriguez secured a fifth of rum from the bartender. Victoria propped up Rodriguez beside the soft drink machine and vended a cola while Rodriguez downed a large portion of the fifth straight from the bottle. By the time the two arrived inside Room 512, a space distastefully decorated and consumed by the sheer size of the king bed, Victoria excused herself to powder her nose. Rodriguez dropped headfirst into the middle of the bed and passed into a deep state of an unintended alcohol-induced state of unconsciousness. Victoria returned, her plan almost completed, crossed Rodriguez's feet, and rolled him via a field maneuver from the center to the left side of the bed. Victoria, fully clothed, as was her passed-out companion, pulled back the daisy-dotted bedspread and slept, much as any other civilian would, tossing through the night to keep a nervous eye out for her bunk mate but sleeping well past the normal blaring bugle of the 4 a.m. predawn reveille.

The sleepmates straddled separate corners of the bed pretty much molded in their original sleeping positions and awakened almost at the same instant that the sun came glaring through the room's window, which spanned the entire length of the east wall. The matching full-length daisy-dotted curtains were fully retracted, allowing the sunlight to pour over the bed's occupants, causing them to cover their bloodshot eyes, turning simultaneously face down into their pillows.

Rodriguez inquired, "What time is it, Pierce?"

"Don't know, sir."

"In spite of my shortcomings of last night, it's never too late to start our engines for an early morning race before returning to the base." Rodriguez rolled over and reached for Victoria, who had escaped to the motel chair beside the bed.

"If you do not cooperate, Pierce, I will be most reluctant to make recommendation for you up the chain of command."

"Well, sir, you blew your big chance last night. If you ask me, you need to know more about what's in a Long Island Ice Tea! But you will keep your half of the bargain that you struck with me last night as the officer and gentleman that I know you are, or face charges for sexual harassment."

"'Sexual harassment'? What in the hell is 'sexual harassment'?"

"You should read your own bulletin board, sir." Victoria retrieved the crumpled paper from her purse and cast it over to Rodriguez, whose solid red eyes were in no shape to read anything.

"Read this! Oh, not reading well this morning, sir? Those blue eyes hurting this morning? It's a little late to give you a refresher course on sexual harassment, so let's just go to the bottom line, Rodriguez. I intend to be stationed in San Juan, Puerto Rico, or else I will go to the post commander and explain how you harassed me until I consented to come here with you to this motel room to satisfy the sexual lusts of my warrant officer. You will be busted to private or run out of the corps altogether.

"That's absurd. No one even knows we were here last night. It's an officer's word against that of a recruit."

"Did you ask who knows we were here last night? Oh, about ten witnesses in the bar downstairs who moved away from a loud and drunken Marine by the name of Rodriguez, the attractive cocktail waitress whom you did not tip on a hundred-dollar bar bill, and, of course, the night manager who was about to call the MPs on such an intoxicated Marine who attempted to register for the night under a fictitious name, not the least bit identical to the one on his name tag."

"We both know nothing happened last night!"

"That may not be my version of last night's events. Besides, that's not even necessary to prove sexual harassment. Now, what I do know is that, with your recommendation, I am going to be stationed in San Juan."

"Can't do it. There's absolutely no way. What I can do . . . is Bogotá," Rodriguez replied, conceding defeat.

"Not good enough, I want San Juan," but Victoria hesitated, not sure that Rodriguez may not actually be telling the truth about San Juan but still unsure of this Bogotá destination.

"Where is Bogotá, anyway?" Victoria admitted her ignorance of geography.

"It's the capital of Colombia. That would be South America, Señorita loco en la cabeza [crazy in the head], and one of the most desirable locations for a Marine anywhere in the world."

"Then Bogotá it is!"

CHAPTER SEVENTEEN

October–November 2008

"Grace, go back over two things. First, you had an obligation, didn't you, to keep your editor informed about what you were doing in Oklahoma? Let's see, we learned about all of this—" a thin man in wire-rimmed glasses glanced up at the clock and then said back to Grace, "it's been about five hours since Legal was called in. So why didn't you do this? And second, can you explain again exactly why you were interviewing— somehow that word doesn't accurately reflect what reporters talking to advanced Alzheimer's patients are doing—but go ahead, tell us again about this 'interview,' as you call it."

Several editors had Grace surrounded in a small conference room on the fifth floor of the New York Times Building. The lead interrogator was one of the paper's lawyers, who was asking Grace to repeat answers to questions she had already answered. As Grace began to speak, the buzz of side conversations ceased. In silence, all focused and listened to her now-repetitive answer.

"OK. I'll start again with Marshal Slaughter. He's the retired U.S. marshal in Oklahoma City. I distinctly had the impression that he recognized Victoria Pierce's photograph as someone he knew from his past as part of his job many years ago. He immediately clammed up, but as he was leaving the interview, he dropped a big clue, hint, or whatever you want to call it, for me to start my search for this 'Vera' under the 'bright lights,' which I took to mean, under the circumstances, New York City."

"This is the really old guy you interviewed while he was on his fourth or fifth draft beer in the bar. Right, but he never said 'New York City,' only the 'bright lights,' correct?"

"Right. So I left the bar and went to my motel room that night, but couldn't sleep. I left the motel to find the answer to the troubling question as to why Lucinda Pierce would refer to her daughter as 'that hoodlum girl,' so I went back to Lucinda Pierce's room at the Sunset Rest Home, and, yes, that was the same night she died."

"No one gave you permission to enter her room, or speak to Ms. Pierce. Matter of fact, you all but broke in by slipping through an unlocked fire exit, correct?" The lawyer's last question, mixed with a singe of both truth and condescension, drove his point home to everyone in the room that Grace clearly violated Lucinda's right to privacy by entering her room in this manner completely without authorization.

Avoiding the trap of a direct admission, Grace continued. "I asked her about her daughter. She denied having any children, and I asked her directly the real name of this 'hoodlum girl,' as that was how she referred to Victoria. As I was leaving her room, Lucinda said her name was Vera."

Grace omitted any reference to the man with the syringe or that "Vera" was her last dying word. She also omitted any reference to the later, untimely death of Gus Margolis.

"That's it? Based solely on such dubious information, and completely leaving your editors in the dark, you surreptitiously approached Victoria Pierce, candidate for vice president of the United States; and then you pretend to be a political spectator on a crowded sidewalk near an Albany hotel, blurt right out your suspicion, hoping for some sort of lame admission; and then divulge to the general that totally without her permission, you questioned her mother, an advanced Alzheimer's patient, from her bed in her private room, shortly before her death, and I hasten to add, to confess that her daughter, Victoria Pierce, is really some bogus person with the first name of Vera. How totally absurd! I'm not sure I can even follow the rationale of the sequencing myself. Imagine what it would be like for Lucinda Pierce to comprehend such a question, on her deathbed no less, dying later that very night from advanced Alzheimer's disease? Ms. Brandon, I'm not even sure a tabloid reporter would go that far, but not even close to the *New York Times'* standards for investigative reporting. And it's a stretch to think that's even what you were doing. I am not going to recommend that you be fired outright, because I may be able to defend this lawsuit as the work of an inexperienced and novice reporter, still wet behind the ears. We will also have to keep you on, in case we later need to fire you as part of a settlement. You will write a letter of apology to General Pierce. But I am recommending to your editors that you be officially yanked from all future presidential election reporting, unless they choose to fire you outright."

Grace interrupted. "What?"

"Quite frankly, I do not want to defend a defamation suit."

"But we get threatened with that all the time," one of the female editors in the room broke in.

"The difference is that Ms. Brandon has established a personal relationship with her subject. No one can argue that a candidate for vice president is not a public figure, but from what I've learned from Ms. Brandon's peers in a very short time is that she has developed quite a personal friendship with General Pierce." Grace was asked, "Do you deny that?"

"Well, no. Let's say we used to be friends."

"My point exactly. She's now a former friend. You have accused your former friend of being someone she's not, an alter ego that you cannot establish, a hunch at best that if untrue could cause her to lose the election, and if this hunch of yours is published, what do you suppose will be the amount of damages your employer will have to pay for a story that a jury may well conclude is false?"

"But she's a public figure, for God's sake!"

"Benefit of a public figure goes right out the window because you have a personal relationship with your subject, and if your accusation is false—frankly, something you cannot prove is true—the *Times* loses its public-figure benefit by publishing a falsehood because its reporter was so personally angry with her subject that when their friendship turned sour she either maliciously made up the falsehood or was so careless that she recklessly disregarded whether it was true. It provides General Pierce with proof of actual malice that defeats your employer's public figure defense. So it would be unsound legal advice to publish your suspicions or for you to continue to cover a subject of this magnitude with whom you have such an established personal dislike."

Grace was stunned and silent.

"But fortunately for all of us at this point, General Pierce's lawyers have not raised the issue of libel—at least not yet. Go back to covering the courthouse beat, and if you ask me, consider yourself damned lucky to still have a job here tomorrow morning. Does anyone in this room, after hearing such a journalistic concoction, disagree with my legal assessment or course of action?"

Their collective silence in the room acknowledged consent. Grace broke a long silence, responding and pointing defiantly at the lawyer. "And just what exactly will the *New York Times* do, including you and every wimp in this room, if my hunch proves to be true and the possible vice president of the United States does in fact have a clandestine past and some other newspaper breaks the biggest story in presidential history?"

"There's a basic tenet of reporting that you're overlooking, Ms. Brandon, and that's the assumption that General Pierce is exactly who she says she is, and is not concealing a clandestine past, and until someone, certainly not you, but some other *Times* reporter, independently comes up with concrete evidence to the contrary, General Pierce will remain who she says she is, and likely, very likely, may well become the vice president of the United States—the first woman to ever fill that office, just in case you have not taken note of her gender."

"I've grown up with a father who is a lawyer—quite a man and quite a lawyer. Believe me, I am not intimidated by lawyers. What bothers me the most is that lawyers can overrule my editors." Grace stared past the lawyer into the faces of her editors, who remained silent. "Where are my editors when I need them the most?"

The next day vice presidential candidate General Victoria Pierce received and accepted a four-page confidential letter of apology, not communicated through some instantaneous email attachment, but by personal delivery in the hands of a *New York Times* courier, officially presented to the general at her campaign headquarters in Lower Manhattan. Both sides received considerable benefit in the apology. The *Times* vindicated itself from a defamatory lawsuit that would allege a clear violation of the federal HIPAA Act, having to admit in such a lawsuit a journalistic lapse of ethics and trying to explain exactly what their agent, though clearly on a lark of her own, was doing in Lucinda Pierce's hospital room minutes before her death, badgering an Alzheimer's patient with absurd questions. Victoria Pierce benefited even more, overtly achieving her secondary objective, by backing down the *Times* into an uncharacteristic apology, but secretly achieving her primary objective by having the *Times* implicitly acknowledge their reporter's reference to an unknown "Vera," a reference heard only by Victoria, to be nothing more than the ravings of her dying, delusional mother and one that would not be raised again, at least not in the foreseeable future, because the *Times* permanently removed Grace Brandon from presidential political reporting.

In spite of her rebuff, Grace Brandon knew much more than what she revealed. Her duty as a professional journalist, spawned in the responsibilities demanded of her by the First Amendment, was to confirm and publish the truth about Victoria Pierce to an informed American electorate prior to her election as vice president of the United States. But Grace was a journalist hanging perilously by a thread, back to the wall, and about to be fired. Desperately, she needed a conclusive lead that would connect Vera to Victoria, all the while trying to dig up such a lead while laboring daily in journalism purgatory. Three people knew something about the identity of Vera. Two were now dead, and the other would delight in having her arrested. The only lead left, with a remotely warm trail, was a real long shot, requiring Grace to go snooping through old invoices stacked in boxes left in the estate of Gus Margolis. Grace told no one at the *Times* about her connection to the deaths of Gus Margolis or Lucinda Pierce. But now that she was officially removed from covering Victoria, Grace assumed she was out of the line of fire and would not be racked up as the third mysterious death. But she knew she had to tell someone about the connection between Lucinda and Gus. She would tell her father.

* * *

Victoria's mission was now to close Sam's presidential aspirations by conquering her objective, much as would a soldier in combat, by delivering solid numbers of women and military voters into his presidential column, not to mention delivering a sizeable portion of crossover male voters who were purely attracted to Victoria's good looks. In addition to Victoria's political contributions, she remained Sam's primary sensual liaison. Nothing had changed. Victoria was still the lifetime lover for a man sexually neglected by his quite frigid, high-society wife of forty years, but also for a man who could not or would not politically divorce this uncaring wife and marry his true lover, or so he said.

* * *

Back on the last weeks of the campaign trail, Victoria returned to a post where she received advanced training on occasion throughout her military career. Victoria visited Camp Pendleton, not just to inspect the post as a visiting general, but to ultimately raise money and votes. As she drove with her military escort through the front gate, Victoria, fidgeting, tried to concentrate on her handwritten notes, a summary of the points that she intended to spring on the commander in chief of CINC PAC, who was one of the most influential ranking four-star generals in the armed services. A major reason for her number-two position on the ticket was to win his support and the support of influential military men like him. Her eyes narrowed and focused. Victoria returned, not just as a brigadier general, but as a candidate for the vice presidency and perhaps the future surrogate commander in chief of the U.S. Armed Forces. She was the candidate whom the base commanders should embrace and who held the key to the deep pockets of the military-industrial complex. She was unsure how the commander would view Sam's reputation as a draft dodger. Victoria reviewed her notes for the last time. She needed to return to the campaign with his military endorsement, and she had no intention to fail in her mission.

Riding along, Victoria remembered Sergeant Judy and Rodriguez and tried to recall the faces of her bunk mates, but not with any degree of clarity and faded in time, before her entourage arrived at base headquarters, a place off limits to her during much of her military career. Exiting to the command, "Atten-Hut," the clicking sound of boots simultaneously coming to attention, and the frozen salute of the honor guard captain standing in front of an abnormally erect platoon, Victoria rose to return his salute according to the exactness demanded of her by military protocol that only an experienced Marine officer would know, illustrating to the assembled, without a word spoken, that she was one of them, finely honed by years of experience in the United States Marine Corps. Flanked by subordinate officers, General Pierce glided with ease through the headquarters' entrance, appointed with military flags waving above and on each side of the doorway, as the honor guard captain barked, "Pa . . . raaade . . . Rest," followed simultaneously with the thud of boots commanded in unison to move to shoulder-width apart. Moments later, she arrived at the commander's office and paused momentarily at the opened door, observing the man behind the desk, reading a newspaper. Finally, he looked up.

Folding the paper in half and dropping it on his desk, he said, "I'm Dan Fowler, General Pierce, welcome aboard. Not often do we get to see a vice presidential candidate on the campaign trail at our base, and by the way, welcome back to Camp Pendleton." Daniel S. Fowler, the rugged, no-nonsense, cigar-smoking four-star, steeped in generations of military tradition, greeted Victoria with an unceremonious handshake as he would any fellow Marine of equal rank. They sat down.

"Thank you for having me. Please call me 'Victoria.' I have many fond memories of my time here, but that was a long time ago. Now I'm on a different mission and hope to elicit your approval of that mission. I know it's impossible for you to align yourself with any presidential candidate, but America must preserve its national defense. This is my campaign message, and why this Marine has agreed to run for national office. My message is simple: support and maintain a strong military and no cutbacks in operational funding, weaponry development, or defense programs as our opponents suggest."

Dan Fowler, seemingly paying attention for the first time, interrupted Victoria's canned speech. He waved his hand dismissively, lit a cigar and, pointing the end at Victoria, asked, "You mind?"

"Of course not." General Fowler could have asked permission to do almost anything, and Victoria would not have objected, given the political importance of her mission.

"Let's stop wasting time beating around the bush here, General. Hell, it's Victoria, right?"

Like with the cigar, Dan Fowler did not wait for permission. "Victoria, one thing's clear, you've already got my vote and the vote of practically every soldier in America, before you ever arrived at the front gate. Like I said, we seldom see anyone campaigning along a military trail on their way to national office."

Victoria looked down at her notes, reviewing her points, about to interrupt, but she realized the general was on a roll.

"Look, you don't have to ask the military to recognize one of their own. We know on which side our military toast is buttered. We've all been watching you, a genuine Marine—one of us. Damned proud you kicked ass in Central Park. Can't say we think much of Sam Eagan's military record, but we know his military spending record in Congress and his astuteness in nominating a decorated Marine, like you, as his running mate."

Victoria again looked down at her notes. She spent a long time fine tuning her arguments, but realized that General Fowler was saying almost everything that she had written down. He was making her speech, so she let him go on.

"Your base commanders, behind the scenes, will deliver the vote of every regular soldier stationed here and abroad, across the branches, mind you. Just wait, you'll see. And next to that, perhaps far more importantly, the brass in the Pentagon will deliver the political bucks from the military budget tit-suckers. Check with your campaign's financial treasurer. It's already happening."

"What do you mean, it's already happening?"

"Look, I've been a commander for five years, been to the Pentagon, wear four stars. Leave it to me, General. I'll see to it that it's all delivered to your side. Really, it's our side, 'cause the support is already there. Hell, you're a Marine. Who else have we got to support? This will be the easiest damned mission of my military career."

Dan pointed his cigar at Victoria. "But we'll counterattack if you start acting like the rest of those candy-assed politicians, who conveniently, after the election, forget their promises to the military!"

Victoria was speechless. All the preparation that went into her well-planned spiel fell into the trash can. General Fowler had anticipated her mission, defused her pretense in salty military terms, articulated her political needs better than she had rehearsed, and completely outflanked her with a maneuver that merged a united military into the Eagan campaign.

"Now that you know, General, exactly where the hell you stand with your comrades in arms, let's drop your canned bullshit, quit wasting our valuable time on a hill you've already taken, get your ass out on a base inspection among your admirers—the men—well, you know—all damned Marines, who have worked pretty damned hard on the preparation for your visit here today, and, let you, like all good jarheads, reminisce for a few hours about your days of training, take a few photos, then get you the hell out of here, back on the campaign trail to catch bigger political fish, 'cause you've got the big military fish wrapped up."

Dan sat back in his chair, dropped his head over the back of his chair, and took a deep draw on his fine Havana, causing the tip's quarter-inch ash to turn charcoal red, before he blew three concentric-circle smoke rings, the last exiting through and ahead of the first two.

"I can tell you're an expert cigar smoker. Well, thank you for your uncompromising support, Dan—a point Senator Eagan, I'll personally assure you, will not overlook after our election. And I'll take your advice. Let's inspect your base, reminisce along the way, and then cast me back into the political waters to catch the next big fish."

Fowler leaned forward, clearing his cigar smoke away from his face, as if it might interfere with Victoria's responding sound waves.

"And what might that fish look like, General?"

"A lady fish!"

* * *

Grace Brandon knocked on the front door of Gus Margolis's home. Frankie answered the door.

"Frankie, I'm Grace Brandon, a reporter from the *New York Times* and one of your many devoted customers. In fact, right before your father died, we were working on a retirement feature. Look, I'm really sorry about your father."

"Yeah, of course, I remember you. You're the reporter Pops was trying to find something for you the night he died. Come in?"

"That's exactly why I'm here. Can you show me where he kept his old invoices? He said there were quite a few big boxes. Mind if I take a look?"

"I have to leave in about fifteen minutes. Could you come back Friday? It's bound to take you more time than we have right now to go through all of those boxes back there, believe me."

"How about letting me take a quick look while you're here? Maybe I'll get lucky. If not, I'll come back Friday."

Frankie, knowing what Grace was about to encounter, reluctantly led her back through a hallway to a small storage room, which was crammed full of nearly seventy-five white corrugated seafood boxes, stacked five high and in more disarray than Mr. Margolis's deli office. Grace surmised that even if she came back for ten hours on Friday, there would not be enough time to go through all of the storage boxes, much less find anything in these cramped quarters in the next fifteen minutes. But she started in, initially undeterred, and then stopped to survey just how exactly to navigate the maze of stacked boxes without toppling them, spilling their contents, or crushing herself under an avalanche.

"Why is everything always so damned difficult?"

Grace questioned her commitment to the arduous task ahead, bringing her right thumb and forefinger up to provide solace to her aching temples, then down to rub them gently into tired eyelids, trying to dam the flood of tears about to come. She was already conceding defeat in the sheer futility of such a search, admitting, in self-pity, her complete failure as a journalist, and contemplating what life might be like in an alternative profession. Then she opened her eyes and glimpsed the sheen of a small envelope atop a single box near her feet, contrasted by its crisp whiteness to the beige dinginess of the room. She approached it with skepticism, seeing in disbelief "Grace Brandon—Times Reporter" scribbled on the outside of the envelope in the cursive script of Gus Margolis. Tearing open the envelope, without permission and not caring, she read the carbon copy of a yellow invoice, dated March 18, 1968, for a single order of four pounds of crab salad, discounted by 5 percent in red pencil and marked, "Bill to Mrs. Benjamin Ochman" at her Brooklyn address, a short distance away. Mrs. Benjamin Ochman must have been the most beautiful woman to have graced the sidewalks of New York, who towed along a daughter, now poised to become vice president of the United States, but not with the name of Vera but Victoria. Grace's despondence erupted into euphoria. Kissing the envelope, she looked up.

"Thank you, Mr. Margolis!"

The next morning Grace knocked nervously at the Brooklyn street address where the Ochmans previously lived in a cramped two-story frame house. The curt response from the woman at the door to her inquiry was, "Never heard of anyone named Ben Ochman. Try over there," she said, pointing. "The lady across the street been here forever."

As the door slams, Grace asked, "What lady? Where?"

Grace canvassed several surrounding addresses before she encountered an older women two houses down and across the street who miraculously answered the door. Whether this was the same lady to whom she was directed no longer mattered, as this woman remembered the Ochman family.

"They were a good Catholic family. Sometimes Mr. Ochman would give me a lift to Mass at St. Patrick's. My husband was raised Lutheran, really wasn't welcome much in the Catholic church, but he didn't go to church, rest his Protestant soul. He's been dead a long time, about as long as the Ochmans. Like I said, a nice family, not like these ones around here now. First she died, then him, then the daughter. Tragic."

"What do you mean by the daughter's tragic death?

"Don't really remember much about it now, but the girl lost her life somehow. Some kind of trouble she got in—died—real sad, though."

"Was the daughter named Vera?"

"Yeah, Vera. That was her name all right. Dead a long time now. Haven't thought about that family in years. They were nice, not like now. Bums, all bums, live around here now."

"Vera's dead? How can that be?" Grace was so close to unraveling the story of how Vera turned into Victoria, but not if this Vera is dead.

"Yeah, she died in high school."

"Do you remember how or anything else about them?"

"Not much. It's been so long. He had a nice funeral at St. Patrick's. Since he had been so nice to me, I went to his funeral."

"Do you know where they're buried?"

"Yeah, the big cemetery on Long Island. I remember that, too. Buried right under a huge marble statute of the Blessed Virgin, the most beautiful I've ever seen." She crosses herself. "Guess Vera was buried there, too, but can't be sure. Didn't go to her funeral."

Grace cut the interview short. The old woman could be wrong. She admittedly was not sure because she had not actually witnessed Vera's funeral. The only way to erase the doubt would be to try to find the Ochman family grave at the big Long Island cemetery, under the marble statute of the Blessed Virgin.

* * *

Grace stared in disbelief at the Romanesque letters chiseled into the stone monument, beneath the marbled, outstretched arms of the Virgin Mary. There, unmistakably, was the name "Vera Ochman," with a birth date of August 2, 1962, and a date of death exactly three weeks after her father's. *How odd*, Grace thought. Solving this conundrum would have to wait for another day. Grace, now defeated, rubbed her temples. "No one would have believed this anyway. Guess I'll spend the rest of my life covering the courthouse, or maybe just marry some rich guy and live at the club. But one thing is for sure: Vice President Pierce will never speak to me again. Time to face the facts. Here's the grave. Vera is dead, and so is my story."

* * *

A week before Election Day, Tom Pearsall's polling predicted the landslide that was about to come. A perception of competence, an alliance of urban voters, and the wildly popular Victoria Pierce were going to sweep Sam Eagan to the presidency. No matter what could come in the week to follow, nothing short of a nuclear disaster could turn the tidal wave about to break over the nation. It was over! The only mystery would be the margin of victory. It was time now to transition from political election to political governance. Tom's all-inclusive campaign notebook included a chapter on responding to your opponent's last-minute acts of desperation. The strategy, simply stated, was to characterize last-minute attack ads as tools of desperation, true or not; make a measured response, if necessary; and stake out the political high ground. Victoria had accomplished exactly what she said she would by delivering solid numbers of crossover women voters and establishing herself as the persona of military competence to offset one of Sam's biggest negatives. But Victoria was not so much a politician as a vote getter. Tom conceded she had done her job well, but her job, in his estimation, was now concluded. It was Sam's presidency, not hers. Victoria Pierce knew nothing about political governance.

The Sunday before the election in their campaign headquarters, Sam and Tom contemplated both victory and a cabinet. Victoria was shoring up voters in Los Angeles before joining Sam on the last day of campaigning, ending with a joint appearance in New York City for the world to watch them watching the election night results together. Like the party's convention, there would be no suspense. It would end early on election night with network projections of victory within minutes after the polls closed and a concession by their opponents before 10:00 p.m. Eastern Standard Time. No one would care about the West Coast balloting because the victory would be electorally sealed with victories in New York, Pennsylvania, Texas, Florida, Michigan, and Ohio, conceding their home states, and a few others.

"You've done it, Sam."

"No, we've done it, Tom, barring some huge last-minute crisis."

"There will be no last-minute crisis, if you'll just listen to me, as you have so far, all the way to election night. Let's be serious for a minute, Sam. You must seize presidential power immediately, look presidential as you interview prospective cabinet members, take a week's vacation with your wife, and never appear uncertain."

"I agree, we'll get started right away. No sense in waiting."

"There's one thing left for you to do and right away. Do it for me, Sam, and do it for your presidency. It's in your best interest that I tell you this now, and you know I wouldn't say this if it were not absolutely in your best interest."

Tom never again wanted to lose his position of influence over Sam, circumvented, that is, by Victoria's bedroom skills.

"We've come through this campaign without anyone confronting my biggest fear."

"Your biggest fear. I didn't think you knew fear, Tom."

"Your affair with Victoria is your best-kept secret. It was hinted at a time or two, but no one really knew or could prove anything. Now it must end, Sam. You have a presidency to protect, and you cannot be pulled down by continuing this affair with your vice president. End it, Sam, and end it now!"

"What on earth could you possibly be referring to, Tom?" Sam responded sarcastically.

"You've done enough for her. What more can you do? Educated her at one of the finest Ivy League schools in the country, developed her military career from lieutenant to general, saw to it that she was a European base commander. Now you're making her vice president of the United States, Sam. What more do you need to do for her? You will be the president. Your legacy by the time you leave office could be that of the greatest president to have ever lived. She will be your vice president, the first women to ever hold this office. That relationship alone will be difficult enough to manage. She'll want power; wait and see. All she really has to do is taste political power, and her demand for it will never end. So stop playing Russian Roulette with her, before she shoots you right through the head. You know I'm right, Sam. End it. I'm the best friend you've got. End it and end it now before it's too late, and no one will be able to spin the damage she'll do to you, not even me, Sam!" Tom waited for an answer and watched Sam think.

"End what, Tom? There's nothing to end!"

* * *

"Eagan Ticket Wins in a Landslide,
Vice President-Elect Pierce Makes History"

The headlines of the unfurled *New York Times* stare up from the bedroom floor at the ceiling. To preserve the intimacy of the inner sanctum, the campaign's outer suite's doors are locked and bolted to bar uninvited entrance into the campaign suite's bedroom. It's now the wee hours following the election night speechmaking, concession, and celebration. Victoria and Sam lie together nude in a giant king bed, next to a nightstand table with an electric clock radio that displays 3:11 a.m. and a champagne bottle three-fourths empty.

"Victoria, time to leave." The president-elect shakes the vice president–elect. "Do you think anyone saw us together?"

Victoria, in a groggy state, responded, "Since when did you start caring about that, Sam? Do you want me to start calling you 'Mr. President'? I think I want you to call me 'Madam Vice President.'" She leans over and kisses Sam passionately.

"Mr. President, you're a stud . . . my stud!"

Victoria stands up. Sam follows her exceptionally curved figure into the illumination of the bathroom's night light. She returns along the same path, still undressed.

"Madam Vice President, there's a matter we must discuss."

"What's that, Mr. President?"

"I want to thank you. You were right on all counts about your role in this campaign. Without you, we would not or could not have won."

"Of course, we make a great team. I'm delighted you will be president of the United States, and I will be your vice president. Some day, Sam, I'll want more, but I'm used to waiting. But it's no secret: I love you. I have since I was nineteen."

"Victoria, we cannot maintain this kind of relationship while we are together in office. Sooner or later, you know, we will be fodder for the tabloids and the paparazzi. It will totally destroy the credibility of my presidency."

"What are you saying, Sam?"

"It's over. Cut this long affair. There's no other choice for us now."

Victoria stared in silence at the clock radio, 3:26 a.m., the only real light in the bedroom. As she stared longer, her thoughts became exhausted and confused. She answered.

"Let me ask you, Sam: why did you think I did this?" Before Sam could answer, she continued. "I'll tell you why. I did it for you because I worship the ground you walk on. This was not about me becoming vice president, this was about you becoming the president. My military mind saw a way for you to conquer your life's ambition—not my ambition, but yours. Yes, I wanted desperately to give something back to someone who had given me so much, but what I really wanted to hear from you tonight is not, 'Thank you, Victoria,' but 'Victoria, I love you.' Words you've never said to me—ever, Sam. Guess I was wrong to think that making you president might . . ." Victoria stopped.

"Look, Victoria, I'm sorry. I told you this would be the ride of your life. You are the first woman to be vice president of the United States. You are the present-day Susan B. Anthony. Don't throw it away on love."

Victoria was not listening.

"If something were to happen to me, you would then become the first woman to be president. More likely, you will be elected president in your own right, but you must start that campaign now while you have all the power behind you as vice president. Our success together will make you someday the president of the United States. Everyone eventually loses at love, with no consolation. Look at the consolation that is laid out before you, ready for the taking. So take it!"

"Sam, you just made the worst decision of your life! Never forget that it was me that made you the president, not your ol' buddy, Tom. Tell that miserable bastard that his polling bullshit had nothing to do with my victory. It was my raw instincts that won this election, and the line for credit starts right behind my ass. Yes, I'll take vice president, Sam. I'll take president of the United States Senate. I'll even take president of the United States, but it's meaningless. This is Tom's plot against me, not yours. Right, Sam? He fears my influence over you. Well, you can tell the spineless bastard his assassination attempt failed. I'm alive. I'll survive. It's his ass that will soon be dead!"

CHAPTER EIGHTEEN

Winter/Spring 2009

From Victoria's perspective, behind the podium, seated with her party's most prestigious dignitaries, she pretended to listen to Sam's inaugural address but stared aimlessly instead out onto a sea of faceless loyalists gathered beneath his podium on Capitol Hill. It was cold, and his words were shadowed by the vapor escaping from his breath. "A new generation of Americans will overcome challenges never before faced with opportunities never before imagined." Sam's inaugural delivery was near perfect. He had ample time to write his address and rehearse its delivery in the days between November and January, the final lame-duck days of his predecessor's administration. Persuasive speaking brought success to Sam as a young Roanoke lawyer and ultimately brought him success in Congress. He wanted his inaugural address to be remembered in history as the greatest ever given by a president.

Some of the faces nearer the front were more recognizable to Victoria. They were the moneyed who financed the winning campaign and sat according to their rank of giving. Tom saw to it that these loyalists were rewarded with the coveted places of honor nearest the elevated podium to hear the flow of Sam's eloquent words drop down over them like water pouring over a dam. Some editorialist decried Sam's victory as one bought by the millions they raised. Tom unknowingly quoted President Jackson, "But to the victor go the spoils," and for once Tom was not concerned with public opinion, preferring instead to reward these benefactors, who would be reminded later, right after the Inaugural Ball, that Sam's reelection would begin the next day.

Numb from the cold and emptied by rejection, Victoria listened to Sam through an emotional filter that caused his words to be nonsensical. "Cut this long affair," Victoria remembered his parting line. "Affair," to Sam, meant the conclusion of an impermanent relationship, a severance as easy for him as discarding worn-out luggage. But for Victoria, ending the "affair" meant the conclusion of a permanent relationship, a severance as difficult for her as separating heart from soul. Losing Sam was not the end of an affair; rather, losing Sam was to become the incense of a burning soul, and the phoenix to emerge from those ashes would be an avian creature more horrific than anything found in Greek mythology.

"And I bring to my administration Brigadier General Victoria Pierce as the vice president." The relentless applause, laced with whistles and shouts, snapped a smiling Victoria back into her campaign persona, modestly waving her acknowledgment, then clapping together her white gloved hands while pointing figuratively to Sam, her president. But Sam was not her president. Sam, that day, became her stepping-stone, the last stone to cross before she became the president.

For Victoria, transitioning to vice president was far easier than Sam's transition to president. Tom had been successful in classifying Victoria as the "titular" head, a vice president with whom the president would not share power and someone with limited access to the president, thus achieving

Tom's twin goals of rendering Victoria politically barren and denying her physical proximity to the president. She would be utilized in her areas of her expertise, as consultant to the president on military affairs and congressional policy, the latter expertise to be acquired as the Senate's presiding officer. Victoria did, however, advocate and then insist that Sam nominate her choice for chair of the Joint Chiefs of Staff— the one political plum given to her in exchange for making him president of the United States. Sam quickly acceded to her choice of General Daniel S. Fowler, who delivered the military-industrial complex for the Eagan camp. Victoria always knew where she stood with Dan. His words were plain and honest. Otherwise, Victoria was relegated to her role as the president's surrogate ribbon cutter, a role spurned by Maggie O'Connor.

While Sam was smothered in the enormity of taking the reins of the presidency, Victoria settled easily into her role as president of the U.S. Senate, a title given to her, not by Sam, but by the U.S. Constitution. Mastering the Senate rules was a daunting task, as it would be for any general who understood little about building consensus through debate— preferring, instead, to steamroll the enemy in combat. But she was a quick study, and there was no shortage of eager coaches who knew these rules better than they knew the Ten Commandments. The vice president also quickly learned that powerful deals were negotiated in the Senate Dining Room, and hobnobbing there commanded far more political power than directing debate on the Senate floor. The country's military bases and the Senate Dining Room would be the staging area for her own presidential campaign. She would learn how to be presidential by observing Sam and by securing a confidant, but not a coward like Tom Pearsall. Her confidant would be a Marine with true mettle, chairman of the Joint Chiefs of Staff, General Daniel S. Fowler.

* * *

January turned to May. Victoria combined a vice presidential visit to Camp Pendleton with a literal ribbon-cutting ceremony, opening a new interstate bridge outside of San Diego that had been five years in construction. Sam's administration had nothing to do with the massive undertaking, but that mattered little to Tom, who was prepared to redirect the converging media from the bridge to Sam. Ever the opportunist, Tom knew he could tap into the media hype surrounding the billion-dollar project and the relief offered to commuters delayed by alternate routes, frustrated by the five-year completion date. Due to the scope and magnitude of the project, the opening ceremony would attract national, perhaps international, media attention. The vice president would today represent her president who by necessity was managing the nation's more serious business back in Washington. Besides, the media always relished following the widely popular and photogenic vice president, much more so than the president.

"This bridge represents the best and worst of what our government has to offer. We stand today atop an engineering masterpiece, a bridge that pulls two shores together, opening a conduit for the efficient transfer of vehicular traffic above and the maritime traffic below. But we also stand on a bridge two years behind schedule and $50 million over budget."

Against this backdrop, Victoria captivated her admirers, mostly dads shouldering small children out to see up close the glamorous vice president, who would soon slice the red, white, and blue ribbon that stretched across the bridge's eight lanes of traffic.

As Victoria continued her prepared speech, her delivery became labored as she tried to elevate her voice over the approaching thunder of jet engines propelling the navy's Sea

King helicopter, *Marine One*, the presidential helicopter, no less. Victoria paused, irritably, as she did not recognize the distinctive rumble of the Sea King helicopter approaching from the rear or the importance of its mission. She heard only an interruption, as she looked up, waiting for the noisy disturbance to clear. Much to her annoyance, the pilot, instead of flying over, descended, hovering over the starboard side of the bridge trying to identify a safe landing area. Touching down with its dual blades and jet engines in a continuous and deafening roar, several Marines and plainclothes agents rushed from the aircraft, like soldiers zigzagging in combat, communicating by wireless military devices in code to the Secret Service guarding the vice president. The agent closest to the vice president grabbed her elbow, trying to forcibly turn her in the direction of the presidential helicopter. Victoria, still misunderstanding the mission unfolding, rebuffed the agent's overture by pulling her elbows away, freeing herself from such a rude interference. Finally, this agent stepped between the vice president and her microphone as all the agents in charge of protecting the vice president descended upon her as if they were about to obstruct an assassin's bullet. Whisking Victoria within seconds beneath the swirling blades of the waiting Sea King helicopter, she disappeared inside the passenger compartment before the crowd could comprehend what they had just witnessed. As *Marine One* thundered away from its perch, a dignitary in a Padres baseball cap approached the microphone and asked the crowd to maintain calm. He said, "There is no danger, please remain calm. We will continue with the program shortly. There is an emergency requiring the vice president to return immediately to Washington."

"So just what the hell is going on here? You guys certainly know how to manhandle a lady in the middle of an important speech. Couldn't this wait?" Victoria yelled, accustomed to talking above the interior roar of a Marine helicopter's engine.

"Madam Vice President, I am Adam McIntyre, agent in charge of the CIA's West Coast operations. We received a communiqué from the White House at 10:30 hours this morning that President Eagan suffered a severe stroke in Washington earlier today. He was rushed for treatment to Bethesda Naval Hospital."

"Say again."

"The president suffered a stroke, is presently comatose, and is unable to communicate. CIA headquarters, according to emergency protocol, has instructed me to return the vice president to our nation's capital in the interest of national security."

Victoria stared blankly into McIntyre's face trying to comprehend the impact of what she knew she just heard. After several seconds, she responded.

"National security?"

"Madam Vice President, you are now or soon will be in charge of our nation's nuclear arsenal in case of enemy attack."

"Is there any evidence of attack or invasion?"

"Negative. You also need to return to Washington immediately as the Chief Justice of the United States Supreme Court is standing by at the White House ready to administer the oath of office in the event of the president's death."

"What's Sam's present medical condition?"

"Critical but stable, Madam Vice President."

"What about the press? What do they know about the president's condition?"

"Nothing official. We did not want the press to be asking you awkward questions about this before you were informed. We tried to intercede before you began your speech, but we were too late. Now that we've publicly shanghaied the vice president in front of the world press, you can be sure that the media knows something major is up. By the time you arrive back in Washington, the nation and world will know for sure. The White House is awaiting your instructions on how to proceed. They have drafted a release for your review." Agent McIntyre handed the release to Victoria. She quickly read it and nodded her approval.

"Release it now. The country cannot be kept in the dark about the president's condition for the next three hours. Add here that I am *en route* back to the White House." Victoria pointed to a spot on the release. "Also, schedule a televised address to the nation no later than 1900 hours."

"Anything more?"

"Yes, I want the chairman of the Joint Chiefs to personally brief me on all matters concerning the president's medical condition and national security issues at Camp David this afternoon. I will not—repeat, will not—be advised by anyone else in Sam's administration, particularly not Tom Pearsall. The briefing with Dan Fowler will begin immediately by secured transmission en route back to Washington, one hour into the flight. See to it that General Fowler is immediately transported by military escort to Camp David."

Fifteen minutes later, *Marine One* landed on the tarmac at Camp Pendleton, where Victoria was transferred, surrounded by intense security, to the waiting and refueled *Air Force Two* for the four-and-a-half-hour flight back to Washington. Along its flight path, a squadron of F-15 fighter jets surrounded each wing of the Boeing 757. Victoria arrived by armored limousine at Camp David at 6:45 p.m. Eastern Daylight Time.

"The United States armed forces are on stand-by alert throughout the world, but intelligence does not reveal any overt or subversive military threat presently to the United States or its allies." Dan Fowler reported to the vice president on a litany of topics, mostly of a military nature, before he briefed her on the president's current medical condition.

"General, there's been no change in the president's status. What the hell do I call you now, anyway?"

"You've never had much trouble with 'Victoria.'"

"Look then, Victoria, everyone knows how close you are to the president, so if I get a little too salty . . . off color—well, you know. Just let me know."

"We're Marines, Dan. I can take it. I appreciate straight talk. Besides, Sam and I have been personally estranged for quite some time. I have no more tears left for him, so just get on with it, General Fowler."

"As we discussed en route, the president suffered a debilitating stroke, but he received early medical intervention and continues to be monitored by the foremost medical experts in the world. Quite frankly, had he not received immediate emergency intervention, it would have been unlikely he would have survived the initial stroke, just like our Marine corpsmen intervening on the battlefield."

"Well, it's not exactly the same, Dan."

"The hell you say. Early medical intervention is early medical intervention."

"Will you please continue your briefing, General Fowler?"

Dan lit a cigar. "OK. The next forty-eight hours are critical to the determination of the president's recovery. Bottom line, right now, the president is unconsciousness, pretty damned near a corpse if you ask me, but the docs say he's got a shot at recovery." Dan read verbatim from the papers in his hand. "His prognosis for making a complete recovery, though possible, is indeterminable at this time." He looked up. "One thing is for sure right now. There's no certainty as to when or if Sam will be able to resume his constitutional powers as president of the United States. How's that for a formal briefing? Cleaned it right up, yes siree?"

"But he's still the president, technically speaking?"

"Yeah, he's still the president, technically, but if the United States were to come under nuclear attack, he could not perform his duties as commander in chief of the armed forces. So I have taken the liberty—"

"So who's in charge of our nuclear arsenal, right now?"

"Right now, he technically is still president with all presidential powers."

"You mean a president who is lying comatose in a hospital bed is in charge of our nuclear arms?"

"I'm getting to that, Victoria, damn it. Let me finish what I have got to say and then ask your questions. You're worse than my damned subordinates at Camp Pendleton— always interrupting before I can finish. Now where was I? OK. The Constitution. Ready for that?"

Victoria nodded, not wanting to interrupt.

"I have taken the liberty of reviewing for you the Twenty-fifth Amendment to the United States Constitution. Are you aware of its provisions, General? I mean, Victoria?"

"Vaguely. Adam McIntyre mentioned something about this on the flight in."

"Because of the threat to national security, I have been reviewing the plain language of its provisions and am prepared to advise you on the transfer of presidential power to you, when you are ready."

"If there's confusion as to who still has control over our nuclear arsenal, I better get some authority PDQ before some rogue government out there realizes there is no one in charge here!"

"The Twenty-fifth Amendment provides for the transfer of presidential power to the vice president in the event that the president is unable to perform the duties of his office.

It's really a rather simple procedure requiring you, as the vice president, and a majority of the president's cabinet to certify that Sam is unable to perform his powers or duties as president, which is clearly the case here."

"Certify to whom?"

"The Speaker of the House of Representatives and the President Pro Tempore of the Senate."

"You mean Maggie O'Connor?"

"Yeah, her name is on this . . . on this letter right here, and the other is the President Pro Tempore of the Senate."

Dan Fowler handed the letter to Victoria. She read it.

"You mean you have obtained the unanimous consent of the president's cabinet for me to assume the office of president?"

"That's acting president, not president."

"Just what in the hell is an 'acting president'?"

Victoria's military aide entered the room, interrupting, "Do you wish to take a call from Tom Pearsall? He's rather insistent."

"Tell him he'll have to wait!" The aide left the room. "Or drop dead," Victoria said in a stage whisper." Victoria snapped back. "Continue, Mr. Chairman."

"I'm really not too sure what the hell an acting president is but I'll get to that, First things first. You need to know that a few members of the president's cabinet were quite hesitant about signing this letter, but I assured them that it was in the national interest to immediately transfer presidential power to the vice president under the Twenty-fifth Amendment. Most agreed that it was in the national interest." Dan chuckled. "One or two held out to see how Sam might do in the next twenty-four to forty-eight hours. I assured them that they were in the minority and that you could assume the office over their dissent, but that you were likely to immediately kick their ass out of your administration—I meant to say 'seek their resignation,' but they got the point anyway—after you became the acting president. That made it unanimous!"

Victoria smiled at Dan Fowler and asked, "What's next?"

"This letter must be signed by you and delivered immediately to the Speaker of the House and the President Pro Tempore of the Senate. That's all it takes."

"But Maggie O'Connor will never go along with this."

"Makes no difference. Neither she nor anyone else has the capacity to overrule the constitutional provision. The transfer of power is not subject to congressional confirmation, popular vote, or any other damned democratic thing like that. It's merely a declaration that the vice president becomes the acting president—that is, until the president is capable of resuming his duties or until the next presidential election, whichever comes first. For all practical purposes, General Pierce, you are now the president of the United States. You are not technically the president, but the Constitution refers to you as the acting president."

At 9:00 p.m., Victoria was seated behind the president's desk in the Oval Office of the White House. She was dressed in a dark navy suit, reminiscent of her military dress uniform. Only one television camera was stationed squarely in front of her to capture her presentation from a single frontal position. After counting down sequentially with five fingers, the cameraman pointed to the vice president that she was now live.

"Good evening. It is with a sad heart that I must confirm what the news media has been reporting to you throughout this day. President Sam Eagan lies in critical but stable condition at Bethesda Naval Hospital here in Washington, the victim of a massive stroke this morning. Faithfully by his side is his wife of forty years, First Lady Betty Eagan, and a team of the best medical personnel our country and the world have to offer."

Victoria's eyes moistened unexpectedly at the mention of Betty Eagan. *Must his solace come from someone who cares so little?* Victoria prayed to herself, *God, please not now. Don't let me lose it in front of the entire world.* She was not going to let her lifelong adversary trip her up. Victoria quickly regained her composure and continued.

"I speak for all Americans when I say, we pray that the president will make a full and speedy recovery. If sheer will and determination could restore the president to complete health, then his recovery is a certainty. But we must face the medical reality that a complete recovery remains less certain. Only time will tell.

"Thus, with the advice and consent of the president's cabinet, and as the duly elected vice president of the United States, I have sought to constitutionally protect our republic during such a time as this by activating the procedures for transfer of presidential power found in the Twenty-fifth Amendment to the United States Constitution. This is an important but rather obscure amendment that has been used sparingly, on a voluntary basis, since its adoption in 1967 after the assassination of President John Kennedy. It provides for the vice president to become the acting president in the event that the president becomes unable to discharge the powers and duties of his office. Due to President Eagan's medical uncertainty, comatose state, and his inability to voluntarily sign over to me his authority to act as president, I am left no choice but to proceed without his consent. There is no doubt, and I repeat no doubt, that at this time President Eagan is incapable of performing his powers and duties as president.

"This afternoon at five o'clock, guided by the able assistance of the chairman of the Joint Chiefs of Staff, General Daniel S. Fowler, I issued a communiqué, signed by me and every member of the president's cabinet. This communiqué was hand delivered to the Speaker of the House and President Pro Tempore of the Senate, officially informing our congressional leaders of the transfer of presidential power from the president to the vice president as provided for in the Twenty-fifth Amendment.

"Again, the assessment of the president's medical condition was acknowledged and endorsed by every member of the president's cabinet and his attending physicians. I will continue to discharge the duties of acting president until President Eagan recovers and returns to his rightful office. In the interim, I am naming General Fowler as the acting vice president.

"Now, it's time to turn our attention to business as usual, carrying forward President Eagan's farsighted policies and programs. I ask for the prayers of all Americans for the president's speedy recovery and for me as acting president in the execution of the office of the president and as the commander in chief. May God be with the president and our great country. Thank you."

The same cameraman who signaled at the beginning of the address cut a signal with his finger across his neck, indicating that Victoria was off camera. Network anchors picked up immediately to offer their commentary on the acting president's speech, explaining the constitutional transfer of presidential power, and recounting for the uninformed the sequence of the day's tragic events. Victoria had just announced the first-ever involuntary transfer of presidential power from president to vice president under the Twenty-fifth Amendment. The vice president had stepped in, not to succeed a deceased president struck down by assassination or a president who resigned, but a living president struck down by incapacitation. With the assistance of Dan Fowler, her new acting vice president, Victoria rose and retreated further into the confines of the White House. Along the way she received the handshakes and good wishes of Sam's cabinet and invited congressional leaders, save one. Speaker of the House Maggie O'Connor, escorted by husband Larry, with not so much as a congratulatory word, fled the White House through a side entrance at the point that Victoria announced Dan Fowler as the acting vice president.

At the dawn of the new morning, alone in her bedroom, Victoria reflected on Sam. Fate made Victoria president, and fate handed Sam what he deserved. Victoria felt pity but not remorse. Reflecting on their twenty-five-year affair, Victoria saw that Sam refused to reciprocate the love she had for him. Sam could not and would not yield his heart. He feared more an unpalatable divorce than a lasting relationship with Victoria in a marriage that from the beginning would never be. Victoria concluded that Sam got what he deserved.

Late that morning, Victoria met with Sam's cabinet, now her cabinet, ostensibly to discuss the president's agenda but actually to give the press the opportunity to photograph the orderly transfer of presidential power and the restoration of governmental business under the acting president. Victoria met privately with congressional leaders and went directly to Maggie O'Connor's office to make overtures to a House Speaker who, but for her misfortune in the stairwell, would herself have now been the acting president.

Before leaving, Dan further briefed Victoria on the constitutional dilemma facing Victoria and the country so early into Sam's first term as president. He pointed out that President Garfield was the most obvious example of a president incapacitated after an attempted assassination in a Washington train station who suffered from an incurable gunshot wound for months before his eventual demise, and Woodrow Wilson actually had a stroke in office. But during these times, there was no constitutional provision to authorize the vice president to act for the president. Government then was far less complicated, and there was no nuclear arsenal to be protected from an enemy's first strike.

Dan also offered another unlikely but theoretical eventuality. If by happenstance something tragic were to befall Victoria, who then would become the acting president? Victoria remained in the office of vice president while exercising her constitutional duties of acting president as long as Sam remained incapable of resuming his constitutional duties as president. If Sam was restored to health, he would resume his office. But if he did not and Victoria tragically died in office, there was no constitutional provision for who then would become the acting president, because Sam would still be quite alive as the constitutionally elected president, albeit a comatose one. Victoria, though she was the constitutional acting president, never relinquished her constitutionally elected office of vice president nor officially assumed the office of president. The Constitution does not provide the acting president with any express authority to appoint an acting vice president, as Victoria did that night. Maggie O'Connor, as Speaker of the House, was next in line in presidential succession, but only if there was a vacancy in the offices of both the president and vice president. Dan reminded Victoria that she had no authority to name him as acting vice president and wished that she had consulted someone in the know before making such a startling last-second announcement. Dan expected that Victoria would have to issue a correction or defend the appointment somehow through her implied powers as acting president. Dan could only surmise that Victoria's announcement of his appointment had drawn the immediate ire of Speaker O'Connor, causing her to stomp away from the White House, in Dan's words, "in a complete tizzy," fearing her continuing presence would be some sort of a silent acquiescence to

Victoria's appointment of an acting vice president. The real question that remained, according to Dan, was who would become the acting president in the event of Victoria's death, incapacity, or resignation? Would it fall to Dan Fowler or Maggie O'Connor?

"You can't do it. I will not permit it. It's unconstitutional," Maggie O'Connor stated firmly as she leaned over her desk, pointing her finger at Victoria.

"It's pointless, Maggie, to bicker about something that doesn't really matter and likely will never happen. Either Sam's going to get well and return to office, or I will serve out the remainder of his term. Then there will be an election. Either way, the question of succession will never arise."

"No, it is an infringement upon the office of the Speaker, and I will not permit it, even if it's merely theoretical."

"Well, had I known you felt so strongly about this, Madam Speaker, I would have never made the announcement last night. I just thought the American public would be relieved to have an acting vice president, particularly someone as competent as Dan Fowler."

"Several congressional leaders agree with me, and we are considering filing a lawsuit challenging the constitutionality of your appointment, that some here have described as a colossal usurpation of constitutional power. Really, just going ahead and naming an acting vice president in a nationwide address to millions of Americans without congressional consultation or a shred of constitutional authority."

"I apologize, Maggie. But this appointment is not about you. It's about the psychological well-being of our country, and your reaction is nothing more than a tempest in a teapot. I cannot and will not lend myself to creating more national uncertainty by retreating from last night's announcement. It would just be too unsettling. I am prepared to ask Congress to amend the Twenty-fifth Amendment to make provision for an acting vice president, and then there should be no doubt about the legality of my appointment of Dan Fowler, subject to congressional confirmation. Amending the Constitution is left to Congress or to the states, as I understand it. What exactly will happen to our nuclear arsenal if I become incapacitated? If Sam had died, no one would have challenged my constitutional succession to be president and then to automatically name a vice president, subject to congressional approval, which is exactly how President Ford became President Ford. He was first named vice president, not elected vice president, by President Nixon when Spiro Agnew left office, and Ford himself named Nelson Rockefeller, not elected, as his vice president after Richard Nixon resigned. Why not have an identical process between an acting president and an acting vice president so the country will not be thrown into a state of crisis?"

"There's nothing to clear up. If something happens to you, I become—I mean, the Speaker of the House becomes—the acting president. That's much clearer than what you did last night. What you cannot do is just create a vice president of the United States merely by announcing him as the acting vice president. Now if Sam dies, then you can clearly name your own vice president, subject to congressional approval. But if you insist on maintaining this constitutional charade, then there are two other branches of government quite willing to stop you. You're not in authority for more than a couple of hours, and already you're seizing congressional power. Some over here on the Hill say you're acting more like a general than a president."

"All I can see is that we are off to a really bad start, Maggie. You can be sure that it's no insult to me to be called a general, because, by God, that's exactly what I am." Victoria rose and left the Speaker's office. Both the acting president and the Speaker of the House ultimately decided not to make a public issue over Victoria's appointment of Dan Fowler as acting vice president, and Congress did not challenge the appointment in court.

The days that followed were uneventful, except that Tom Pearsall was dispatched to meet with the president ostensibly to report his medical condition to the press, but in reality this assignment was designed to remove him from the confidential confines of the White House to permanent exile at Bethesda Hospital. As Sam's presidential spokesperson, Tom made press announcements twice a day. Both Tom and Betty waited daily for Sam to regain enough consciousness to sign his name to a letter that Tom prepared for delivery to the Speaker and President Pro Tempore of the Senate declaring that Sam could resume his lawful presidential powers. Of course, that would mean that Tom would assume the role of Sam's stand-in president. In reality, Sam was not close to resuming his presidential duties, incapable of even scrawling his name on Tom's letter. If Tom could present such a letter to Congress, Sam's cabinet, remarkably responsive to Victoria in her first few days, would have to decide the issue of the president's competency, but if they sided with Victoria, the determination would switch to Congress to resolve the disagreement between the president and vice president.

Sam, as a former United States Senator, would likely have the political edge. This circumstance put Victoria on the horns of dilemma. She needed to incur favor with Sam's appointed cabinet members, but she needed to be firm with them about their allegiance to her as long as she was the acting president, which in all likelihood would be for the remainder of Sam's term of office. Or she could, as Dan suggested, dismiss the unfaithful, deriving the power of dismissal from an implied interpretation of her authority under the Twenty-fifth Amendment. Fortunately for Victoria, in the weeks that followed, this issue did not arise as Sam remained in medical limbo, drifting in and out of consciousness, and clearly incapable of resuming the powers and duties of president. Sam's cabinet was painfully aware of his condition, though Tom spun his recovery as best he could in his twice-daily press announcements.

* * *

In the summer months that followed, Sam showed signs of improvement, but with no real ability to communicate and certainly not ambulate. His medical team predicted that Sam would regain some mental capacity, but he would likely remain permanently bedridden. Victoria and Dan continued their daily contact with Sam's handpicked cabinet in order to solidify their support, using Victoria's considerable presidential powers as the acting president.

What was unexpected was Victoria's approval rating among American citizens. At one point during the summer, Victoria captured the highest approval rating of any president ever to have held office. She was viewed more like a rock star than a president. Foreign heads of state rushed to her side in a stream of highly publicized diplomatic visits to the White House. Victoria made a point of visiting Sam at the hospital and reporting directly to the media herself, always upstaging Tom in carefully worded, less optimistic tones, at the afternoon press conferences on the hospital grounds. Americans rallied around the first woman ever to command the powers of the president of the United States, albeit as acting president, and her approval ratings, although fluctuating, escalated beyond what Victoria, and certainly Tom, ever imagined. Victoria governed well as the acting president, but the real president, Sam Eagan, lay vegetating in a Bethesda hospital bed, daily gaining an improving prognosis under the best medical care that the world had to offer.

CHAPTER EIGHTEEN

* * *

The skeleton of a bony hand emerged from the water's edge of the Chesapeake Bay. Two small children, one holding a crab line and the other a dipnet, dropped both and ran screaming to their mothers, who were aimlessly chatting away while spreading a picnic lunch underneath a green and white beach umbrella. Twelve minutes later, the Chincoteague Rescue Squad arrived with sirens screaming in a rushed attempt to rescue a man who had been dead for almost thirty years.

From inside his brown and white sheriff's vehicle, a deputy picked up his radio and said, "Looks like this guy's been here one hell of a long time."

"Ship the ol' buzzard to the morgue," the response crackled back.

The corpse, a skeleton remarkably intact, was transported to the coroner's morgue for possible identification from a national data bank of missing persons and a determination of cause of death, if that even remained a possibility after so many years in a watery grave. A balding man in a white jacket with pockets stuffed and spilling over with various metal implements peeked under a sheet at the assembly of bones and walked back to his telephone.

"Sheriff, DNA is probably our best shot. Hold on. Looks like this ol' boy's been gone longer than we've been collecting DNA. I better check for dental records that might be a match. Tell you what, I'll make a radiograph and send it to you. . . . Yeah, that's an X-ray." The coroner hung up, walked back over to his skeletal riddle, and scratched his head as he examined a broken jaw still full of teeth.

CHAPTER NINETEEN

Summer 1981

Rodriguez reluctantly kept his end of the bargain. He did not want to, but Victoria left him no way to wiggle out. She had him dead to rights; his death knell was a copy of the motel registration and bill for Room 512, with the signature of Enrique Rodriguez scrawled at the bottom. What Rodriguez did receive was valuable on-the-job training from Victoria as to the meaning of the Marine Corps' newly issued unclassified regulations on sexual harassment. He vowed never to again fall prey to such trickery. He was not at all repentant of his own tactics but indeed savvier as to the tactics of a shrewd woman.

On the day of Victoria's basic training graduation, Rodriguez decided to attend the ceremony, both to avoid a last-minute snafu in her ordered assignment and to be sure she permanently shipped out that day, never to get tangled up with her again. Appropriately enough, her graduation fell on July 4. The parade field at Parris Island was filled with dignitaries reviewing troops marching in perfectly called cadence, perfectly pressed dress uniforms, and perfectly polished shoes. As each company passed in review, they saluted in unison, preceded by the command, "Eyes right." The brass were seated from the rear of the stage to front in neat rows, with the highest-ranking officers at the front, but all wore stern and faceless expressions. The reviewing stand, because of the military significance of Independence Day, was draped prodigiously in the Stars and Stripes with no spot bare of the red, white, and blue.

Sergeant Judy paraded her platoon past the reviewing stand with her Smokey the Bear hat tilted so low in front it was a wonder she could see where she was going, but behind her professionally called cadence there was more than a hint of pride for this platoon, a pride in fact more significant than ever before. Sergeant Judy's platoon took its place within its company after Judy ordered, "Pla . . . toon, Halt," followed by "A . . . ten . . . hut!"

Before the dawn of this Independence Day and without naming the person outright, Judy's CO announced that one recruit from her platoon would be recognized as Marine of the Cycle, a coveted award always given before to a man.

The words "Platoon Leader Victoria Pierce" rang out through the loudspeakers for all to hear on the parade field. "Front and center." Victoria saluted the post commander as she came to attention in front of the reviewing stand. He descended from the elevated stage by the stairs, approached Victoria, pinned the ribbon on her dress uniform above her left pocket, and said, "For the first time in Marine Corps history, this award will be given to a Marine, the finest of this cycle, who outperformed every other Marine on this field today and who on this Independence Day so happens to be a woman. Congratulations, Private Pierce." Victoria saluted the commander again, acknowledged the recognition with only a stern, "Sir, yes, sir," and stepped back in the ranks of her platoon.

Sergeant Judy beamed her pride as she was the D.I. who produced and quite frankly politicked as hard as permitted internally to have Victoria win the award. Victoria stood swaying, locked at attention, knees wobbling, literally about to faint from the acute shock and the broiling sun, mentally telling herself she must avoid the embarrassment of being recognized as the first woman Marine of the Cycle, yet wimpy enough to fall out in front of God and country on a field with five hundred witnesses.

Victoria managed to hold up, and after the final command, "Com . . . pan . . . eeeee . . . Dis . . . missed," she was flooded with congratulations from every quarter of the field. Victoria, with genuine affection, embraced Sergeant Judy in an all too short and tearful good-bye. There was no time to celebrate or to bask in the first major recognition of her life. Victoria collected all her personal gear to ship out for advance training as communication specialist aboard a military plane bound for Bogotá, Colombia, at 2400 hours.

After touchdown in Bogotá and transportation to base, Victoria would have been making up her rack in her barracks and not sauntering through the Bogotá market where she met Walter Clarke on that infamous Sunday afternoon, had it not been that her assigned quarters were all but deserted when she reported for duty. The only person on the premises was one lone sergeant who, after taking a good look at the female private, granted her immediate afternoon leave under the strictest condition that she report back to the sergeant's desk no later than 1800 hours, where she would become some other sergeant's problem to figure out how to billet a female soldier in an all-male barracks.

After their late afternoon excursion through the Bogotá marketplace, Walter Clarke and Victoria Pierce stood beside Clarke's Land Rover with his bamboo furniture spilling out the back. Having agreed to give her a ride back to the barracks, Walter Clarke dropped Victoria at the front gate, smiled broadly, winked at his chief negotiator with his pipe extended through the passenger side window, and drove away. For all Victoria knew, this would be the last time she would ever see the nice Englishman.

Victoria figured out that Enrique Rodriguez had played a vengeful practical joke on her when she observed that her billeting orders incorrectly identified her as "Victor Pierce," assigning her to an all-male barracks full of Marines who were milling around in clusters outside, eagerly awaiting her arrival. Once she pointed out the typo to the night sergeant on duty at the front desk, Victoria was transferred immediately to a more gender-appropriate quarters reserved for civilian personnel.

Without elaboration or explanation early Monday morning, a sergeant banged on her door at 0500 hours and ordered Victoria to report directly to the base commander's office at 0700 hours. Victoria paced down a long hallway, floored with dark linoleum squares so brightly polished that she feared she would slip if she walked too fast, to the door of a back corner office draped in front with both the American and Marine Corps flags. A sergeant checked her identification and said, "Major Sparks will see you now." Passing through the door, Victoria removed her cap, stood at attention, and gave the major her best Marine Corps salute. "Sir, yes, sir, Private Victoria Pierce reporting for duty, sir, yes, sir." The major, seated at his desk, lifelessly returned the salute. Victoria, seeing in the corner of her eye another person seated to her left, turned to salute this officer, but her right hand never made it farther than shoulder level, when she exclaimed, "Mr. Clarke, sir, what are you doing here?"

Clarke, dressed much as he was the day before, turned to Major Sparks and said, "Absolutely, the best American I've ever seen communicating in the marketplace. Her Spanish is flawless. What's more, she's comfortable in the culture. Get rid of her green eyes, she will fit right in as an ordinary Colombian—perfect for this undercover assignment."

Major Sparks, looking up from an open file, said, "Have a seat," pointing to the chair in front of his desk, "and tell me, Private, what is it about a farm girl from Oklahoma that makes you so comfortable in this culture?"

Victoria, sitting down, replied, "I adapt well, sir."

"You see, Walt over here is really not what he appears to be. He's an Englishman, alright, but he's also a Marine, like you, just undercover. His assignment was to observe Americans in the city marketplace to find the right soldier for this job. He's been at the selection process for quite some time now. Seems you're it, but Walt did not count on finding a woman. Sit down, Private Pierce, relax, and let's discuss your fitness for this assignment."

"What assignment, sir? I thought I was here to be trained as a Spanish-speaking communications specialist—a desk job.

"That was yesterday. Today, you may well be headed in a completely different direction. Now, the streets of America are being bombarded with Colombian drugs, particularly cocaine. Militant drug lords hide out in the jungle outside the city in tightly fortified impoundments. They buy their drugs locally and ship them directly to the United States, trafficking mostly on the streets of New York."

"Yes, sir, I've heard how readily available cocaine is on the streets of New York City." Victoria paused and then suddenly her complexion turned jet red at the thought, *These guys know I'm Vera, the real me. . . . They know exactly how expert I really am on the New York City drug market. But then again, if they really do know about Vera, they're not saying anything. But if they do know I'm Vera, shouldn't I just go ahead and confess it?* Victoria analyzed her dilemma, further studying the faces of her questioners. *Maybe not. What they need is a Spanish negotiator, not a streetwise drug dealer.* Somewhat relieved,

Victoria concluded they knew nothing about Vera. Victoria's complexion returned to normal.

"We've decided a woman, this time around, would be perfect to infiltrate the compound of a drug lord named Raul."

"This time? What about the other times?" Victoria began to sense this assignment was far worse than any war zone and totally inconsistent with the cushy destination that she pried out of Rodriguez. She began backpedaling, constructing the reasons that these officers had found the wrong Marine for the job.

Clarke responded, "Honestly, we've had some poor luck with our male chaps. They seem to get caught. Just about the time we locate his jungle compound, a constantly moving target, preparing to destroy it, Raul moves again. His intelligence has an uncanny ability to root out our undercover Marines. Now we have gotten some out unharmed, but some have been tortured, and some have given the full measure for their country."

"Sounds like a job for a combat-tested Marine, not me, sir."

"Well, not really," Clarke pressed ahead with his proposal. "This time we will plant a woman inside as a domestic servant. The Latin culture, as you must know, is far less suspicious of women. You will be allowed more freedom and access to move about the compound—a lot safer for you and much more productive in stopping Raul and eliminating his trafficking."

Major Sparks added, "A big plus for you is that Raul is a sucker for a pretty woman, particularly such an attractive woman as yourself, Private."

The conversation was going badly and entirely in the wrong direction. Victoria wanted to spend her time at a desk and on the beach. She might as well have been assigned to a combat zone.

"Look, sirs, I'm grateful for your confidence that you have placed in me, but, believe me, if you knew the real me, you would know you've got the wrong Marine here for this assignment. I'm way too raw—never even been in or even near live combat—and I'm certainly not the bravest Marine you've ever seen. Bound to be others here much better suited—much, much better suited than me!" Victoria, now desperate, thought she might have to go so far as to disclose her true identity as Vera Ochman, collared in an FBI drug bust at the Wicked Whiskey Bar, sent to the federal Witness Protection Program instead of prison for numerous drug violations, and saved only because she snitched on one of the city's biggest drug dealers. *Don't these guys know that? Why was Marshal Slaughter so damned good at covering my trail? Apparently, these men know nothing except what's written about me in the thin file open on Major Sparks's desk.* The major shuffled through the papers in the file.

"Apparently, you've not read your own file. You're totally fluent in Spanish, your intelligence scores are through the roof, you are an expert marksman, you just graduated as the first woman in history to be Marine of the Cycle at Parris Island, and you are, if you don't mind me saying so, drop-dead gorgeous."

"Tell me, is there anything in that file there that was written by an NCO named Rodriguez?"

"Not that I see. Who is Rodriguez?"

"A real jerk in a Marine's uniform!"

Victoria realized that this conversation was almost at the bottom of the hill and about to go down the rest of the way. There was no question in Victoria's mind that she could handle this assignment. It was not a question of her ability. What she questioned was her willingness to give her life to stop the flow of drugs onto the streets of New York. This was a job reserved for a male Marine. She worked hard for this Bogotá assignment, the closest thing she could find to permanent Rest and Relaxation, known to all combat Marines as R&R. She would learn a few skills, muster out after four years, get married, and live a normal life—not wind up dead or tortured in some war lord's jungle compound.

"You really, and I do mean really, sirs, don't know me and the big mistake that you are about to make. You gotta believe me when I say you've got the wrong girl. I mean, the wrong Marine."

Major Sparks looked over to Clarke, "I agree, she's perfect. We already know how and where Raul gets his domestic help. Private Pierce will infiltrate Raul's camp as a domestic servant. She should be ready to go by Monday of next week after her special training and intelligence briefing." Sparks turned to Victoria. "Actually, Pierce, I would have preferred you would have jumped at this assignment like the few good Marines before you, but that's OK. You're a good Marine, too. Certainly you can follow orders. Report back here, ready to start your training, at 1200 hours. Dismissed."

Victoria rose from her chair, stood, and saluted. She said, "Sir, yes, sir," not shouting as she had before when she reported for duty, and this time without even a hint of enthusiasm.

* * *

A bearded Raul, dressed in green jungle fatigues and a soft cap, was a dead ringer for a younger Fidel Castro at age thirty-five, better looking, and far more ruthless. Bumping along a barely cleared path through a bamboo thicket with his entourage, consisting of five army jeeps filled with armed passengers—except for one man with his hands tied behind his back—Raul stopped suddenly at the top of a cliff a hundred yards above a cascading waterfall. Raul stepped out of his jeep and motioned for the prisoner. This man was blindfolded in a red bandana and was led by four guards to a position above the fall. Raul said to the captive, "¡Puede vivir pero dígame el nombre!" (You can live but tell me the name!) A pause of less than three seconds ensued.

Obviously, the man did not respond quickly enough with the name requested. Before the fourth second elapsed, Raul took his sidearm and fired a single bullet into the back of the man's head. The executed man fell forward, tumbling down the cliff through the waterfall and into the water below.

Raul's entourage loaded up, circled in a tight U-turn, and returned along the same bumpy path. In order to combat the unpleasantness of the day, Raul took a fifth of rum from the glove compartment and started chugging large gulps. Raul said aloud, "So easy for him, really. One little name. He could have told me that one name. Instead he dies. He was my brother-in-law's youngest nephew. Now, how I am going to explain this to my sister, Rosa? She will not understand that he betrayed me for money. All she'll talk about is how cute he was as a baby!" Raul drew another chug from the bottle and tossed it angrily out the door.

* * *

Victoria successfully infiltrated the compound as a domestic maid and was learning her responsibilities from Rosa, a younger but quite rotund Colombian, who was Raul's chief servant and eldest sister. Rosa was loyal to Raul and could be trusted inside his bedroom. She demonstrated for Victoria the technique required in making Raul's bed. Victoria said to herself over and over how much she had to remember to answer to "Maria," her undercover name, and, confusingly enough, her second alias in just over a year.

From a distance down the hallway outside the bedroom, Rosa, for years, and Maria, for the first time, heard Raul's drunken singing growing progressively louder until Raul burst through the bedroom door chugging the last drop from his day's second fifth of rum. Rosa escaped her drunken brother by slipping out as he entered. Maria was not so fortunate. They spoke in Spanish.

"Excuse me, sir, I was just finishing making the bed."

Raul sat on the corner of the bed and said, not recognizing Maria in his stupor, "I killed another one of my relatives today. Holy Mother, forgive me." He sat there saying nothing for a long time. Maria backed out behind him toward the door.

"But he was trying to have me killed. Maybe that would be for the best." He looked to see who he was talking to. Maria, caught in her attempt to escape, turned to dust one of the two mounted brass lamps beside the door. She had almost made it out.

"Hey, who are you? Are you another one sent to kill me? Come here. What is your name?"

Victoria, completely rejecting a truthful response to Raul's second question, responded correctly to his third, "Maria."

Raul swayed as he sat on the corner of his bed and stared blankly at the floor. He looked up and squinted through the dim light across the room to see Maria approach to render assistance. Raul halted all wayward motion at the sight of the beauty in front of him. He reached out unexpectedly, firmly grasping Maria's wrist.

Raul said, "Come lie with me and make me forget today."

Maria responded, "I am working, sir."

Raul replied, "Work, work, my orders are not to work! I own everything and everyone under this roof."

Maria pulled her wrists free. A sudden anger spawned a New Yorker's sharp retort: "You don't own me, sir."

Raul stared again blankly at the floor. "Please remind me tomorrow to have you killed…I'm just too tired to do it tonight."

With the last utterance and his day now complete, Raul dropped backwards across the foot of the bed, still grasping his rum bottle. In a matter of seconds he was snoring.

Maria, thanks to her Marine Corps strength training, dragged Raul backward to the front of his bed, rolled him over with the same maneuver she had employed on Rodriguez, and covered him with the bedspread. By the time Maria slipped out the door, the room shook under the ferocity of Raul's snoring. Rosa, waiting for Maria in the hallway, put her finger to her lips. "Shoo." Rosa led Victoria by the arm down the hallway. "Tomorrow, he will remember nothing."

In the bamboo outside the sleeping quarters of the compound, Victoria had hidden her two-way walkie-talkie to be used for communicating with rescue. She boldly slipped past the posted guards, retrieved the walkie-talkie, and blared away.

"Come in, Walt. Do you know what that son of a bitch, first damned day on the job, now, said to me, Walt? I'll tell you what he said. He threatened to kill me. No damned reason at all. Straight out asks me if I have been sent to kill him." She paused.

Clarke replied, "Private, when you are finished talking, you are supposed to say, 'Over.' Then I speak."

"Well, 'Over,' then, you skinny bastard!"

"That's better, but not so loud. Please just settle down. What on earth have you done to make him so angry? Over."

"He was drunk. He shot his nephew today or someone like that. Decided a little late-night sex with me would ease the pain, I guess. Over."

"You said 'no,' of course. It's way too early for that on your first night there. Over."

"You've got that right, but I wasn't exactly thinking it was too early to have sex. I was thinking more what it would be like for him having sex with a corpse."

"Well, of course, you were frightened. Completely understandable. Wish we hadn't told you about the others. Over."

"He's not gross looking or anything, but I hate obnoxious drunks. Just ask Rodriguez. Raul really pissed me off."

"The sex will come later, Pierce, won't it? Over."

"Alright, Clarke, now I really get it. So let's cut all the bullshit about me being the best you've ever seen negotiating in the Bogotá marketplace. My selection for this mission had nothing to do with that, did it, Walt?"

"Say 'Over' when you're finished. You keep forgetting to say 'Over.' Now, Pierce, that's not altogether true. You've got many fine qualities . . . qualities you can use to accomplish our mission there. But face it, Victoria, you can't help that you are a beautiful women. Can you? Over."

"Know what he said, Clarke? 'Please remind me tomorrow to have you killed. I'm just too tired to do it tonight.' Over."

"We've been on too long. It's more dangerous for you to be talking to me now than worrying about Raul. There's really nothing to this. I know Raul. He's definitely a lady's man. Never known him to kill a woman. Lots of men. It was his rum talking. Remember, a smitten Raul is your best protection. Over . . . out."

"Hold on a damned minute, Walt. That's easy for you to say. He was not talking about killing you. By the way, if you don't hear from me tomorrow, be sure to remember how wrong you were, OK, Walt? Walt, are you still there?" Victoria paused, but there was no one on the receiving end of her communication. "OK, out, you bastard!" Victoria threw the walkie-talkie into the darkness.

Late the following afternoon, Rosa and Maria were quickly changing the sheets in Raul's bedroom, scurrying around like two squirrels in hopes of completing their room service before Raul completed lathering and shaving around his beard in the adjoining bathroom so Maria's presence would not trigger Raul's memory of the "tomorrow" issue. Too late. Raul exited the bathroom, looked at Maria, grabbed her hand—gently this time—and apologized. "I am very sorry for my conduct last night. It was a tough day for me. I wish to make amends by inviting you to have dinner with me tonight in my room."

Rosa responded to Maria, "It's not necessary."

Raul stated, "I insist."

Maria nodded, "If you insist."

After they left, Rosa stopped Maria in the hallway and said, "Raul loves all the women, and he will try to love you, too."

Maria's beauty, even in her modest domestic attire, radiated. She arrived at six o'clock for dinner. Raul stood, bowed, and assisted Maria with her chair. Raul's dinner table was, as usual, covered in white linen, but tonight it was also set with the finest china, crystal goblets, and silver.

Looks like a rush to me, Victoria thought to herself. Remembering Clarke's advice about a smitten Raul being Maria's best protection, Victoria made sure that Maria turned on her charm, and so she stared across the table into Raul's eyes. Dinner began with a fig appetizer, extended over four courses, and ended with Raul sipping sherry while smoking an expensive Havana cigar that was at least a foot long.

He said, "Care to join me in a glass of sherry?"

"No, I'm tired from a long day's work and am ready for sleep." Maria pushed her chair backward, stood up, and prepared to leave. Quickly, Raul reached across the narrow table, adept at ensnaring her wrist.

"Please accept my apology?" Raul opened Maria's hand and placed a double-strung necklace of mother of pearl in Maria's palm. "I would never harm such a pretty woman."

"Thank you. Apology accepted."

Maria ignored Raul's invitation for a glass of sherry and excused herself, but before leaving leaned over and kissed his cheek. Maria exited quickly through the door as Raul caressed the outline of her kiss with the back of his hand. She returned to her small sleeping quarters, wearing her mother of pearl necklace, and opened the door to a room filled with cut flowers, so many she could hardly reach her bed. Victoria forgot momentarily that Raul was the object of her undercover mission. She thought Raul to be handsome, a suitor who really knew how to treat a woman. Her superiors never expressly ordered her to do so, but nonetheless they expected her to bed Raul at some point. Victoria thought to herself, *Now what's the harm in combining a little pleasure with business?* Victoria genuinely believed Raul when he said he would never harm such a pretty woman.

Raul was now clearly smitten and intensified his pursuit. Rosa was not to join Maria in cleaning his room so they could talk privately, and they did for hours at a time. Soon, Maria was no longer a domestic servant at all. She was relieved of her duties as Rosa's assistant, which sparked a sharp disagreement, vociferously argued between siblings. The guards in the compound had seen Raul smitten in the past, but not quite like this. The gifts delivered to Maria's room become extravagant. She wore the finest lingerie and silk gowns in complete idleness throughout the day, except now she slept alone in the family's bedroom next door to Raul, and from there she would soon move into the lord of the manor's quarters. Maria planned her final seduction, but her plan was delayed by Raul's weeklong absence to conduct business in the jungle. But for each day of his absence, Raul surprised Maria with gifts hidden in her pathway that daily grew more lavish. By Raul's return on Saturday, diamonds were the order of the day, each in a minimum setting larger than three carats. Certainly, Sanchez had never pursued Victoria like this back on the streets of Brooklyn. She became accustomed to the luxurious life, which sharply contrasted with the Pierce Farm and basic training. Victoria slept longer hours than even on Saturdays in her Brooklyn home. She enjoyed sleeping, dining, and lounging one day at a time. Victoria tried in vain to find her lost walkie-talkie in the bushes after the first night, so all communications were suspended. *What really did they care about me anyway?* Besides, Rosa was suspiciously watching her every move. Perhaps remaining incommunicado would extend her reign as the palace queen. Victoria even began directing Rosa on how to arrange the amenities in Raul's quarters.

Servants moved all of Maria's things to Raul's bedroom on the Saturday of his return. Rosa worked furiously and irritably to appoint the room as Maria had directed. Rosa deeply resented this treatment directed by her domestic hire, and she intended to report her growing suspicions to her brother. But Raul was now so obsessively in love with Maria that Rosa's suspicions would not be enough. Rosa would have to produce the hard evidence.

For Saturday night, Raul ordered the most sumptuous dinner he could imagine. This time Maria elegantly wore a black sequined gown, suitable for a queen, adorned with a diamond necklace, the likes of which she had never seen, even in the storefront window of Tiffany's. As Victoria stared at herself in her dressing table mirror, lost in a daydream, she saw the reflection of her mother's image, the goddess suspended over the mantle in the Ochmans' Brooklyn living room. Victoria's hair and eyes returned to their natural color and mirrored her mother's natural beauty, a beauty that haunted her father every time he looked at her portrait. Victoria picked up a red rose and gazed again at herself, assured that her mother would approve of what she was about to do. Her mother, too, had used her beauty to her advantage. Victoria had but a different theme on the same motive.

After dinner, Raul extended for a second time an invitation to Maria to sip sherry with him, reclining next to him in bed. Maria accepted without hesitation. The sherry was forgotten in the passion of their embrace. Maria expected to yield herself completely, not just for her mission but for her pleasure. To engage in this activity, men and women must disrobe. For Maria to step out of her sequined gown was not altogether uncomplicated. It would take time and effort. Besides, Maria wanted Raul to see her lingerie. She disappeared through the adjoining door into her bedroom's walk-in closet, slipped out of her tight gown, and into a see-through black negligee.

As she returned to surrender into the arms of her lover, automatic weapons rang out throughout the compound much louder than Victoria had ever heard before. Bullets exploded the remnants of the expensive china on the dining room table. Raul jumped up, grabbed his machine gun from underneath his bed, and returned fire through the window behind the outside balcony. Lying completely prone on the floor on the opposite side of the bed, Victoria heard Marines lobbing grenades and armored carriers roaring around in the distance. Raul was badly outgunned, seconds away from being killed, losing his compound, or being captured by the Colombians, which meant death by firing squad. Victoria thought, *Clarke, damn it all. Clarke should have found the walkie-talkie and rung me back up. He thinks I'm dead. Geez, he's called in rescue. Guess he had no way of knowing how much I was enjoying my mission.*

Bullets from automatic weapons blasted everything in the room. Victoria dropped the persona of the palace queen and resumed her identity as Private Pierce. Quite a shock! She heard Marines shouting in the hallway, "You move, I'll cover." In minutes they would be inside the bedroom, gawking at the woman in the lingerie. But Victoria's survival instinct at the moment trumped embarrassment. She decided she would be delighted to come up with a reason for her combat nudity, if she could survive long enough to offer an explanation.

Victoria pulled together a quick plan as she low-crawled her way to a position on the opposite side of the bed next to Raul and yelled in Spanish, "Raul, throw me your machine gun and jump down from the balcony. I'll cover you while you jump. I'll throw you the machine gun, and you cover me while I jump. Your attackers are at the door and will be coming through it in seconds. Now jump!"

Amazingly enough, Raul listened to his lover's advice, threw the machine gun to Maria, waited for Maria to pick it up, and then jumped from the balcony's ledge just as the Marines stormed through the bedroom door. Victoria screamed in her strongest military voice, "I'm a Marine! I'm a Marine! Don't shoot! Don't shoot!" Her semi-nudity caused the attacking male forces to hesitate just long enough for Victoria to check to make sure Raul's automatic machine gun was still loaded as she stepped out onto the balcony. She looked down at Raul, who looked up expecting Maria, his lover, to throw down his weapon. Instead he saw Maria spray bullets across his torso. Raul stared up at his lover in disbelief as Maria stared down into his eyes. With his final gasp, Raul took his hand and blew Maria a kiss, smiled, and died. From that moment and for the rest of her military life, Victoria never again forgot that her mission came first and that she was always a Marine.

Clarke, strangely dressed in full combat fatigues, rushed to Victoria's side, stopping in his tracks to admire Victoria in her combat lingerie.

Clarke inquired, "Why on earth didn't you ring me up? We thought you were dead, like the others."

Before Clarke could ask another uncomfortable question, Victoria explained. "Thank God, Clarke, you got here when you did. I've been held captive for a week, completely trapped as Raul's slave mistress. Rosa wouldn't let me out of her sight long enough for me to find the damned walkie-talkie. It was just a matter of time before Raul would have used me up and tossed me into a shallow grave. What a ruthless man!"

Just as Victoria was about to supplement the part about being trapped as Raul's mistress, she looked past Clarke to Rosa, who squinted and raised one black eyebrow higher than the other. Rosa knew just enough English to realize that Maria had lied about her treatment in the compound.

Victoria pointed at Rosa. "She's one of them, Clarke, Raul's sister. Arrest her." Marines quickly took Rosa into custody and led her away.

Clarke said to Victoria, "Well done, Marine. You'll be up for a commendation and promotion to lance corporal. Better put on some fatigues before you start a riot!"

* * *

Two mornings later, back in the security of his headquarters office in Bogotá, Major Sparks handed Victoria a copy of the front page of the local newspaper, showing Raul shot dead beneath his bedroom balcony next to an unflattering photograph of Victoria, with squinting eyes, uncorrected by her green contact lenses. This was the face of Victoria

Pierce, but a face hauntingly similar to Vera Ochman's that accompanied the headline story of her extraordinary bravery in bringing about the demise of Colombia's worst drug lord.

Victoria's only comment was, "What an awful picture! My eyes are even closed!"

Major Sparks congratulated himself and Clarke. "A stroke of genius, Clarke, sending a woman in undercover. What better way to trap a womanizer than with such beautiful bait as this?" pointing to the bait.

"So that's how you used me, as bait?"

Clarke interrupted, "I should say not, Private Pierce. You're a genuine hero. You will receive a battlefield commendation and a pay raise, not to mention a promotion in rank."

Major Sparks continued, "Your picture is not just in the Bogotá press." He lifted a stack of newspapers off the floor with both arms and piled them up on the top of his desk so Victoria could see all the editions from around the world. As Victoria leaned forward in shock, she could see the *Washington Post* and the same grainy photograph, accompanied by an AP story of her heroics.

"That's all really nice, sirs, but all I want is to return to my assigned duty station with perhaps a few days off to go to the beach, lay out, and rest up. By the way, is there some type of reward for this guy?"

"Yes," replied Major Sparks, "quite a large reward, but too bad you were on active duty as a Marine at the time. Regulations prohibit accepting rewards. It's your duty as a Marine to kill or capture the enemy."

Major Sparks's intercom buzzed, then buzzed again, and finally an elongated buzz for a third time without ceasing. Irritably, the major picked up the phone. "Sergeant, I told you that I did not want to be disturbed during this debriefing. I don't care if it is the president of the United States on the phone. . . . What was that, Sergeant? You didn't say 'the president,' did you? Are you sure?" Silence filled the air. Sheepishly, the major continued. "Well, did he happen to say what he wanted? God, yes, Sergeant, put the commander in chief through and be quick about it!" He quickly changed his tone.

"Yes, sir, Mr. President! Well, yes, the story is correct. Yes, sir, we were just conducting a debriefing when you called, sir. Yes, sir, by all means I would recommend her for that medal. . . . Sir, of course, sir, she can be in Washington by Thursday." The major held out the phone, covering the lower end with his hand, and pointed it at Victoria. "It's the president."

Victoria did not move and in no way seemed inclined to take the phone from the major. The major reached across the desk with his hand over the receiver: "*of the United States of America!*" Victoria finally took the receiver.

"Thank you, sir. I am delighted we got him, sir. Yes, sir, the streets of America will definitely will be safer without his drugs. . . . Oh, that will not be necessary, sir. . . . I'd rather just stay here and decompress, sir. . . . But, yes, indeed, you are the commander in chief and those are my orders. . . . With the major's permission . . . no, no need for that either because you are the commander in chief. . . . Yes, I can be in this rose garden for a Friday ceremony. . . . OK, sir, thank you."

Victoria handed the phone back to Major Sparks, leaned back in her chair with both hands extended over her face, slumped down lower, almost falling to the floor. "What rose garden is he talking about?"

Clarke leaned over and whispered, "I believe you'll find it on the south lawn beside the White House in Washington, DC."

Major Sparks said, "Yes, sir, Mr. President, she will be on a flight to Washington early Thursday and will be there for a Friday morning ceremony in the Rose Garden. Thank you, sir. . . . Good day, sir."

CHAPTER TWENTY

Summer 1981

In a sudden crosswind that caused the tip of the starboard wing to narrowly miss scraping the runway, Pan American Flight 825, a 747 jumbo jet bound from Bogotá, slammed down on the south runway at DC's Dulles International Airport at exactly 4:31 p.m. The jolting landing awakened First Class Passenger Victoria Pierce, who ached from a champagne-induced hangover, and heard, inexplicably, the buzzing conversations of startled passengers relieved to be safely on the ground. The flight captain—who knew, had the tip of the starboard wing actually touched the runway, his career as a professional aviator would have ended that very afternoon—nervously announced over the cabin public address system, "My apologies for such an unexpected rough landing caused at the last second by a severe crosswind. Now that we are on the ground safely, let me be the first to welcome you to our nation's capital."

Pan Am 825 taxied toward the Dulles terminal, jostling passengers along a bumpy runway. The slow ride across the expansion joints of the tarmac reminded the passengers that they were no longer gliding effortlessly through stratospheric thin air high above South and Central America. As the plane's brakes grabbed suddenly and whined to a halt, yielding to a departing flight at an intersecting runway, Victoria glanced out of her cabin window at the black exhaust belching from the departing flight. She pressed her index fingers simultaneously into the sides of a forehead still throbbing from the residue of two complimentary glasses of champagne downed too quickly at twenty-five thousand feet. Her conscious thoughts returned to the apprehension of tomorrow's White House ceremony, where the president of the United States would pin a ribbon representing the Marine Corps' highest medal in the space just above a name tag that read "Lance Corporal Victoria Pierce," a totally bogus name. She wondered, *Doesn't even the president of the United States know her true identity as Vera Ochman, a would-be felon from Brooklyn, New York, masking now as a farm girl turned Marine from the plains of Oklahoma?*

Mindlessly walking to the front exit in her full dress uniform, Victoria thought, *Just how long can this charade go on?* Still deep in thought as she reached the front cabin doorway, Victoria managed to return the perfunctory wave of a smiling flight attendant who blandly thanked her for flying Pan Am.

Moments after retrieving her luggage, Victoria on the crowded street in front of the terminal hailed the first taxi in a neat line of yellow Checker Cabs, all with faceless drivers wearing black narrow-brimmed caps, waiting impatiently for their turn at the big fares for the long ride to the inner-city hotels. A rotund man in his thirties jumped out from the driver's side door, snatched Victoria's Marine duffle bag from her hand before she could object and placed it in the trunk, opened the right rear door, and motioned for her to get inside. Victoria slid mechanically across the Checker's backseat to the middle, so accustomed to the interior of cabs from her many rides along the jammed streets of Manhattan. She knew well that the driver expected a larger tip for assisting her with her luggage. Shrugging indifferently, she did not care. All of her out-of-pocket expenses were to be fully covered by the Marine Corps.

"Where to?" said the driver, glancing at his passenger in the rearview mirror.

Victoria paused and pulled her travel voucher from her purse and located the name of the hotel. "The Mayflower Hotel. You know that one?"

"Oh, yeah."

"About how much?"

"Should be no more than fifteen dollars, depending on afternoon traffic."

Victoria retrieved a crisp twenty from a zipped side compartment and replaced her voucher in her purse as the driver pulled away from the terminal, his eyes glancing up to admire the beauty of his fare framed in his rearview mirror. He removed his hat and placed it next to him on the seat, looked up through his mirror at the beautiful face in the backseat, and asked, "Your first trip to DC?"

Victoria, preoccupied still with how she would resolve tomorrow's charade and looking for a distraction to break a potentially prolonged conversation with this cab driver, spotted a copy of the *New York Times* discarded on the floor in front of her. "Yes, it is," she said as she retrieved yesterday's paper from the floor. She unfolded the front section to conceal her face behind headlines unreadable in reverse through the refracted light of his rearview mirror. The driver got the message as Victoria pretended to read.

Her mind drifted ahead to the Rose Garden rendezvous with the president of the United States. *Perhaps,* she thought, *there will be another article chronicling her heroics in Bogotá, accompanied by a better photograph.* She smiled as she turned to an inside page and pretended to read while she dreamed of what it would be like to meet the president. She mindlessly glanced at a headline above two photographs. "Lawyer Disbarred, Cop Killer Freed." She turned the page and continued the daydream. *What will the president of the United States say to me? What will he look like up close? Will he wear cologne for the occasion?*

Victoria's subconscious mind interrupted her conscious mind's daydream and whispered a warning, *Go back to the photographs on the previous page.* Victoria, without thinking, returned to the previous page. She reread the headline and glanced at the photographs. Victoria's eyes dropped to the caption beneath the photographs.

"This can't be real!"

The right image was a photograph of Felipe Sanchez, and the left image was a photograph of his disbarred lawyer, Angelo Siffo.

Panic stricken, Victoria's vision narrowed to read the fine print of the article beneath the headline and photographs.

"Imprisoned cop killer, Felipe Sanchez, was released from a Connecticut federal penitentiary today where he was serving a twenty-year sentence for the cold-blooded murder of an undercover FBI agent in August of 1980. He served slightly more than one year of his sentence when a federal district court judge granted him a new trial for ineffective assistance of counsel. His then defense lawyer, Angelo Siffo, was disbarred by the State of New York in July for an admitted chronic addiction to cocaine and heroin."

"Disbarred?"

The cab driver looked up, thinking his passenger had just asked him a question.

Victoria leaned forward in her seat and read quickly through the article. "Sanchez claimed his constitutional right to effective assistance of counsel was violated. . . . His lawyer . . . Siffo . . . addicted to drugs. . . . Federal judge agreed with Sanchez. . . . U.S. attorney Michael Brandon . . . unable to dissuade the judge . . . argued that it would be impossible to retry Sanchez on the murder charges as the government's key witness, Vera Ochman, had been the victim of a Mob-style assassination. . . . No other eyewitnesses. Sanchez's court-appointed counsel argued that Siffo had forced him into the plea bargain. . . . Sanchez steadfastly maintained his innocence throughout his incarceration . . . claimed it was Vera Ochman, the government's eyewitness, who had committed the murder."

"Holy shit!"

The cab driver looked up again, this time realizing that something in the newspaper caused his passenger's reaction.

Victoria continued with the story, sitting erect on the outside edge of the backseat. "Michael Brandon conceded today in a called news conference that his case against Sanchez . . . hopelessly lost with the death of . . . Vera Ochman. He will not try Sanchez for the crime of murder or any of the related charges that had been dismissed in the plea bargain. The federal judge apologized to Sanchez for the conduct of his lawyer and . . . awarded Sanchez the statutory sum of $50,000 in full settlement of his civil case against the government for false imprisonment in a federal penitentiary."

The driver stopped beside a uniformed doorman who stood on the circular drive, and after a protracted silence with no sign of movement from his backseat passenger, announced, "Mayflower Hotel, ma'am." The driver jumped out of the cab, pulled the duffle bag from the trunk, handed it to the doorman, and opened the rear passenger door for Victoria to slide out. Victoria, still reading while exiting the cab, mindlessly handed the driver a darker-than-normal twenty-dollar bill soaked through completely from the sweat accumulated in her tightly clutched left palm. The driver acknowledged the five-dollar tip with a "Thank you, ma'am," slammed the rear door, jumped back into his cab, and sped away from the hotel, eyeing his fare's finely contoured frame in his right rearview mirror on his way out the drive. Victoria stood obliviously in the exact location where she exited the cab, incredulously leaned into the paper, and reread the article for the third time, clutching the *Times* in outstretched arms spread as wide as an eagle's wings in flight.

The doorman correctly identified the uniformed Marine blocking the portico as the arriving White House VIP and waited patiently while Victoria completed her driveway reading. He walked up to her and asked, "Would you be United States Marine Corporal Victoria Pierce?" Victoria nodded. "Right this way, please. Bellman, front." The doorman passed off Victoria's bag to the diminutive bell captain. "Show Corporal Pierce to the Diplomat Suite."

Added to the stress that the president of the United States might already know that Victoria Pierce was a complete fraud, and of course, being dishonorably discharged instead of decorated, it was a distinct possibility in Vera Ochman's mind that she would be arrested on the spot in the White House Rose Garden and returned to the Manhattan Courthouse to face murder charges. In that case, Sanchez would probably have her killed for a second time, or do it himself to make sure she really was dead.

In spite of the luxuriously appointed comfort of the spacious Diplomat Suite, reserved by the White House for only the top-ranking ambassadors and dignitaries, Victoria lay awake all night swallowed up in a gigantic bed staring up blankly at a pink silk canopy. She could not have been more ill at ease had tomorrow's sunrise presented her with a black-hooded executioner. At least she could have dealt with that certainty instead of the uncertainty of not knowing whether tomorrow she was going to be decorated as hero or arrested for murder.

* * *

The south lawn of the White House was nothing like Victoria had imagined. It sloped sharply downhill to a landing pad for the president's helicopter. Although well maintained and manicured, the lawn was otherwise unremarkable, similar to the grounds of any other public building. While she waited for the president to return from Camp David, the Marine Corps color guard rehearsed its entrance. No one seemed to be paying much attention to Victoria at all, which came as a relief. If the FBI intended to step in to make a surprise arrest, there was no sign of any preparation.

Within minutes, *Marine One*, the president's Sea King helicopter, thundered and whirred to a landing precisely on its landing pad, as the president of the United States, dressed in a dark blue suit, stood at the door and waved to the assembled press, paying special attention to wave directly at the masses hidden behind the live coverage television cameras.

* * *

Far removed from the White House Rose Garden, in a smoke-filled bar in the Bronx, two men, dressed in biker leather weighted down with an assortment of chains, sat on uncomfortable bar stools while they drank from the necks of dark brown beer bottles. They watched a news interruption of the regularly scheduled programming, from a small television set suspended on a platform right above the shaved head of a bartender with a long scar carved down his left cheek. One man, the smaller and dumpier of the two, said to the bartender, "Another," pointing to his bottle.

The bartender pulled out another brown bottle from the cooler underneath the bar, twisted off the cap, and set the beer in front of the man. The man pointed up to the television above the bartender's head and said, "That's the Marine bitch who collared our supplier in Colombia."

Without looking up, the other man, the taller and stronger of the two, pointed to his empty beer bottle held at the end of a forearm emblazoned with a lightning-bolt tattoo and then glanced up at the television. "Me, too," said Felipe Sanchez as he sat on a bar stool, easing back into motorcycle society, nineteen years ahead of schedule. The bartender thought that Sanchez should have pointed to his beer at the same time as his friend to avoid a duplication of his effort, twisted off the cap to the second beer, rudely jerked the empty from Felipe's hand, and slammed the full bottle on the counter. Uncharacteristically, Sanchez ignored the bartender's rude behavior. This was a night for celebrating, not fighting—at least not immediately.

Sanchez appeared no worse for the wear after a year in the federal pen. His biceps still bulged through the short sleeves of his T-shirt, larger than before from daily workouts in the prison yard. His sense of humor was razor sharp as he joked with the patrons on the occasion of his return to the streets as a free man before he got back down to the serious business of recruiting another gang to recapture his lost territory. Every member of the old gang was still doing a ten- to fifteen-year stretch behind bars for conspiracy to commit murder arising out of the arrests at the Wicked Whiskey Bar. Unlike Sanchez, the rest, unfortunately for them, had effective assistance of legal counsel before entering their plea bargains, and all remained unemancipated in the slammer, with no hope for parole because the murder victim, also unfortunately for them, happened to be an undercover FBI agent. Sanchez would gladly have exchanged the biker bum beside him for Amber Morelli, but she was working on a hard thirty-year sentence, thanks to Vera's vengeful and shaded testimony before the grand jury. Unlike Vera, Amber would have never betrayed him. Even though Amber's performance had been less than consistent, it was caused legitimately by chronic inebriation, nothing major, but she had always been loyal and even warned Sanchez of her suspicions about Vera, suspicions that Felipe had blindly ignored. Felipe and Amber corresponded while in prison, each expecting the other to be incarcerated until the expiration of their maximum terms. After Sanchez made an early exit, he decided to look Amber up, acknowledge she got a bum wrap, and apologize for his defection to Vera. With his settlement money, Sanchez even contemplated hiring a lawyer for Amber to assist with her parole, but that was for another day. This afternoon, Sanchez had some serious celebrating to do.

Turning to his companion beside him at the bar, Sanchez said finally, "You will have to forgive me, compadre, I've been a little out of touch over the last year."

The television camera panned to a tight close-up of the president. The president of the United States, his voice barely audible above the roar of the bar's noisy patrons, was about to honor the Marine corporal standing at ease in front of him as he lauded her conspicuous gallantry and intrepidity in action. "Corporal Victoria Pierce represents all that is good about the United States of America."

As the man who sat beside Sanchez spun his stool to his left, he said, "The bitch pretended to be his girlfriend and then shot his ass dead. Raul was the best damned supplier of quality cocaine to ever reach the streets of New York City . . . and now the president's giving the bitch a medal."

Sanchez finally looked up at the screen. "Yeah, an old girlfriend, still in prison, got busted with me last year, cut out this article about her . . . didn't say why. Got it in the mail yesterday." Sanchez pointed up at the screen. "She said to take a look at the photograph to see if it reminded me of anyone. You don't have to tell me about bitches who turn on your ass. Lost one full year of my life on account of a bitch like that." Sanchez pointed again at the television set above the bartender's head. "Even looks like her . . ."

Sanchez noticed for the first time that the Marine about to be decorated did bear a remarkable resemblance to Vera. She was the same petite size, same dark hair, but different colored eyes. Everyone knew what happened to Vera. "Vera's dead. Score's even."

His biker friend said, "It doesn't pay to cross drug money. That bitch will get hers. Wait and see."

In the lull of the conversation that followed, the two continued watching the medal ceremony in the Rose Garden. A camera behind Victoria zoomed in for a tight shot of the president's head that clearly placed the back of Victoria's head and neck in the foreground.

Marshal Slaughter had been successful in his mission to remove all traces of the life of the former Vera Ochman—all except one. The tattoo removal technology of the early 1980s in Oklahoma City was at best poor. There, on the back of the medal recipient's neck, for the entire world to see, was the bleached outline of the lightning-bolt tattoo. Sanchez, frozen, stopped guzzling from the upright neck of his bottle, rose from his bar stool, and crossed into the forbidden domain behind the bar to within inches of the television screen.

The bartender threatened Sanchez with a nightstick. With lightning-bolt speed, Sanchez coldcocked the bartender with a single right hook to the jaw—something he should have done before in response to his surly behavior. While Sanchez stood with one foot on the bartender's chest, positioned to verify what he thought he had seen moments earlier, Sanchez watched intently in a bar suddenly gone silent.

"I guess he finally realized this same bitch cut off his street supply of cocaine," snorted the biker from the other side of the bar. No one could have guessed the unbelievable circumstance about to unfold before Sanchez's eyes as he watched the president pin the medal on the Marine standing in front of him. The president saluted and from the viewpoint again of the camera behind the Marine standing at attention, who crisply returned the president's salute, there, unmistakably, lay the outline of the bleached-out tattoo, matching perfectly the tattoo on Sanchez's forearm.

"Vera, you sorry-assed bitch. Could that really be you? But how could it be?" Suddenly, the government's ploy was made clear to Sanchez. Amber would not have sent the identical article to him had she not suspected the same thing. An inmate locked up in prison library has a lot of time to study a photograph in a newspaper. Sanchez in his own mind unmistakably confirmed that Victoria Pierce and Vera Ochman were one and the same. The rage of a year's incarceration erupted within Sanchez. He bounded over the counter, shoving patrons out of his way as he pushed through the crowded bar. Sanchez crashed the bottom of his beer bottle on the brick wall next to the exit, simultaneously making a sharp, jagged weapon, while cutting his hand on the neck and splattering his blood everywhere as a warning to any patron who might have thought about avenging the assault on the bartender, who was still out cold.

Sanchez reached his bike, started it with a single kick, and blasted his way into the middle lane of traffic onto the crowded street in front of the bar. First gear screamed at the highest possible redline RPM before he mercifully shifted into second gear. Bright red blood blew backward in an airborne trail off the grip on his left handlebar, while Sanchez headed at maximum speed to the interstate connecting New York City and the nation's capital.

Victoria breathed deeply with the Medal of Honor pinned neatly above her name tag by the president of the United States. The ceremony abruptly closed. She watched intently. No one came. A minute passed and still no one. The press corps left, everyone left except Senator Sam. He made his way back across the lawn to Victoria's side.

* * *

Innocently, Victoria accepted the senator's evening invitation, the exquisite dinner that followed, the frolic between the sheets, and the stark awakening in the dimness of the following dawn at Sam's exclusive Connecticut Avenue apartment. While Sam snored brusquely in the darkness, Victoria decided it was time to abandon her overnight lover as she scribbled jesting words on his copy of the ceremonial program, thanking the United States Senate for her dinner along with her room number at the Mayflower Hotel.

Outside, Victoria hailed a passing cab and, as if in a daydream, directed the driver to the Mayflower Hotel, handed him cash, and walked through the doors straight to the elevators for the ride up to her sanctuary high above.

Will he call?, she wondered.

The lock yielded to her key. Inside her suite, the sun's yellow fingers entered the room from across the Potomac River through curtains left undrawn. Victoria walked across the room to block the dawn's early light. She wanted to fade her fairy-tale lover into a dreamless sleep. She was tired. But lodged unnoticed in the stealth of the silence behind the front door, an armed and familiar intruder rushed at Victoria, ensnaring her in a death grip, covering her mouth and muffling her scream as he pointed the tip of a long bowie knife into the side of her neck. He centered his left leg between hers. His arms constricted her chest like a python enfolding its prey.

"Vera, could this pretty body really be yours?" Felipe Sanchez whispered, inches from her right ear.

Recognizing immediately the voice of Felipe Sanchez, in desperation, Victoria responded, "Wrong girl. There's no one registered in this room by that name. Just back out of here and find this 'Vera' somewhere else."

"You always were such a shrewd bitch, Vera. There's only one way to be sure." Sanchez dragged her body like a rag doll over to the window to the light of the sun's morning rays, flipped up her short hair on the back of her neck, and examined the unmistakable shadow of her lightning-bolt tattoo.

Victoria conceded the charade, "How did you find me so quickly, Felipe, before I could escape back to Colombia? The Marine Corps will be looking for me, you know."

"Very simple, señorita, you had to land at the airport. Start there and show the cab drivers enough money, and they will tell you anything. You made quite an impression on your driver. I think he fell in love with you. The room service bellmen are just as crooked as in the big city. You remember the big city, Vera, and the good times we had together, until you gave me up to rot in jail for twenty years."

Stalling, Vera responded, "I only told the truth, Sanchez. You shot BB in the back of the head and then blamed it on me. What was I to do, go to jail for your crime?"

"Wrong answer. I had it worked out where we could both have walked. I told them it was an accident. You told them I killed the snitch in cold blood. It made me believe that you didn't love me anymore, Vera. You must know how I reward such disloyalty."

"Look, Felipe, I'll make it up to you. We both know we were just hours away from a passionate night together. There's a big canopy bed over there just waiting for us."

"Who says that I won't enjoy your body while it's still warm?"

The point of his blade pressed closer to her jugular, and Vera realized she was moments from death. *But wait,* she thought, *I'm a Marine.* Sergeant Judy taught her the counter-maneuver to an opponent in this very position. But Victoria's hope faded further into desperation as Sanchez said, "Don't try anything stupid that will only make matters all the worse for you. I can kill you quickly, or you can die slowly."

The telephone rang. Sam had awakened to his lover's absence. There was hope. He was calling her room. Sanchez looked at the telephone on the second ring and was distracted just enough that Victoria felt the point of his knife retract slightly, and in an instant Victoria's right arm flew out and fired backward solidly connecting into his groin and making direct contact with the dual targets in the middle of his crotch. Simultaneously, she pulled his wrist and knife away from her neck, grabbed his elbow, flipped his body over her shoulder, and crashed him face down into the credenza next to the curtained window.

"Damn, Sergeant Judy, it actually worked. He's out cold!"

Instead of completing the drill by smashing his head with the heel of her dress shoes, which would have broken his neck, Victoria turned instead to pick up the ringing phone to summon emergency rescue and later complete the job if need be. Instantly striking her ankle from across the floor like the snake he was, Sanchez tripped Victoria from behind and sprang toward her with his knife extended to nail her prone body permanently to the hardwood floor. Victoria rolled instinctively to her left a millisecond before the point of his long dagger lodged into the surface with such force that it penetrated an inch into the polished oak where Victoria's head had been only an instant before. With both hands, Sanchez struggled to retrieve his deeply ensconced knife. Victoria, up from the floor, landed a solid kick squarely into his nose, knocking Sanchez away from his weapon and sideways into the legs of the nightstand. The telephone on its last ring shot straight up into the air, landing in silence on the floor.

Victoria saw that another blow to the groin and then to the head would be sufficient to repel her attacker long enough to at least flee into the hallway. But her next kick to the groin fell harmlessly onto his thigh and only served to infuriate an adversary twice her size. Sanchez intercepted his victim's attempted flight for the door and instead of flattening her immediately with combination punches, he grabbed her by the hair, dragged her backward, and loosened his grip long enough to retrieve his murder weapon from the floor. Victoria, the moment he relaxed his grip, jerked free and faced her attacker.

Brandishing the knife and alternatively flipping it from hand to hand to disguise which hand would be used to impale his victim, Sanchez found his sense of humor. "I should have known you would be a tough bitch to kill!"

"Not yet a fact, you sorry-assed Puerto Rican." Victoria punted the knife high into the air the moment it moved into the center of its traverse. Her next karate kick, landed to his head, sent him reeling him backward into the credenza. Seemingly unfazed, Sanchez immediately countered, striking Victoria a hard blow in the solar plexus, turning her around and knocking the wind completely out of her lungs so perilously that, without a sudden recovery, Sanchez—with knife retrieved and securely in hand—would within the next instance have shoved the full length of the twelve-inch blade into her back before finishing her execution.

Victoria, after Marine Corps training and a year of survival on the farm—summoning the very last ounce of her strength and the necessary determination to save her life— grasped the base of one of the twin brass lamps from the end table beside the sofa. She concealed it from Sanchez in a crouched position, pretended to be totally incapacitated, and turned at the last second on her advancing assailant, striking him across the jaw with all the force she could muster, knocking him backward through the bathroom door where he landed face down squarely in the middle of the bathtub. This time, Victoria rushed her attacker, kicked him repeatedly in the side of his motionless face until she noticed the knife he so ineptly wielded against her, its full length embedded into his own chest, oozing streams of deep red blood around the pearl handle into the white porcelain below. Sanchez was dead.

* * *

In her rented Ford Granada engulfed in fog at 4:00 a.m., Victoria crept through Chincoteague, Virginia, the last of many desolate villages below the southern tip of the Eastern Shore. Victoria's eyes strained to discern the shape of the dockside piers, close to the road, extending far out into the bay. She rounded a sharp curve. A bright yellow triangular sign warned of the road's end one mile ahead. In the next second, she spotted a long, isolated wooden pier. Shrimp boats had sailed long before dawn as none were docked beside their mooring posts. Dropping off the road onto a shoulder of wet sand and shells, Victoria halted, peering out into the fog-enshrouded landscape to see if she noticed anyone or anyone noticed her.

Waiting, she recalled how Sanchez impaled himself and died instantly, bleeding lifeless blood into the bathtub drain. She wrapped him in the shower curtain where he lay motionless for the whole day. She, too, sat motionless for the whole day, not allowing room service to enter, not answering Sam's persistent telephoning, and later in silence, tearfully ignoring his banging at the door. She could not call the police. What name would she give to the cops? She could not give them the name of Vera Ochman. A dead woman cannot commit murder. She could not give them the name of Victoria Pierce. What was Sanchez doing in her hotel room in Washington, DC, anyway? It was hardly a case of mistaken identity. In no time, investigators would make the connection between Victoria and Vera. Besides, Michael Brandon said he could not prosecute Sanchez because the state's key witness, Vera Ochman, was dead. How would that make the U.S. attorney look? Why stir this all back up when the government had given her a legitimate second chance? Victoria Pierce had now killed her second victim within the span of a single week, the first in combat, the other in self-defense. She was lucky that neither had killed her. They both got what they deserved. She had done what a Marine was trained to do: "Kill, kill, kill."

By late Sunday afternoon, Victoria left Sanchez resting in his shower curtain pall, darted through the lobby unobserved by either the bellman or doorman, shot down the street to the car rental lot, leased a red Ford Granada, purchased a zipper-locked duffel bag made of a strong synthetic material in the pawn shop next to the car rental lot, and returned to the suite she shared with a corpse. A laundry cart transported the body down the hall to a back elevator and then to her Granada, parked behind the hotel in the predawn darkness.

Minutes passed, and not a soul appeared from any direction. The fog lifted slightly as the sun peeked over the surface of the Atlantic Ocean. This was to be Felipe Sanchez's final resting place. There was no time to search for another grave. Victoria noticed an upstairs light in a distant house shine like a beacon. Another check through the fog revealed she was still in total isolation.

Victoria jumped from the front seat of the rented red Granada, inserted the round key into the trunk, turned the key clockwise, and there in the heavy duffle bag lay Felipe

Sanchez curled up into the identical position as the day he was born. With the strength of a Marine pumped up by adrenalin, Victoria dragged Sanchez's lifeless body out of the trunk and down the pier to its midpoint. Her breathing turned labored from nerves and exhaustion. Physically incapacitated for the moment, she had to stop to survey the seascape and then resumed her trek to the end, half-pulling Sanchez, half-bouncing him along the remaining saturated boards that were so graciously lubricated by the morning dew. Two cinder blocks, used for mooring small boats, sat stacked on each other at the edge of the pier. Victoria opened the duffle bag that smelled of human decay, inserted one block on each end, zipped it back, fastened the lock, and tumbled the bag over the side of the pier into the water. For a long moment Felipe Sanchez would not sink. The duffle bag floated as upright as a life preserver before it finally deflated, listed upward, and gurgled bubbles to the surface from its downward descent into the black waters of the bay.

"Thank God!"

As the last remnants of her past life as Vera Ochman sank into the abyss to be entombed forever with Felipe Sanchez, Victoria Pierce knew she had to make a transition from the mistakes of her former life, and so she kept her 3:00 p.m. appointment with the dean of admissions at the university. In preparation for her new life, Victoria Pierce would have to also bury forever the murder of Felipe Sanchez. And she did.

CHAPTER TWENTY-ONE

August 2009

Grace Brandon sat in her father's kitchen in his Manhattan condominium.

"Look, Grace, the DA's not going to give up that kind of information right before trial. You can't expect that of him, no matter how important it is to your story," said Michael Brandon.

"But he's a public official, and the public has a right to know. You prosecutors are all alike, finding some damned ethical excuse not to give up information to the press during a criminal investigation."

"When are you going to get back to political reporting? Lot more interesting stuff happening there—not that I ever pay attention to any of it—but I'm not sure you're cut out . . ."

Michael Brandon's ringing telephone offered an opportune interruption. As he walked to the other side of the kitchen to answer it, he said, too loudly, "Good," thankful for the reprieve to disengage his daughter's relentless assault on his professional ethics.

Grace said, "I heard that. We're not finished!"

"You can stay or leave, but my answer is going to be the same." Michael picked up the receiver and said, "Hello." Grace grimaced, thumbing through a magazine at the kitchen table, and decided to stay. She was definitely not satisfied with her father's answer.

"Yeah, this is Michael Brandon speaking." There was almost a minute of silence in the kitchen as Michael paused, listened, and paced.

"Yeah, I remember a Puerto Rican gang leader by the name of Felipe Sanchez. Let's see, went up on a felony murder plea years ago. Best I can remember now, undercover FBI agent bought it in raid, girlfriend turned state's. Yeah, got out of prison on ineffective assistance of counsel. . . . No, he wasn't retried. . . . No, I don't recall her name. Why? What's he done now? . . . Dead? . . . Well, good, can't say that bothers me much. Sounds like he finally got what was coming to him. . . . Matched dental records from his stretch in the pen. . . . What's all this got to do with me? I'm retired. No, I can't help you. . . . I said, I'm retired!"

Michael glanced over at Grace, flipping through the magazine purely as a diversion for calculating her next attack on prosecutorial ethics. It dawned on Michael Brandon that his daughter intended to stay the entire afternoon to tie him up in an unwinnable ethical debate. The press, not to mention his own daughter, never understood why prosecutors cannot give up information in their files before trial. Grace, as she'd done many times before, would not give up her position until her father eventually yielded or, in this case, he left his home.

"You should have been a lawyer. No, not you. . . . I was talking to someone else here. . . . Go on, I'm listening." Michael Brandon listened, watched Grace pretending to read, and decided to change the course of his afternoon.

"Well, you know, it does sound very important, now that I think about it. Yeah, it could take you weeks to cut through all the bureaucratic red tape in that particular closed file. Most of what you want would be redacted anyway. Tell you what, I'll go down to the courthouse this very afternoon"—

Michael elevated the last words to make sure Grace heard them—"and check out the file myself, and I'll get back to you tomorrow. . . . That soon enough? Yeah, I am leaving right now. . . . Give me your number." Michael Brandon scribbled the number down on a pad beside the phone and turned to Grace.

"Got to run down to the courthouse. Looks like we will have to continue this conversation another time."

"I'll be back tomorrow at lunch. I'm not finished with you, and you're not getting off that easy."

"My answer will be the same tomorrow."

"We'll see about that!"

Grace hugged her dad affectionately. "I love you, and it's my job to take care of you, now that Mom's gone."

"No, it's not your job to take care of me. You need to start taking care of a husband. I want grandchildren. What about that nice photographer friend of yours, Lennie Callahan?"

"I like Lennie—good-looking guy—but, you know, he can really get on my nerves sometimes! Besides, he's never asked me out."

"Well, ask him out!"

* * *

Grace returned to her father's apartment the following day around lunchtime. The note on the table beside the front door read, "Grace, I have an appointment. Will be back around 2 p.m."

"He knows I can't take more than an hour for lunch. He's avoiding me because he knows I'm right," Grace whispered to herself, as she read the note and walked back to the refrigerator to see what she could scavenge for lunch.

Had Grace not been hungry, she would have never seen the file. There on the kitchen table, where she and her dad often staged their debates, disguised as discussions, lay a dark brown manila file, but not just any file. Stamped in large green letters across the outside of the file was the word, "Confidential."

On the white file index, Grace read in small type, "Vera Ochman," which she immediately converted to an audible, *"Vera Ochman!"*

Grace flipped right past the cover marked "Confidential" without the slightest ethical hesitation and began reading through eyes that alternatively narrowed and bulged. Grace quickly realized that her apolitical father had neither grasped nor understood the magnitude of what this file revealed about the vice president of the United States. In less than fifteen minutes, Grace mentally assembled all of the facts for the biggest exposé in presidential history. Her own father was the U.S. attorney who arranged the plea bargain that put his star witness through a feigned assassination on the courthouse steps and funneled her into the federal Witness Protection Program in Oklahoma, where she later emerged as the farm daughter of Lucinda and Ezekiel Pierce. Grace remembered nothing about this case as she was less than four years old at the time, and her father, to her knowledge, had never mentioned it.

Grace dropped the file for a second. She had turned over Marshal Slaughter's parting phrase in her mind a thousand times: "The answer is right under your prying nose, but it ain't here in Oklahoma City." Now Grace understood his phrase, "right under your prying nose," to be a reference to her own father. "And no damned wonder Vera Ochman lies in a grave on Long Island. She had to be shot, and they had to bury a corpse. If the acting president of the United States denies she's Vera Ochman, we can just go out there and dig up an empty coffin."

Once and for all, Grace could authenticate her story for her skeptical editors and announce the truth about the president to the entire world. Acting completely on impulse, Grace tucked the file under her arm, walked out of her father's apartment and down the crowded sidewalk to the copy center three blocks away. For twenty dollars and twenty-five cents, Grace photocopied her father's entire confidential file. She returned by the same route back to his condominium, replaced the original file in its original location on the kitchen table, and dashed to catch the subway to Times Square. As she dodged pedestrians on the way to her stop, Grace rationalized the magnitude of the public's right to know about Victoria's surreptitious past and that she would ultimately win the debate with her father as to the propriety of her actions, explaining that she could not just sit on a story of this magnitude, waiting hours for her father to stop circumventing the truth, and still make her deadline. Besides, her father was always forgiving, and he would certainly forgive such a minor indiscretion, particularly if she could base her action upon some lofty journalistic principle that compelled her to publish. Grace further rationalized that he should have never left such an important file on the kitchen table, right under a reporter's nose, had he not intended for her to publish the contents.

As Grace waited for the subway's first car, she organized the chronology of her story in her mind to shorten her writing time to make tomorrow's late edition deadline, just in case the *Times* might lose some of its ethical apprehensiveness for endless confirmation and rush to publish the most sensational story of the century, perhaps under threat of a competitor's scoop. The official U.S. attorney's file confirmed, without the slightest speculation, every detail of Vera Ochman's transition to Victoria Pierce.

Several distracting trains clacked, banged, and screeched their way along the rails before Grace spied the light of the Seventh Avenue Express about to roll into the subterranean station. She edged all the way forward to the choice spot at the edge of the platform, all but guaranteeing her a seat, or at worst a handrail, on the first car. Just as she turned, leaning forward, a pedestrian from behind jolted her in the back with such force that she careened down onto the tracks below. Desperately grasping her file on the way down, but landing fortuitously in the middle of the graveled bed on one foot, as might a track star competing in the triple jump, her momentum carried her stumbling across the rails before she collapsed on the other side—miraculously avoiding being smashed under the wheels of the car that she so desperately wanted to occupy seconds earlier, and also miraculously avoiding the electrified third rail, which would have killed her instantly. A man who saw what happened exclaimed, "That woman pushed you!" But the woman, if she had pushed Grace, was not there, nowhere to be seen. Yet Grace was alive, and so was her story.

Thirty minutes later, Grace burst through the office door, sans knocking or permission to enter, of the editor who not only did not defend his reporter after her interrogation with the paper's lawyer but instead banished her to the courthouse beat as punishment for pursuing such an implausible story, now proven true. She tossed her father's copy file about three feet high into the air before it landed on his desk, flopping open. He looked up, startled. "What are you doing in my office? Can't you knock like everyone else?"

"Read this, you prick!" Grace leaned over the desk, grabbed him by the collar, and whispered sarcastically about an inch away from his nose. "Let me know, you cowardly bastard, when you're ready for me to write the whole truth that almost got me fired. And you better be pretty damned quick about it. I estimate that you've got less than two minutes to give me the go-ahead . . . before I lose what little professional loyalty I have left for this newspaper and run over to the *Post* with the biggest story in presidential history."

* * *

Tom Pearsall was startled as he tried immediately to silence his musical cell phone, walking away from earshot just as Victoria concluded one of her front-yard status reports on Sam's medical condition at Bethesda Naval Hospital. "Hello," Tom whispered. "Hold on." Without asking the identity of the caller, Tom returned close enough to hand Victoria his cell phone as she backed away from the podium.

"Who is it?"

Tom shrugged.

Victoria picked up the phone and walked away to the privacy of a park bench beneath a cherry tree about twenty-five yards away from Tom and the press. "Yes."

"Vera, I tried my best to avoid making this call!"

"What did you say? My name is Victoria . . . Vice Presid—."

"Yeah, yeah, sure. Whatever you say now, but by tomorrow morning it won't make much difference what you call yourself. But I wouldn't hang up just yet, 'cause you really need to hear this."

Victoria listened, recognizing all too well the steely voice that shocked her early in the morning after her nomination.

"I estimate—max—you've got about five hours before the *Times* final national edition hits the streets exposing your entire clandestine past. I never really knew much of the details about Vera, but I knew damned well enough that was not the name you go by now. Two nobodies were silenced because of it. Gone for good. Sorry I missed knocking off the most important source of the leak. Like I said, I tried, but now I can't silence the entire *New York Times* readership."

"Are you saying that the *Times* has the story about Vera?"

"Oh yeah. That so-called reporter friend of yours, Ace— no, sorry, she's not much of a friend of yours anymore—she's probably writing the last words of her exposé as we speak. She may even call you for comment. So I'll say adieu, my sweets, a permanent good-bye, unless you can figure out a way to survive this one, which is really why I'm risking this call anyway. You're really pretty damned good at surviving."

"Well, at least tell me your name? Maybe I can thank you personally sometime."

"Oh, I would really love to whisper sweet nothings into your ear while we're making love, but I only make love to presidents. By tomorrow night, you'll no longer be the president."

The line went dead.

Victoria called her press secretary at the Oval Office.

"Just checking in. Any messages?"

"Nothing out of the ordinary, but there have been repeated calls from the *Times* for comment on some big story that they're working on. . . . No, they won't tell me, but it's Grace Brandon. You know Ace. She's calling every five minutes. And then several minor . . ."

Victoria clicked off the cell phone in mid-sentence, sat back down on the park bench, fidgeting in her panic, and then began to think. She imagined that she was in combat, surrounded by enemy artillery on a ridge high above about to rain down a barrage of eight-inch shells on her troops caught completely in the open.

"Wait a minute. Resignation. That means surrender. If you cut and run, that's certain death. Howitzers do the most damage at a distance; they are vulnerable up close. . . . Have to dig in and charge up the hill no matter what, but is there time to dig in before being destroyed? Is there time to counterattack? I've got some time . . . at least until midnight to make a plan before press time for the final edition, but no time at all if they release the story in an early edition. Must buy some time to plan. Dig in early, prepare a counterattack."

Victoria redialed her press secretary on Tom's cell phone. "Call back the *Times*. Tell Ace personally that I cannot get back to her before 9:00 p.m. Make up some excuse, any damned excuse, but promise her I'll get back to her for comment before nine.

"Tom . . . hey Tom, get over here," Victoria screamed. Tom was smoking and pacing in the distance, preparing to leave as soon as he retrieved his special cell phone, knowing that the words just shouted by Victoria were the most she had directed at him since Sam's stroke. "Can you get Dan Fowler on this thing, right now?" Tom found the number in his cell phone directory, pressed automatic dial, and handed her the ringing phone. She talked directly to Tom, covering the receiver. "Meet me back in the Oval Office in thirty minutes. I need the best political PR person in the country, and regrettably that happens to be you."

Then she spoke into the phone, "This is the vice president. Put me through to General Fowler."

Victoria looked up at Tom while waiting for Dan to connect. "But, listen to me, if you try to screw me again, I'll cut your nuts out personally. Bring my latest approval numbers with you and anything else you've got, and don't give me that bullshit innocent look. I know you've got the damned numbers, and I'll need more, much more within the next twenty-four hours, so get your overnight polling guys ready, focus groups, or whatever the hell you do." She turned her attention back to the telephone.

"Yeah, Dan, get to the Oval Office no later than 1830 hours. Drop everything. Cancel everything. No one in the administration will have a job by tomorrow morning if you're not there. Let's put it to you this way, General Fowler. Pretend I'm on the ground. My entire unit is in the valley about to be pounded into smithereens by incoming. No, actually, it's worse than that. . . . Yeah, just wait till you hear this one. So you'll be there. Thirty minutes max, Dan. No longer."

* * *

At 6:30 p.m. in the Oval Office, Victoria told the two men sitting parallel in high-backed leather chairs across the desk from her what was about to hit them squarely in their disbelieving eyes. Victoria started at the beginning. "My real name is Vera Ochman, a child born to a Polish New York City architect and a Puerto Rican mother." Victoria in her thirty-minute yarn spared no details, except one: the fact that she had to kill Felipe Sanchez in self-defense.

"This is unfuckin' real. Please tell me it ain't true. First Sam and now you." Tom Pearsall reflected momentarily and summarily declared, "All the press and half the country will be screaming for your resignation by tomorrow night!"

"Listen carefully, Tom, you've got about two hours to come up with a strategy that will save my ass, your ass, and Sam's administration. Got it? This is no time to let your political legs turn to jelly, and you've got probably less than two hours. Grace Brandon will call for my comment at 2100 hours, and you better have something good by that time."

Dan Fowler swallowed hard, the only one in the room who was really thinking about national security. "Who deploys our armed forces if something happens to you? Who's the commander in chief? Who's in charge?" Dan did not wait for the answer but continued. "We already know the confusion surrounding the answer to that question, not to mention the nuclear issues. We've been talking a lot about that. If you resign, we have a very sick president still out of his gourd, no acting president, no vice president, and no way to replace the vice president. Consequently, no rational person is in charge of national security."

Tom knew, too, there was no way for Sam to resume his office. He saw a glimmer of a defense in what Dan said, but was it in his best interest to try to save Victoria? "You know, dear, it would have been really nice of you to have told me this during the campaign. I'm sitting in a room now with two Marines, and I don't even know what time it is. Will someone please tell me what fuckin' time is 2100 hours?"

"That would be 9 p.m. in civilian time, which is less than two hours from right now," Victoria answered sarcastically.

Before deciding to craft a plan to defend Victoria's political life, Tom had to decide his own fate. "Why not just deny it, Victoria? What can they prove? Sandbag 'em. Tell a lie long enough and loud enough, pretty soon the gullible citizens will start believing it. The ones you can fool all of the time, start with them. Who knows? Stall long enough, and Sam might be right back in the saddle, and you can bow out gracefully."

Victoria responded, "Just like you, Tom, right out of the gate, to think of lying. Let me tell you, it's not only disingenuous. It's too late, and what's more, it won't work. The *Times* has the whole truth right, and they're putting the ink on my story as we speak. Better to meet it head on, right now. Take their hit and be prepared to charge up the hill tomorrow. There's no time to play dodgeball here!"

Dan Fowler stood up and walked over to the trash can, cutting the tip off of his cigar and watching it drop inside. "Marine Corps taught you something: when in doubt, attack! What the hell? I like it!"

Tom, now chain-smoking, lit up his fourth cigarette. "Will someone please save me from these gung-ho leathernecks? The truth? You want to tell the truth? Admit to the world what you have just told us as the truth? You gotta be out of your mind! You can't admit that. Madam Acting President, if you tell the truth, the press is going to hang you from the highest cherry tree in Washington by sundown tomorrow, so if you want to swing, just go out there and admit all this bullshit! Besides, if the press doesn't hang your ass, Maggie O'Connor will have articles of impeachment lodged against you by the end of next week, and the Senate will remove you from office by the end of the month."

"I'm not swinging yet, Tom, and I'm not impeached, so you better start doing what you're paid to do, or I'll get someone in here who will. If you want to jump ship, there's the door! Believe me, the only reason you're even in here right now is that you just so happen to be the best PR guy in town. Now, we've got two hours. Pretty damn lucky, I'd say. Right? Now I've seen you in action before. You know and I know that you can pull this off, but for some reason you're stalling. You really don't want me to think that you don't have your heart in this, Tom. Do you really want to see what a desperate general looks like in combat dealing with a hesitant infantry lieutenant?"

Victoria reached into her desk drawer, pulled out her holstered service revolver, and placed it on the table. "Now, Lieutenant Pearsall, come up with a strategy just like you did that day at campaign headquarters when you had to flatten my nuclear weapons gaffe. You were quick and you were good, so start thinking. Start with a briefing on my latest approval rating."

Tom absentmindedly reported, "Frankly, it's a record high . . . has been since Sam's stroke!" Tom snapped his fingers. He was a natural at his work and now had an added incentive to cooperate as he watched Victoria's hand resting atop the handgun beside her on the table, but Tom was equally convinced of the uncertainty of Sam's political future. He figured he might as well throw in with Victoria.

Besides, if Sam made a recovery, Tom could always reverse field. He decided it was in his best interest to help.

"You know. That's it. You've got a half-assed shot at surviving, and I'm not saying you will, but if you can give the American people a plausible answer, they might—just might—give you a break. The American people have always loved you—God only knows why—and you have the highest damned approval rating of any president I've ever seen as long as I have been tracking it. A good desperation strategy to save your presidency is possibly based on those high numbers. The American public will want to believe in you. Let me hasten to add that after this little disclosure, it will be really hard to say just how long they will remain in love with you."

"You gotta fight, 'cause you can't resign," Dan Fowler thought out loud. "Victoria, resignation is not an option. In case you two have not been listening, let me say it again. The United States has no president. It's that simple. If you resign, there's no right of succession to the vice presidency, even though Victoria named me as the acting vice president, which everyone seems to know is unconstitutional. I'll have to start a political civil war to decide who is in charge. Hey, I like my chances, frankly," Fowler continued sarcastically, but he made his point. "I have a better shot at controlling the military than does Maggie O'Connor, and that may be the bottom line. Who will the generals listen to? Just watch me. I'm personally going to take command of our nuclear arsenal and settle a few scores. Believe me, every general has imagined blowing his enemies into smithereens. Now, do you really want me, or some general like me, moving up to be acting president right now? So look, let's get real—and I mean real seriousness now. It's really that simple. You resign, and you create a void at the top, and military fools like me will rush in." Dan sat back in his chair and finally lit his cigar, smugly knowing he'd found the bottom-line argument.

"OK. If I cannot resign as the vice president and as acting president, what's my best defense?"

Tom talked out loud in a stream of consciousness, trying to connect his public relations defense with Dan's constitutional defense. He stood and paced. "OK, you were not even eighteen years old at the time. Youthful indiscretion. You didn't kill anybody, you just hung around with the wrong crowd and got burned at a tender age. Look, Teddy Kennedy survived a worse disclosure, much older at the time, turned it all around, and later ran for president. People gave him the benefit of the doubt. I could tell you some stuff I did at that age. Almost any conduct at that age is understandable and defensible. All eighteen-year-olds are nuts. And just look at how you overcame the odds and turned out to be one the most popular vice presidents ever. It's defensible. You were left with no alternative but to conceal your real identity from the American public. I assume you were required by law to keep all this top secret—confidential. If you're lucky, who knows? The press might be, as I speak, publishing something that's lawfully protected, and if not legally protected, they may be callously publishing the terms of a minor's plea bargain that has been held in confidence for over twenty-five years. Vera—that was your name—is legally dead. She lies dead in a grave dug by the government for that very purpose so she would remain permanently dead. *She's dead.* What were you supposed to do? Go dig her up yourself in violation of the law? You were bound by plea bargain not to disclose it. That's what you were told. That's what you believed. No way you could ever go back to Vera. She's dead. Her youthful indiscretions were buried with her, and you became someone totally different."

"See, Dan, I told you he was good. Give the devil his due," Victoria said with pride.

Tom continued, "You helped put the real bad guys in prison—not just bad guys, but hardened, dangerous criminals who would have killed again. Besides, you never had any reason to disclose your past because after Sam's election, you were supposed to return to military life in Europe, not become the vice presidential nominee. Had the Speaker not so clumsily fallen down the steps, she would have become the vice president—not you—and I might add at this juncture it was no secret that I did everything I could to prevent that from happening. The Speaker should have been on the winning ticket, not you. You wanted to return to an overseas command, and no one would have heard from you again. Just didn't turn out that way. How's that?"

Tom had just stepped over an invisible line. Victoria moved her hand back on top of her weapon and thought how many men on and off the battlefield she had killed or had others kill. "Yes, Tom, that's pretty damned good, but you just might want to remember right now how stressed I am and how many times you've tried to screw me over the past year. Dan, of course, it goes without saying, that's figuratively 'screwed.'"

As Victoria clutched her weapon and fingered the trigger, she thought to herself, *I really hated him for thinking that I was not good enough to be on Sam's ticket, and then advising Sam that I was not good enough—all of this without a backup candidate after Maggie O'Connor dropped out. Then he thumbed through a list of 'anybody but Victoria for vice president,' and how unapologetically wrong he had been about me all along. I should have killed him the night Sam broke up with me, now that I am remembering all of this. How many ways has the Marine Corps actually trained me to kill jerks like him?*

"And by the way, Tom, while we are on the subject, you might want to remember that you had no contingency plan.

There was no 'next' on Sam's vice presidential short list, was there? I was all that you had, and actually a much better choice. Right, Tom?"

Tom turned sheepish. "Of course you're right, Madam Vice President."

"So, Tom, the only thing right now saving me from pulling the trigger—remember, according to you, I have no real way out—is that I need you and your political mind. A minute ago, Tom, you were thinking like my political consultant. But there's a lot we need to talk about, so don't push me to the edge again.

"What about Tom's plan, Dan?"

"Yeah, it fits. True, all this happened almost thirty years ago, and you've led an exemplary life since then. But it's really even more simple than that. No matter how you cut it, we've got to have you as the acting president, fully on board. You're the only presidential game in town. You may be all that stands between us and nuclear disaster. Doesn't anyone get it? I'll say it once more: If you leave while Sam is still in his present condition, there is no commander in chief. Ultimately, I have to decide who, besides the chairman of the Joint Chiefs, can authorize a nuclear counterattack. Sam is neither competent to take command nor competent to name a vice president. We are all in a nuclear limbo here. All this other stuff that Tom has thought up does merge into your strongest argument, but never forget it's all founded on PR. The real reason you cannot leave is that the United States of America will have no president."

Tom found his courage, glared straight at Dan, and responded, "Look, damn it, don't you ever forget the power a president with such a high approval rating has over the American people. They will believe anything she says right now, and they will want to help her out of this mess, if she will show them how to respond."

"Not really. The Twenty-fifth Amendment creates the office of acting president, not just someone acting as president, with no provision for what happens in the event of the vice-president's resignation, so Americans have no choice," Dan countered.

Undaunted, Tom continued because he saw the full picture. "The problem is how to ask for their help. That's what we've got less than an hour now to figure out. We have to play these cards right, bring all these strategies together. You've got a shot, Victoria. It's a damned long shot, 'cause there is a political tidal wave out there, the likes of which we've never seen before, that's about to come crashing over our heads tomorrow morning, and we better be ready! General Fowler, you're an excellent Marine Corps general, but remember I know politics and you don't. Victoria does not need to hang her defense on a single issue, no matter how persuasive that issue may be. It's too risky. If the air comes out of the single issue, you're sunk. Believe me, my experience confirms it."

Victoria was convinced that Tom had it right. "OK, now, this is what I'll tell Grace Brandon in fifteen minutes. She'll try to blindside me because she thinks I don't have a clue of what's coming."

"How did you know about the *Times'* story, anyway? Was it the guy on my cell phone?" Tom checked the called numbers.

"You will be supplied that information on an as-needed basis. I have my sources. Now, listen: I hit Grace squarely between the eyes with the truth. She'll be stunned. But that will be my statement to her after her lengthy accusation in the form of a reporter's question for comment. It will be totally unexpected, and there's nothing she can do because she's waited too long. She's too late to withdraw or modify her story based upon my admission instead of the denial she's expecting. So she's left no choice but to quote my comment verbatim, right before she hits the send button on her story. My response to her question will simply be, "That's correct," and no other comment, but it will confirm the truth of her story. No elaboration, no stuttering, no stammering, and no bullshit denial or coverup. Just a simple admission. Then tomorrow morning, I'll address the nation and hold an hourlong press conference to answer all incoming questions and then do a series of individual conferences with my network favorites."

Tom immediately interrupted. "You can't have the address tomorrow morning. It's not enough time to let the news sink in. Not enough viewers will know to watch. Wait. Stonewall all day. No public comment from you for the entire day. We'll tell the press to wait for your official response tomorrow night at 9 p.m., which will be in prime time to garner the largest number of viewers, and it better be good, Victoria, because the entire world will be watching you. By the way, Marines, 9 p.m. is 2100 hours. I'll get back some mostly unreliable early polling numbers by noon tomorrow and tweak the language in your speech. We will be prepared to do the follow-up polling to see how far your approval rating drops overnight, really to see if you have a pulse the next day."

A voice over the intercom broke in. "Grace Brandon from the *Times* is on line one. Says she can't wait any longer and will be forced to go with her story without comment."

"Hold for one," Victoria responded. "Now, are we ready to execute this plan? Fully committed?" Dan silently saluted and Tom mockingly followed, but with the Boy Scout salute, the only one he knew. "Call the staff back to the White House immediately, and I'll personally brief everyone here early tomorrow morning. Anyone who wants out can get out. Dan, call each member of the cabinet tonight around midnight. Wake them up if necessary—less chance for an early leak before the *Times* hits the street, a leak we will not have time to answer. Give the cabinet the substance of the *Times* story with as little detail as possible, and please use a little more diplomacy this time. Don't run over 'em like you're driving a tank. Set a cabinet meeting for 0700 hours at the White House. They need to be in here by 0600. After that we will call in the congressional leaders and take it from there."

Victoria punched line one. "Hello, Ace." Victoria knew just how much this epithet irritated her. If Victoria made Grace feel ridiculed, Grace could go on with her story as written even though some of the air would go out of it with Victoria's candid admission. "What's on your mind, Ace? What do I call you now anyway? Is it Ace or Grace? Oh, it's Grace, now that you seem to be back on the political beat. Look, I'm so sorry I couldn't get back to you sooner. Do tell, what is it that's on your mind, Ace? There I go again. Of course, it's Grace!"

"The *New York Times* has reliable information that suggests that you were once arrested on multiple felony charges, including the murder of an undercover FBI agent, and charged under the name Vera Ochman." Grace's question went on for several sentences and concluded with, "What does Victoria Pierce, vice president and acting president of the United States, have to say in response?"

Victoria says, "That's correct."

The pregnant pause that followed Victoria's succinct admission illustrated just how much Grace was knocked off her pins. It was as if Victoria knew the question before Grace asked it, which, of course, she did. Victoria was quick to cut off Grace's follow-up questions by hanging up the phone. Grace proceeded to polish a story that seethed through two full pages, sparing no detail or even a modicum of restraint to save Victoria from embarrassment.

The reality of the admission permeated the Oval Office. Tom joked, "Mistaken strategy. Call her back and lie, and it may not be too late to turn that gun on yourself instead of me!" But the gravity of what Victoria admitted was as suffocating as the tobacco smoke that filled the Oval Office. The three knew they were in the midst of an eerie calm, like being in the eye of a Category Five hurricane, before the storm wall winds—the likes of which Washington had never seen before—would come crashing into the White House. Two hours, maybe three at the most, was all the time they had to draft Victoria's saving defense before the chaos of the breaking news began. Three hours later, Tom and Dan had their first draft of Victoria's speech just as the *Times* final edition hit the streets with a three-inch bold headline: "Clandestine President Has Criminal Past."

CHAPTER TWENTY-TWO

August 2009

The White House press corps and the national media, in the flood of predawn camera lights on the grounds and sidewalks in front of the White House, trumpeted the breaking news in telecasts beamed around the world. Fortunately, Dan Fowler's early-morning reconnaissance report spared the cabinet the initial shock of the *Times* story as the members assembled in a White House conference room at 6 a.m., one hour ahead of their scheduled meeting. Most arrived early enough, as directed, to dodge embarrassing questions from the assembling press, and the few who were stopped did not know enough to even comment, but neither did the press know enough to ask. None left the White House before Victoria's speech at 9 p.m. Tom blanketed the world with silence until Victoria made her explanation to the nation. He directed the cabinet further on how to respond to press inquiries as they left the White House in the late evening. Dan's assignment was to make the cabinet believe that Victoria was left no constitutional alternative, and that her presidency would survive the *Times* story because of the void at the top. Tom's assignment was to make the cabinet believe that Victoria acted as any teenage minor might under similar circumstances, and that her presidency would survive the

Times story because of her lifetime of personal achievement. In between their briefings, both men shuttled between the Oval Office and the cabinet's conference room, alternatively placating them and assisting Victoria's speechwriting team, who were continuously redrafting her address, an address that had to be perfect in every respect to revive a nation awakened in political shock.

By 9 p.m., Victoria was rehearsed and ready. On camera she responded, "Americans are indeed in a state of shock this evening, just as I have been, by today's story first published in this morning's edition of the *New York Times*. Shocked, because I myself believed that the young teenage woman, Vera Ochman, who was supposed to be permanently buried in a grave on Long Island, has now been figuratively exhumed almost thirty years after her arranged death and who now lives again as the one speaking to you as the vice president of the United States. But I am no longer that young wayward girl who made mistakes long ago as might any other teenager under the same circumstances might have done, what many of you watching tonight might well have done yourself. This young woman's only fault lies within the decisions she made under the tragic influences of youthful indiscretions, indiscretions born in the heartbreaking loss of her mother to cancer and by her father's all-consuming grief. I say that I am shocked because this young woman, who lived and grew up as a typical high school teenage girl in Brooklyn, New York, was to never have again been seen and was to be forever forgotten.

"That was before today. And it was done because of the harsh and shameful decision of the editors at the *New York Times* to publish federally protected and confidential information, information designed to embarrass me as the acting president of the United States during a crisis when Americans watch their president struggle to regain his life. This was a disclosure that not even I could legally or morally disclose to you myself, no matter how much I may have wanted. But now this ancient confidence has been shockingly revealed, and I now, amid all the consternation surrounded this administration, must defend the actions of that precocious teenage girl who made a single major mistake almost thirty years ago.

"First, this defense comes just less than twenty-four hours after this shocking revelation was made to me. I was notified for comment last night less than thirty minutes in advance of this reporter's story, a reporter who holds a great deal of animosity toward me, evident to anyone who reads the venom she wrote. What did I do immediately when confronted with the facts presented to me? You already know what I did. I did what the Marine Corps has taught me to do. I told the truth and told it honorably when many other presidents might have taken a different course of action, a political course of action. I'll ask you again to imagine my devastation at learning of this personal invasion of my legally protected privacy.

"Now I am called on to explain the life of a teenage girl named Vera Ochman, a name I readily admit was buried and all but forgotten in 1980. Because of Vera's youthful indiscretion to seek companionship among the wrong crowd, whose leaders preyed on a desperate young women's need for companionship, she began an association with a despicable gang who made themselves appear to be what they were not, portraying themselves as a rebellious group out for harmless fun, but in reality they were hardened criminals bent on a course of profiteering from illegal vice. Caught up in this charade, a young, impressionable woman found herself locked into another tragedy that led to the death of a federal agent.

"This agent's tragic death at the hands of the leader of this gang led to my arrest and ultimately to my entry into the federal Witness Protection Program. I was merely there that night, caught in the wrong place at the wrong time, innocent of all wrongdoing and all alone, with no one to help me because my father died that very night when he was informed of my involvement. I was left alone in a frightening legal system with no parents, no family, no relatives, no one to turn to for help. Yes, the very young and frightened Vera Ochman bravely volunteered to give up her life in order to protect herself from this gang's retribution in exchange for grand jury testimony that led to the conviction, incarceration, and removal from society of seriously hardened criminals, who professionally trafficked in drugs and other heinous crimes, crimes concealed and unknown to me."

Tom intently observed the reaction on the faces of his focus group, who in turn watched Victoria deliver her address on the large-screen monitor attached to the wall high above the entrance to one of the White House's interior conference rooms. About fifteen individuals, all selected and screened by the Pearsall agency, reflected the profile of a cross-section of Americans. Tom assembled the focus group at the White House in the early morning hours to give him an early indication of how all Americans would be reacting to Victoria's speech as she delivered it.

"OK. OK. Not bad. So far so good," Tom surmised as he surveyed his focus group privately watching Victoria's performance. Victoria masterfully and persuasively articulated the quickly devised initial themes of her defense to a nation wanting to believe her. She explained in powerful language—words carefully designed and sifted by Tom, that would link the themes of innocence and indiscretion to an orphaned and confused young woman who was forced into a deal to produce convicting testimony before the grand jury in exchange for her entry into the strict confidentiality of the Witness Protection Program. Next, Tom would gauge the group's reaction to an awkward new identity, followed closely by her subjugation and oppression on the farm.

"I escaped the abuses of my adoptive parents who treated me as farm slave labor. I was literally shot at from the sights of my adoptive mother's handgun as I fled, rescued by a long-distance truck driver, and then abandoned to the streets of San Francisco. It was there, out of sheer desperation, that I voluntarily enlisted in the United States Marine Corps. That day changed the direction of my whole life. It led me to the harsh but liberating discipline of Marine Corps basic training. It was there I realized that I had to get stronger on my own or perish in this world. I owe a great debt of gratitude to the outstanding Marines who trained me at Parris Island and who gave me a new family. I responded by becoming the first woman to ever win the honor of the most outstanding Marine of the Cycle, a competition that I won over many other deserving men and women. Later on, in active duty in Colombia, South America, I personally eliminated one of the world's largest suppliers of cocaine, a feat recognized by the then president of the United States for gallant and conspicuous bravery, above and beyond the call of duty, as to merit the Medal of Honor, the Marine Corps' highest commendation, awarded in a ceremony that took place literally a few hundred yards from where I now sit. I went on to be commissioned a Marine Corps officer and to graduate with honors from one of the finest universities in the country."

Tom watched the collective body language of the focus group relax, and some members leaned forward, intently listening to Victoria's speech. She was winning. Victoria closed with Dan's "no choice but to stay" final argument.

"From there I worked my way up in the ranks of the Marine Corps, decorated many times as an officer, rapidly advancing from second lieutenant to brigadier general in a rough-and-tumble military world. I served as commander in charge of a Marine base in Germany before Senator Eagan tapped me as one of his key military advisors for his campaign that led him to the White House. Most of you know the rest of my story, including what some reporters have written about me. In fact, one of the authors of today's story in the *Times* described my act of single-handedly subduing a drug gang in Central Park as, and I quote, 'One of the most significant acts of courage by a woman that I have ever witnessed.'"

A man in the focus group spontaneously chimed, "Damn right it was!"

"I went on to become vice president of the United States, quite by accident. I never intended to do anything of the sort but only wanted to return to my command. The military in this country owed a great debt to Senator Sam Eagan, so I joined my old friend in his campaign. It was fate that led me into a last-minute selection as a vice presidential nominee on a victorious ticket with President Sam Eagan. The whole nation suffers with me, knowing that Sam Eagan can neither physically nor mentally serve you as the president you elected as he labors daily to recover from the effects of a devastating stroke. And it is that stroke that leads to my final comments before I close. With today's revelation of the circumstances of what happened to me at age seventeen, some have already called on me to resign. But many have not. Notably among those is my friend, Speaker of the House Maggie O'Connor, who called me just before airtime to offer words of understanding and support. I want to here publicly acknowledge her act of courage.

"It is not my nature to quit, and I know it is not best for America, particularly now as your president remains in such an unstable and tenuous state. And this is the very reason why I cannot abandon my post, no matter what the circumstances. If I resign, there is no constitutional provision for my replacement as the acting president. An acting president serves until the president is restored to health or until the next presidential election. Only a vice president can be placed in the office of acting president. By the Constitution, no one else in presidential succession can assume the office of acting president. If I were to resign as the vice president, the Constitution says that the president must name a replacement, something that Sam Eagan is not presently capable of doing. Thus, if I resign and leave office, by the express terms of the Twenty-fifth Amendment, there is no one left in charge as president of the United States, and no one to discharge the constitutional authorities granted to the commander in chief to protect our national security until the next presidential election, over three years from now. No, I cannot and will not resign under these circumstances.

"Others have suggested that the Congress may impeach the vice president. If the vice president were to be impeached, hypothetically speaking, this would, similarly to the vice president's resignation, place the country in the identical indeterminable state, given the inability of the president to name a vice president. Besides, I have done nothing that could lead to articles of impeachment or a conviction. I have neither committed nor ever been convicted of a crime or offense deserving impeachment. All I've ever tried to do in my adult life and as vice president is to honorably serve my country. If someone were to suggest that I have committed an impeachable offense, I would vigorously defend my honor against such a scurrilous attack.

"I plead with the American people tonight, a nation of good citizens, known as a good people throughout the civilized world, to understand my personal and our country's predicament. Given the state of these affairs, let's now move on and forward from this scurrilous and unnecessary attack upon my personal honor and reputation by this awkward revelation, forget now my ancient youthful indiscretions, and realize that the United States of America must have a competent president who is in charge. I am, have been, and will be that president at least until such time as President Eagan can resume his lawful office.

"Thank you and good night."

Light applause scattered at first across the room, and then spontaneously erupted. Tom saw immediately in their faces that Victoria had just scored a victory, but he knew, too, that the group had not yet heard the opposition's calls for her resignation that would surely come. No matter, Tom did not expect such a positive response. His initial feedback far exceeded his expectations, notwithstanding that he personally orchestrated most of Victoria's defense. After watching the pundits' reaction for the first thirty minutes, the ultimate surprise was that no one recognized that the Constitution made no provision for the removal or replacement of an acting president. Any attempt to remove an acting president would create a constitutional crisis. This constitutional bottom line sustained Victoria's administration from the calls for her resignation or removal. Dan was right.

The network anchors' commentary, viewer call-ins, and emails followed on the TV screen for several more hours under Tom's watchful eye. After observing this commentary, Tom moved to a deeper level of analysis, soliciting first the group's verbal answers and then individual written responses. Tom's inescapable conclusion was that Victoria achieved a sustainable victory. If his carefully selected group reflected, as it should, the aggregate mood and opinion of all Americans, then a majority of viewers did not care what happened to their popular vice president when she was seventeen years old, and, instead of being disgusted, they positively responded to her forthright disclosure of such an embarrassing situation.

There was more than a suggestion that they agreed with Victoria's characterization of an uncaring and scurrilous press that would divulge such a matter on such short notice. Now, thoroughly confident of his assessment, Tom dismissed his group with the promise of a check in the mail, and then moved to refine further his overnight polling questions, before congratulating Victoria on her command performance.

The overnight polling confirmed the early focus group results. Synthesizing all of his data, Tom was now certain that America would forgive Victoria and was prepared to move on with the nation's business. Tom's later data surprisingly confirmed an unexpected spike in Victoria's already high overall approval rating. Tom had never seen numbers such as these for any president and could not explain Victoria's surging approval rating.

As Victoria moved through the press conference the following morning, responding to and deflecting a barrage of questions, never straying far from Tom's established talking points, she convinced the nation that she was an orphaned victim who overcame implausible odds to achieve unprecedented success in both military and political life. Her candid interviews with, as she described them, "her favorites," further reinforced her defense to the American public.

Victoria's political instincts, always the subject of surprise to Tom for a military woman with no political underpinnings, directed her, yet again, to the correct course of action in the heat of a political battle. Victoria usually opted for an honest approach, and it worked, yet again, but this time on a colossal scale, which saved her from what most believed was a certain defeat. Tom was never one to weigh in with the truth, unless he could confirm a truth strategy through hard polling numbers, and he was surprised how the American public bought into a truth strategy.

Tom, always one to look out for number one first, knew he had reconciled with Victoria and in no way damaged his relationship with Sam in the event the president should make enough of a recovery to return as president. Tom, too, had a knack for political survival and once again landed safely on his political feet.

Victoria had told the truth, but not the whole truth. She knew America was not ready to forgive a president for murder, even in self-defense, and all the lingering questions as to why she neither summoned the police nor reported the Sanchez murder in the dawn of that fateful morning at the Mayflower Hotel but instead tossed his impaled body into the depths of the Chesapeake Bay.

True, Victoria did not suffer the expected defeat from her somewhat veiled and incomplete disclosure of a clandestine past, but it was Grace, the harbinger herself, who suffered not one but multiple defeats. Grace expected that Victoria would either resign immediately or suffer a swift impeachment, the seemingly natural progression of unraveling Victoria's secret past, but these alternatives never even came close to fruition, due mainly to Grace's constitutional naiveté as to the consequences of the removal of a vice president while serving as acting president. But Grace, in journalistic defeat, did what her profession required. She disclosed the truth.

What she grossly underestimated was the severe consequences of her second defeat, a defeat far less altruistic than the compulsion to publish a hidden truth about a vice president, but a defeat that hurt her profoundly. Grace made it appear that her father had compromised his professional ethics, an ethical reputation that he had toiled a lifetime to earn and preserve. Nothing could have prepared a daughter for her father's fall from grace. In her blind ambition to publish the truth and justify herself to her skeptical editors, Grace lapsed in her assessment of just how unethical this story would make her father appear. What was the honorably retired United States attorney to say in his own defense afterward? What was a father to say in defense of his daughter?

Michael Brandon made the honorable choice, just as he had done his entire professional life. He took the fall for his daughter's lapse of judgment, falsely admitting that he was complicit in the disclosure. Besides, no one would have believed that he had not voluntarily turned over the file to his daughter, no matter how much he denied it. So Michael Brandon would be the one—not his daughter, the ambitious reporter—who breached Vera Ochman's confidentiality, a confidence lawfully protected in the U.S. Witness Protection Program. Brandon would feign acceptance for his own lapse of judgment when in reality he had done nothing except, perhaps, be too careless with a confidential file, instead of overtly committing the unpardonable transgression of revealing a federally protected identity in his capacity, no less, as the very United States Attorney who had prosecuted, bargained for, and guaranteed Vera Ochman's anonymity and then just blithely handed over a top-secret file to promote his daughter's journalistic career. No matter the vehement denials of his daughter to the contrary, no one believed her, particularly as Victoria bore down on these lapses, both morally and legally, as part of her own defense. Michael Brandon, to escape the hounding tabloid reporters, fled the city for the seclusion of his country farmstead in upstate New York. He lost a lifetime of professional honor, bitter now and totally disgraced, at the hands of his unthinking and overzealous daughter.

For Grace, her only means of redemption for herself and her father was to chase the winds for the missing clues. What had she overlooked? What question remained unanswered? Her search led inevitably to Felipe Sanchez. How had he died? He was not the type to commit suicide. Too many gangster competitors had motives to kill him, and it was probably one of them who did him in. But his criminal territory was New York City, not even close to his final resting place on the Eastern Shore of the Chesapeake Bay. Who killed him?

* * *

Grace returned to her father's condominium and retrieved the sticky yellow note with a return telephone number that eventually led her back to the Chincoteague Coroner's Office. The doctor would gladly speak to anyone who might lay claim to the skeletal remains of Felipe Sanchez still residing in the morgue's stainless steel body drawer, awaiting the statutorily mandated time before unceremoniously cremating his remains.

"So, Doc, what can you tell me about this guy?" Grace inquired as the two stood on opposite sides of the sliding drawer holding the skeleton of the once-proud Felipe Sanchez.

"See here, his jaw is broken." The coroner pointed with an expandable stainless steel implement, which he retrieved from the floor after spilling out the entire contents of his overcrowded white jacketed pocket.

"But you cannot die from a broken jaw, can you?"

"You can, but it's unlikely. I would have even put that down as the cause of death but for this." The doctor again points, but this time to a break in his neck at the top of his spine. "Someone or something broke his neck, with a great deal of force."

"'Something'? Don't you mean 'someone'?"

"You gotta remember this guy was pulled out of the bay. Hard to say what a cadaver might encounter tossed about on the bottom for all those years. But as skeletons go, this one was in excellent condition, like it might have just emerged from its casket. If that was the case, then the skeleton likely remained in the same condition as the time of death. So taking the broken jaw with the broken neck, you have to believe that this guy Sanchez was in one hell of a fight right before he died."

"You don't say."

"You're right, I don't say. This is all speculation. The cause of death is officially undetermined. If you can give me any reason at all, I will let you take charge of these bones. But you gotta do it. Let's see." The doctor turned around and looked back at the calendar on the opposite wall, one adorned with a buxom brunette in a red swimsuit and inscribed across the top, "Jakes Body Shop." "You got another fifteen days before this guy's goin' in the furnace."

"Thanks, Doc, I'll get back to you on that one."

According to the coroner's speculative conclusion, Sanchez died as a result of blunt trauma to his spinal column, severe enough to break his neck, not to mention the trauma sufficient to cause a broken jaw. The totality of the circumstantial evidence connecting Sanchez to Victoria surrounding his death was not sufficient to publish, not even for a tabloid, and certainly not enough for the *New York Times*. For Grace, there were too many unanswered questions. How did Sanchez know where Victoria was that night or even who she was?

Grace turned to the archival stacks of the press accounts of the sensational murder and trial, resulting in Vera's supposed execution. All the gang conspirators had disappeared or died or been murdered in prison, all except one. The one who remained incarcerated, still doing hard time, went by the name of Amber Morelli, but before Grace could make contact with her, Amber, after the press hoopla, had already dropped a letter to Grace at her midtown apartment. The handwritten letter was easy to distinguish in a mailbox full of Grace's bills and computer-generated junk mail: Amber's envelope had an unusual script and a return address from a New York women's correctional facility.

CHAPTER TWENTY-TWO

Dear Grace Brandon,

    Thank you for telling everyone the truth about Vera Ochman. She lies all the time. I know because she lied about me many years ago and that's why I'm still in jail today. She's still lying by not telling the truth about what she knows about my old boyfriend, Felipe Sanchez. I think she knows how he died. Maybe she killed him.

    In August of 1981, I saw Vera's picture in the newspaper (now she goes by Victoria and is the president . . . what a joke). Way back then, I sent it to Felipe. He may not have believed it was her . . . turns out now that it was. . . . But if he did believe it, Felipe would have followed her into hell to get even. Felipe dumped me for Vera. . . . Felipe was hot for her like he was for a lot of women. Felipe and me didn't get along so good back then. . . . I drank too much. But Felipe wrote back to me after he got out of prison and was going to help me get out too . . . but I never heard from him again after I sent him the story in the newspaper. . . . There's a lot I need to tell you . . . but they read my mail in here all the time (you may not even get this letter at all) so it's better if you come to see me and I'll tell you everything.

Amber Morelli
Inmate 2055408
Women's State Correction Institution of New York
Rochester, New York

PS: Felipe was in Washington, DC.

Grace would never learn how Amber knew that Sanchez had been in Washington, DC. Just like Lucinda Pierce and Gus Margolis, Amber Morelli died of stab wounds in jail three days after her letter arrived at Grace's apartment.

* * *

Tom Pearsall, now officially Victoria's White House press spokesperson, entered the Oval Office. Victoria said, "Tom, I just watched your briefing. You're getting pretty damned good at making long-winded statements that say nothing."

"Thank you, Madam Vice President, I do try. . . . I wish they would let up a little on questions about your past, particularly from Grace Brandon."

Tom's cell phone rang. He answered. "It's that guy again." Tom knew he would only learn this guy's identity on an as-needed basis, so before being asked to leave, Tom handed the phone to Victoria and excused himself to go down the hall.

"Hello, Madam Acting President. Let me add my congratulations on another brilliant performance. Tom's not listening, is he? You're not on speakerphone, are you?"

"He's left the room. Why are you calling?"

"Well, now, it's impossible for you to call me, isn't it? Please don't linger too long and make me suspicious that you are tracing my call. But you're smart enough not to do that, knowing just how much I've helped you over the last few days—saved your ass really—and you must be certainly aware of just how much trouble I can cause you now."

"You know I am desperate to meet you. Just say when."

"I would love to meet you, Madam Acting President. Perhaps a little phone sex might suffice, but meeting you now would be out of the question. You're not yet the president. I have a thing for powerful women, in case you haven't noticed. My ultimate fantasy is to lay the president of the United States. But that's not why I'm calling."

"So why are you calling?"

"It's that meddlesome reporter again, Grace Brandon, and her sources. She seems to be getting closer all the time. But there's one source you will not have to worry about."

"And who might that be?"

"Amber Morelli. Grace was desperate to talk to Amber about her letter."

"What letter?"

"The one I opened, read, and resealed. But everyone reads letters from prisoners without their permission. Anyway, Grace got this scandalous letter from Amber that said some pretty terrible things about you, not to mention that Felipe Sanchez had been in Washington, DC, about the same time you got your medal. But no need to worry about what Amber knows. No one will be able to find that out now, not Grace, not anyone. It was so unfortunate what happened to Amber. But I thought you might want to know, because I'm certain Grace will be asking troublesome questions about Amber."

"Who are you, and what have you done this time, you despicable bastard?"

"Now, now, just remember, all I want is to sleep with you when you are really Madam President, but you first have to become the president, Victoria. That's what it will cost you. Believe me, you'll enjoy it as much I will. So it's all smooth sailing from here until then, so, Madam Acting President, better get started on your campaign right away!"

Victoria stared into silence as Tom's cell phone went dead.

Victoria's secret admirer discarded his prepaid cell phone into a trash can outside of his Georgetown apartment and returned inside to continue a discussion with his wife.

"Maggie, please excuse the interruption. Now, where were we?"

"Larry, it's always the same topic with you. Listen, once and for all, there are no grounds for articles of impeachment. Even if there were, Sam Eagan either has to get well or die before the House would even consider taking up the issue of impeachment, and given her popularity, it's doubtful even then. We've gone through all of this before. Please, Larry, can't we for once talk about something else?"

"Of course, dear, we can always talk about your running for president three years from now."

"But, Larry, I'm perfectly happy being the Speaker of the House. It's only you, dear, who keeps insisting that I run for president."

Larry O'Connor, MD, told Victoria the truth when he said he wanted to sleep with the president. In fact, he was obsessed by it, night and day. One way or the other, Larry intended to be the First Gentleman, whether the president was Maggie O'Connor or Victoria Pierce. That's why Larry secretly followed Maggie and Victoria into the hotel stairwell, to make sure that Maggie would go through with her meeting with Sam, the same day Maggie fell down the stairs on her return, the same place he decided to wait in hiding, and the same place that he fortuitously pointed his cell phone camera at Victoria, hesitating for three minutes at the top of the steps. Larry, too, in his darkened corner also hesitated, thinking the same thing Victoria was thinking, while both stared at Maggie from different perspectives. Larry believed that Maggie had died or was going to die from the fall and, if she were not dead, Larry surmised that the severity of his wife's injuries were so devastating that the fall would surely end her status as Sam's running mate and his as the vice president's First Gentleman. After Maggie survived and was taken to the hospital, Larry, oblivious to her condition, spent hours in the hospital that night trying to persuade Maggie to run in spite of her injuries, but eventually even Larry had to concede the inevitable. Had Maggie died in the stairwell, Larry believed his cell phone pictures would be enough to blackmail Victoria into accepting his marriage proposal. It was also in the stairwell that Tom found a way to communicate with Victoria. Victoria had used Maggie's cell phone to call Tom on his secret number, so it was equally as simple for Larry to retrieve Tom's top-secret number from Maggie's cell phone and make his initial threatening call to Victoria as she stood framed through the window in her campaign headquarters in the early morning hours after her convention speech. Larry, through binoculars, truly enjoyed watching Victoria squirm as he watched her from the darkened building across the street.

Larry O'Connor personally murdered Lucinda Pierce with his own syringe filled with an untraceable toxin. It was a snap to smash Gus Margolis on the hood of a colorless rental car as he crossed the street in a complete daydream about Grace's retirement feature. But it was much more difficult for Larry to follow and then shove Grace in front of the headlights of the Seventh Avenue Express and make a hasty getaway, disguised as a woman in drag, but even Larry was astonished as to how simple it was to commission a murder inside prison walls in exchange for narcotics transferred through a corrupt intermediary to a rival gang member who stabbed Amber Morelli as she showered alone in solitary confinement.

Grace, meandering through a stream of unsubstantiated clues, was nevertheless now more convinced than ever that Felipe Sanchez breathed his last in Washington, DC, dying from blunt trauma severe enough to break his neck, not to mention trauma sufficient to cause a broken jaw, at the hands of Victoria Pierce. Grace envisioned Victoria's stonewalled denial of such false innuendo, all manufactured by the same reporter who victimized her before. The vice president would, like every time before, spin Grace's story into oblivion.

As Grace was now a more seasoned reporter than before, she had only one last credible shot at Victoria. This time there could be no loose ends. Grace would have to wait, keep her leads to herself, avoid tipping off the tabloids, and pursue the evidentiary connections that would surely evolve. But she also would have to blockade her subject's avenue of escape. It was a gamble, but one she would have to risk, to do the unthinkable, to inform her subject and stake her out now on her positions, ahead of the story.

Grace telephoned Victoria at the White House to make an inquiry ostensibly before forever closing her file on her failed story, or so she said. An acting president, filled with confidence, for one last time would field Grace's closing questions.

"Madam Acting President, I was going over a letter from one of your former criminal accomplices by the name of Amber Morelli. Do you remember a gang member by the name of Amber Morelli?

"You must remember, Ace, that I was never convicted of a crime and therefore could have no criminal accomplices, and, no, I do not remember this person. But go on, maybe I will. What's your one last question?"

Indeed, Victoria remembered Amber, not just because of Larry O'Connor's warning, but because she still held Amber in contempt and certainly felt no remorse for someone she still despised.

"You see, Madame Acting President, I am trying to understand why Amber would have known that Felipe Sanchez was in Washington, DC, near the time that you received your Medal of Honor."

Victoria paused to comprehend all the ramifications of this disclosure—questioning whether Grace already knew the answer, and then rejecting that as impossible—but Victoria nervously squirmed nonetheless before answering.

"Ace, you must appreciate just how behind I've been lately in my official responsibilities as the acting president of the United States, all at your expense, so please try not to waste any more of my time with more of your trifling speculations. Tell me the foundation for your sheer speculation."

"Well, Madam Acting President, you were staying at the Mayflower Hotel in Washington DC, right?"

"I don't recall now. It's been a long time ago. I was very young at the time. Tell, me, Ace, did you ever do anything that you were ashamed of when you were seventeen years old?"

Completely ignoring the attempted diversion, Grace continued. "Madam Acting President, unless I am badly mistaken, you stayed at the Mayflower Hotel, and I think it's a safe bet to say that you slept at the Mayflower Hotel on the last night that anyone ever saw or heard from Felipe Sanchez again."

"Like I said, Ace, I don't remember where I stayed."

"I'll be brief, Madam Acting President. And I'll ask my final questions with a certain trepidation because I don't relish the specter of being tossed in front of a subway again, but I must ask you on the record and for attribution, my last questions. Was this just some wild coincidence, or was Sanchez in Washington, DC, that same day looking for revenge? Do you know the circumstances surrounding the death of Felipe Sanchez?"

"My answer for attribution to your final question is, of course, it must have been a coincidence if he even was in Washington. I am certain that Sanchez must have believed, like everyone else, that Vera Ochman was dead. Now, is that all?"

"But do you know the circumstances surrounding the death of Felipe Sanchez?" Grace, more for harassment, asked,

"Well, then, how about the deaths of your adopted mother, Lucinda Pierce? Or your old buddy, Gus Margolis? Or your longtime nemesis, Amber Morelli?"

Victoria responded calmly, "Ms. Brandon, I've answered your one last question and will not suffer listening to the rantings of a desperate reporter a second longer. You can be sure this will be the last call."

Victoria hung up, knowing all too well the real reason that Sanchez was in Washington, DC, that day and knowing all too well there would be other calls from Grace. Likely, it would only be a matter of time before Grace uncovered the hard evidence of the Sanchez murder at the Mayflower Hotel, and Grace would be right back at her doorstep with more troubling questions for the acting president.

But Victoria always knew that the murder she committed was completely justified, clearly in self-defense. It was his life or hers. Even so, Victoria knew it would be difficult for the acting president to later admit to a murder that she had now officially denied, even if she had been attacked at knifepoint by Felipe Sanchez, a man bent on revenge on the morning after her return from an adulterous tryst that started the night before and continued for well over twenty-five years with the now president of the United States. But Victoria knew, if she was called to explain these circumstances to the American public, she could defend the murder, because the circumstances were more justifiable and understandable than her concealment of a clandestine past.

Victoria reclined on the couch in the Oval Office with her forearm covering her eyes, uncomfortably trying to contour her body into a position of relaxation as she listened to Bach's *Piano Concerto Number 1 in D-Minor*.

Before drifting off to sleep, she summarized to herself, *I've survived the revelation of a clandestine past, without the man I loved and depended on since I was nineteen—a man who himself now lies comatose in a hospital bed, struggling to survive—a man whose love—no, not love—whose lust I satisfied as a surrogate for his frigid wife who cared nothing for him. I survived an attack on our administration, with no help from him—all accomplished by my own wits and with my own selected counsel. And I can damn well justify to the American people killing Felipe Sanchez, a murderous stalker who attacked me unmercifully in a life-or-death struggle that I should have never survived in the first place, had it not been for my Marine Corp basic training. Yes, I survived that assault to become vice president and acting president of the United States. How could I have revealed then what I had done without compromising my identity as Victoria Pierce? The American people would understand both the bravery and immaturity of a nineteen-year-old woman just as they understood the bravery and immaturity of an eighteen-year-old woman.* These last words she would remember if she had to write such a speech for the American people. These words reassured Victoria as she fell asleep, at ease now in the quiet of the Oval Office, amid the balm of Bach's piano concerto.

What would have been unreassuring to Victoria, had she known, was how Larry O'Connor planned to play both sides of the presidential matrimonial game, positioning himself to win with either Maggie or Victoria, and how unrelenting he would push Maggie until she appointed a special congressional committee that would lead to articles of impeachment, all fueled by the public disclosure of Victoria's concealment of the crime of murder. But Victoria did not know that it was Larry O'Connor, the husband of the Speaker of the House, who tormented her, so she dozed blissfully, exhausted.

Tom entered the Oval Office and saw Victoria on the couch asleep, as if she were dead. He intentionally slammed the door. Victoria woke up and stretched to face Tom's voice.

"You won't fuckin' believe this! I can hardly fuckin' believe it myself!"

"What is it now, Tom?" Victoria rolled back on her side, thinking this would only be a momentary interruption.

"You better sit up to hear this, Madam President."

"What did you call me?"

"I said, "Madam President." Sam just died at Bethesda Naval Hospital from a second massive stroke!"